OUR GUARDIAN RENEGADE

HARLEY ZED MONA

Cover Design – Kostas Lagos
Icons – Libuse Klechova

ISBN-13: 978-0692878668
ISBN-10: 0692878661
Library of Congress CN: TXu 2-015-823

PROLOGUE:

They stood in a unified line by the inner edge of the frozen dome, all prepared to face the dangers lurking inside their own great city.

 He was a monster, a brute of a man, a fearsome giant. The wicked raven perched on his shoulder, the scar that drained the pigment from his eye, his towering height, his massive muscles, and his assortment of gadgets and weapons contributed to make him appear a beast forged from nightmares. He grinned from ear to ear, unable to contain his excitement for his next battle. The spiteful berserker was nothing short of a terrifying sight.

 He was the color of night, from his beak to his talons. The pitch-black raven seemed to smile just as his tall friend did, the two an inseparable duo of fearsome creatures. Various parts of the bird had been augmented with metal, making his wings, beak, and talons razor-sharp. Steel also covered his eye, the eye that held steady a damning gaze, forming a hexagonal shape over it. The haunting raven was nothing short of a terrifying sight.

 She was a petite, pretty woman, dressed in the fashions of youthful spunk. Her brunette hair shimmered in the daylight, and a pink headband held it together. With her white blouse and white shoes, she looked angelic, and her charming face radiated with sweetness, completed well by her bright, hopeful smile. Yet the rifle clenched in her arms warned that she was a capable fighter, and her eyes were already scanning, watching for targets coming from every possible direction, every possible angle.

 He was a shadow, a young man able to fit into the crowd with ease. A glassy, yet peaceful stare was hidden in a darkness cast by the hood hiding his head. He had simple armor, mail beginning to collect rust, yet his cape and hammer were icons of justice and heroism. He was quite short; shorter, in fact, than all of his human comrades next to him, and yet his presence did not lack in demanding attention. His skin was not visible in any spot, his clothing not willing to betray his true colors.

 She had the appearance of a reaper, yet death was her greatest rival. Her black lips, dark hair, and sensual clothing made her a beauty, but her tall shape, wicked scythe, and countless daggers menacingly dared one to touch her. Tears of black streamed down her face, a haunting visage. She was an eerie, curious sight, and yet all she felt inside herself was curiosity.

 She was a young witch in modest clothing. A dull sweater covered her chest, a simple skirt fluttered around her, and her blue boots shimmered brightly, as if they were made of glass. Her long red hair stretched to her shins, a beautiful mane. Her sleeves were rolled up, revealing permanent markings on her body that pulsed bright blue. Gripped in one hand was a grimoire, her book of frozen arts and out of the palm of her other hand a snowflake had manifested.

 He was a great hound, a shepherd dog turned war machine. His mouth was ajar, revealing a row of teeth adorned in a mysteriously glistening metal. The helmet on his head and the protective coat that hugged him indicated his readiness for battle; it almost seemed he was covered in an armored shell, the various gadgets on his body serving to boost his ferocity, and there was no remorse to be found in his angry eyes.

 He was a military man, stern and firm, cynical and unforgiving. Various guns and gadgets were scattered across his body, preparing him for every

occasion, and he had equipped a thick coat and cool urban look. Two revolvers he had drawn, one tinted in red and the other in green, and a bulky machine pistol clung to his thigh. As their tactician, he was lost in thought, already imagining every possible outcome of the important battle that sat before him.

 She was their dark-haired leader, a strong warrior capped in a beret decorated with four stars, clad in the uniformed garb of her high rank. An exoskeleton suit surrounded her body, stretching from her neck to her shoes. Her black pumps were quite extraordinary, fit to more uses than simply their style. She looked almost willing to take to the skies with a small pistol gripped tightly in her hand, but in truth, she was nothing less than ready to lead her people into the fray of battle.

Behind them stood soldiers of a sanctuary and soldiers of an empire, side-by-side for the first time in history, fierce red-skinned warriors seeking justice, guards of a dark order wielding weapons as terrifying as their ghostly visages, even sanctuary civilians willing to take up arms to defend themselves.

"Are we ready?" asked the red-haired girl, prepared to melt the dome of ice before them. When it opened, it would begin their crusade to defeat the enemies within their homeland.

Their leader took a deep breath, then spoke: "Let's go!" she said, in a loud enough voice for her entire army to hear. "We have a city to take back."

CHAPTER 1:

She had been working on her plan for months, and now here she was, finally ready to present it. She looked down at her legs to find them shaking involuntarily, but there was little she could do to quiet them. She adjusted her beret, straightened her skirt, and fixed her blouse, hoping the satisfaction of tidying herself up would take the stress off her mind.

After what seemed like ages, a secretary with austere bearing stepped out of an office and walked towards a woman who looked prepared to receive a prison sentence.

"General Leavett," said the secretary. "The Chairman is ready to see you."

Amber Leavett rose from her chair and picked up her suitcase. She took a deep breath and followed the secretary, who led her down a flight of stairs and into a basement corridor flanked by many doors. "First one on the right," the serious woman stated, almost robotically.

"Thank you," Amber replied, but the secretary didn't seem to hear. She was already walking back up the stairs, her shoes boisterously clacking on the marble steps. Alone now, Amber turned back to the corridor. She followed the secretary's directions until she reached a door marked "Chairman's Office," then her anxious hands reached for the knob.

The door opened to a large but cozy room. A colossal rug sat comfortably on the wooden floor, and windows crawled high on the wall she faced. The walls cowered behind giant racks of books on every side, except for the one behind Amber, which was replaced by a grand fireplace on her right.

A man, older but not elderly, sat at the worn, wooden desk opposite the general, signing what looked like an important document. His dark hands shoved it aside as Amber stepped towards him.

"Have a seat," he said, pointing to two chairs on the other side of his desk, identical to his own. Amber promptly chose one.

"Sir, I would like to...," she began.

"No need to address me as 'Sir,'" he interrupted. "I care not for formalities. Please, call me 'Chairman,' or whatever else you prefer."

"Chairman," continued Amber, with fragments of excitement strewn across what was almost a smile on her face. "I would like to propose an idea to you. As I'm sure you know..."

The Chairman cut her off with no words this time, simply a deep stare that silenced her before she could go on. "I know why you're here," he said, his voice smooth and deep.

Amber tilted her head in confusion. "You...you do?"

"Oh, I would think so. You're here because you want to reinitiate the Guardians protocol. Is that correct?"

"Yes, it is," Amber spoke, nearly stammering. "How did you know?"

He flashed a warm smile. "Amber, I haven't forgotten your face, even after all these years. I remember how fond you were of the concept when it was first proposed, and how you took the position as leader without hesitation. It was tragic what happened to your group, yes, but I knew it was a matter of time before you were ready to reinitiate it. Now that you've climbed the ranks, and aged a bit, I'm certain you've grown more mature, as well."

He paused with a sigh, then his tone quieted. "Our world, our beautiful Senia...it's taking a turn for the worse, I fear. The Syndicate Empire of Avalon intends to conquer all of it, to control everyone, and someone has to be there to protect those who cannot fend for themselves. I will fund your project once more, Amber, because I know you of all people can destroy the evils in our presence."

Amber was at a loss for words. Part of her never believed the Chairman would be on board with the pitch, let alone jump at the idea himself. "Thank you so much," she finally managed to say, and she laughed awkwardly.

"So, have you any idea of who will be in this new task force?" he asked as he sat back in his seat.

"Oh, absolutely." Amber reached into her suitcase and emerged with a neatly organized portfolio folder of files. She pulled seven papers from it, then tidily spread them on the Chairman's desk for him to gander at. They were reports, one for each would-be member of Amber's group, complete with pictures and information.

"You've got quite the cast here!" he proclaimed. "Well, go on, let's hear about them!"

Amber gave him a proud smile, then pointed to the dark characters on the very left of the Chairman, a scarred man and a corrupted raven. They were the one exception, as they shared one report together, unlike the rest of the group. "Let's start with them."

. . .

Lightning flashed against a pitch sky, illuminating the shiny raven perched on the roof of the tavern. Its brother, Thunder, then shouted at the darkened world of Senia.

The sleek, black bird's hexagonal eye widened as he let loose his metallic wings, cawed with sinister pride, and flew inside the pub for cover before the rain hit. He landed comfortably on the shoulder strap of the only person in Senia he truly trusted.

As Tyreesius Black set his mug of ale on top of the counter, he realized he was attracting the bartender's stare. The bartender quickly diverted his eyes, but the man with the raven on his shoulder had already caught him in the act. He chuckled, loud enough for the bartender to hear, and continued sipping at his drink.

This wasn't uncommon for the pair; everywhere they went, they caught the eyes of nearly everyone around them. He was called Reese by those who feared him, so that his true name had mostly been forgotten by now. With his astonishing height and ugly scar that had long since rid his right eye of any color but white, he certainly stood out amongst a crowd. His jet black, half-mechanical friend didn't help them blend in, either. Senia surely was a strange and scary world, but Reese and Hex were surely among the strangest and scariest inhabitants to roam its mighty realm.

Reese took a dogmatic glance around the room. As expected, he caught the stares of at least three others. They hastily diverted their attention, much like the bartender.

It was then that he saw two armed figures enter the bar, sporting the rugged clothes and fearsome masks of bandits. At the sight of them, Reese slumped in his stool, but that did little to help, as his massive body stood out sorely amongst the crowd. He kept watch on the two from the corner of his eye, carefully surveying their movements. It was hard for anyone else to notice them in the chaotic hustle and bustle of the bar, with stewards running around frequently and drunken patrons bellowing with graceless voices.

Reese brushed Hex, giving the hand signal to take cover above. The raven accordingly did so, quietly flying to a loose tile in the ceiling.

He turned back towards the bandits just in time to watch them nod to each other. One proceeded to pull out a revolver from her holster. She fired two rounds into the ceiling, and it was a wonder how quickly the room silenced. Everyone in the pub froze in fear and turned towards the disrupters of peace, save for Reese, who tried to shrink in his stool even more, and Hex, who kept close surveillance on the intruders.

"Attention!" the bandit to the right announced. Anticipation drew a smile on the scarred man's face as he awaited the words he so wished to hear: "We are looking for a Reese Black!"

He laughed at his cue, menacingly and wickedly. Slaughter was imminent, he knew, and he was nothing but thrilled.

"Stopping the party so soon, officers? Why don't you sit down and have a drink," his gruff voice spoke aloud, turning from the bar and chuckling unnervingly. The bandits looked at each other in disbelief as the other patrons eyed him fearfully. "After all, it's happy hour!"

Suddenly, Reese let out a sharp whistle. Hex, on the signal, dashed towards the bandit with the gun in her hand, lunging for her exposed throat with incredible speed. As a blur of black zoomed past her, she let the pistol fall from her grip and placed her hands on her neck, choking inaudibly, save for the sound of bubbling blood from within her throat.

The other bandit jumped back, a moment of fear taking over his body: hesitation, the sign of weakness Reese was waiting for. The beast of a man got up from his chair and unclipped his throwing axe from its waist strap, flinging it just before the remaining bandit managed to draw a weapon. The axe soared over the heads of the crowd and straight into his forehead, thieving him of his life instantaneously at the sound of metal meeting organs.

His job done, Reese slowly walked towards the exit. The crowd, in utter fear and submissiveness, gave path to let him pass. Once he was towering over the lifeless body of the bandit he had just killed, Reese opened his hand, leaving his palms exposed. His dark axe flew back into his fingerless gloves, as if on command. Hex soared up, returning to Reese as well, and landed on his shoulder pad.

After he rubbed his raven's beak in caring praise, he began for the door, but in a second he was back, as if he had forgotten something. He stepped over the mangled bandit bodies and walked back past the parted crowd. The silent stares of the people around him couldn't have been heavier, but he indulged in the attention he so loved to receive.

Reese made his way to the bartender once more, pulling a few credits out of his pocket. He placed them next to his nearly empty mug of ale.

"Thank you, kind sir," he said with a nod, a smile, and the tip of an invisible hat, and once again, he made for the exit. On his way there, he noticed that one of the bandits, the poor soul that Hex had targeted, was still alive. Her head wobbled awkwardly against the floor, and a puddle of blood slowly crept from her broken body, but her raspy, desperate breathing was hard to miss. Reese, imposing over her, raised his foot and crushed it into the horrified face of the bandit, as one might squash a bothersome bug. If she wasn't dead before, she surely was now.

Just before he left the tavern, he turned to face the terrified onlookers. He saw the faces of traumatized stewards, of customers who came for a gay time but received just the opposite, and of the bartender, the innocent, afraid man. They all bore expressions of disgust, fear, and shock.

Reese gave a slight chuckle at them. How amusing it was to be naïve.

Meanwhile, a bereted woman at the bar had witnessed the entire scene unfold before her eyes. As Reese and Hex left the pub, she pulled out a card from her pocket. Parting from the dumbfounded crowd, she chased after them, her heels loudly clacking on the stone pavement. Outside, the rain beat down on them ruthlessly. Lightning and Thunder followed suit in making a gloomy city even gloomier.

The darkness of the night immediately hugged her body as she stepped out. The sky was completely black; it was if someone had placed a box over Senia.

"Excuse me!" she called out. Reese turned around to face her, a ragged cloth hanging from his belt flapping in the wind. "My name is Amber Leavett," she continued, holding out a hand as she approached.

Reese shook it eagerly. "Can I help you, general?" he responded, noticing the stars on her beret. His mouth stuck itself in a twisted and curious smile.

"Please, call me Amber," she continued in an irenic tone, as she handed Reese a card with his name written on it in careful calligraphy. "I would like to propose to you an offer."

■ ■ ■

Evangeline Bates adjusted her pink headband as she sat idly on the rooftop of an apartment complex in the sprawling, modernized, corrupt city-state of Greenwood, one leg dangling freely over the side of the building and a rifle in her hands. Across the street from the sniper was a modernized mansion, a house that had been holding her gaze for some time now.

After a few more minutes of waiting while leaning on her gun, Eva heard the sound of footsteps in the distance. She peered over the rooftop, and surely enough, a pretty blonde in a stunning red dress was walking alone along the sidewalk. Eva watched as the woman made her way to the mansion across the street and rang the doorbell. A muscular man with a stubby beard opened the door and let her in.

A grin found itself upon the sniper: now the fun would begin.

Eva hastily shimmied down a pipe that crawled up the side of the building, descending to a few feet above ground-level before pushing off. She threw in a graceful flip before swooping onto the top of a van parked near the sidewalk. Once she landed, she bowed out of habit, to no one in particular. Instead of the long-familiar applause, she heard the chirp of crickets and the distant sounds of moving cars.

She climbed down from the vehicle's roof and onto the street. Fortunately, she still had not witnessed any pedestrians or vehicles coming down the lonely avenue. Darting across the street, she scaled the fence to the mansion's backyard, hopped over the side, and approached a back door. She pulled a hairpin from the pockets of her short shorts as she came to the lock. It was a surprisingly simple pick, and she managed to get the door open faster than expected.

Eva sneaked into the room and closed the door behind her, albeit more loudly than she desired. She cringed in suspense, hoping the owners of the house did not hear the unwelcomed guest. After a few seconds of silence, no angry gun-toting resident had put a bullet in her yet, so she decided to move on.

She searched the house for some time, quiet as a mouse. Finally, she came to a closed door and heard the faint sounds of pleasure from the other side of it. With rifle in hand, she shoved the door open and was presented with a man tearing a woman's dress off her body. The unclothed couple turned to Eva with blank, fearful expressions.

"I'm sorry, am I interrupting something?" Eva asked mockingly, before emptying a few rounds into both of them.

Within an hour, she was dragging two nude bodies to the door of a fancy house. She set the two aside and rang the doorbell, and the next thing she knew she was face-to-face with her customer.

"One cheating wife with a side of young boyfriend that has everything you don't, coming right up!" she said, turning to the bodies and pulling the darts lodged in various places out. "Don't worry, they're just tranquilized."

"Oh dear," murmured the man across from her, with a heavy breath. "Oh dear, oh dear, ohdearohdearohdear..." He paused, blinking his eyes a few times, almost as if hoping to wake up from a nightmare. His hand went to his sweating forehead, and his mouth fell ajar. "Why? Why, why, why? This," he said, pointing at the two, "this is a felony! I'm an accomplice to a crime!" More groans and other sounds of disapproval from the man, followed by uninterested sighs from Eva as she waited for him to finish. "I didn't ask you to do this!"

Eva stood on her toes, raised a finger to his lips, and made a gesture in her other hand that demanded payment. "You said for me to bring you evidence that they cheated."

"This is not evidence!" he screamed, pushing her away.

Eva laughed. "Oh, right. Silly me, I almost forgot. Here ya go." She rummaged through her pockets to find a series of photographs taken on previous nights that depicted the now deeply sleeping woman and man in bed together. She pointed to a particularly lewd photo she seemed strangely proud of. "That right there is what they call the 'money shot.'" She tried to keep from laughing, which grew easy when she found the man looked back at her with a grim, angry expression. "You're giving me a look that suggests you won't be paying me, so I'm just going to leave," Eva said, turning around.

She walked a few steps before she turned back, darting past the man and into his house, finding his wallet on the counter. "Hey!" he shouted, pathetically attempting to chase her down with clumsy steps.

She dove under his legs with ease, abandoning the mansion and fleeing into the depths of the city of Greenwood, leaving behind a very upset customer swearing profanities that nearly made her burst out in laughter.

With her great endurance, she planned to run until her legs gave out, but tripped over a figure that suddenly manifested in her way and landed painfully on the stone road below her pretty face first. A hound lapped at her rosy cheeks as she picked herself up, and Eva realized he was what she had stumbled into. As she opened her eyes to see the dog, she wanted desperately to be upset with him, but his consistent licking and big, sweet eyes were too much for her, and she found herself giggling loudly. As her laughing died down, she noticed something tucked inside the dog's collar. She reached out to touch it, finding something paper-thin and plastic touching her back. She tried to remove it, but as soon as she did, the hound ran off in haste. Eva prepared herself to take off after him in curiosity, but the object stole away her interest; it was a card, an invitation, and the name *"Evangeline Bates"* was printed in big letters on the front of it.

■ ■ ■

A mysterious man in a hood walked down a busy street, a small hammer clipped to his belt swinging at his side. Many pedestrians walked past, but he went unnoticed by them. He didn't mind the ignorance of the crowd; he felt more in power when working from the shadows.

He reached to adjust his necklace, the jewelry almost as strange as its owner. It was a dog tag with a skull on it, elegantly carved with onyx, swinging from a bronze chain.

He walked past an alleyway, to which he paid no attention at first, but something in the corner of his eye caught his interest; had he actually seen someone? His curiosity got the best of him, and he turned and walked towards the intriguing scene.

The alley continued for a short distance and then split into two opposite directions, but for all he could see, it was completely vacant. He told himself he had seen nothing and turned to leave, but just as he did, he heard a cry for help: someone in great pain pleading for a passerby's assistance. He looked back into the crowd from where he had come. It didn't seem as if anyone heard the agonizing wail, or if they did, didn't care.

Unlike them, the mysterious man heard it, and he was determined to be the catalyst of judgment.

With silent footsteps, he ran towards the back of the alley, leaning on the left side of the wall and peeking his head out. Three men were in front of him, with one lying on the ground, kicked and beaten by the other two. The witness to the crime noticed that the victim was no ordinary man: his skin was red, but not due to blood or bruise.

One of the assaulters stopped and picked up the victim by his hair. Angrily, he said, "Don't you know you're not welcome here?" The red-skinned man's face hit the ground with a shove, and another desperate cry of misery escaped.

The strange onlooker cringed; he could no longer bear to be merely a witness. The hammer unclipped from his waist, and he tightly gripped it in his hands. Stepping out from the corner, he dared to betray his cover. The thugs didn't notice him at first, their backs turned towards him, but the victim, struggling on the ground, did. A look of hope glimmered in his terrified eyes.

The onlooker stepped forward into the fray with a fierce cry, both two hands on his weapon. He took a swing at one of the thugs, crushing the man's head between the wall next to him and the hammer. The thug cried out, hit the floor, and consciousness faded from him. His friend, upon noticing this, rushed to pull a gun from his back pocket and aimed it straight at the hooded man with the hammer. Bullets went off and struck the man's armor, but it did little to stop him, as the hammer swung once again. This time, his weapon struck the thug's gun, sending the pistol flying, but the mysterious man kept spinning, a tight grip on his hammer.

The thug, an expression of utter disbelief upon him, turned to run, but the onlooker now let go of his swinging weapon. The hammer soared through the air and landed precisely on the nape of the attacker, who dropped to the ground, stuck into a deep sleep by instant justice.

The man in the hood walked towards the unconscious assaulter's body to retrieve his hammer, then walked back over to the weakened innocent on the ground.

"*V-vaz eff,*" was all the victim could mutter under his breath before he collapsed. The man in the hood hastily clipped his hammer back onto his belt and lifted the enervated civilian onto his shoulders. Now side-by-side, the innocent's mysterious guardian pulling his exhausted body, they both appeared relatively short in stature.

He led him out of the alley and back onto the sidewalk, where the two received many curious stares from nearby pedestrians. Despite the dead weight he was carrying, the rescuer continued to trudge, looking for any place that would offer them hospitality.

At one point, he felt a hand near his pocket and assumed someone was attempting to steal from him. When he turned, something brushed against him, and he witnessed black hair rustling away. He yelled after the thief, but received no response. The man checked his pockets to find out what had been stolen, but nothing was missing. However, he found a card inside a pocket he was certain had been empty earlier. He pulled it out and read it over, quietly noticing that it addressed him simply as *"Skullgem, the Lionhearted."*

■ ■ ■

The marsh's fog engulfed the deep green topless jeep as it drove past skyscraper-sized trees and massive lakes of murky swamp water. Brutus McCallister sat at the steering wheel, while Charlie rested with his head down in the back, tail tucked between his legs.

The man leaned towards the dog behind him and stroked his neck. He watched Charlie pick his head up as if he saw something in the path in front of him, and Brutus turned back to the wheel. Out of nowhere, the fog parted to reveal a curved wall of tall, dangerous spikes that leaned against a gigantic hollowed tree, this one much bigger than its gargantuan siblings nearby. An enormous iron gate, currently closed, stood as the only noticeable entrance. As they drew closer, they noticed four guards were posted as sentries, two outside the gate and two inside. Brutus stopped the car nearby, disembarked, and approached, the hound curiously trotting beside him. The guards, as they noticed the duo, took out various weapons and pointed them threateningly towards the duo.

Casually raising his hands, Brutus spoke: "I don't want to hurt anyone here, I just need to talk to whoever is in charge. I believe that would be Xela..." he paused, taking out the card he had to deliver and reading the name once more: "Zamora. Yes, Xela Zamora."

The guards passed around reluctant gestures and hushed whispers until one hastily sent another off. Brutus leaned against his vehicle casually, the stern, serious stares of the remaining guards focused on him as they waited nervously for the return of their comrade. After a period of silence, one on his side of the gate piped up: "On what grounds are you here?"

"Xela, right? That'd be your leader?" Brutus asked, crossing his arms. "I've got an offer for her. A job opportunity, if you will," he explained, leaving much to the imagination.

Shortly after, a tall woman appeared at the gate, a weapon stowed behind her. Her face was adorned with black makeup that dripped below her eyes as if she were crying ugly tears. Glancing back to the guards, Brutus noticed that all of them wore the same makeup; he had missed it earlier because of the concealing helmets they wore. While the guards were clad in thick armor, the woman that paced towards him was dressed in sultry, flowing clothes, beautifully tailored, entirely black save for some brighter accents.

Amber had called them an order, but Brutus was beginning to consider whether "cult" was a more appropriate title.

The woman, whom Brutus could only assume was Xela, drew a long, wicked scythe. As she approached, so did Brutus, slowly but casually. She readied as if to strike, then swung her weapon between the slits of the gate. The cruel edge of its blade stopped just before it impaled itself into an unflinching Brutus' chin. He felt no pain, only the tiniest drop of blood running down his neck as he swallowed.

"Talk," Xela demanded.

Brutus reached for his pocket to fetch the card Amber had given him once more, noticing the guards tightening their weapons. "Relax, killing you is the last thing on my agenda. This is for you," Brutus spoke confidently, as he brought the card towards Xela. She plucked it from his hand through the iron bars separating them. Her wary gaze never left him.

"Consider it," he simply said, as Xela's blade eased off his neck, and with that, he got back in his jeep. Charlie hopped in with him, and they left the strange village in the marsh behind.

Meanwhile, a confused Xela pondered the strange card, her eyes boring a hole into where her name was written on it. It was certainly a curious case, and she was certainly a curious person.

■ ■ ■

Alyssa Lincoln pushed up the sleeves of her dull sweater as she reached for a book on a high shelf, selecting a tome entitled *Relics*. It was a very old book, controversial and feared for its claims of teaching dark, mystical arts, as it covered the topics of the ancient and magical runes of Senia. Due to the rarity of gifted people able to control these relics, many even doubted the existence of them. Alyssa, however, knew firsthand that they were real, and furthermore, what they were capable of.

"Excuse me," she heard a voice call to her, "but I have to close down for tonight." A startled Alyssa turned to face the embodiment of every librarian stereotype, a wizened woman wearing wide-eyed glasses, clutching a book in one hand and a pen in the other.

"Of course, of course," Alyssa murmured as she reached to return the book to its shelf space.

"If you'd like, though, I can check the book out for you," suggested the librarian.

"That would be nice, thank you," Alyssa responded, giving the woman a smile of innocence.

She led Alyssa to the front of the library, walked behind a counter, and took the book from Alyssa's hands. "Do you have a library card?" the librarian asked.

"Of course," answered Alyssa, handing it to her. The old woman took it and wrote a few things down. She then handed back both the card and the book.

"Good night," she said with a faint smile to the girl in front of her. Alyssa nodded sweetly and bid her farewell as she took her leave. Behind her, the lights shut off, and the library fell asleep. Outside, however, the city was alive with celebration.

Book in hand, the redhead stepped out onto the crowded streets of White Heart, but was quick to stray from the parade of merry drunks and partiers, completely uncaring to the session of gaiety. The more vacant side streets were much more her friends; she followed them ever-enthusiastically. The sounds of fading celebration behind her brought her a strange, nostalgic aesthetic: she was alone, in bliss with herself. This was what she lived for.

As she entered a particular alley, she heard the alarming sound of footsteps in her trail. They followed on for quite some time before a demanding voice behind her forced the girl to stop in her tracks.

"Wait," she heard a call. Alyssa pretended not to hear, but she could feel his presence approaching. She sensed a hand reaching out to stop her, but grabbed at his arm before he could touch.

In one terrifying, sudden movement, Alyssa turned, her expression cold and angry. Her eyes shined a bright blue, almost blinding the man. He screamed in pain and pulled his hand away. A hound was at his side, howling and barking at Alyssa. The girl covered her ears, loud noises blending together and masterfully triggering her anxiety. Filled with abashment, she gave a remorseful look at the screaming man and the shouting dog, then raced off to seek inconspicuousness in the more crowded streets of the great city.

She left behind an angered Brutus and a confused Charlie. The former's groans faded as he pushed the pain from his system. At first, when she had held him, he had felt a strange tingling sensation, but it quickly turned into a feeling of an agonizing burning, like frostbite. Brutus had been skeptical about her at first, but the stories Amber had told him about Alyssa Lincoln were seemingly true. He was fearful of the unknown extent of the power of which she was apparently capable.

When the pain in his arm finally subsided, Brutus picked himself up from the ground. He made haste to follow Alyssa's trail, and Charlie chased close behind. She had disappeared somewhere into an alley, he knew, and as Brutus stepped into one, he noticed a familiar object: a grimoire, identical to the one Alyssa had been holding, lying abandoned on the ground. He waved it in front of the dog's snout, who caught a whiff of the book's recent holder's scent and showed Brutus the way.

Meanwhile, as Alyssa ran through an alley, she turned, her fear of pursuit growing. Fleeing with her gaze not where she was running, she accidentally hit a pipe and fell with a clumsy trip. Her heart grew faint when she felt the heavy book fly out of her arms and land somewhere nearby. As she picked herself up, knowing in that moment that when she took off her boots again, she would be greeted with bruises and scabs on her knees, she searched around for *Relics*, but to her dismay, failed to locate it. Not far away, the man and the hound turned a corner, and she abandoned hope of finding her borrowed tome. She continued on, not willing to trade her life for a book, and found her way back to the bustling parade on the wide streets, hoping she would lose her chasers in the chaos. Unfortunately, her crimson hair and shiny boots were much more harm than help. However, several times she stole frantic glances behind her, and she did not see a strange man or a vicious dog.

Just when Alyssa thought she lost them, a dreadful bark pierced her heart, a hound's cry loud enough to be heard through the commotion of the crowd. She welcomed a panicked run back as she shoved her way through the cluster of people, found her way into an alley on the opposite side of the street, and began to run down it. The alley took a sharp left turn that she hoped would lose her pursuers in, but to her alarm, she realized it was a dead end. As she turned, she was privy to the sight of the duo walking towards her where she lay; so if flight had not worked for her yet, she closed her eyes and focused her mind as she prepared to fight. Her fingers grew cold to the touch, and when the girl opened her eyes again, she had conjured a spear of ice in one hand and a frozen shield in the other.

"What do you want?" she asked in a hostile tone, her makeshift weapons raised, as the two cautiously approached.

"I think we might have gotten off on the wrong foot here," said the man. "I don't want to harm you, and neither does Charlie," he proclaimed as he peered down at the hound. Brutus shot a short, high-pitched whistle to signal Charlie's attention, and he patiently sat without delay. The man, however, continued his gentle pace towards Alyssa.

"What do you want?" Alyssa asked again, a touch more danger in her tone now.

He pulled a book from his coat, and Alyssa almost gasped when she recognized it as none other than *Relics*. He then slowly reached for something in his pockets, sticking it in her tome like a bookmark, and slowly bent to place the borrowed book on the ground so that he could slide it to her without approaching further.

"Don't just leave it on the floor! Do you have any idea how dirty it'll get?" she snapped, startling Brutus.

With an exasperated and slightly sassy sigh, she tossed her weapons aside, ignoring them as they shattered like glass. With the sound of her rapidly treading heels on cobble floor, she groaned in complaint and stepped forward to yank the book out of his hands. Once it was back in her possession, she hugged it in her arms tightly.

"My name is Brutus," he continued, as Alyssa gave him a glare that suggested he get to the point. "We know who you are, and we know what you're capable of. All we want is your help, and in exchange, we will protect you and give you a place to stay." He paused as he looked into her childlike eyes, blue like a deep ice. "Please visit us. We just don't want you falling into the wrong hands." With that, Brutus motioned to Charlie, and the two turned away. They left the alley behind, as well as a perplexed girl hugging a tome in her cold arms.

She waited idly until the two were long gone, then finally opened *Relics* again. Interest struck her when she realized that in the aging book, Brutus had placed a card with her name on it.

CHAPTER 2:

A bulky white cargo van driven by a pretty brunette pulled up to a long line of cars waiting for access to the east entrance of White Heart.

Massive walls loomed above Eva from a distance, walls surrounding a city of opportunity in front of her, captivating her with awe. The architecture was built to look as sturdy and defensive as it truly was. Several posts and buildings lined the wall, beyond which were even more structures, so far off in the massive city-state that they were lighter in color than the nostalgic sky clouding them from Eva.

The easternmost gate was the only vehicle-friendly entrance, the eastern section the only one to allow vehicles on the streets. Cars instead were parked in a large parking garage next to the gate.

Behind the wheel of the van, Eva sighed. She was safe now, her corrupt city far from here. White Heart and Greenwood were not allies; Greenwood officers had no authority to search for her on White Heart grounds.

Sooner than she expected, Eva found herself at the gate. A White Heart officer briefly checked her and her van, then allowed her to park in the massive garage nearby.

As she exited the van, Eva reached for the passenger seat, grabbing a thin piece of paper: a map of White Heart. On it, she had circled the address that the card had given her in bold red, a place directly in the center of the massive, sprawling city-state. She began to make her way down the overflowing streets to her destination.

With many streets not wide enough to even allow the passing of vehicles, the numerous cozy houses of White Heart huddled and clustered, pushing wandering civilians closer together than Eva had seen before. With so much energy packed so tightly, it was no surprise to her that the city was always alive; she had certainly never known a place so blind to gloom. Even from the tops of houses, commotion sounded, as the more urban, knowledgeable White Heart citizens navigated both the streets below and the roofs above with ease.

Eva had long been lost in thought, the city-state so new, foreign, fresh to her. As she jolted out of her pondering, she was thankful that her feet were guiding her to the location noted on her invitation.

The building, if it was the correct one, ducked beneath an underpass. The booming sound of a train passing on tracks above deafened her ears. As she looked up from her map, Eva noticed that the building looked like a station of some sort, perhaps for police or some form over government security. A woman in a blue beret leaned on an open-roofed army jeep in the parking lot in front, her eyes fixed on a holo-device tablet. She was the sole soul there.

"Excuse me," spoke Eva, as she approached and reached in her back pocket to fetch a card. "I'm here because of this. Might you know anything about it?"

The woman's eyes widened. "You must be Evangeline Bates. It is truly, truly an honor to meet you. Please, follow me."

She took off with haste and led Eva to a back door of the station, but stopped before opening it. "I'm sorry, perhaps I should introduce myself. My name is Amber Leavett." She held out her right hand, her other clutching the tablet, and Eva shook it. "I'm sure you have many questions, but please, hold them off for now."

With that, she opened the door and took Eva to a waiting room with a table at the center and a one-way window on one side. A dog lounged on a plush bed nearby. She recognized the hound as the one that brought her the invitation card.

"I believe you've met Charlie," Amber said, facing the dog. "Perhaps the best multi-service dog we have on the force. Vicious on the field, but very playful at home, so don't you worry about him."

Several other people sat at the table, all of whom looked just a bit more outlandish than Eva. One had a very ugly scar spread across his face and a bird covered in steel on his shoulder. Another, a woman with overdone black makeup covering her eyes, wore a scythe strapped to her back. A hooded man heavily-clad in armor sat nearby, as well as a young girl in a dull sweater with crimson hair so long it could have been used as a rope.

Maybe I'm in the wrong place...

Eva's thought went away soon, as Amber pulled up a chair for her. "Everyone has arrived, so I have a report to file," Amber announced, her voice pleasant and calm. "It should not take too long, mind you, but in the meantime, get to know each other better."

She smiled and began to leave, but a slightly crooked portrait of a honey-colored flower caught her attention on the way out. She fixed it back into place and abandoned the room, leaving the motley group behind.

■ ■ ■

"Is everyone present? Shall we begin?" asked the man, clipboard in hand, as Amber entered the room.

"Yes and yes," she replied, taking a seat next to the recorder. From the other side of the one-way window they sat across from, she could see the odd group, unaware yet of why they were there.

"Who would you like to start with?" the recorder asked in a monotone voice. Amber stared at the window, eyeing her options.

"How about her?" She pointed to the red-haired girl hiding behind a sweater. "Alyssa Lincoln." The man capped his pen, signaling he was ready to start.

"Her mother died not long after childbirth. She lived with her father, an ex-con. When sixteen-year-old Alyssa and her father were dining out one night, a group of gangsters ambushed them; Alyssa's father and a few other civilians were killed in a shootout. Somehow, this girl single-handedly managed to survive for two years on her own. Sometimes, she was reported seen in major cities, but every so often, she would venture out into the wilderness.

"I've been told that one such time, she was lucky enough to stumble upon a relic; I'm sure you've heard about them in myths and legends. If these stories are true, Alyssa is capable of immeasurable power, so I would like to take her in to prevent her from falling into the wrong hands. Moving on..." Amber paused to rummage through a few of the files in her hand. "Ah." She glanced at the recorder. "Shall we proceed?" The man indifferently nodded his head.

"Him," she said, selecting another character in the room. "The one with the hood. Very mysterious man, he is. Not much is known about him, but his most common nickname is Skullgem, on account of his bulky pendant. He's rallied public protests for racial equality and seems to have a particular focus on Assossian rights. But since he's mute, he has others translate for him."

"Is that all?" the recorder asked, after a pause from Amber. "On him, I mean."

Amber nodded her head. "It's all we've got on him. He's an enigma."

■ ■ ■

Meanwhile, on the other side of the one-way window, a cloud of awkwardness plagued the group of strangers brought together for reasons still unknown to them.

Finally, someone broke the silence.

"Okay, if we all somehow end up working together for...whatever this is, it might not be a bad idea to get to know each other."

31

The dialogue had come from the woman in heavy makeup sitting in the corner. Looking around, she realized the others still looked uninterested; it was almost as if she hadn't even spoken. "Fun crowd," she murmured to herself, just loud enough for the others to hear. Her pale hand ran through her short, black hair. "I guess I'll start." She tried incredibly hard to feel enthusiastic.

"My name is Xela, and I work as the leader of an order that specializes in resuscitation research, as well as the philosophy of life after death."

"Interesting," spoke the taller man with a bird on his shoulder. "Religion and science? That's a new one."

"And now you talk? Who might you be?"

He chuckled. "My name is Reese. Berserker, outlaw, badass..." He paused to turn to Eva with raised eyebrows: "...lover." A very vocal groan of disapproval sounded from her, followed by a roll of her eyes. "And this," he continued, giving a slight and strangely friendly nudge to the macabre raven, "this is Hex." The bird announced himself with a loud caw.

"I've got an extremely short temper, a serious addiction to both alcohol and drugs, and a deranged brother that rules an entire fucking empire." He sat back in his seat and crossed his arms. "Top that."

After a short period of silence, the woman across from him sighed.

"Very well. I might as well get this over with," she said. "My name is Evangeline, and I'm a vigilante, of a sort. I make my living doing the necessary deeds that others are afraid to do, for money." She paused briefly. "Oh, but I have a policy against killing. Only tranquilizers." She tapped the tip of her rifle idly.

"No killing?" Reese asked, chuckling. "Sounds like torture."

"I think having to listen to your obnoxious comments for the rest of my life would be torture," Eva retorted. A quiet laughter and a resounding *ooh* came from the others in the room. Even Reese himself gave a slight snicker.

After the room had silenced once more, the red-haired girl pulled her beige sweater away from her face. She shyly cleared her throat and tried to raise her voice.

"My name is Alyssa," she spoke, then paused. Here she was to choose whether these were people she would trust with her story. Deciding it was too late to go back now, she continued on: "I've survived life in the streets for a while now, and I'm hoping I can stay somewhere with people I can depend on."

She shocked both herself and the others with her sudden statement. She could see the pity in their eyes, and abashment struck her heart. Thankfully, the attention soon abandoned her, as Xela shifted her focus to the last person in the room: the mysterious man with a hood covering his face.

"And what about you?" she asked him directly. It was a strange hood; somehow, despite the bright lights illuminating the room, his face was indistinguishable.

He stood up silently, seemingly at ease with the spotlight on him, and it became obvious he was the smallest in the room. After a short silence, he began signing with elegant hands.

"Cat got your tongue?" Reese joked.

"Anyone know sign language?" asked Xela.

"Here, I have an idea," Eva said, standing from her chair. She took a pen from her backpack and placed it on the table, walked over to a bulletin board on one side of the room, and unclipped a flier from it. She turned it over and placed the paper, blank side up, in front of the hooded man, and handed him the pen. "Maybe you can't speak, but you can write, at least. I hope."

The stranger gave an affirming nod. He began to jot on the paper, as the others waited for his response. Once he finished, he slid the paper towards the center of the table. The others crowded around to read it. In neat handwriting was written:

"Please excuse me, for I am mute. The most common name I have been given is Skullgem, the Lionhearted. I am a public speaker and a civil rights activist."

"Interesting," Xela noted out loud.

"How can you be a public speaker if you can't talk?" Reese asked.

Before he could answer how his 'speeches' worked, the door opened, and Amber hastily rushed in.

"Dreadfully sorry to keep you waiting," she said. "I hope at least I left you enough time to learn more about each other." She gave a quick smile to Xela, who had first encouraged them to speak, and

34

Xela meekly returned one back. "Hopefully, now I can explain to you why you're all here."

Amber paused, recollecting her thoughts, as the group waited expectantly. "Have any of you heard of the Guardians?"

No one answered.

"For those of you who haven't," Amber continued, "the Guardians were an elite White Heart task force team dedicated to protecting and serving the people by taking down large-scale threats. A tragic accident a few years ago forced us to take it down before it got far, but now, a new threat arises: the Syndicate Empire of Avalon, led by a man named Boss Gareth. Our city-state, our sanctuary of protection, will be brought to ruin next, so long as their string of chaos remains uninterrupted. We are currently looking to reinstate the initiative, however, which is where you all come into play." Amber paused to pull up a chair and sat at the front of the table. "I have spent quite some time researching to make a list of the best of the best when it comes to the varied skills necessary for this job. The people in this room, sitting around this table," she said, her words exploding with wonder, "fit the description better than no other.

"We want people who are dedicated, strong-willed, and able to make tough decisions in the face of danger, and I have found that all of you fit those requirements. Together, we can put an end to the Syndicate's campaign of conquest. But join us or not, the choice is ultimately yours."

"What's in it for us?" Reese said.

"As compensation for the good you will do for the people, we will put you all under White Heart's protection," Amber answered. "No longer must you worry from the threats present in other city-states, and from the savage disorder of the Borderlands. Oh, and of course, all the renown and people's glory you can imagine will be yours."

"Is there any chance that protection can extend to more than one person?" Xela inquired.

Amber tilted her head at her. "How many are we talking?"

"A whole order," said Xela. "A hundred or so."

"We, the people of White Heart, are powerful," Amber assured contently. "We would be more than happy to take your people in, Ms. Zamora."

"Then you've got yourself a deal, general."

"I've always had a taste for adventure," said Reese. His raven cawed in agreement. "I'm in."

"M-me too," quietly spoke Alyssa.

"I mean, I could use the protection," said Eva. "But what about money?"

"White Heart could handle all of your expenses. You'll all certainly get a free home, too."

Eva thought it over, then gave an assuring shrug. "What else am I gonna do with my life? Count me in."

The only verbal response not received was from Skullgem, who promptly raised his hand in agreement.

Amber gave a smug look, clearly impressed with herself. "I had never expected it to come that easy," she said proudly. "Well, I have some time on my hands. Your new home is less than a block away, so long as you don't change your minds on the way there," she jested. "Why don't I give you all a tour?" In agreement, they got up to leave.

"Wait a minute," Reese spoke. "That's it? No contracts? We just magically become 'protectors of the realm'?"

"Guardians of White Heart is more like it, but yes, that's it," replied Amber. "I hold a solemn belief in trust; you trust that we will protect you, and we trust that you will help us." As she spoke, Amber opened the door to the streets of a sprawling city. Charlie, the hound, leaped up and followed her enthusiastically. "Come along now, I have much to show you."

She led the unlikely group to a new home.

■ ■ ■

Amber had not prevaricated; the house was incredibly close to the station where they had gathered. A curious sight, it was sandwiched tightly between two much larger buildings. It appeared quite commonplace both inside and out, giving a look that it was just an average house. A nice place it was, but much less a grand mansion and more a cozy cottage. Not that they would likely have minded; Alyssa didn't have a home, Reese lived furtively in scattered safe houses, Eva in her van, Xela in a swamp, and Skullgem a vagrant's life, often traveling from city-state to city-state to spread his messages of peace.

"Rest easy now," Amber spoke, as she let the newcomers into the house. "You have a long day tomorrow; I wish to begin your first mission. Nothing too drastic, just a sort of training exercise, the purpose of which is to see how we work together on the field. But make no mistake: the risk will not be small. It will still be a live operation. I'll fill you in with the details tomorrow morning."

Sleep engulfed all of them rather quickly that night.

CHAPTER 3:

Alyssa's face went numb as she was painfully pushed against the snow. Frost crept up to her cheeks like a spider crawling up its web, stealing a shiver out of her and forcing her onto her feet. Her assaulter, who had tossed her from her seat, was a man in the back of a truck that had carried them to this forsaken, frozen corner of Senia.

"We're here!" he announced in a cheerful, but sarcastic tone. "Nothing but ice, snow, and unforgivingly freezing wind for..." he looked around, "...for quite a distance.

"Your father managed to survive for a while until we finally caught up with him." He clapped his hands. "Now we've finally caught up to you! Run off then, little girl. Get a little taste of your daddy's medicine. But hey, then again, you're lucky, we're not lining you up in front of a firing squad or chopping your head off or yadda yadda, whatever boring method of execution we're talking about. Nah, I think we'll give you a chance. Maybe you'll survive the below-freezing temperatures, or the lack of food, or whatever fucked-up creatures roam around here. If you do, just come to me and prove me wrong, alright?" His tone was painfully stained with false concern.

"Oh, and you better come back!" yelled the woman at the wheel, clad in the same coattail uniform as the man who had pushed Alyssa. "I have fifty credits on you saying that you will!" she joked. The man scoffed, and with that, the truck abandoned her. The next minute, Alyssa was alone.

She chased after it for a few feet, but soon realized it fruitless; she might as well save her stamina for actually enduring her new habitat. She was glad for the sweater her body clung close to; it might give her an extra few hours of survival. Food was also a problem; unsurprisingly, nothing chose to grow in the brutal, arctic side of Senia.

The red-haired girl trudged on for about an hour. She had been following the trail marks of the truck in the snow, but flakes had begun to fall, starting to cover up the tracks. She quickly grew tired of the crunching of snow beneath her boots, and often glanced up at the horizon in hopes to see it change to the comforts of shelter. For quite some time, it remained flat and unhopeful, until she journeyed further, and finally...

Up ahead, a hill brought a difference to the landscape. Upon closer inspection, Alyssa found an opening in the middle of it; it was not a hill, but rather a cave. She ran to it, as it was better than standing out in the near blizzard conditions outside; the trail of the truck was practically gone, anyway.

Her instincts had been right, she realized as she approached the entrance. She wasted no time in plunging into the darkness of the cave, quickly realizing that it was much bigger on the inside. A tunnel led below ground and a light of the brightest blue shined on the walls of the cavern, tempting Alyssa to explore. She hesitated at first, but drawn to the possibility of warmth inside, ultimately gave in, and permitted the light guide her through the winding tunnel.

It grew brighter and brighter as Alyssa crept deeper and deeper. After blindly following it for some time, she finally came upon a room that looked as if it had been dug out by someone from a long-past time. An ancient pedestal stood at the center, and a strange rock, apparently the light source, sat on top of it. It looked like a meteorite, with holes in it that revealed a blue core, shining so brightly that the girl had trouble looking at it. Its outer layer gave off a chrome luster, paining her eyes even further. Creepily, it pulsated, like the beating of a heart, which hypnotized Alyssa despite the overload of brightness. A glimmer of concern whispered to her that the rock might be dangerous, but she felt a queer urge to touch it, as if it beckoned to her. Her feet moved for her, towards the shining mystery.

As Alyssa stepped closer, the core of the rock began to pulsate faster, almost furiously. She could swear she heard it beating, too, to the rhythm of her footsteps, drawing closer and closer. Finally, she reached the pedestal, bringing her hand down to it and touching the outer chrome layer. Nothing happened at first, but then the exterior of the artifact began to shrivel. Alyssa flinched and stepped back from it, fear suddenly striking her. The outer layer melted away seemingly into nowhere, betraying its glowing interior. She walked up to a beautiful blue crystal, now free from its shell. Picking it up in her hands, she found it freezing to the touch, but she felt more bliss than pain. A blue aura seeped from the crystal and found its way into the sleeves of Alyssa's beige sweater, crawling up her arms and around her body, caressing her with a gentle, yet cold touch. A strange calm descended upon her, and she steadily held the artifact in her anxious hands. Eventually, the relic began to lose its light. Its bright glow was soon gone, and the cavern grew darker until it became once again engulfed in pitch-black.

She stumbled about, feeling around for a wall. The touch of a rough surface to her side told her that she had found one, but navigating her way out would prove a new challenge. She rolled up her sleeves, hoping to rely on her sense of touch to get out of this predicament. Instead, strange markings on her arms greeted her, shining just as brightly as the crystal she had touched, providing her a torch in the darkness. She followed the way up, back to the overworld, the light in the tunnel above her growing closer and closer. As she trudged back up the cavern, the sounds of howling winter touched her ears, as did the whiteness of the world outside the reach of her eyes. It was not long before her boots touched snow again, and she had found her way out.

A snowstorm had picked up outside, but she somehow did not give even a sliver of a shiver. She was no longer weary nor cold; in fact, she felt invigorated, and despite the disappearance of the tracks, she seemed to know her way, almost as if a strong instinct had implanted itself within her. Although she still felt the frozen wind upon her, it inspired her now rather than threatened her life. It greatly puzzled Alyssa, and her mind was astorm, attempting to understand the situation. She took her sweater off. Nothing changed, she felt no pain. She knelt down to rub snow on her body. Nothing changed, she still felt no pain. She laughed, in part amazement and part disbelief, pondering what the relic in the cave had done to her.

Alyssa reached to put her sweater back on, but was then caught by her markings again. They reminded her of sprawling tribals, and they ran everywhere on her arms. Like the relic she had found in the cave, they too mysteriously pulsated, and the beating of color against her eyes entranced her. Hypnotized, she slowly felt herself slipping away, away from the blizzard, away from her past...

Alyssa opened her eyes. She found herself back in White Heart, in one of the many bedrooms of her new home.

It was the same dream she witnessed about once a week since obtaining the relic, the one that told the story of how such an event occurred. It was a constant, haunting reminder of the rare, perplexing life she was stuck with. She pulled her arms out from under the bedcovers to find that the markings shone just as brightly as they did that fateful day.

She got up, dressing in her sweater and skirt, and left the room. Locating the stairwell, she made her way downstairs, finding Amber already in the kitchen.

"Good morning," they said to each other in unison.

"Did you sleep well? Have any dreams?" Amber asked.

"Yeah. No dreams," lied Alyssa. "Is anyone else awake?"

Amber pointed to her right, at a shepherd dog lapping away at a bowl filled with water. He noticed Alyssa and ran over to her, his mouth still dripping, but coupled with the oblivious smile he donned, he was quite possibly one of the sweetest sights she had ever been privy to. An uncontrollable smile graced her too, as she knelt down to pet his soft neck. As he panted, she noticed something shining in his mouth and glanced at Amber with a look of inquiry.

"Titanium fang implants. Sharp enough to bite through steel." Amber responded.

"Whoa." Alyssa's amazement was noticeable.

Amber chuckled. "Yeah. He's quite the fighter."

A silence then found them, and a question flowered in Alyssa's concerned mind. "Can I ask you something?"

"Of course, anything!"

Alyssa sighed. "These people here, they seem very strong-willed and ready to do something good for the world..."

Amber nodded in agreement. "That they are."

"I can understand why you picked them for this," continued Alyssa, "but why would you pick me? Just a day ago, I was nothing but a street urchin. I mean, that's still the same girl you're talking to."

Amber sighed. "I had a feeling you might ask this. I can understand where you're coming from, too. Why in the vast majority of Senia, among a very exclusive group of the most skilled people in the world, was an orphan girl chosen?" She paused, then gave Alyssa a sweet smile. "You're a survivor. You've lived on the streets for longer than most could. You've faced misfortune and misery with every step, and yet you still trudge on. You've learned how to be better, and how to overcome challenges, rather than give up. That takes a lot, Alyssa, more than you realize." She walked over to the redhead and took a seat next to her. "Trust me, I know everything I need to know about everyone here. Including," she lightly touched Alyssa's arm, "the secrets you may be wishing to hide."

Amber got up and walked back to where she stood, her pumps loudly echoing her steps. "The people amongst this group may seem intimidating, but remember: a team can't accomplish much if the people within it can't cooperate with each other. Believe me when I say you are just as qualified to be here as anyone else in this house. They may be older than you, but no one is going to treat you any differently because of it. Make them realize who you are. Show them Alyssa Lincoln's true potential, her true power."

Alyssa nodded, doing her best to give the general a happier countenance. "Yeah. Yeah, I think I will. Thank you, ma'am," she said, clicking her boots together lightly.

"Please, call me Amber," she said, with a facilitating smile. "My dream is that one day, the Guardians will become the most powerful face of meritorious justice Senia has ever known, and will ever know," she said, breaking out into a slight chuckle. "We can all dream, can't we?"

In the next two hours, the rest of the unit began appearing downstairs. Amber gathered them all together eagerly, ready to brief them on their mission.

"Good morning, everyone," she began, once she saw that the seven of them had assembled in front of her. "Tomorrow will not be practice; you are going to be put in dangerous situations, to be frank. Do not underestimate the risks at stake here and be cautious with your choices. This will be, however, a test to see where your best skills are, how you operate in the field, how well you cooperate with teammates, and how well you act under pressure. Charlie and I will accompany you out in the field. That being said, are there any questions so far?" Not a word was spoken.

"Good," continued Amber. "A bandit group has been reported plotting to poison the water filter station outside of White Heart, as well as to hijack supply trains that make stops at the city. According to our mole in their system, a huge raid is scheduled for tomorrow. A train running from the north is anticipated to make its run around that time. You are to stop any and all attempts made in the endeavor to hijack it.

"Meanwhile," she said, shifting her focus, "a water refinery sits outside the walls of White Heart. All water that goes into White Heart's systems passes through there first. As my insider says, a plot to sabotage the purifying station will accordingly be made tomorrow.

"I want one team to prevent the hijacking of a supply train and another to stop the poisoning of White Heart's water supply. Who goes on which team is up to you to decide, but I want the final decision to be made today." Amber reached into her purse and pulled out a small bag. "Inside this are unique badges for each of you, and they identify you as official Guardians. Do not lose these!" She took them out of the bag and tossed them, one by one, to their respective recipients.

"Oh, and one more thing. Watch your fire. Our insider will likely accompany these raids, and will promptly present himself to you if he sees you. So please, be careful where you aim."

CHAPTER 4:

A young girl trotted up to the man working the register, an expression donning on her with touches of enthusiasm. "Excuse me," she said, as she parted her scarlet hair. "Do you have any books on relics?"

He looked up and got up from his seat, walking around the counter. "I believe we do. Follow me, please." He led Alyssa through the store and stopped upon a certain bookshelf. "Last I checked, they were somewhere around...ah." He bent down and pointed at the lowest shelf. "All of these books should be about relics. I hope that helps."

"Thank you very much," Alyssa replied, as the man started to walk away. She began to browse among the books when she noticed the sign atop the shelf that told her what part of the store she was in. "Hold on," she called out to the bookstore attendant.

He turned to face her. "Something wrong?"

"Why are these books in the fiction section?" Alyssa inquired.

The man looked at her strangely and gave a slight laugh. "You don't actually believe in those fairy tales, do you?"

Alyssa's mouth cracked ajar, and her eyebrows twitched in frustration, crestfallen and offended at his remark. In front of the man's eyes, she grabbed one of the books and placed her palm on the cover. As she pressed on it, the surface began to cover itself in a glass-like substance. When the book had been sealed completely, Alyssa tossed it to the shocked clerk. He couldn't believe what he had just seen, but it was confirmed by the man's sense of touch, as he could barely grip it, the book threatening to slip out of his shaking hands at any moment:

It was completely encased in ice.

"Fairy tales, my ass," she remarked with a smirk, pointing towards the nonfiction section. "When this thaws, it goes over there."

■ ■ ■

The open-roofed army jeep braked on the icy terrain, a few feet from the train tracks. They were miles from civilization now, just on the outskirts of White Heart territory, not far from the reaches of the Borderlands.

The tracks curved to the south, through a grassy area of nostalgic plains dotted by pretty flowers, until they finally darted straight to White Heart. The great sanctuary stood out far in the distance, an elegant, yet humongous cluster of buildings surrounded by grand walls. It sat between the plains, a huge dark forest, and the large arctic biome they had found themselves in. The city was truly built in a unique place.

Charlie's ears perked up, and he picked up his head. Amber leaned over from the driver's seat to face the others in the vehicle. Along with her and the dog were Xela and Skullgem.

"It should pass here in a few minutes," Amber stated. "Keep your eyes peeled for any other vehicles."

Soon enough, they noticed the train steaming ahead on the tracks. Its booming sound coursed through their ears, growing louder as it approached them. Amber waited until the train screamed and chugged merely yards from them, before starting up the jeep again to follow the tracks. By maintaining this pace, they could drive parallel to the front car of the train. When the conductor noticed them, Xela pulled her badge out, waving it in the air. The conductor seemed to recognize it but was unsure of what to do. Finally, he asked his assistant to step outside.

The assistant opened the train door and attempted to speak with them, but over the clamor of the train, nothing was audible. After a bit, Amber yelled to Xela.

"Get closer! I need you to get on the train!" Amber called. She wasn't sure if Xela heard her at first, but as Xela started to stand up, it seemed as if she did.

Amber slowly, patiently moved the jeep as close as possible to the stairs of the first train car. When they were close enough, Xela dauntlessly leaped forward.

Her arms grabbed the rails, but her feet slipped off the steps as she landed, and they hung dangerously free, dangling precariously close to the train's churning wheels. Amber let out a light gasp. Xela, however, had the will to find her footing, and the conductor's assistant helped pull her to safety. He opened the door to the inside, the two ran in, and Amber exhaled a sigh of relief. She knew she shouldn't have been doubting her Guardians so soon, as Xela proved capable, but that was only the first sign of danger. Much more was to come.

Meanwhile, from within the train, where the sounds of the great roaring machine were suppressed: "What's wrong?" the conductor asked. "I'm sure they didn't just send you over for a tea party for three and some comic relief."

"We came to warn and protect you," the Guardian began, "from a raid. Bandits are going to come for your train to steal whatever you're transporting, and we're here to stop them."

"I wouldn't know shit about what I'm carrying," the conductor said. "I just drive, lady. Anything you need me to do?"

"Just keep your head down and man the train. Don't go into any other cars."

"I was doing that before you got on," he remarked. "And my life wasn't in danger." While the conductor remained sarcastic yet collected, his assistant wasn't doing so well with the news.

"Hold on, hold on," he said. "A raid? This is ridiculous. I better be getting paid extra for this."

"Get your head out of your ass and show some respect for this woman!" the conductor harshly scolded. "She's coming over here to save your sorry butt, and you're thinking about money? For shame, kid."

Xela tried hard not to chuckle at their less-than-intimate banter. She was about to head back out to consult Amber when a strong jolt almost swept her off her feet.

"Speak of the sinner," she whispered. "Where is that coming from?"

"Has to be from the caboose," the conductor replied.

"Whatever you do, do not stop the train," Xela cautioned, as she left their car, treading forward into danger.

■ ■ ■

Meanwhile, a girl sat in the back of a van, attempting to read a clustered book. The many bumps along the ride that shook the vehicle, however, made this a difficult process. Alyssa had barely gotten to take in a page of her new tome when Eva pulled the van over, shouting, "We're here!"

The filtering plant was huge. Like White Heart, it was fortified by colossal walls, something of a cross between castle defenses and regal architecture fit for a museum. Various hangars were visible, with open spaces reaching far below them, ending with swirling rapids at the very bottom.

They followed through the entrance to the plant. Eva's van was only the leader of a small convoy; a few other White Heart agents followed close behind.

A man at the gate stopped them. As Amber had instructed, Eva flashed him their badges, and the guard let them in. Alyssa went back to reading her book, but was interrupted by a cluster of arguments arising from in front of the van. She crawled over to the front and peered out the window.

"What's going on?" she asked.

"No idea," Reese replied. A brutish man was angrily yelling at the guard who let them in. Eva rolled open her window, and the vexed man trudged up to her.

"What are you doing here? Who are you?" he inquired.

Eva pulled out her badge again, growing irked. "Convincing enough? I'd like to speak to whoever's in charge around here."

"You already are. And I say that I have never heard of you 'Guardians.' I cannot let you in."

Eva was noticeably angered, but not as upset as Reese, who was clearly biting back his ire. He looked ready to initiate a fistfight with the man.

Eva sighed. "We're not leaving. We're here to protect you from a raid. Your lives are in danger."

"Do what you want," he said, "as long as it does not involve you getting through these walls."

Reese viciously opened the van's door and walked up to the man, opening his mouth to start an argument, while Hex stayed inside the van, his talons gripping the front seat. Just as Reese was getting ready to let loose a barrage of inappropriate insults, he was interrupted by a truck that came screeching around the path to the entrance, loaded to the brim with kegs in the back. A heavily-armed and armored man stepped out from the passenger seat, a rifle in his hands. Without hesitation, he opened fire on the van and anyone around it.

They witnessed Reese take multiple gunshots, blood spilling from his body in many directions. Hex quickly flew outside the van and threw himself at his partner, maintaining a spot in front of him by light flaps of his wings. At first, Eva and Alyssa were perplexed at what he was doing; though possibly deadly, Hex was still but a fragile bird. Then they noticed the bullets vaporizing a foot from the raven. From the bird's mechanized eye, a few quick moving projectiles were being shot out, as if he had some sort of anti-projectile system hardwired inside his body. Hex's cover worked like a charm, allowing enough time for Reese to crawl back into the passenger seat, and when the raven saw that he had made it back to safety, he flew into the van with him.

To their left, the White Heart agents returned fire. From the back of the van, Alyssa noticed more bandit vehicles careening down the path, on their way to join the fray.

"Now can we come in?" Eva sarcastically yelled to the panicked manager running to safety. "Dumbass," she murmured as she slammed the gas pedal down, speeding inside the plant. The agents followed suit, as did the raiders.

"Pull over here," Reese harshly spoke through gritted teeth, the blood in his mouth making his voice even scarier than usual. Eva did as he instructed, parking her van behind the cover of a row of water tanks.

Reese lifted his shirt to reveal the belt at his waist, holding strange capsules filled with red serum across the front of it. He pulled one out and uncapped it, the thick needle attached revealing it to vaunt the appearance of a syringe. A painful groan escaped him as he stabbed it into his arm, but the noise quickly faded away. Eva glanced at him, finding his entire body gone limp, almost as if he were dead.

"Reese?" Eva frantically spoke, shaking him.

Surprisingly, his bird friend didn't seem to be traumatized, giving no reaction to Reese's lack of animation. Eva checked his pulse as Alyssa crawled over, eager to understand the panic. For a second, she felt nothing, but out of nowhere, it began to beat abnormally quickly, gaining speed at an alarming rate. Suddenly, Reese let out a huge gasp as his body violently convulsed. Eva and Alyssa yelped and looked on with some curiosity and a great deal of fear.

A heavily panting Reese wordlessly picked himself up and bolted out of the van, no longer twitching, but his movements jagged and unfriendly, as a bandit approached the door with a weapon in hand. Before the raider could react, Reese brutally grabbed for her throat and picked her up from the ground, only to slam her back down with such force that the splintering and crushing of her bones could be heard by everyone around them. Eva almost felt sorry for her, until one of her armed allies approached the driver's side door. In a split second, Eva pushed the door open, pulled her rifle from her back, and raised it forward, hitting the bandit with the butt multiple times. As he stumbled away, Eva shot a dart into an exposed spot just below his neck. He reached for it, pulling the dart out, but the heavy tranquilizer had already taken effect. His eyes shut as he fell into deep sleep, and toppled over onto the ground.

Alyssa pushed open the back doors of the van and jumped out. As she witnessed more vehicles pulling up to the hill leading to the plant, she knew the fight was only beginning. Afraid at first, her worried thoughts fled as she knew the sniper to her right and the berserker to her left were there fighting with her.

CHAPTER 5:

Another sudden jerk of the train pushed Xela against the sides of her car. She steadied herself and gave a glance through the windows to see outside the train. She could still see Amber's jeep running parallel to Xela as she traveled down the cars.

Holding a railing nearby for support, Xela steadily progressed to the back of the car, crossed the threshold, and opened the door to the next car. As she did, she came upon the sight of three bandits making their way towards her from the opposite side. All wore helmets with tinted visors that masked their faces and bore pistols, rifles, swords, or other scary weapons. In retreat, Xela closed the door with a slam and ran back to the previous train car. From her thigh, where a small holster strap was placed, she pulled a throwing knife, preparing for her attackers to approach.

Instead, she heard two shots ring out, so loud that they brought shame to the clacking of train wheels below them. Weapon drawn, Xela waited patiently, the sound of boots approaching the door blending with the staccato beat of her own heart. Before she could open it again, someone on the other side did it for her.

A man stepped out, no weapons in hand, reaching for his helmet to unmask himself. Instinctively, Xela threw the knife, which dug itself into the man's hand, sending him flinching backward. He cried out in pain and quickly reached his other hand out to remove his helmet before she could attack him further.

Xela was speechless. It was Brutus, the man who partook in her admission, whose hand she had just impaled.

"I'm so sorry!" she blurted, her eyes widening. "Are you alright?"

"Just fine," he said, in a slightly sarcastic tone, ripping the blade out of his skin. He wiped the bloodied knife on his sleeve, tossed it to its owner, and Xela caught it and put it back on her thigh-strap. "You just nailed my good hand pretty nice, is all."

"I'm sorry," Xela repeated. "I am so sorry."

Brutus gave her apology no attention. He ripped off part of his costume and used it as a makeshift gauze for his hand. Little did he heed to the pain from his injury, as as soon as his wound was covered, he went on and opened the door again, standing in the gap between the cars. Upon noticing the jeep following them, he waved, catching Amber's attention. It was hard to tell from where she stood, but Xela could swear Amber grinned at Brutus, perhaps out of her happiness to see him alive and well.

"Let's go," he said, leading Xela down the train.

"Are you sure you'll be fine?" Xela inquired. A hurried "yeah, yeah" was the only response she received from him.

The gruesome display in the car beyond left little to the imagination. The two bandits who saw Brutus as a comrade were now reduced to mangled and sanguinary corpses. A crimson liquid dripped down the elegantly decorated train walls. It was nothing Xela hadn't seen before, especially considering her occupation, but it triggered a series of pondering questions about post-necrosis in her head that trailed on, much like the train she journeyed down.

Outside the speeding train, Amber's vehicle followed Brutus and Xela as they made their way to the end of the line. "Haven't forgotten your role, have you?" she asked aloud.

The hooded man next to her clenched his hammer and promptly flashed a nod of his head, armed and ready. The Guardian general nodded back at him, then applied the brakes so that their jeep could parallel itself with the back of the train.

As Amber drove just behind the caboose, two menacing, open-roofed vehicles came into view from the other side. They were cluttered to the brim with crooked outlaws and adorned with spiked poles which they were using to push the train in hopes of tipping it over. As Amber noticed, they were doing a decent job at it; the train's last few wheels were almost levitating off the ground. No doubt more vehicles would come to the assistance of their comrades quite soon, and when they did, the train would stand no chance.

As they approached the bandit cars from the back, Skullgem stood from his seat in preparation, just as they had planned. Even closer now, he climbed the hood of Amber's jeep, tightly clamping onto the front windows for balance. The general accelerated, slamming the gas pedal. As they picked up speed, Skullgem picked himself up, now standing on the very front of the jeep. His pitch cape fluttered behind him with little care, and though his expression was not visible, it was clear he was serious and ready. Closer and closer their vehicle crept, but not one of the bandits noticed them; their focus was elsewhere, and the boisterous noises emitted from multiple vehicles gave Amber, Charlie, and Skullgem a stealthy advantage.

Finally, however, they drew too near; as a bandit in the back turned, he noticed them and made an attempt to draw a weapon.

Now was the mysterious hammer-wielder's time. As the bandit aimed a pistol, Skullgem made a daring leap, hammer over his head, toward the bandit vehicle. The gun went off, but the bullet found itself stuck harmlessly in Skullgem's shoulder plates. The hammer proved victorious, clubbing the bandit over his head and knocking him out cold.

Meanwhile, Amber drew her pistol with a flip from the driver's seat and aimed it at the bandit squad. Before she could fire, however, she was interrupted by a jolt that rocked her, and her head slammed against the steering wheel. She turned and was shown to an identical bandit truck ramming the back of her car, with yet another following close behind it.

A highwayman with a wicked dirk in his hand performed the same maneuver Skullgem had attempted, only this time, Amber's vehicle was the victim. He landed in the back seat, where Charlie sprang up and began biting the hijacker's legs frantically. He delivered a good kick towards the hound's snout, sending Charlie whimpering onto the vehicle's cold, metal floor. Struck with ire, Amber focused her pistol upon her attacker, firing a few rounds into his chest. He stumbled and fell back, landing across the hood of the truck, blocking the driver's view.

As Amber fought, so did Skullgem in front of her, and though he was largely outnumbered four to one, sharing a technical with no one else but bandits, he battled valiantly.

One bandit lay on the ground incapacitated, having been taken down by the hooded Guardian, and another was busy tending to the wheel. Skullgem was menacingly approached by the other two in the vehicle. One with a club in his hand attacked first, but Skullgem parried, and then struck him down. He gave no moment for hesitation and instantly followed through with an attack that the second bandit didn't see coming, and she was quick to fall from the vehicle. As he recovered from a heavy swing of his hammer, he received a kick to the stomach from the first bandit, who had already brought himself to his feet, and Skullgem flew back into Amber's windshield. He picked himself back up as Amber covered him with her gunfire.

Inside the train, a tall woman with a scythe in hand and a gruff man with revolvers at the ready made their way to the caboose. While passing through two cars, Brutus stopped Xela; the fight would begin here. From the side of the train, a sliver of a truck's hood was visible. Brutus peeked his head out at the situation, then reported back to Xela.

"Shit, they're trapped between three Syndicate trucks. They need our help."

"Syndicate?" Xela shot a confused stare at him.

"I'm going to head to the back of the caboose and handle the truck behind them. I need you to take out the front crew. Don't worry; there's less in that one than there are in the other two. Think you can do that?"

She promptly nodded and put aside her massive weapon, and with that, Brutus stepped into the caboose. Xela climbed over the guardrail between the train cars, creeping along the edge, slowly making her way to the bandit truck.

No one was driving, as the truck was impaling the train, allowing it to do the tugging. The two bandits in it didn't seem to notice her at first, busy with tormenting Amber, Skullgem, and Charlie behind them. Seeing her opportunity, she edged just a bit further before leaping onto the hood of the truck, scythe in hand. With a swift sweep of the blade, she made elegant cuts into the two unnoticing bandits. They fell from the truck and tumbled onto the grass below, quickly disappearing from view as the train and trucks sped by and abandoned them.

Shame precious lives had to be wasted on this, she thought to herself. Her pondering was interrupted by a loud explosion that deafened her ears, coming from the truck farthest back. As the smoke subsided, Xela saw not a crew manning the truck, but a single man. Having dealt with the technical's crew with an explosive device, Brutus sat in the driver's seat and began to pull the truck away from the train. In correspondence, the train began balancing itself, but the trouble was not over yet. Xela looked over to see the last remaining crew, between Amber and Brutus, focusing their aim on the former.

Amber seemed to notice just in time and swerved away from the action, towards a hill in front of her that elevated the car from the train. It granted her cover from fire, but for unfortunate Skullgem, the curve of the slope was too much. He lost his balance, fell from the hood of the jeep, and barely caught onto it as he tumbled; his hands clung to the passenger doors, but his feet were dragging behind him.

Brutus, upon seeing this, called himself to action, pushing the gas pedal and slammed into the bandit truck's rear. His enemies lost their aim for a second, providing Skullgem some safety, but upon recovering, directed their bullets towards Brutus. Outnumbered, he pulled back, but not before slipping them a present: he yanked a pin off, tossed something towards the bandits, and a grenade clanked on the metal floor of the bandit truck. Unlike in the first truck, it was noticed, to his dismay. One amongst the crew quickly picked it up, hastily throwing it far away, and it exploded harmlessly behind them.

Meanwhile, Skullgem's grip began to falter. Amber noticed this, and from her elevated position, devised a plot.

"Hey!" She could only hope he heard her over the ruckus and chaos. "I'm going to need you to drop on my mark! You're going to have to trust me!" She wasn't sure if she saw a tiny nod from him, but she hoped he picked up what she was saying.

Amber punched the gas as she allowed her jeep to steer slightly to the left, before she pulled the wheel clockwise with all her force. "Now!" she screamed, just before her vehicle flew off the hillside, up and over the bandit technical, and landed on the top of the train. She slammed on the brakes and breathed a sigh of relief as she turned and realized Skullgem had let go, dropping onto the bandit technical.

He hit one bandit with his knee as he fell, and another with his hammer after he landed. Then, he kicked a clutch next to the driver with a sweep of his legs. As he had hoped, the spikes on the side retracted, and the train was no longer pushed over by the truck. The bandit driver, noticing this, picked up speed, and one of his allies grabbed Skullgem by his chest plate. He easily pulled the Guardian from the floor and pushed him against the train. The steel of Skullgem's armor clattered, and his body violently thrashed as his back grinded against the train car behind him. The bandit dropped him, however, after receiving a bullet to the arm.

From behind them, Brutus had drawn the revolver usually holstered to his left side. It was green-streaked, and along its side was inscribed the word "GOOD." He wasted away at the bandits, bullets of green streaming into them, as a now free Skullgem leaped into the seat by his side. The bandit driver pulled away from the train in retreat, he and his severely wounded bandit comrades drenched in failure.

Their mission complete, Xela looked up at Amber with a grin. "How are we going to get you down?"

Amber chuckled, sending a smile back Xela's way. They laughed now, but soon they would be called back to action: a fight was still taking place elsewhere.

■ ■ ■

War still raged at the White Heart purification plant. When one bandit went down, three more would take its place. The battle went from a zoned skirmish to a bloody blitzkrieg for supremacy. Numbers of bandits made their way to the hangers, hauling barrels of toxins to the distillation chambers and attempting to toss their worth of poison in the waters. Most were stopped by Guardians, White Heart agents, or sometimes even workers of the plant themselves.

An eagle-eyed Eva crawled up to an elevated position, where she carefully targeted bandits making their way towards the large entrance. Reese and Alyssa were below her, and agents and armed workers fighting for their lives were scattered throughout the plant, but the rest of the battlefield was dominated by bandits. It seemed, from her nest, that the line she and her allies were holding was beginning to weaken, and would soon fall to the hordes of storming criminals at their gates.

Suddenly, however, a convoy sped in through the front entrance, almost halting the battle with the screeching of demanding tires. Eva's heart was taken by gloom, expecting more bandits, but the familiar faces of the drivers and passengers brought a smug grin to her face.

Before the approaching jeeps and trucks came to a full stop, a dog jumped out from one and darted into the fray. Charlie gnarled at a bandit firing at the vehicles with a rifle, selecting him as his victim. With terrifying speed, the hound jumped at him before he could react, and with paws on the man's shoulders, tackled him to the ground. He let his ferocious fangs tend to the rest, ignoring the bandit's desperate pleas for help.

Meanwhile, Amber pulled her car over and beckoned to Xela, who had been sharing the vehicle with her. "Come with me," she said to her.

Xela did promptly, following suit as the two snuck away from the conflict. Amber stumbled upon a few workers hiding from the firefight, and to one of them, she asked if there was any way to blockade the water flow after it passed through purification.

"Through the back entrance," a worker responded, pointing to a secluded door behind them. "First left on the hallway. Door marked 'control room.' Can't be missed."

Amber thanked him, and she and Xela ran for the door. Before they could reach it, however, a bandit vehicle wheeled towards them, closing in on them with breakneck speed.

"Amber!" Xela shouted, noticing that her fellow Guardian was still oblivious to the truck darting towards her.

In the nick of time, Xela dove, grabbing Amber and pulling her towards safety. The driver of the bandit vehicle, having missed the target, began to turn the truck as a few bandits dropped from the back.

Xela was up and ready, her menacing scythe already gripped tightly in her hands. She ran towards the bandit group as they disembarked from the truck. One of them pulled a shield from her back just as Xela slashed away with her own weapon. Scythe and shield clashed, and Xela pushed off of the bandit. When she tried to attack again, her swift strikes found themselves parried by the bandit's weapon.

Meanwhile, bullets from the other bandits whizzed past them, directed towards Amber. Xela immediately forgot her attacking stance in concern for the general and turned to check on her. The bandit woman with the massive shield in her hands saw her chance and struck Xela's chest with the side of her weapon. As Xela fell to the ground, the wind knocked from her, the bandit peered over her and raised her weapon to deal a final blow to the Guardian, a twisted smile of victory on her face. Her expression changed to a grimace as a bullet caught her throat, and she reached to her wound, dropping her weapon and crumbling to her knees as blood shot out onto her shield.

Amber lowered her smoking pistol and made her way to Xela, firing into any bandit that threatened them. She knelt and quickly helped her fellow Guardian up, pulling her towards the door. They managed to get inside just before a barrage of bullets laid waste to them.

"I underestimated you, Xela," Amber murmured, as she locked the door behind them and led Xela around a corner. "You're quite the protector."

"I'm used to it," Xela admitted. "I've had to protect a lot of people. You'd know what that's like, I'm sure."

"Then I made the right call. You were born to be a Guardian."

As Amber spoke, she put her hand on Xela's arm in a friendly manner. The other woman flinched, and it was then that Amber noticed the blood seeping onto her black sleeves. "It just brushed me," she said, her voice unwavering. "I'll be fine." Amber surely hoped so.

Outside the building, the Guardians and White Heart agents stood outside the large entrance to the purification chambers, struggling to keep the army of bandits at bay.

Reese was at the front of the line, swatting and punching away with his massive fists. Next to him, Alyssa fended off opponents with knives of ice, freezing those that drew too close. Eva stood behind, firing sedatives into the few bandits that threatened to break their ranks. Hex was darting from enemy to enemy, taking them down with wing or talon as he zipped by and through the crowd.

"You sure you'll be okay?" Reese yelled to Alyssa over the chaos of gunfire. His voice was deep and terrifying, pulsing with anger and rage.

Alyssa drove an icicle into a bandit's chest, then pushed him aside. "You don't take me for innocent, do you?" she shouted back.

Reese drew his lever-action shotgun and fired a round at a cluster of bandits. "Well, no, but..."

"Oh, so you do?" she interrupted, eyeing an opportunity to prove herself.

A man with a sword in hand charged at her, steaming with battle-rage. Before he reached her, Alyssa stomped her boots on the floor. Ice crawled from her heels to the ground, and along the ground to the man. Hastily running, he slipped on the ice, but before he hit the ground, Alyssa conjured a frozen spire beneath him. The bandit fell back and impaled himself on it, giving a bloodcurdling wail as life began to desert his body.

"You've got your tricks, girl!" Reese exclaimed, clearly in awe. "But I have mine, too."

Before he could impress her with his savagery in combat, a man with a mace in hand took a swing at Reese from his blindside. The weapon struck Reese, and he let out a groan, but it did little to falter him. Foolishly, the bandit raised his mace over his head and attempted to slam it into Reese again. Bleeding from his side, Reese grabbed the mace by its hilt just before it clubbed him. He pushed himself up and the bandit away, just as another bandit charged at him. Reese let out a shrill whistle from his lips, his call for backup. Hex immediately shot to help, slashing his metal wings into the approaching highwayman. As his opponent struggled, the raven dug his talons into his shoulders, shredding the man, tearing the skin from his face with a fluttering of his dagger-like wings and pecking of his razor-sharp beak.

Meanwhile, Reese gave a punishing throw of his fist towards the man with the mace. When he struggled backward from the painful blow, Reese grabbed him and threw him to the ground. He advanced towards his downed opponent, but was stopped by a battle cry that screamed from behind him. Reese had no time to turn before he felt someone push off of his head, using him as a footstool. Looking ahead, he saw Eva soar and fire a dart into the bandit. She rolled onto the ground below her, and the man, benumbed from the sedative, fell back down, letting out a light groan.

Reese chuckled at her in the midst of chaotic fighting, loud enough for her to hear. Eva flashed a proud grin, then the two brought their focus back to the battle.

The berserker grabbed his axe and slammed it into the ground with such force that it stuck there, the cement below it broken in fragments. From his side, he pulled a thick green disk, tossing it behind a pursuing bandit. Where the disk landed, Reese immediately appeared, his body teleporting from one place to another instantaneously. From his new position, Reese opened the palm of his hand, and the implanted axe flew from the ground into his fingerless gloves. It cared not for what was in its way and passed straight through the bandit. He bled much and fell quickly, a large hole torn in his chest.

"Can't say I've seen that before," Alyssa spoke to him. He smirked at the young girl, then tossed another disc away, somewhere into the fray. In the blink of an eye, his body was gone once more.

Alyssa focused once more, looking around for a new quarry, and she found a bandit rushing into the hangar with a barrel in her hands. The young girl chased her down and jumped on her, and the bandit dropped her heavy load in shock. She struggled to get Alyssa off, but the ice witch stabbed two frozen daggers into her and held on with all the might in her petite body. She pulled the screaming bandit into the hangar and stopped just before a metal railing, then kicked herself off of her opponent's back, pushing her forward. The bandit's screams were drowned out as she fell over the railing and plunged into the roaring waters below.

Meanwhile, away from the chaos of battle, Xela and Amber snuck their way to stop the already poisoned water from entering the city's pipelines. As they progressed down the hallway, they came upon a door identical to the description the worker had given; conveniently, the words "control room" were painted on it in red.

Amber was ready to enter the room, but stopped herself once she glanced out the small window on the door and saw that someone had beaten them to it: a bandit with a gun in hand was checking the control panel. The two Guardians lined up on opposite sides of the doorway.

"How good's that aim of yours with those knives?" Amber asked, turning towards Xela.

Xela smiled and drew them from her thigh with a skillful spin. "Good enough."

With that, Amber nodded and kicked the door down with her heels, and they barged into the room together.

"Weapons down!" she yelled. The bandit turned, witnessing the two armed women approach him. He began to slowly put his gun down towards the ground, but then in a sudden movement, abruptly raised it, letting loose a bullet at Amber. Xela tossed a knife that struck his arm, and as he stumbled back, Amber stepped forward, emptying a few bullets into his body.

"Are you okay?" Xela asked as the bandit fell to the ground.

Amber put her pistol back in its holster. "I'm fine, he didn't get me," she said quickly. "Don't worry yourself too much about me. We've still got a mission on our hands."

She approached the panel, a cluster of countless buttons and switches spread in every direction. Across from it was a window to the vastly open area where the waters of the plant flowed beneath. Her hands touched a random assortment of toggles, and she hoped that one of them would seal off the circulation of the current.

"What did that do?" Amber asked Xela. She looked at the water across the window from them, shrugging when nothing noticeable occurred.

"Nothing, it seems," she said. Amber undid a flip on a switch.

"How about this?" she asked Xela. Again, her response was the same. Amber undid another flip.

Тя докосна един ключ близо до нея, който не беше опитала още. Зела поклати глава, когато пак нищо не се случи. "Губим време," каза Амбер. "Всеки момент, в който се забавяме тук, отровната вода ще прелее в Уаит Харт." Тя превкючи ключа и опита един бутон.

A large door came down on the flowing rapids across from them. It stopped the current flow, forcing the water to stay in the room they could see from the window, and in turn, prohibit it escape from the plant. "That's one problem solved," Amber said.

"But we've still got a few more," said Xela, pointing to the fighting outside the window.

They hastily turned to leave the room, but before doing so, Xela grimaced at the bloodied body lying on the floor. "Almost as if he had nothing to live for," she murmured to no one in particular, and ran to Amber.

Outside, the bandits were thinning out. Few took to fleeing, but many had fallen. Even with their downed brethren lying lifeless beside them, their fighting did not cease; it was almost heroic, if not for their intentions. Eventually, it came down to a group of twenty or so bandits that grew surrounded. They saw their disadvantage and slowly surrendered their weapons. Xela and Amber made their way back outside to aid their fellow Guardians.

"Check each corner," Eva said to Reese and Alyssa, as the other Guardians approached them. "We've rounded up the most of them, but we—"

She was interrupted by a booming explosion that left her losing hearing for a moment. The newfound team collectively turned to face the side of the gigantic wall surrounding the facility facing opposite the entrance. Smoke wisped from a huge hole in it, remains of broken barrier strewn about, having been thrown aside violently. From within the battle-fog arose an even bigger threat; hordes of bandits poured into the inner courtyard, some armed with bombs and grenades, which they promptly tossed into the havoc. More explosions followed.

Amber, Xela, Charlie, Brutus, Alyssa, Eva, Reese, Hex, and Skullgem regrouped to face the new threat head-on. They slowly pushed toward the battle, but their line was broken when one of them ran ahead in blind, thoughtless ire.

"Reese, wait!" Eva shouted, as Charlie barked loudly at him, yet his movements failed to falter.

A trauma trigger empowered Tyreesius Black's actions; when the smoke cleared, standing behind the line of soldiers, a man in white armor appeared, wearing a robe and a conical hat to match. He was someone who Reese instantly remembered for the pain and suffering inflicted on him.

He darted as fast as he could, shoving bandits away like they were nothing. The rage inside him was too strong to be contained, and nothing could hinder his urge for vengeance.

They were moving fast and in sync, Reese and Hex, one sprinting and the other soaring. Hex attempted to shoot down a few bullets as they sped, but there were many, coming from every direction, and the raven found it difficult to protect his partner. Clad in his armor of anger and hate, Reese screamed the pain away as he felt the projectiles strike his body, yet remained in unfaltering pursuit with his eyes dead-set on his quarry.

The man in the white armor, who had stood still as a statue, now calmly withdrew a claymore and prepared to stab the brute bull charging for him. He aimed for Reese's heart, but got in nothing more than a slash, which drew blood, but did not stop his attacker. After Reese struck with such force that the swordsman flew back several feet, the latter man rolled down a hill behind the open section of the broken wall.

Reese readied a disc, prepared to give chase, but two bandits that had been attempting to guard the man in white hit him with painful electrical charges. Reese tried to shake them off, but found himself caught in a struggle. He watched one of Eva's darts hit a guard, who fell to the ground, trapped in slumber. The other still had an electrically charged rifle on him, but Reese fought through the stunning pain enough to slowly get up and push the gun out of the fearful man's hands. Once the bodyguard had no weapons, a cackling Reese delivered a punch that sent the bandit soaring until he hit the facility's great wall, cracking it behind him.

Eva ran to her partner's assistance. "Who was that?" she asked frantically, her rifle firing away at any enemies that drew too close.

Reese swerved to look behind him but found his rival gone from where he had fallen after having been struck. He turned back to Eva, spitting on the ground, where a crimson substance splattered. "A coward."

There was something he was not telling her, but Eva had no time to worry about it at the moment. She helped Reese regain his senses, then pulled him back into the fray.

It was astonishing how fast he regained his energy; immediately after he got up, a bandit charged at him with a dagger in hand. With little effort, Reese picked him up by his legs before he got in a decent slash. He tossed the attacker onto his shoulder, only to slam him back down, spin him around, and humiliatingly toss him at one of his comrades. Eva and Hex were at Reese's side, covering his blind spots.

Meanwhile, the other Guardians fended off their enemies, stealing glances at the horde pouring further towards them.

"Did you know that he'd be here?" Amber asked Brutus, referring to the man with a longsword that Reese had sent tumbling away.

"No, not at all," he responded. "I don't know why he showed his ass up now."

"Who's that?" Xela curiously inquired, hoping they would provide an answer to her question this time.

A loud sigh sounded from Amber. "Long story, I'll tell you once it's over," she quickly assured. It was the best she could give her for now.

Alyssa approached them to inquire what to do. She ducked as the generator on their right, one in a long line of many, exploded in a column of flame.

"If those go out, the entire plant shuts down," Amber said to her group. "Even if we win this battle, it likely won't be up for weeks."

"I have an idea," Alyssa said, "but I'm going to need all of you to protect me."

She ran over to the generators as her allies cut in front of her to deal with the bandits already there. The sorceress set herself next to one and placed her palm on it, beginning to encase it in ice, but Alyssa didn't stop there: she ran around the generators, her finger tracing their circumference. Once she had completely encircled it, a protective dome of ice began to form, until it completely covered the generators like a snow globe.

"Smart thinking," Amber commented. "But do you think it will last?"

"It's made of ice," responded Alyssa. "It'll at least buy us some time."

The bandits, upon noticing their leader topple down the hill, began retreating from their positions and back from whence they came. Some fought harder upon seeing their allies give up. One ran up to the ice barrier, firing upon it with an automatic rifle. He didn't get far, as Charlie leaped, tackling him to the ground and feasting on his flesh.

Their forces quickly grew weaker and more scattered, succumbing to the impenetrable defense of White Heart. Reese placed himself between those who fled and the destroyed portion of the wall. The ones who tried to escape from him were butchered mercilessly. Those who chose to flee to the main entrance were forced to surrender by the rest of the Guardians.

Strategically stuck between two of their enemies, the horde of bandits stood awkwardly, pushed against each other, with nowhere left to go. One by one, they dropped their weapons onto the ground. Some fell to their knees as well, and more followed suit as they witnessed their comrades surrender.

Not long after, they were herded up like lambs. White Heart trucks pulled over next to the entrance, into which the bandits were pushed. They fled with haste, back towards White Heart, where a massive batch of bandits would soon become a sorry cluster of fresh prisoners. Their mission complete, and the sun of Senia beginning to set in the distance, the Guardians finally got around to heading home.

During the aftermath, Amber spoke to Brutus alone.

"Something wasn't right back there," she said.

"What are you talking about? That was a success if I've ever seen it." His voice was as monotone as usual.

"I could have expected the initial wave, but they brought Gareth around as well? The plant is important, but is it really *that* important to them?" Amber thought out loud.

"Boss Gareth hasn't been leader for that long. We don't know his style as well. We don't know whether he's the one to charge out on the front lines or to command from behind closed gates," Brutus responded.

"I suppose you're right," Amber concurred, her voice drained. It had been a long day, and rest would be well deserved. With their first mission a success, the Guardians returned home to their sanctuary.

CHAPTER 6:

Blazing sparks flew in every direction as beautiful steel met dull stone. The claymore shrieked in agony as the young bull pressed it against his spinning wheel.

Nearby, a stern leader clad in armor paced near an even more armored, taller man standing still as a statue, a bronze battle axe idly resting in his grip. From his head to his toes he was covered by bronze; even his face was barely visible under the horned helmet he wore. What could be noticed, however, was the bushy autumn beard poking out from under his helmet, the large bronze ring hanging from his nose, and the angry countenance with which he was seemingly always equipped.

"As I suspected, our favorite general has formed a quaint little group, it seems," spoke the leader. The Syndicate emblem of two crossed swords emblazoned on the back of the leader's pale robe was visible as he faced away from the taller man. "Amusing, amusing. Worse off, it seems she's hired my moronic brother to aid her in her evil efforts. What fun this will be, Minotaur, what fun indeed."

The Minotaur grunted loudly, his expression unfaltering.

"No matter. White Heart is just like the rest of the city-states and tribes we've conquered. They will fall in no time, as will all that oppose the great Syndicate Empire. Senia will be ours soon, very soon, and the people will thank us for gifting them the peace they so desperately desire."

It was just then that the blacksmith's spinning stone slowed to a stop, the sword successfully shined and sharpened spectacularly. The young boy flipped up his small-horned welder's helmet, revealing a face blackened from intense work, and gave a content stare at the claymore's glimmering visage, then carried it over to the armored Boss cautiously.

"I believe this belongs to you, Boss Gareth," he said as he handed the fabled blade to his leader. "No sharper could I make it; you have my oath."

"Caliburn...there is certainly nothing more beautiful in this world than you," said Gareth, as he gripped his sword, took up his combat stance, and closed his eyes. The boy and the Minotaur could have blinked their eyes just then and missed the clean slice that silently cut the crafting table in front of them into two.

"I will pay for that," said his serious voice as he spun his claymore and sheathed it in its holster with practiced dexterity. Then he pulled a pouch from a pocket at his side and tossed it to the boy, the credits inside clunking boisterously as he caught it in his open palms. "Impressive work you have certainly done, young..." Gareth paused as he attempted to recall a name.

"Calf," said the boy.

"...Calf. Next time I will be sure not to forget it."
He reached over to pick up the sawed conical hat
resting on a nearby bench and placed it on his pitch-
haired head, then turned to the still man looming
above him. "Much pride is to be had in your son. Even
I was not such a hard worker in my age. He certainly
makes our empire proud, that much I can say. But
now, let us make haste, Minotaur, for our planning of
retaliation begins today."

The bronze beast nodded as he parted from his
son's forge and followed Boss Gareth to his throne
room.

■ ■ ■

"You'll show them who the true enemy is?"
Brutus asked Amber.

They stood around the table in the kitchen, the
only ones awake in the house. Outside, the sky was
overcast, and rain was falling upon their world
mercilessly.

"I have to," Amber replied regretfully. "They
need to know exactly what they're up against."

"The Syndicate, you mean?"

"Yes. These attacks prove that war is coming,
faster than I wished it would. If they're not willing to
fight our fight with us against this particularly
dangerous threat, then they should leave while they
still can."

"And what if they don't? What if they're not
prepared to be in the middle of a war? What will we
do then, with no Guardians to protect us?"

Amber shook her head. "Always negativity with you, Brutus, isn't it?"

"Not negativity. Just being the realist here."

"I suppose that's why you're the tactician, not me." She sighed loudly. "It's a shot I'm going to have to take. They're either in, or they're out."

Brutus nodded. "But look, you're the leader, the general, you know what's best. The call is yours."

As Brutus parted from her, a pondering Amber left the room, catching a messy-haired Eva running down the stairs. She was so excited that she almost collided into Amber.

"General Leavett!" Eva started.

"Please. Amber," she corrected in a friendly tone.

"General Amber, I stayed up late last night to plan ahead, and I realized it may be a good idea to take advantage of the bandit captives we have in custody. Do some interrogations, maybe—"

"Whoa, whoa, slow down! Are you always this overachieving?" Amber joked, a slight chuckle in her voice. "First thing's first, I have to talk to you about something."

"Oh." Eva's tone dropped drastically in energy. "What would that be?"

"No, not just you. The entire team."

Eva smiled. "Of course! Call me when you're ready, ma'a—uh, Amber."

They waited for the team to gather. As they came together, the Guardians engaged in small talk around the house.

"Can I ask you something?" Reese questioned Eva, as the two of them shared the living room.

"Go ahead."

"What's with you and killing? I get it, for some people it can be hard, but why?" he inquired her.

Eva sighed. "There's just some line that you cross when you purposefully cause someone to die. I can never bring myself to even imagine crossing it."

"Mmhmm," he replied. "Like losing your virginity?"

She shook her head and laughed. "I don't even remember having *that,* honey."

He laughed back with a heartfelt roar. "Yeah, I can bet that. You're a pretty little thing," he joked, receiving an embarrassed blush at first from her.

"What's that supposed to mean, sugar?" Eva asked him, using her particularly charming tone.

"Just messing with you." Reese's chuckling slowly died down.

Her serious expression remained in play for a few more seconds before she cracked down, smiling somewhat sweetly at him. Neither had noticed that they had spent an odd amount of time staring at one another rather than engaging in conversation.

Meanwhile, in the kitchen, Xela stole constant glances at Brutus.

"How's your hand?" she finally asked. He opened his palm to reveal it to be wrapped almost completely in gauze wrap. She apologized again.

"It's all right," he responded flatly. "I'm used to taking one for the team." Pity brought a silence to Xela before Brutus parted from her.

Soon enough, everyone was up and around the house. Amber, seeing this, started to gather them around the kitchen island table.

"I have some announcements to make," she said, her eyes darting without pause. "Firstly, those 'bandits' weren't bandits at all." Though they may have been unaware of this, none looked too surprised, as Amber could tell from a brief study of expressions around the room. "We called them that because we wanted this to seem to all of you as a simple mission: stopping a bandit raid, just like the ones that happen every other day. But the fact of the matter is it's more than that. Bigger than that. That being said, if you desire to drop from the team, now is your chance, so I bid you speak up."

"What were they?" Eva asked.

"The Syndicate." Amber had intended to say it, but the voice came out deep and gruff. Reese was the one who spoke, as he was looking down with a melancholy gaze upon Hex eating from a bowl of grains on the table. "I used to work for them, long time ago. I didn't roll with them, so I helped start an escape group, but they kept everyone dumb. Friends, family...so many idolized the Syndicate as protectors, guardians, with no idea what they were capable of. Many didn't want to leave." The group stared at Reese, astonished at his sudden unbosoming. "My brother," he continued, his voice beginning to crescendo, "betrayed us. Butchered innocents right before my eyes. In our time of escape, he took advantage of us. And he left me a good scar to remember him by!"

He shot up, one fist slamming into the table, the other pointing at the permanent stretch across his left eye. His teammates were aphonic. He sat back down, his face red, and tried to collect himself. With a sigh, he went on.

"Know where I found this beautiful creature?" he asked, pointing to Hex, who was peering obliviously into space. "In chains. They were messing with him, for whatever fucked-up reason. Labeled him as an 'experiment gone wrong,' a failure. This," he stated, pointing to his raven again, "is anything but a failure." He slumped down in his chair, tired from his indignation.

The Guardians stood there, a silence lingering in the room, until finally, Amber broke it.

"Since we're on the topic, and Reese has done it already, why don't we go around the room and share something with each other? Your stories, if you will. Where you come from and why you fight." They waited for a volunteer, and Eva was the next to speak up.

"My story is more of a drifting one. I was born in Greenwood, corrupt and awful city, kinda like what I'm hearing from this Syndicate place, and I was trained extensively and painfully by my parents. I took off from them as soon as I could. For one of my first jobs, I took to the circus. I was an excellent acrobat, and it was wonderful, but eventually, they shut the place down. Ironic really, corruption was what killed it. I joined a brothel, but I abandoned it when I came under the mentorship of a vigilante by the name of the Hangman."

"Wait a minute," Reese interrupted. "You joined a brothel?"

Eva raised an eyebrow. "Sweetheart, I've done a lot of things in my past. But...never killing. Somehow, despite this unshakeable cloud of evil following me, I've never murdered a soul. I became a markswoman who refused to take lives. A paid vigilante, as opposed to an assassin. That's how I ended up here, and that's all I've got to my story so far."

Another silence followed, until Skullgem cleared his throat, attempting to direct the attention towards him. All eyes bore into his body as he pushed a previously unseen button on the side of his cowl. A shadow wall desynchronized at the front of his hood, revealing why his face seemed so obscured, as he slowly pulled the cowl down. To the shock of his friends, the skin on his pretty, boyish face was completely red. He took out a piece of paper and a pen and began writing.

"Uh, that won't be necessary here," Amber broke off. "Brutus is quite fluent in sign language." At that, Skullgem looked Brutus up and down, took haste to begin signing, and his translator started translating.

"My name is..." Brutus began, waiting for Skullgem to finish signing his full name, "Geronimo Ao-Shi. I am an Assossian, a race that lives in this world in fear of hate. Long ago, Assossians and humans battled for this land. We lost the war, and we poorly chose our representatives, letting an extremist group take control. They wanted to take humans out of the picture, to eradicate them, and because of this, we were hated by humans for centuries after our conflicts ended. This generation of Assossians still faces this pain, though we have nothing to do with the spiteful ones from years ago. That is the power of history."

He paused, as blank, yet dreamy-eyed Skullgem thought of where to go from there. Brutus himself was full of admiration, realizing how carefully the civil rights leader chose the words he desired translated. "A few years ago, my tongue was ripped out by humans, humans that tortured and humiliated me, yet when I escaped, I remembered the actions of the extremists, and ignored the thirst for revenge. Since then, I have devoted myself to being a public speaker and protecting those who can't protect themselves. I chose the symbol of the skull-gem, onyx, to represent me, as it is the stone of justice and compassion, hence my name: Skullgem the Lionhearted."

Nothing but silence for an anxious many seconds. Finally, Reese, albeit in half-jest, clapped loudly at his speech. The Guardians around him joined in with genuine applause, however, struck with reverence, and Geronimo smiled. He was happy to finally see people who accepted him in spite of his differences.

Alyssa slowly stood next, volunteering to speak up:

"I never got around to know my mother, but my father took care of me for a long time by himself. He did what he did to try and support the two of us.

On my fifteenth birthday, he gave me these," she said, clacking together her blue thigh-high boots; a strange fashion, but the young girl loved them so. "They were so expensive, and despite all our troubles, he bought them for me. He really loved me so, so much."

As she sighed, a small tear rolled down from her eye. She went to scrub it off, but it seemed to have frozen; she was peeling a tiny icicle from her cheeks. "I guess he owed a lot of money, or he pissed off someone he shouldn't have, but for some reason, some horrible, terrible reason, someone wanted him dead, and they didn't care who they harmed in the process.

"It was a nice night, and he took me out to dinner, a special occasion. We were all happy, everything was going great, then the people with guns came in and..." She struggled to finish the sentence. "I knew they were there for my father when I saw them checking his body to make sure he was dead. I ran then. I ran as far as I could, but of course, I'm no match. They caught me and tried to dump me in the middle of an arctic wasteland, and look what good that did them." She rolled up her sleeves. The runic carvings still pulsated on her arms. "They tried to kill me, but only ended up making me stronger. I hope that we can one day bring them to justice, and anyone who brings harm to those that don't deserve it."

Once again, the silence sank in, as the rest of them took in Alyssa's revelation. Her tear faded, her face cleared up, and after a long sigh, she awaited the next to speak.

Then, Brutus chimed in:

"I was raised by my mother way in the lawless Borderlands, where I learned to use a six-shooter from a young age," he said. "I haven't seen her in many years, due to unfortunate circumstances, as I was forced to part with her long ago. I came to White Heart in seek of somewhere I can use my skills, and it was here I learned the arts of war, the tactician's game. I met Amber some time ago, and the rest was history.

"She and I were part of the original Guardians. A serious accident forced us to disband, but we think it's time now to reinstate it. Conflict approaches, and we need people we can trust to help us. A Guardians 2.0, if you will."

After taking his monologue in, they all turned to Xela; all that remained was her. She took a calming breath and spoke up:

"For most of my life, death fascinated me. The thought that one day, everything you've known and will ever know will mean nothing anymore is...much to take. I founded my own order, an assemblage of people not afraid to think like I do. In the past, we were involved in a scandal, someone spreading false rumors that we killed people in our research. Of course, we did nothing of the sort. We had to move anyway, and we made ourselves look more fearful than we actually were, for our safety. I mean, look at me. It's hard to believe I'm a scientist, right?" She scoffed, then blew the short hair from her face. "I had to step up to protect my order, but now I've been getting the chance to step up and protect more lives. You can bet I'm going to jump at that, as no one understands how permanent death truly is better than I do. And now I'm here."

Eva smirked at her. "How can you say that and still kill people? Don't you see the hypocrisy?"

Xela sighed, not in anger, but in understanding. "It was hard for me to accept it, and I know exactly where you're coming from. But in the end, sometimes it's necessary to take the lives of those who do not respect life, so that those that do may live on."

Eva took this in quietly, and another silence followed before Amber decided to conclude the session:

"Stop me if you've heard this one: what do a general, a tactician, a hound, a vigilante, a civil rights leader, a thanatologist, a cryomancer, a berserker, and his guardian angel have in common?" she said, circling the room. "Enemies. We couldn't be more different from each other, I agree, but inside, we all want the same righteous things. I want everyone here to remember that when they're out there, fighting for a good cause. You represent protection, as the guardians of those who are unable to protect themselves. But don't forget, you'll be there to protect each other as well." Amber looked at each of them, then finished with a smile. "Thank you."

They roamed free for some time after, most pondering her words. She soon found herself staring out the window as the rain dropped from the sky, pattering carelessly on the streets below.

"Good speech," a voice said behind her.

Amber turned. "Thank you," she proudly said to Xela.

"I admire what you do, Amber," Xela began with reverence. "There's far too few people like you in this world."

The general smiled at her. "Let's hope we can all change that together."

CHAPTER 7:

Alyssa's relic markings almost glowed as she read on, and her face radiated with interest. Once again, she was deeply lost in an ancient tome.

"Thanks again for the book," Alyssa, with her gaze still glued on her reading, said to Amber, who had given it to her as a gift. The teenage Guardian sat on a stool, one hand on her tome and another in her beautiful, bright hair.

"Of course," Amber said. "What's it about? Is it any good?"

"I like it so far," Alyssa enthusiastically responded. "It's pretty interesting. It takes place in a war-torn world, and it's about goddesses, priestesses, sibyls, oracles..."

"I have no idea what any of that means," said Amber, smiling, "but it sounds like you're enjoying it. What's it called?"

Alyssa peered at the cover of the novel. The only word that wasn't so faded from the title as to be illegible was *Volcanic*. "I wish I knew. Where did you find it?"

"Oh, I uh..." began Amber. "My old house, a while ago. I polished it a little bit, and I've had it with me for some time. I tend to have a habit of finding random junk."

"It's far from junk, I can tell you that," responded the teenager. "It's quite the read. Thank you once again."

Alyssa's leader smiled at her. "Anything for a fellow Guardian."

Elsewhere in the house, Reese ascended the stairs with a heavy silver case in his hands. He walked over to the door to Xela's bedroom, and after a slight moment of reflection on his aversion, knocked loudly.

"Come in!"

He opened the door to find Xela in her typical garments, packing a small bag. "Didn't catch you at a bad time, did I?" he inquired.

"No, it's fine. I'm just getting a few things to bring back to my order's base. I should fill them in on what's going on."

"Oh, good," Reese said. "Before you leave, I wanna to give you this." He pushed the case across the bed to her.

She stared at it curiously. "What is it?"

"It's called 'Rage Serum,' but I like to think of it as steroids on steroids. One of the many tricks up my sleeve. It lets me punch things really, *really* hard, but it also has killer regenerative properties. Figure it might help in your research."

As he spoke, she opened the case. A few vials of a red-orange liquid tempted her inquisitiveness. "That's incredible!" she stated in awe. "Doesn't it make you...invincible?"

Reese sighed. "I wish. It's got its long-term effects, apparently. Every time I get a hit, I'm shaving off days, months, or even years my life, depending on the severity. It's incredible, yeah, but it causes serious strain on my body."

"Intense," she spoke, solemnly and slowly. A frown appeared upon her face. "If the long-term effects are so bad, why do you still use them?"

"Gotta live life to the fullest, do the shit everyone else is scared to, right?" Reese walked over to the bed and tapped a vial. "Besides, these things got a good grip on me. I couldn't quit if I wanted to."

Xela looked up at him with her dark eyes. "Well, thank you, that's very kind of you. What do I owe you?"

"Please, you don't owe me anything. Just, uh," Reese began to leave, one foot out the door, his head not turning to face her. "Be careful with them." With that, the door closed behind Xela.

On Reese's way down the stairs, he noticed commotion by the front entrance: Amber speaking with someone in front of the house. "I'm sorry, I have no idea who you are. I really can't let you in," she was saying to him. Reese walked past the scene, heading into the living room.

"Reese!"

The giant Guardian slowly turned, barely recognizing the voice. When he saw a man behind Amber wearing the face of an old friend, he gave her a look of approbation.

"Amber," he said, his tone filled with awe. "Let him in."

■ ■ ■

"I thought you dead, Ezekiel!" Reese said to the man across from him. His raven partner had gathered on his shoulder to analyze the long-forgotten face in his midst.

"I thought of you the same," he responded, taking a seat. "I'm glad to see you alive and well, as well as that raven of yours."

"Hex."

"What?"

"Hex. His name." Reese paused to take a seat.

"Oh, right," Ezekiel awkwardly uttered.

"It's been so long, Zeke! How you been doing these years? Oh!" Reese exclaimed, suddenly remembering the times he shared with his old friend. "How's the family? Your son's gotta be old now!"

"It has been so long, hasn't it?" Ezekiel chuckled, remembering the years past. "Saturninus is almost an adult now. I had another kid, too, Virtua's his name. I don't see them often, actually. They love to go out into the Borderlands together. Natural-born adventurers, they've never been one for the cities, sure, but they worry the shit out of me sometimes."

"Ah, it's good to get the kids out of the house," jested Reese, "I wish 'em the best of luck. And your wife? How's she doing these days?"

Ezekiel donned a sorrowful countenance. Reese read the grief in his friend's eyes as he stared blankly into space.

"Nami passed some time ago, bless her." Very quiet now, his enthusiasm drained. "Drowned. Like that, she was gone."

Reese sighed. "I'm really sorry to hear that. And I'm sorry for...reminding you of things you'd rather forget."

"No, no," began Ezekiel. "You didn't know, it's not your fault." He took a deep breath, then decided he wanted to change the subject. "Have you seen any of the others lately? The alchemist, Seared? The doctor, Mary? The creator...ah, what was his name again? Reveck, was it?"

"Everyone we escaped the Syndicate with?" Reese gave a sad shake of his head. "We all split not far from the city. Haven't seen a single one of them since. Although, I do still have a gift from Seared!" He gave a slight lift of his shirt, revealing his belt.

"Is that what I think it is?"

Reese nodded. "I still have a stash, but I always worry they'll run out."

After a long pause, the other man spoke up. "Reese, you haven't become dependent on those things, have you?"

There was no response from the tall man. After some quiet, Zeke spoke again. "Never mind, forget I asked. Listen, I came to ask for your help. The others we had to split from during the escape...I'm searching for them. Just to make sure they're safe and in good hands, you know? "

"Right, good on you," Reese responded. "We gotta have someone looking out for us in this crazy world. Well, wish I could help, but I'm with a new group now. I got new duties. Funny, now that you mention it, I guess I'm doing just that: looking out for people."

His old friend sighed. "Very well. I'm glad to see that you've moved on. I just want to make sure that the others have been given that chance as well."

He reached behind him to pull out a case he had been carrying with him. "Before I go, I would like to give you something." Opening it, he revealed assorted equipment and wires strewn about.

"What is it?" Reese asked.

"Before we abandoned Avalon, I worked on a prototype for long-distance communication. I finally finished the invention only recently, and I would like to give part of that to you. It'd be good to be able to check in on all of you, make sure you all are doing okay."

Reese was bewildered but fascinated. "How does it work?"

"It has separate channels through which you can communicate to others who have their own piece. For example..."

He picked up two identical pieces, putting one in his ear, keeping the other in his hand. He pressed a few miniature buttons on each, then sat back contently. "Now anyone on my own channel can speak to me as if I'm right next to them."

"I see. And you're gifting this to me?" Reese asked.

"Well," Ezekiel pondered. "Perhaps not just to you. How many people are in your group?"

Reese thought it over. "Seven or eight?"

"Very well. Take the whole case. I considered giving only one to you to keep in contact with me, but I feel like the least I can do is aid your cause. And I'll be able to always be there if you feel like having a nice reunion."

"You got a name for this?"

The inventor laughed. "I find it easier to create an invention than name it."

"Zeke," began Reese. "You gotta have a name. Names define, and if you don't got a name for something...well, what does that thing mean then? Not much, if you ask me."

"I was thinking...'talker.'"

"A...talker? Wow, I wish I had your creativity," Reese jested.

"I'll come up with something better, don't you worry." Ezekiel chuckled to himself, only to be interrupted by a blaring siren sounding from outside.

"What's going on?" Reese asked to no one in particular. Ezekiel was just as confused. The two held their breath as Amber rushed into the common room.

"Arm yourselves," she gravely directed. "White Heart is under attack."

CHAPTER 8:

One by one, the Guardians assembled downstairs. The whole house was in a frenzy as all of them frantically collected weapon, gear, and armor in preparation for battle. The stentorian emergency sirens screaming outside only worsened their hurried state. Reese quickly handed out the talkers given to him by Ezekiel and explained how they worked. After he did this, he turned to his old friend.

"I trust you'll be fine, Zeke?"

"I left my weapons in the city garage. Do you happen to have anything I could use?"

"Hold on. You don't have to do this. This isn't your battle to fight. Your ass is staying put here where it's safe."

"The enemy of my friend is my enemy," Zeke said, flashing a smile. "Besides, I'm sure you could use all the help you can get."

Reese sighed, no time to argue. "No, I don't have any spares, but I'm sure Amber's got something." They began to approach her to ask, but upon seeing most of the Guardians downstairs and present, she seemed ready to raise her voice. A holo-tablet in her hands, she was motioning to a point on a three-dimensional holographic map of White Heart. Four bright dots on the westernmost part of the graph flashed as they made their way towards the center of the city, and a few dots outside the city walls were beginning to close in on White Heart.

"Listen up!" Amber yelled at the top of her lungs. The room instantaneously froze and quieted down. "We've got a couple problems on our hands. Firstly, we've got a few Syndicate choppers soaring above the walls like mosquitoes; White Heart's defense will take care of them, don't you worry. I have a different task for you: we have four heavily armed trucks making their way down this street, firing away at anything that moves. Fortunately, most of the city has fortified itself. We have minutes before it passes this very spot, so we need to think of a way we can stop them before they get any further."

Suddenly, Reese's recent confession gave Xela an idea. "I have a plan," she announced to no one in particular. She walked up to Reese, quickly yanking a syringe from his belt before he could react. "Where do I stab this?" she asked.

Reese stammered and began to protest. "Wait, wait. It doesn't work like that. I need something to—"

"His arm," Zeke interrupted.

"Sorry, sweetheart," Xela whispered as she jabbed him accordingly. The fluid oozed into his veins, and Reese shouted in pain and collapsed quickly onto the floor. "What's wrong with him?" asked Xela, slight panic in her voice.

"Give him a moment," Eva said, looking on at the scene.

After a few seconds, Reese began to pick himself up, panting and twitching. Xela led him to the door hastily, her hand tugging his wrist. Peeking out, she saw the trucks speeding towards them, though still off in the distance. She ducked inside until she heard the roaring of engines passing in front of them. At this exact moment, she jumped out and unsheathed her scythe. Aiming and holding it by two side-handles, she pressed a button on the hilt, and a chain with a spear-tip on its end shot out from her weapon, attaching itself to the back of a truck speeding ahead of them. Before the chain reached its end, Xela handed it to Reese. "Hold this," she sternly said. He simply grunted, but obeyed. "And do *not* let go."

They waited a few seconds, Xela counting down in her head. "Brace yourself!" she warned Reese, just before the chain ended. Reese was almost launched forth by the pulling of the truck, but the immense strength of his current state stopped him. The truck abruptly halted, though the driver was pushing the pedal as hard as he could. Slowly but surely, Reese counteracted the truck's force and began pulling it towards them, locking his opponents in a dangerous game of tug-of-war.

Amber saw what Xela was trying to do and took up her role. "Move in!" she commanded the Guardians.

While Reese pulled the truck with all his might, his comrades advanced on the enemy. Eva fired a shot into the nape of the man in the back of the vehicle, and he soon fell. Charlie cornered the driver and Amber the passenger next to him; they were surrounded.

Zeke, who stood by Reese and Hex, was in awe. "That was incredible!" he exclaimed. "I've never seen a group work so well together!"

Reese said nothing, simply panting as the chain retracted back into the scythe. He thrust it back into Xela's hands with so much unwitting force that she almost fell over. Then his breathing slowed as he collapsed to the ground, bone-weary from battle. Hex hopped off of his shoulder and pecked his forehead with his sharp beak. As the massive man slowly opened his eyes, he groaned in discomfort.

"All right, all right," he growled at Hex. "I'm getting up, relax." When he noticed the stares of his allies around him, he responded with a casual and hurried, "I'm fine, don't worry."

After guards arrived on the scene to take away the three criminals, Amber led Zeke to the side alley between the Guardians' house and another tenement, with Reese and Hex promptly following. The alley led them to a locked garage door. Amber took out her holo-tablet, fiddled with some buttons on it, and the door promptly opened for the four. Two army jeeps, exactly like those used earlier by Amber and Brutus, were parked directly in front, but in the back stood a wall stocked with weapons of a huge variety.

"Make your choice," Amber said to Zeke. "But make it quick."

He and Reese examined the wall of weapons. Zeke fleetly chose a shortbow, complete with a quiver of arrows.

"You still know how to use that?" Reese asked.

"My personal bow is much more... technologically advanced, as you can imagine. But I'm sure this will do."

"Let's go then," Amber said, but Reese did not follow.

"Oooh," he said in awe, selecting a rocket launcher from the wall. To most, it would have been too arduous to carry, but he easily picked it up with one hand. Turning to Amber, he asked: "Can I use this?"

She sighed. "No. Today's battleground is our home city. Too risky."

"Ugh, fine." Reese put the weapon back on its shelf, like a little boy being denied a toy by his mother, and followed the others out.

■ ■ ■

The droning blare of machine guns in action sounded outside the command room, adding its noise to the symphony of chaos erupting from the scattered military inside. Commands shouted to and fro, and so paced the generals, commanders, and lieutenants within, as outside, helicopters laid waste to the walls of White Heart.

"Those choppers have to go!" someone called out.

"Prepare the mortars!"

"Ready for fire!"

One went down in a fury of flames as a surface-to-air rocket struck it dead-on, and it tumbled into the forests of the Borderlands outside the great city-state. Still more remained, closing in on them ever so slowly from many feet above them, firing away with automatic machine guns with little care. A battle was truly commencing now.

"Sir, one's going into the city!"

"Who will stop it?"

There was a long silence as they pondered an answer, until one voice spoke: "I know just the guys for the job."

■ ■ ■

An enemy truck headed to the north, to the higher, more suburban district. It was decided that Amber, Charlie, Brutus, Skullgem, and Xela would follow that truck, while Eva, Reese, Alyssa, and Ezekiel trailed the two combatant vehicles heading east.

Eva had a holo-tablet of her own, and Amber had managed to get the map onto it, complete with blinking lights to signify the trucks. The trucks appeared to split up, so Eva tracked the closest one, yet both were heading towards the eastern gate. Reese peered over Eva's bare shoulder at the unfolded tablet in her lap, carefully studying the movements of the trucks.

At that moment, the four heroes were steering parallel towards lower-level, open-roof train tracks ahead of them. Reese, seemingly hatching another plan, promptly told Eva to drive faster, and she did so accordingly. A train began to pass on the tracks, as he had hoped.

"Sharp right!" he shouted out. "Stop!" and Eva obeyed, watching him leap out their jeep.

"What are you doing now?" Eva asked, a little annoyed at his abrupt idea.

"Don't worry about me. Just try to cut off the truck," said Reese, his partner cawing in harmony. Eva sighed, yet complied.

They had passed the train, which moved slowly through the populated city with its many curves and turns. Reese peered over the edge of a bridge overlooking the tracks, his ears on alert for the sound of the train growing closer and closer. After backing up, he took off with a running start, leaping over the bridge's railing and onto the train that just began to pass below, landing with such force as to dent the boxcar beneath his feet.

Unfazed, Reese began running towards the rear of the moving train. The enemy truck he was waiting for came into view, and now it was speeding parallel to the train. A sprinting Reese, attempting to keep pace so he did not follow the train away from his targets, readied a green disc in his hands, spinning it in preparation. He tossed it directly in front of where the truck was about to speed and leaped with one fist raised behind him. When he translocated himself onto the hood of the truck, he lowered his hand with his fearful might. The front window shattered and Reese grabbed for anything he could, thrashing around once he felt the skin of the driver's neck. The truck began swerving as the driver panicked, choking and gasping for air.

The twists and turns of the vehicle were too much for Reese, however, and he finally slipped off, his hand parting from his enemy's neck. He plummeted to the ground below, his massive body tumbling over the concrete street pavement. Hex flew to him and perched on his shoulder as Reese pulled himself up. Like an angered bull, the truck revved around, preparing to crush its attacker. There was an interim moment of hush as Reese and Hex faced the technical and its marauders.

"Eva, I'm by the closer truck," he spoke in a gruff voice to the talker on his ear. "If you're going to help me, do it..."

"...Now!"

He was interrupted by the war cry of the driver of the vehicle, signaling his comrades to open fire. The gunner in the back let loose a barrage from a mounted turret, most of which were harmlessly terminated by Hex, while the passenger unloaded his rifle, firing ahead. The truck began to charge, but Reese bravely stood his ground. As it drew closer, Reese opened his palms in preparation.

A massive machine of metal collided with a behemoth, yet the vehicle did not continue moving. Reese still stood, his hands on the front of the bandit truck, having completely stopped it in its place. The driver was attempting to accelerate, but to no avail, as Reese barely budged an inch.

The muscular Guardian realized the gunner had stopped firing. Rather than manning the turret, he was slumped over it, a pink and white dart in his neck. The driver, now aware that moving forward was a fruitless cause, tried to shift into reverse. However, this didn't seem to work either, as he was stuck, going nowhere, his back wheels frozen in place. Seeing no other option, he opened the door and ran. Reese whistled, and the driver was immediately cut down by Hex.

Meanwhile, the passenger hid in his seat, rifle in hand. When he saw his chance, he got out and aimed his gun at an exposed Reese.

He heard a swooshing noise and a thud, turning to see the marauder collapsing onto the hood of the truck, an arrow impaled in his head.

"Yeah, I still got it!"

The voice came from behind the truck; Zeke and Alyssa approached Reese from one side, and looking behind him, Reese saw Eva and the jeep. He noticed why the driver could not move backward: the wheels of the truck were encased in ice and hiding in an icy clump, courtesy of Alyssa.

"Thanks," he gratefully replied with a sigh, his strength exerted.

Alyssa pointed at the driver a few feet from them, who was attempting to get himself up, only to be tormented by Reese's raven. The dark bird pecked at the back of the man's head every time he attempted to raise it.

"He'll be fine," Reese assured.

Hex, through with his sadistic fun with the man, finally threw his talons upon his neck and reached his beak over his head. The man let out a shrill wail as Hex reached his beak into his socket and violently ripped out a juicy eyeball. The raven then proceeded to throw it in the air, catch it skillfully, and swallow the eye whole, all while his victim moaned in utter agony.

"You said...he'd be fine..." Alyssa stammered, horrified.

Reese laughed, clearly more amused than she. "Oh, sorry! I thought you were talking about Hex. Sorry you had to see that, but my sweet little birdy has to eat something." He made a kissy face towards the raven, who looked up at him, his metal beak covered in blood, and tilted his head.

■ ■ ■

To the northernmost part of White Heart was a rich suburban district, full to the brim with chic, massive houses. Where the city ended there, the trucks split up, and the Guardians decided it would be smart to diverge there, too. Amber and Xela headed to the west, while Charlie, Brutus, and Skullgem trailed east.

"Hang on," Brutus muttered to his allies with him, as he gunned the vehicle. "We're gonna try and flank them."

He cut across whole streets precariously, taking shortcuts he knew from the mental map of White Heart branded into him. After a particular turn, he swerved across a long lawn, and when they emerged back onto the streets, the hostile technical was straight in front of them, speeding away, firing into houses with no care.

"I'm going to need you to board them, alright?" Brutus said to Skullgem, with an oddly calm tone. The Assossian Guardian nodded and climbed up in his seat. "Be careful."

Skullgem barely heard his words as he stepped one foot onto the door of their roofless vehicle. Shouting could be heard from in front of them, and the technical's gunner swerved a massive turret towards them. Brutus pushed forward with all the might his car could manage. Before any bullets could strike them, Brutus caught up with the enemy vehicle and rammed into them, catching the gunner awry and in unbalance.

"Now, now!" he shouted.

Skullgem made haste to board. The gunner was helpless to stop him, and he quickly fell off the vehicle after a few good hammer swings. Meanwhile, Brutus backed his car slightly, then sped up to catch his quarry. He swerved sharply left, nudging his enemies into the walls of White Heart next to them. They broke off for a moment, and Brutus opened his driver's side door.

As the technical's passenger opened his front-seat door to get a better shot, Charlie promptly sprinted out of Brutus' vehicle and pounced on the hostile inside. Within a matter of seconds, the dog had ripped a hole in the man's throat. Charlie moved towards the driver and attempted to jump him, but was pushed back towards Brutus with a kick. Brutus caught the dog by his collar, not allowing his ally to touch the speeding street below, and was quick to place the hound on the passenger seat next to him. He glanced back at the driver of the enemy truck and noticed one hand reach for a holster. With an impressive draw, Brutus retrieved one of his revolvers, masterfully quick, before the other man could reach for his weapon. The gun itself was identical to its twin holstered at Brutus' other side, save for that it was tipped in red, with the word "BAD" scribed onto its side. It shot out a powerful projectile in crimson, which smote its target before he could fire at Brutus. The driver slumped onto the wheel, and the truck drastically slowed down.

Brutus then stopped the car and pressed against his talker. "We've neutralized them," he said to his fellow Guardians, breathing a sigh of relief.

■ ■ ■

Meanwhile, Eva, Hex, Reese, Alyssa, and Zeke tracked another rogue vehicle to the east. They followed it into the market district, and when the truck caught sight of them, it briefly stopped. A tall man, clad in bronze armor and sporting a huge nose ring, climbed out from the passenger seat and pulled out an incredibly broad battle axe. The truck left him behind, and he pulled his weapon over his shoulder as the Guardians' vehicle sped towards him.

"He's not going to pull a Reese, is he?" asked Eva, to no one in particular.

"Only one way to find out," Alyssa responded. Their vehicle inched closer and closer, but the man did not budge.

"He's not moving," Zeke worriedly pointed out. To that, Eva responded by pushing harder on the pedal. The man pulled his axe over his back and prepared to fling it over his head. "Guys, he's not moving!"

The next instant, he dropped his axe upon the hood of the jeep, causing it to jump its back wheels off the ground and come to a screeching halt. Everyone inside flew out, landing flatly onto the concrete ground, save for Eva, who bumped her head into the steering wheel.

The man selected her as his victim, as she was the closest to him. As she struggled to regain her senses, the bronze man raised his axe over his head once again. However, when he brought his weapon down with mighty force, it did not connect with flesh. Reese was in front of him in a flash, narrowly saving Eva, stopping the man's axe with his own.

"Grab the others and get out of here!" he said to her, as he pushed the other warrior off of him. "Stop the other truck!"

Eva did not argue. She put on her aviators and let the others board, while Reese and Hex minded the bronze man.

As his friends departed, Reese held his ground, growling at his opponent. The two charged at each other, but Reese's axe was much smaller than his attacker's, and as their weapons connected, the former's flew out of his hand. He leaped back, his palm open, and his axe was quick to fly back into it. The other man swung once more, missing Reese, his axe cracking the ground where it struck. He pulled it out, his giant nose ring moving in unison with his heavy panting, as the Guardian collected himself.

"How's my brother?" Reese asked him, a furious countenance donning on his face.

116

■ ■ ■

The monorail train that encircled the great walls of White Heart passed above Xela and Amber as they continued on the same high-speed chase, sirens still blaring across their city. It was not difficult to catch up to the truck, as its heavy turret and bulky build wore it down.

When they were close enough, Xela stood and aimed the tip of her scythe at the man in the back. She fired, and the chain-spear dug itself into the marauder's leg ahead of them. He stopped shooting his turret and clutched his thigh as he attempted to pull Xela's spear-tip out. Before he could, Xela pressed another button along her scythe, and the chain flew back towards them with tremendous force, dragging the bandit along with it. The man hit the hood of their car and spun above and behind them before tumbling on the ground. Within seconds, he was long abandoned, his crippled body left to suffer in the streets.

The others in front of the truck noticed the ceasefire of the turret. When they looked back, they realized they were a man short, and a car was attempting to cut them off.

Amber pressed a button on the side of her talker. "If anyone can hear me, we're requesting help with a truck approaching the center of the city." It took about a minute, but she received a response:

"I'm a little busy at the moment," replied Reese, sounding quite so, "but I'll try my best."

...

The man in bronze armor swung his axe at the Guardian, who parried it with his shotgun. Reese then landed a punch to the man's chest, and his opponent staggered backward from the blow. He took this opportunity to repeatedly fire shotgun pellets into the bronze man, who barely seemed affected. He swatted at Reese's bullets with an angry fist and charged the Guardian. They collided, tumbling backward together, before finally rolling away from each other.

Reese boosted himself up with his shotgun and spit on the ground. "They call you the Minotaur, is that right? Funny, must be why I'm smelling so much bullshit."

The Minotaur roared like a beast, swinging his axe and tossing it with tremendous momentum. Hex flew in front of Reese, firing an anti-air projectile from his eye. The axe was too large to be destroyed, but the raven managed to shift its course away from Reese. The soaring battle axe chipped away at the market's cobblestone road as it skidded away from its owner, before finally landing, hilt up, stuck inside the ground.

Reese saw his chance, tossing his own axe at the Minotaur. It grazed the bronze man's arm, briefly stunning him as he clenched his shoulder. An opportunity provided, Reese launched himself like a bullet, his fists a furious blur as he threw punch after punch. Finally, he opened his palm out again, and his axe flew back into his hands. It grazed the Minotaur's other arm, and blood spurted out as he gave a feral shout of agony.

118

Reese moved in close to throw another fist, but to his surprise, the Minotaur dodged it. The bronze man tilted his head down, revealing the razor-sharp horns on his helmet. He charged at Reese before he could recover, stabbing his horns into the Guardian's chest. Reese gave a feral shout as the Minotaur pushed him back with all his force. The horns parted with his body now, but not before pulling out some blood with them. As Reese struggled to get himself up, he heard a familiar voice speak into his ear:

"If anyone can hear me, we're requesting help with a truck approaching the center of the city."

"I'm a little busy at the moment," replied Reese, the holes that had just been gored in his chest forcing a groan out of him, "but I'll try my best."

His sharp whistle sounded over the screaming emergency sirens. Upon hearing it, Hex dashed to the Minotaur. He dug his talons into the man's helmet and flapped his wings frantically in an attempt to disorient him. The Minotaur pulled and clawed at the raven, who endured the pain until he saw his best friend at a safe distance. His job complete, he unhooked himself from the Minotaur, flying off with a throaty caw. The bronze man attempted to throw a fist at the bird as he flew away, but missed sorely. Hex planted himself back on Reese's shoulder, his one true home.

"Face me, coward!" the Minotaur hollered at Reese, far away from him, shaking an angry fist. "You have a fight to finish!"

Reese proceeded to flip him off and blow an immature raspberry. He was not fast, but he was definitely faster than the armored man, so his escape was not arduous. To his surprise, the next time Reese looked behind him, the man was gone from where he had stood, along with his massive bronze axe.

■ ■ ■

A car holding Ezekiel, Alyssa, and Evangeline sped through White Heart's streets, chasing another group of enemies on the loose.

Zeke loaded his bow in preparation, standing as Eva's vehicle approached the rampaging truck. He fired an onslaught of arrows, none hitting his targets, although some lodged into the sides of the truck. Once Eva realized Ezekiel had caught the attention of the enemy gunner, she quickly sped up towards the truck. Ezekiel let another arrow fly, and this one shot through the window, lodging itself in the back of the driver's neck. The truck momentarily stopped, but the turret in the back was still active. The gunner fired back at the group, and a few bullets got inside the vehicle. Zeke's shoulder was clipped by a pellet, and he promptly sat down, clutching himself in pain.

"You alright?" Eva shouted behind her. Zeke shot her a prompt grunt of confirmation.

While bullets flew everywhere, Alyssa conjured walls of ice on the sides of the jeep that swerved sharply towards the dormant gunner. Taking the damage for them, the tall, frozen barriers gave Zeke time to pick himself up the best he could, and when their jeep made another round circling the immobile gunner again, he did not miss. A swift arrow pierced the marauder's chest, and down he fell.

A final truck remained; Xela and Amber had chased it out of the suburban neighborhoods and to the safer market district. As it sped ahead, Amber removed a hand from the steering wheel to reach for her small pistol, but just as the truck emerged from under an overpass, it exploded in a magnificent flood of brightness. Amber stopped the car in surprise as flames licked away at the demolished wreckage of what was a war technical.

The two women stood next to each other, stupefied, their jaws slightly ajar. Their surprise was only increased when they noticed a familiar face walking through the smoky ruins, a heavy weapon in hand, and a bird perched on his shoulder.

"Damn it, Reese!" Amber shouted. "What did I tell you?"

He approached her with a wicked smile. "You needed help. I helped."

"Before that," she said, her voice lowering. "When I said something about not using a rocket launcher in a tightly populated city...do you recall that conversation?"

"I do," he answered. "I just chose to ignore it."

"How did you even manage to sneak it past me?" a bewildered Amber asked. Reese shrugged in an almost childish manner. "Well, you certainly helped. I'll give you that," she admitted with a hesitant tone, sighing in the midst of the wreckage behind her.

Two jeeps then drove by, and they all turned their attention onto them. Out of one came Eva,

Alyssa, and Zeke, and out of the other that came from the street opposite to them disembarked Skullgem, Charlie, and Brutus.

"Mission complete?" asked Eva as she approached and stretched her arms.

Amber smiled. "I believe so. Good work out there, Guardians...and company." She glanced at Ezekiel. "You've proved that you are a strong, inseparable unit that functions as one, a threat to those that threaten us, a protector of those unable to protect themselves, and...is that a damn chopper I hear?"

The sound of helicopter blades whirring towards them had been crescendoing since she began to speak, and now it was far too loud to ignore. She turned just in time to see it emerge from behind the tall building that had provided it cover from them. It carried its pilot hiding behind what looked like a sturdy glass and two gunners to the side with their weapons at the ready, approaching at an alarming pace, a soaring death machine prepared to bring carnage to the readied decuplet of heroes.

Amber groaned. "You have got to be kidding me."

The whirring sounds of manned chain guns charging their fire were sirens to their ears, alarming them that death was imminent. There was nowhere the Guardians could hide.

"Let's see you get past this!" a young voice shouted.

As the bullets began to fly towards them, a colossal wall of thick ice emerged from the ground up, blocking the fire, and yet the fear-mongering volley pressed on. Alyssa's abilities were not omnipotent; soon, the wall would crumble, and so would the Guardians, lest they did something about the massive threat in front of them.

"We need a plan!" Ezekiel shouted as they grouped against the wall for protection. He was shouting to the point his throat hurt, yet he was still barely audible in the midst of the boisterous chaos.

"Listen up!" screamed Amber, and the attention she demanded was instantly received. "We're going to need a distraction!"

A bark sounded from Charlie that couldn't have been a coincidence of timing.

"Someone's gotta take out the gunners!" she continued.

"On it!" Brutus exclaimed.

"Got you covered!" Zeke added.

"We need a way to hold it in place!"

"I'll handle that!" shouted Xela.

Reese chuckled. "Not without my help!"

"The pilot needs to go!"

Eva readied her rifle and smiled. "But someone's gotta take out that glass for me to get a shot!"

Skullgem began signing with speedy fingers. "If someone can get me up there!" translated Brutus in a booming voice.

Hex let loose a throaty caw.

"Then let's get it going!" Amber shouted, and their plan began to take form. "Charlie!"

The hound ran out from behind the wall on his nimble feet, attracting the attention of the two gunners. They moved their weapons onto him, attempting to spray him dead to little avail.

"Brutus! Zeke!"

The gunslinger and the archer emerged from behind the wall, weapons at the ready. A barrage of high-caliber bullets struck the gunner on their left, while the gunner on the right took an arrow to the hip, then the arm, finally losing his footing and spiraling out of the machine onto the concrete below.

"Xela!"

The wall of ice crumbled before her, and the scythewoman gripped her weapon and aimed it at the helicopter. With the press of a button, a spear-tip shot out, its chain uncoiling as it flew towards its target, and impaled itself into the metal machine.

"Reese!"

Xela handed her scythe to the berserker, who steadily took it in his arms. It was then that the pilot realized what was going on and tried to flee. Reese shouted with all of his might as the helicopter attempted to escape, but due to his massive strength, it stayed put right where it was.

"Hex! Skullgem!"

The raven dug his talons into the warrior's pauldrons, then prepared for takeoff. Thrusters on his wings sounded akin to jets as they exploded, and the two propelled into the sky. When Hex let go, Skullgem yet soared upwards and landed onto the helicopter's windshield. The pilot froze, eyes aghast, as his opponent drew a hammer, made a sign by rubbing his fist against his chest in a circular motion, and bashed his weapon into the glass. Soon the hammer had shattered a large hole. His job complete, Skullgem leaped back with an elegant flip. Hex caught him on his fearless descent and carefully carried his petite body onto the ground below.

"Eva!"

The sniper donned her aviators and aimed her rifle at the machine in the sky. Her sights lined up with the perfect shot, she squeezed her trigger, and a dart shot through the air and into the pilot's neck, bringing him to sleep.

The Guardians were overjoyed at their victory for a brief moment, until the chopper's blades slowed their whirring, and the machine began to tip. It tilted itself downwards, and the victors below bore fearful faces as the massive metal object threatened to crush them.

Its descent slowed, however, and it gradually grew blue in color as it went from crashing to creeping down towards them. Just when it seemed it would bury them in the ground, it slowed even more drastically, until it was simply frozen, unmoving. Ice had risen from the ground up, overcoming the helicopter, and encased it before it could even touch the ground.

Alyssa lowered her hand, and her relic marking went from a brilliant glimmer to dark again, as if they had simply been drawn on her. Her serious, stressed countenance faded, and she let out an exhausted sigh of relief as she accepted her task as complete.

A helicopter, trapped in an enormous clump of ice, stood present in front of the ten. It seemed all of them sighed just as Alyssa had, relieved to be rid of their attackers, relieved not to have lost their lives in the process. Had they not been tired to the bones, they would have gloated in their stupendous victory.

■ ■ ■

The Guardians soon returned back to their home base. Xela went on her way to the marsh, as she was so rudely interrupted, and Alyssa volunteered to help clean up the mess, as her abilities proved quite serviceable to putting out fires. The other Guardians roamed in and nearby their home, all seeking ways to remove the stress of their mission.

After Ezekiel and Reese talked some more, the old friend saw it fit to leave, before their sky darkened. Reese followed his friend out with Hex on his shoulder, walked with him for a bit down sprawling White Heart streets, then bid him farewell when they reached the garage.

"It's been a pleasure," Zeke said to him.

"Good luck on reuniting our group," Reese replied. "Keep me updated."

"I most certainly will." Zeke looked around with a grin, his eyes finding the beautiful, dark colors of dusk above. "I hope to see you again."

"Likewise, friend," said Reese, a slight smile dawning on him too.

"I feel like a hug would be appropriate now."

"I, uh," the massive hulk of a man began. "I've never been much for hugs...oh, alright."

Ezekiel didn't hear him, as he was already wrapping his arms around Reese. "Ah, shut up, you old hag. Have some emotions for once."

Reese chuckled slightly, embracing Zeke back. The two friends stood in the cold, dwelling in their resumed friendship from a lengthy hiatus. Even the raven curled his head against the two and closed his eyes.

Finally, Ezekiel let go and gave Reese one final smile. He turned and walked down the abandoned street, the cold wind lightly pushing against him, the streetlights lighting up as he walked on. The Guardians he left behind were hopeful to see him again.

CHAPTER 9:

Weeks passed before Reese heard a voice in his talker once more. He jolted up from the living room couch as it spoke to him again, forgetting he had left it on, unsure of who was talking at first.

As she walked past, Eva noticed him conversing with what seemed like no one, but realized, upon closer inspection, that he was speaking over the talker. She fixed her hair in her headband, sat next to him on the couch, and waited for him to finish.

"Who was that?" she asked.

"Zeke." The answer was prompt, and Reese didn't explain why his friend had decided to speak to him then.

"And what did he say?"

"Eva," he started, slowly. "I have a son."

Eva stared at him, unsure of how to react. Finally, the words "You're shitting me," poured from her. "I'm sorry, I'm sorry," she spoke, shaking her head and covering her mouth, "but what?"

"Yeah. I'm finding it hard to believe, too." Eva had never seen him so calm; it was quite an eerie sight.

Silence touched them once more, and then Eva spoke. "So, who's the lucky girl?" she finally queried, in partial curiosity and partial jest. It seemed strange to her; though she hadn't known him for very long, Eva had quickly grown used to Reese's narcissistic and angry personality. Now, seeing him turn from loud-mouthed to serious, she was taken back a bit.

"Hardly would call her lucky. I hate that bitch, and she hates this one," he said, pointing to himself. "We used to have a thing, back when we worked for the Syndicate."

"Does she still work for them?"

"No. She helped us escape, but I haven't seen her since we decided to split up our resistance groups."

Eva took a deep breath, deciding what to say next. "And you're sure you two...don't have anything going anymore?"

"I haven't seen her in over a decade!" He looked at her quizzically. "And why would we? I just called her a bitch."

"Yes, but you also called yourself one."

A sigh from Reese. "No, we're not still in a relationship, and I'm real thankful for that."

"Alright, just checking." Reese heeded her not-so-subtle hint no mind as he picked himself up and began to head for his bedroom wordlessly. "Where are you going?" she asked.

"I'm gonna get my shit together," he responded. "I don't care if it means I have to see her again; I have a son, and I need to meet him."

"Well..." Eva began, as she watched him walk away. "You're gonna need a ride."

Reese stopped in his tracks. "Yeah, you're right."

She smiled to herself. "Which is exactly why I was thinking—"

"Remind me to ask Amber when I get the chance if I can borrow one of her jeeps. Thanks, Eva."

"Ughhh," Eva groaned out loud, her hands in her face. She removed them once she heard Reese laughing at her.

"I'm just teasing you." His eyes were on her, and a smile was cracked on his face. "Could you be ready in ten?"

Her smile reappeared. "Absolutely! I'm pretty much ready already. It's a good thing we all wear the same clothes every day, for whatever reason."

Soon, Eva and Reese, accompanied by a macabre raven, stood by the door.

"Amber gave us permission, we're good to go," he said.

"You ready, then?" she asked him.

"Let's get going."

They walked for some time down the main street of White Heart, step after step down the cobblestone road on the path to the garage, before one of them spoke again.

"Hey, Reese," Eva began. "What do you do if you have feelings for someone?"

"Hmm?" He hadn't been paying attention, engulfed in indulging Hex with affection.

She flashed him a pulchritudinous smile. "Nothing, just thinking out loud."

■ ■ ■

Amber flashed her security card to the guard's scanner. He granted her access, moving out of her way as she walked down a long hallway to an interrogation room where the four remaining prisoners from the battle in White Heart were held. The front door guard

130

saluted her, and Amber did the same, glad to see a sign of respect. He stood aside to give her pass, but before she entered, she inquired of him:

"Did you manage to get the names of any of them?"

"Good thing you asked," he replied. "They refuse to speak, but I managed to pull their tags from their uniforms. They go by the names Brandon Derringer-Crimani, Jack Bahal, Mov Dormin, and Weylin Graves. Be wary, Ms. Leavett, they were clothed in Syndicate uniforms."

"I noticed. Hmm," she grumbled, her gaze unfocused. "Strange. The Syndicate, or at least, the new Syndicate, led by Boss Gareth, almost always opts to deceive. It is unlike them to now bear their own uniforms proudly."

"Well, you could always ask these fine four gentlemen," the guard offered with a chuckle.

Amber nodded, taking his suggestion seriously. "I'll get to that."

The four perpetrators said nothing, nor did they look at the general as she stepped into the room. Rather, they focused their minds elsewhere, in hopes of ignoring her as best they could.

"Alright, let's get started." Amber sat across from them and equipped herself with a stare, serious and threatening. "I warn you, if I can't do this the easy way, you can bet I'll make the hard way a nightmare."

■ ■ ■

The clamor of dishes and chatter of various conversations brought the restaurant to life. Amber approached the counter, four criminals following behind her like embarrassed children.

"Table for five, please," spoke Amber. A waiter promptly guided them through the restaurant and seated them at a booth.

After some time, one of them finally spoke up: "Why are you doing this?" he asked in a frustrated tone. It was the first thing any one of them had said to her.

Amber casually picked up a menu, going through her meal options. "Secrets can be learned through trust or through fear. I firmly believe that fear is the last resort."

"Hiya, I'm Nils!" a loud voice boomed.

Amber slowly shifted her head upwards, finding a young boy clad in waiter attire staring at them, a toothy grin on his youthful face. He held a notepad in his hands and seemed to be eagerly awaiting a response from the general.

"Hi...Nils. Can we get a—"

"Should I get y'all waters right now, or are y'all good to order?" he interrupted, his boisterous, slightly obnoxious voice ever-present.

"Uh," Amber stammered, at a bit of a loss for words. She continued on, ignoring the youthful server's awkward presence. "Can we get the pasta platter? Would anyone else like something different?"

"Oh, definitely a salad," another criminal said. "I'm on a diet." He received disappointed and insulted stares from his comrades, and with that, he sulked

down in his seat.

"Comin' right up, folks!" Nils announced, then left in a hurry.

Amber waited until he was out of earshot, then turned back to her guests. "To tell you the truth, I only do this to people who haven't committed serious crimes."

One of the criminals turned his glare towards her, a bit of anger in his eyes. "What are you talking about?" he said. "We broke into your city and wreaked havoc."

Amber scoffed and snickered. "If you mean minor damages and no deaths on our side, then yes, you certainly 'wreaked havoc.' And truth be told, you did less than all of your friends combined did. No, I don't think I could trust you four to kill a fly."

The man grumbled to himself, and Amber chuckled. She was getting to them, and she knew it well.

■ ■ ■

Dusk was breaking as Eva pulled her van over the rarely-treaded road. Reese stepped out into the cold air and opened the back of it, there finding what he was looking for: a box full of various bottles. He selected two and seated himself in the back. Eva joined him soon, and he tossed a bottle to her as she relaxed herself opposite him. The road adjacent to them was shining with moonlight, barren, forgotten, lonely. They hadn't seen another car for miles.

"Can I ask you something?" Reese asked, after a long silence.

Eva shrugged. "Sure."

"Can you explain to me why you choose not to kill?"

Eva sighed, sipping her mead. "I just can't bring myself past the threshold of killing anyone. It's a big deal to me. I don't think I'm qualified to make a decision like that. I'm not sure if anyone should be." She paused, her eyes fixing themselves on the sky. The moons were making a brilliant display of their celestial beauty.

Senia had two moons: one gave off a purple shine and was home to a massive crater visible even to the three Guardians huddled in a van. Its sibling orbited nearby, much smaller and paler, but still beautiful in its own sense.

Eva silently got on her knees, crawled to the man across from her, and curled up next to his massive body. Though she was still, inside, she was overcome with peaceful joy, enjoying Reese's close company.

He couldn't stop himself from glancing at her petite body next to his, and every time he stole a look, he noticed a different part of her that he found fascinating.

On his other shoulder, Hex had one eye closed, the other metal one staying ever watchful. There was a moment of quiet, as the three rested together, and Reese's eyes slowly shut, permitting sleep to engulf him.

Suddenly, Hex jolted at the sound of distant gunfire, and when he saw Reese and Eva sleeping, he pecked their heads lightly. They woke up irritated, but snapped to their senses when they heard the violent sounds. The three packed up quickly and got into their seats. Within seconds, they were gone.

"What should we do about that?" Eva asked after she was sure they were far away.

"I'm not sure," Reese responded. "But maybe we should just keep going."

"What if there are people in need?"

Reese grumbled. He didn't respond at first, only because he wasn't sure what call to make. Finally, he spoke up: "Turn the van around."

"Good choice," Eva said, in agreement.

■ ■ ■

Xela placed the remaining electrodes onto the peaceful corpse, readying the experiment. "Stand back," she warned the people working amongst her. She reached for a lever on the other side of the room and pulled it. A few seconds passed before she shut off the electric current again.

"Measurements?" she asked one of her fellow workers with a clipboard in hand. He didn't respond at first. Xela repeated herself: "Measurements?"

"Oh my, Miss Zamora," the man said, in a low and quiet voice.

"What is it?" she anxiously asked.

"There was a beat! Brief and slow, but it was there!"

A cheer came from around the room. Xela breathed a sigh of relief.

"Today, we took a step!" she announced at the top of her lungs. "Tomorrow, we will take another!"

The scientists around her gave cheers, the room erupting into joy. Xela glanced around the room with a grin, reveling in the proud faces of her coworkers, but her gleeful countenance faded in surprise when she noticed Amber watching her from the back of the room. She quickly turned to the remaining thanatologists. "Pack up the body. Remember," she reminded them, "preservation is key."

"What a fascinating job," Amber said, approaching her. "Do advancements like this happen every day in your work?"

"Not every day. But they're happening more often lately. I think we're really getting somewhere!" Xela's outburst of cheerfulness made Amber laugh sweetly to herself. "What brings you here?"

Amber looked around the room. "Just curious as to what you do here."

Xela nodded. "Everyone," she said, turning to her remaining colleagues next to her, "this is Amber! For the next few months, I'll be working with her and a few others to bring down a larger threat. In exchange, she's agreed to bring us under her protection."

Amber waved, and they waved back. One of them approached her with a hand extended, and Amber shook it.

"It's a pleasure to know there's someone else out there watching our backs," he said, before quickly getting back to his work.

"It's a good feeling, caring for others," Amber said as she watched the science being conducted in the room around her, before turning to Xela with a sweet stare. "I'm a bit curious myself. Would you mind showing me some more of how your work gets done?"

Xela smiled and chuckled. "I'd be more than happy to."

CHAPTER 10:

The stinging smell of smoke and blaze worsened as Eva drove closer to the gunfire. They were in thick woods now, far off the road they had treaded on, and the burning trees grew more common and clustered as they drove deeper into the forest.

"Damn it," Eva said, as her van drew to a halt before a cluster of bushes on fire. "This is as far as we go in this thing."

They disembarked and ran on foot. Far in the distance, an ominous volcano gloomed, poking its head through the layer of ash clouds that masked the sky.

They had just reached a clearing in the forest when a fiery explosion nearby took their attention: a battle was in progress. On the closest side to them, they witnessed red-skinned soldiers clad in grey and orange disembark from army vehicles. They took off into the forest, into the fray of conflict.

"Reese, they're..."

"Assossians." he finished. Their red skin and short stature quickly betrayed their race. However, it did not seem like they wished to hide it.

There was a moment in which the three of them, raven, woman, and man, watched on with frozen stares, unsure of what to do. Reese was the first to snap into action.

"Reese!" Eva called, as he ran into the clearing, Hex perched on his shoulder as he almost always was, but the brutish man failed to heed her cry. She could do little but watch as he grabbed an unassuming soldier running into the fray and disappeared back into the woods with him.

"*Ushe tea ai!*" the Assossian screamed, struggling for his life. "*Madad! Madad!*" The crackling of rifles in the distance and booming of explosions silenced his pleas from his comrades, and Reese held him in place with ease.

"What are you doing?" Eva called out nervously.

The tower of a man ignored her. "Listen to me," he said to the Assossian. "I ain't gonna hurt you if you stop struggling."

"What do you want?" the captured man queried, anger garbling the words in his throat. He relaxed his squirming, but only slightly.

"Who are you fighting?" asked Eva, giving in to Reese's impetuous tactics. "And why?"

He scoffed. "Ungrateful *marhwa* who want to take more from us than they already have."

"You're going to have to be a bit more specific," Reese said, his arm still around the Asssossian's neck.

"Ever hear of the Syndicate?"

Reese and Eva's eyes widened, and they exchanged looks of intrigue.

"Ever hear of 'the enemy of my enemy is my friend'?" Eva asked as Reese let go of the man. "Take us to whoever's in charge around these parts. We'd like a few words."

■ ■ ■

"General Leavett?" a guard inquired as Amber prepared to enter the interrogation room. "Before you ask them anything, I would like to let you know that Weylin wishes to speak with you in private."

"Which one is Weylin?" she asked, intrigued, as they walked together to the one-way window displaying the inside of the interrogation room. Four soldiers sat at the end of a table, their hands cuffed. The guard pointed out the closest prisoner to Amber. He was clad in a striped black-and-white fedora.

"Very well," Amber said as she stepped into the room and grabbed a keychain from her pockets. With it, she uncuffed Weylin and pulled him away from his comrades. As they left, the guard dutifully closed the door behind them.

Amber led the prisoner into a room identical to the one in which he was holed up, only this one was void of his allies. "I heard you wanted to speak with me," she said, leaning against the wall. "So speak."

After a long sigh, Weylin began: "I had nothing to lose by volunteering to help the Syndicate do this. The other three soldiers in here agreed to do this because they saw an opportunity to aid the Syndicate, maybe to die for them. I don't care for glory, and I really regret what I did.

"When I saw you care for us by feeding us even after we attempted to destroy your precious city, I was inspired by your compassion and forgiveness. I want to help and serve your cause because it brought meaning to me when I believed there was none."

Amber took a moment to take his words in. "Well said, Mr. Graves," she complimented him. "But the Syndicate are naturally deceptive folk. How do I know you're not trying to play me for a fool?"

Weylin sighed and shrugged. "The best I can do is feed you information about the Syndicate which I can only hope you would find helpful and, if you permit me, fight by your side against them."

"Very well, but we start small. Your sentence will be reduced, but you will need to serve some time. I know you understand. Do your penance, and I will be back in due time to check on you. Impress me, and you'll see yourself accepted by this city-state with open arms."

She opened the door for him, but rather than take his arm forcefully, she trusted him to bring himself back to the interrogation room down the hall, under her supervision. Before he re-entered the room, Amber turned to the man. "Goodbye, Mr. Graves. I truly hope we may work together in the future."

Weylin sat back down and let the guard handcuff him again. Those few words had saved him from longer imprisonment and given him the chance to serve her? He couldn't believe she let him off the hook like that; she truly must have been either crazy or a shade of compassionate the world had never seen. Perhaps a bit of both.

■ ■ ■

Skullgem grasped the edge, his feet planted on the rails of the balcony, as he attempted to pull himself onto the roof of the Guardians' residence. A faint gasp escaped him as he lost his footing and almost fell into the alley below him. Just then, an arm reached out and grasped his, giving him enough time to yank himself to safety.

When he found himself lying on the roof, he was surprised to see Alyssa had beaten him there. Her tan sweater was removed, revealing a blue tank top. The markings on her arms were bright and visible in contrast to the darkness around them. She sprawled herself next to him, her incredibly long hair serving as a cushion for her back.

"I'm assuming you like to come here to clear your head as well?" Alyssa asked. He simply nodded, having no other way to communicate with her. "I like to feel the cold winds against my skin. It's relaxing to me."

They then lay in silence for a while, gazing at the black sky of night above them. The brief hush was interrupted by the sounds of footsteps on the concrete street below them. Alyssa shifted herself and peered off the edge of the roof.

"Xela's back." A smile found itself on her face.

The teenager reached for her tan sweater and put it on, then pulled her mess of hair out, letting it flow behind her lawlessly. After she climbed down onto the balcony, she looked up at Skullgem. "You coming?" He shook his head, and Alyssa disappeared inside. The Assossian continued to lie there peacefully, permitting sleep to close his eyelids.

■ ■ ■

When the doors opened to a disorganized, darkened room, Reese, Hex, and Eva were uninvitingly greeted by a man in a grey vest.

"What is the meaning of this? What are these humans doing here?"

"*Laa oten effe*," the Assossian with them reassured. "They want to help us. They fight the Syndicate as well."

"Bah!" said the Assossian wearing grey. "They are humans, just like the Syndicate. Get them out of my sight, before they stab us in the back."

"Wow. That's a little racist," Reese whispered to Eva.

"Sir," called Eva, ignoring Reese and addressing the grey-vested Assossian. "We're part of a special group dedicated to fighting the Syndicate. We have another member who's an Assossian civil rights leader."

"Oh, really?" The voice came from another Assossian dressed in garb of warm, bright colors walking into the room. Majestically long black hair flowed behind him, and where it almost touched the ground, it ended in a fiery hue. His arms were covered in strange orange markings. "And who would that be?"

"Skullgem," she announced proudly. "The Lionhearted."

"Really?" the other Assossian said, slightly taken aback. "Like, as in *the* Skullgem the Lionhearted?"

"Uh, yeah. Who else would we be talking about?"

"Could you, uh..." the man began, leaning on a desk awkwardly. "Could you get me his autograph?"

"Brother," said the grey-clothed Assossian, a groan hidden in his voice.

"Right, sorry. Who are you again?"
"We're under the allegiance of White Heart," Eva stated. Hex cawed, as he did periodically. "The Guardians, we like to call ourselves. We're only here to offer our help."

"My name is Blaze," the ombre-haired Assossian said.

"This is my brother, Smoke. Of course, those aren't our real names. They're just—""With all due respect," Eva interrupted, "I understand the concept of a codename."

"*Yaa'i,*" Blaze continued. "We were just attacked by a squadron of Syndicate soldiers. Thankfully, they've just retreated, but it likely won't be for long."

"We waste time," Smoke said, as he took up a grenade launcher in his arms. "If we wish to retaliate, we must do so now."

"Will you help us?" asked Blaze. He raised his fist, opened his palm, and a beckoning, bright ember emerged.

146

■ ■ ■

The red sea swirled, waves of crimson surrounded in glass, as Amber set her wine on the table. Adjacent to her, Xela took another sip of hers. They were seated on a couch in the living room, facing each other.

"Listen, Xela," Amber began. "I wanted to thank you for all your help. You're a valued member of a team now, and I'm very glad to have you on my side.

"It's what I enjoy doing, really," Xela spoke with a light voice. "You know how much I love to help people." She looked away for a moment, then back at the general. "But please, can you do me a favor, Amber?"

"Of course."

"Stop thanking me."

The room fell silent for a moment, and then Amber laughed quietly to herself. Xela smiled at the sound of the light giggles coming from her friend.

"No, seriously!" Xela continued, hardly suppressing a giggle herself. "I love the appreciation, but that's the millionth time I've heard that spiel about how you're grateful for our help. Tell me something else, something I haven't heard yet." She paused, wondering if she should ask the question on her mind. "Something about you."

"Oh, please," chuckled Amber. "I'm not that interesting. I doubt you'd want to know about me."

"Come on," persisted Xela, tilting her head in disbelief. "You're a general, and your people love you, idolize you, and you're going to pull that bullshit, cliché 'my life's not that interesting card'? Give me something to work with here. Whatever it is, I promise I'll listen."

"Okay, okay, if you say so. I guess since I've been a little girl, I've always been inspired by—" She was rudely interrupted by Xela's flawless impression of someone snoring. "Haha, very funny," Amber mocked, smiling when Xela opened her eyes and grinned.

"I'm kidding, I'm kidding. Go on."

"I've always been inspired by stories and tales of heroes, but I was upset at how few of those heroes were real. I decided that I want to be just that: a hero. I joined the defense corps when I was a teenager, and I've been serving White Heart ever since. I just climbed the ranks, and here I am."

Xela nodded in interest. "Was it hard?"

A sigh from Amber. 'There were times that I didn't even know who I was fighting for. I mean, not everyone in White Heart is as good a person as you or me. I end up saving a lot of bad people, but what can I do about it?"

"I know what you mean."

Amber looked up and peered at her. "You do?"

"I know it too well. Thanatology is a dangerous study, especially in the world we live in," began Xela. Her voice was much more sorrowful and serious now. "People die so, so often. It's no wonder everyone's scared of death. Even mention the very word and someone riots. People want to forget that it exists, but unfortunately, the world doesn't work like that. My life and the lives of my colleagues were threatened by scared and confused people."

"So you moved to a secluded marsh and decided to go through your goth phase again?"

Xela laughed as she ran a hand through her short hair. "It sounds a bit strange when you put it that way. But yes, we needed to conduct our research...elsewhere. For our own safety. Now that I think about it, though, you're really doing me a great favor, Amber."

"Am I, now?" Amber asked sweetly.

"You're bringing my order out of the shadows. You're making people realize who we are, and why we're on their side."

"I guess that means you must be a hero, too."

"Oh, no no no," retorted Xela. "No, I'm still far from that. Far from that..." Her voice trailed off, and quiet once more. "But maybe one day, I will be."

"Oh Xela, love, that day has already come," Amber assured. "When I look at you, I see bravery and leadership, and I see someone who wants to do the world a favor. Isn't that what a hero is?"

Xela was silent. She thought about this for quite some time. "You're so kind, Amber."

"Thank you."

"I mean it, you know."

"I get it, I understand."

"No, you don't understand. You're so, so kind." Xela could have sworn she saw Amber blush slightly.

"And I appreciate you saying that. It means a lot to hear the approval of my teammates."

"You're really not clicking, are you? It's more than approval."

"I'm not..." Amber stammered for a moment. "I'm not sure I comprehend what you mean, Xela. I'm sorry."

"It's okay," Xela said, sighing as she reached for her wine glass. Once she took a sip and set it back down, she turned to Amber. "Do you know what love is, Amber?"

Her friend next to her searched for an answer. Her words lost her, and the few sounds of stammering she made sounded incredibly anxious. "I've cared for a lot of people," Xela continued. "It's my duty, after all. But it's been quite some time since someone's cared for me. I've forgotten what it feels like, and now that you're here for me, I'm not sure what I'm feeling. Perhaps you can help me understand my emotions."

Amber finally found her voice then. "Miss Zamora, I don't quite understand where you're going with this.

Xela peered into Amber's nervous eyes as the room turned quiet. It was always death that made her so curious, but now something else caught her prurience. Something came over her, and she quickly leaned in to kiss Amber. After a moment of their lips together, the other woman pulled back, her cheeks red. The sight of her surprised and embarrassed face snapped Xela back into sobriety.

"I...I'm so sorry," she apologized. "I'm sorry, I'm sorry. That was incredibly out of line. I should go."

She departed quickly, heading up the staircase to her bedroom. She left a confused Amber behind, unsure of what to think or what she would say to Xela when they saw each other again.

. . .

"The Syndicate Empire established an outpost near our settlement a week or two ago, just at the foot of Mount Reverie." Smoke pointed to the dark volcano up ahead in the distance as he explained, then set to opening the garage doors.

"Since then, we've constantly been constantly harassed by Syndicate raids," his brother continued. "Our full-scale retaliation attack was to begin tomorrow, but your arrival means we can pull it off sooner."

"If you don't see this as a chance to stab us in the back," Smoke muttered just loud enough for the Guardians to overhear. If they heard him, they were ignoring him.

A military light truck stood idly in the garage, which the two brothers hopped into with haste as the Guardians followed along.

"Hold on a moment," Eva said, before she boarded. "Is it just going to be only us against the Syndicate stronghold? No backup?"

"Actually, we're going to have an attack helicopter protecting us, and snipers everywhere around us in the woods," said Smoke in his painfully sarcastic tone.

"We'll have another two trucks on standby as backup, if we need it," Blaze said.

"Don't forget about the army of tanks that's going to be protecting us," his brother added.

"He's joking, obviously," Blaze said.

"Take it as an opportunity to prove your worth," Smoke said with a slight grin. He climbed into the turret seat in the middle of the truck.

"And how many Syndicate populate this outpost?" Eva asked.

"About fifty," estimated Smoke.

Before Eva could complain, Reese hushed her. "We can handle that. Although the helicopter would have been arguably cooler."

"Someone's confident," Smoke commented. "You sure you've got what it takes, big man?"

Reese laughed, and Hex cawed along. "Clearly you haven't seen me when I'm angry."

Before they left, an Assossian girl with an orange dress and black hair worn in a beehive barged into the garage. She walked toward them with a youthful swagger, her muscled legs very prominent. "*Aivaso!*" she called, a flame floating above her hand just like how Blaze had posed when they first met him. She seated herself inside the truck, next to the Guardians. "Don't leave without me!"

Blaze signed. "I'm not gonna stop you, but this is going to be dangerous. Are you sure you know the risks and know how to be responsible for yourself?"

"Yeah, yeah." She turned to Eva and stuck out a hand. "*Narha!* My name is Burnellia."

"Is that a nickname, too?" Eva inquired, chuckling and shaking Burnellia's hand. Burnellia was nonplussed. "No. Why would it be?"

Eva held a blank expression, unsure of what to say. "Never mind." Her eyes drifted downwards, and she noticed the familiar tattoos imprinted on the girl's arms. "Are those...?

"Relic markings? You bet." She held her hand open, and a small ember burst from her palms once more.

"Oh right, I probably should have mentioned," Blaze said. He flexed his massive muscles, and the orange markings glowed on his arms as well. "Most people don't know that relics can be passed down genetically."

Eva turned back to the Assossian girl. "I have someone you should meet. I think you and her would make great friends."

Dawn was approaching, but the forest fire had not quelled. It only took a few minutes for them to spot the outpost ahead of them.

"Brace yourselves," Smoke warned, "they've spotted us." A rocket zoomed past as Blaze swerved the car sharply.

"They're already shooting?" Burnellia asked to no one in particular as she was jerked against the car door. A loud explosion rudely sounded somewhere behind them, and Burnellia's words were lost.

As they entered the outpost, which was about the size of a small village, Eva opened her door and began crawling up to the roof of the truck.

"What are you doing?" Burnellia frantically inquired.

"What I do best," Eva blankly responded, as she pulled herself onto the top of the vehicle. She held

155

onto the truck for balance, but when they sped close enough to the rooftops of the outposts' houses, she leaped onto it. She skillfully flipped and landed with a somersault.

Meanwhile, Reese, taken by the overwhelming sight of how many Syndicate were already in arms around them, pulled a syringe from his belt. He injected it into his arm and collapsed back onto his seat, as Burnellia watched on in serious confusion. Once he regained consciousness, he kicked open the vehicle's side door and leaped out.

"And I thought we were strange, *aivaso*," she said, as Reese ran into battle.

"Yeah, you're telling me. I love 'em already," the Assossian driver chuckled out loud, as he slammed the gas directly toward danger.

With a clenched fist, Reese headed towards a group of troopers firing at the technical, grabbing two by the neck and smashing their heads together. The other two in front of him turned to face him, but had no time to fire in retaliation; Reese pulled his axe from his side and slashed at their knees, sweeping them off their feet. As one fell, Reese brutally swung the axe into his chest multiple times, spraying blood on his own body. The other Syndicate soldier was already on his back; easy prey for the raven to tear apart.

Most of the Syndicate soldiers, upon seeing the massacre of their comrades, fled for cover in the few buildings lining the walls of the outpost. The Guardians raided the buildings on the left side, while the Assossians took the right.

Smoke selected several particular namesake grenades and shot them into the houses with a heavy launcher as Blaze drove the car by. Once the grey gas was visibly seeping from every open space in the houses, Blaze drove the car back for another round. They had practiced it many times before: Burnellia and Blaze tossed their flames at the gas, which endured extreme pressure from the heat. One by one, fiery explosions engulfed the houses, and the entire strip of buildings was decimated into a charred ruin.

On the other side of the outpost, Reese and Hex went through the buildings one by one, while Eva moved parallel along the rooftops. When Reese entered the first house, he came across two soldiers viewing the explosions from the window. They turned to face Reese too late, as he was already swinging his fist. One Syndicate trooper flew several feet from his position into a wall, while the other fired at the hulk of a man. Thanks to Hex, the bullets fell to the ground harmlessly before they reached his partner. Reese threw his axe, but the soldier quickly ducked. As she stood back up, he made a terrifying leap for her neck. She attempted to push him away, but it was of no use. The soldier choked and gasped for breath, but eventually collapsed, succumbing to the merciless grip of the monster of a Guardian literally squeezing the life out of her.

Meanwhile, Eva made her way down a spiral staircase from the roof, and came across a few soldiers who weren't paying her attention. With her rifle, she managed to tranquilize three before being noticed.

The remaining two readied their weapons as Eva took cover.

"Reese!" she began into the talker, taking cover hastily. "I could use a little help!" Bullets soared around her as one Syndicate soldier emptied a clip near her position. Another slowly made his way towards her, a spear in hand.

Reese ran from house to house, searching for Eva, knowing he found the right house when he witnessed gunfire directed towards someone not in his sight. He charged the door down in a fury to save his fellow Guardian. As he ran towards the soldier shooting his gun, he rammed into him with fearsome force, sending him soaring back. With a draw of his shotgun, Reese blasted the Syndicate man in his chest before he could get back up.

It was then that the spearman drew his attention towards the raging brute. As he did, Eva exposed herself from cover and shot him in the neck. As the man fell, Reese fired at him as well.

Eva hopped down from the staircase. Instead of thanking Reese as he expected, she gave him a vexed glare.

"What?" he asked, unsure as to why he was receiving such a response.

"What is wrong with you?" Eva asked in a shrill voice.

Reese was quite confused. "What did I do?"

"You killed him!" she shouted as she stormed to him.

"Of course I did." He looked very uninterested.

"He was tranquilized! He didn't need to die!"

Her hands flew forward to push him, and he stumbled back, startled by her sudden burst of frustration. In a move of anger and retaliation, he turned to her and shoved back. Unsurprisingly, she fell to the floor with a tiny yelp, her strength much outmatched by Reese's. Immediately, shame hit him as a tall wave of guilt, and he reached to pick her up. Eva scoffed, but reluctantly took his helping hand.

The army truck made its way around to the Guardians. As the victorious Guardians entered the vehicle, Blaze congratulated them.

"Now do you trust us?" Eva asked.

"With your help, we managed to take on an entire Syndicate base. Outnumbered." Blaze drove the truck away from the outpost, leaving it in flames. "I can't thank you enough for your help. What do you make of it, brother?"

Smoke, his head poking from the gunner seat and his arms leaning on the roof, either didn't hear Blaze or chose to ignore him.

The vehicle's occupants were silent for a short time after that. Eva sat against the door and crossed her arms.

"Why are you always so angry?" she finally asked Reese, a pouty countenance equipped on her face.

"I'm only angry, like, ninety-five percent of the time," he responded.

She rolled her eyes and stared out the window, not wishing to have her eyes on him.

■ ■ ■

"Well then, what do they want?" the Chairman asked Amber.

"The Syndicate wants war," she responded.

"Then I say we give 'em war."

They sat in the Chairman's office once again. It was common for Amber to ask his advice before doing something that might have results on all of White Heart.

Amber fixed her collar. "With all due respect, sir, I don't think that that is the best course of action."

The Chairman sat back in his chair. "Then what would be?"

"They want war?" said Amber. "We give them peace. We give them a treaty. While they consider their options, we rally our troops, and we call our allies. If they attack, which they likely will do, we will be prepared."

"Hmm," murmured the Chairman, considering his options. "Very well, Amber. Send this treaty to them. We shall see where we will go from there. Will that be all?"

Amber nodded. "Good day, Chairman."

She walked out of the room with anticipation in her heart, wondering what the Syndicate leader would make of her play.

■ ■ ■

"A treaty! They dare send an olive branch?" Boss Gareth's words echoed in his massive chambers. A throne loomed behind him, the seat from which he ruled over his soldiers. "Here is what I think of their damned treaty!" He unsheathed his longsword, the fearsome, shining claymore, and impaled the papers with little effort.

"Your brother fights willingly with them," said the soldier who delivered the treaty.

"I don't care that he is my blood," said Gareth, uninterested.

"That's not what I mean. He and his raven have been deemed invincible by many of the other soldiers. And paired with the rest of his group..."

"Bah! No one is invincible." He put away his longsword, the papers flying off the blade. "I have cut his eye, and he has bled. And what bleeds can be killed. I will conquer them all; both the Guardians and their wretched city."

CHAPTER 11:

The three Guardians had gone on to continue their journey. The burning forest only worsened, and now they were in a grove clustered with dead trees, following a road even less treaded.

The inside of the van was silent for quite a while after they left, until Reese finally broke the quiet ambiance:

"I can't take this. I'm sorry for what happened earlier." Eva declined to respond, her focus fixated on the road. "I promise I'll try not to kill anyone you tranquilize in the future."

After some time, she sighed. "Whatever. The past is the past. Check the map for me, will you?"

Reese unfolded a massive map and scanned it for their location. "Oh. We're almost there," he said. "It should be only a few minutes from here."

"That's good. This was a bit more of an adventure than I had bargained for."

The road ran parallel to a cliff, the forest around them filled with barren trees. Eva felt as if she was one of the few people in history who had traveled down such a desolate road.

Finally, they came upon a simple house jutting off the cliffside alongside the road. Reese stepped out and looked over the edge of the cliff, where far below even more dead trees were visible. Where the grim forest ended in the distance, it was met with arid desert badlands, plains of dry sand with massive formations of rock scattered near and far. It was an endless, unexplored landscape, with few calling it home.

It was then that the door of the cottage opened, and out stepped the woman awaiting them. She wore two strange devices on both of her wrists that seemed to contain a volley of syringes inside of them, and her dark hair was tied up in a bun with a pin shaped like a caduceus staff holding it in place.

"And I can already feel my heart shriveling," commented Reese at the sight of the doctor. He slowly, reluctantly opened his passenger-side door and, with the massive bird on his shoulder, stepped out towards the woman he had wished never to see again. "You comin'?" he asked Eva, who was sitting in the driver's seat as if she had nowhere to go.

"I'll, uh, let you two sort out whatever you need," she responded.

"Good call." Reese shut the door and grudgingly took leave, approaching the house and the doctor brooding over the entrance like a beast guarding its den.

"Reese," she greeted him as he approached in a monotone voice. She noticed the raven attempting to bore an evil eye into her, and she returned the favor with a scowl directed towards Hex.

"Mary."

"Who's that behind you?" She motioned to the pretty brunette waiting in the van.

"Just a friend," he was quick to respond.

Mary gave an obnoxiously loud scoff and parted to let the two into her house. "He's upstairs," she said, knowing Reese would only be interested in

what he had come for, but she stopped him before he could head up the staircase to his son's room. "Before you see him, I need to tell you a few things."

"Alright."

"The boy is only thirteen."

"Don't remind me how long you've been keeping me from him," responded Reese, already growing vexed. "All that time and he hasn't asked about me at all? He's never wanted to know who his father is?"

Mary sighed. "Not hiding from you. Ire is a special boy."

"Ire?"

"I named him after you...in a way. I figured if I had to keep him from you, I had to give you something."

"And why, exactly, did you hide him from me?" he demanded loudly.

"Lower your voice," she sternly spoke. "Again, I wasn't hiding him from *you*. I had no way to contact you, and this place is very remote for a reason: it's for his own damn protection." She tapped her boot against the wooden floor, her sign her temper was beginning to flare. "You're always getting yourself into trouble, anyway. I didn't want him involved in your dangerous work."

"Then why tell me about him now?"

"Because it's now my turn to get myself into trouble." Footsteps pattered in the hallway, and Reese turned his attention to the noises, witnessing Ezekiel emerge from a nearby room. "An old friend wants my help in gathering our other old friends."

"Right," Reese said, understanding the situation. "You have a duty. Don't we all?" A low sigh. "Hello, Zeke." Ezekiel waved in response, a touch awkwardly.

"Reese," Mary spoke with a serious tone. "I mean it when I say he is special." Reese paused for a moment, then nodded and headed up the stairs.

Mary turned to Eva, who had left the van and walked to the front of the house. Her elegant blouse whirled in the mild wind. "Who are you?"

Eva was slightly chagrined at her upfront question. She thought for a bit, then, with a hint of pride, answered: "His girlfriend."

Mary scoffed and fixed her glasses. "Of course you are," she murmured.

"Excuse me?"

Mary laughed. "I mean, come on; what could you possibly see in him? It's clear to me what he sees in you, though."

Eva was quickly growing vexed at her. "What did *you* see in him?"

Mary chuckled. "I must have been blind."

Eva's mouths suddenly opened a few inches. "You know, I've never killed anyone in my life, but I might just end that record here."

"Are you threatening me in my own home?" Neither of them noticed Ezekiel slowly, carefully and awkwardly backing away from them.

Inside, Reese reached for the door closest to the staircase. Opening it slowly, he noticed the boy sitting in the center of the room, counting and ordering a handful of credits. His black hair matched Reese's perfectly.

He turned, stood, and looked up towards the giant entering his room. "Are you Tyreesius?" he asked, as he flipped a coin in one hand and a card in the other.

"Yes, I am," replied Reese.

The boy smiled. "Hello, father." He stood up and hugged him, taking Reese aback with the sudden, yet casual gesture. "That's a cool bird," he added, looking up at his shoulder.

"Yes," said Reese. "Yes, he's one cool bird. He's a raven." Reese thought he saw Ire smile again, but the young boy actually hadn't stopped smiling.

"What's his name?"

"Hex. Would you like to hold him?"

Ire nodded. Reese stuck a finger in front of the raven, and Hex hopped onto it. Reese then moved the raven towards Ire, the boy following his father and sticking his own finger out. Hex hopped once again, now onto the young boy. Despite his sharp talons, he knew to be careful not to dig into the child's skin. Son and father simultaneously laughed, Reese's a cheerful, yet awkward laugh, as if to him they were two strangers breaking the ice. Ire's laughter was natural, pure, full of untainted love and joy. Reese hadn't felt this sense of happiness for a long time, and he had Ire to thank for the reminder that emotions were not the worst things to feel sometimes.

At the sound of Reese and Ire's verbal happiness, Mary and Eva's quarrel ceased; both were astonished and dumbfounded. It was as if Ire was the

key to a happy, normal Reese neither of them had seen much of.

. . .

Ire and Alyssa sat in the living room together, one flipping coins in the air and the other freezing them with a beam of frost before they fell. It was amazing how fast they had gone to that; Alyssa was shy, yet the young boy was anything but, his gleeful nature contagious to all who came across his path. Hex kept a careful eye on them from a nearby shelf.

Reese watched his son from the kitchen, next to Amber, who watched the ice sorceress like a caring caretaker.

"It's good to see Alyssa finding some friends," Amber said.

"Aren't we her friends?" asked Reese, with a slight jest.

"I mean kids her age. Peers."

Reese shrugged. "She's got some years on Ire, but I guess you gotta make a few compromises when you've been living alone for a while." But here sat a happy, red-haired girl, laughing without a care for her past. "Where's Xela?" Reese asked after a silence had found itself in the room.

Amber sighed. "She, uh, went back to the Order."

"Really? I thought she just came back."

"Yeah for a night," she said quietly. "Something came up, and she had to go. Why, what's up?"

169

"I was gonna ask how the serum I gave her was working," Reese said, eyeing the syringes strapped to his belt.

"Well, her work seems to be going very well, from what I've seen," Amber assured.

It was then that Alyssa got up and approached them, practically dragging a smiling Ire behind. "Can we go to the next-door tavern for dinner?" she asked.

Reese shrugged, looking at Amber for an answer. "Sure, why not?"

In a matter of minutes, they gathered all the Guardians, save for Xela, and walked over to the nearby bar for a night of settling down. There they sat and shared food, drink, and chat, hours on end of bliss between the Guardians and Ire's tirelessly jovial aura. They were free from conflict, able to spend time with each other almost as a family might, albeit a particularly strange and diverse family.

Reese excused himself at one point to relieve himself, but returned to find Ire and Alyssa at a different table. Ire peeked at a hand of cards while Alyssa watched over his shoulder, inconspicuously whispering words into his ear. They had joined a group of gamblers playing some sort of card game, clearly for money, as Reese witnessed Ire claiming victory over one round and pulling a large stash of credits towards himself.

"What in the fuck?" Reese muttered to himself. "What is going on here?" Now his voice boomed with concern.

"Ire is incredible at this!" Alyssa stated. A huge grin found itself on the young boy's face, stretching almost from ear to ear.

"Nuh-uh," Reese said. "Not under my wing." He picked little Ire up with ease, and the boy grabbed for his pile of credits, managing to carry a few handfuls in his arms, as Reese placed him down in his original seat.

The other gamblers seemed happy to see him removed from their game, but Alyssa did not share their feelings. "Oh come on, Reese. Don't be such a buzzkill."

The words struck him like a stone. He laughed and slowly turned to the red-haired Guardian. "I am NOT a buzzkill," he sternly spoke, as he picked Ire up again and placed him back at the gambler's table. "Did mom know you did this?"

Ire shook his head. "Nope."

Reese smiled wickedly. "In that case, gamble ahead!"

They continued their card game, and Ire continued claiming credits. Eventually, the whole bar crowded around the table to watch as a young boy bested any challengers, his pile of credits serving as a token of his victories. Money flowed towards him, drained from the losses of the gamblers who attempted to oppose him.

When the night grew old, the group eventually left the bar, Ire clutching a bag of credits and Reese clutching his son and laughing amongst friends. None of them were spared from smiles at the scene of father and son joyous in each other's presence.

...

The skies above Avalon were overcast that day, as they were most days. Surrounding the Syndicate's city-state was a lush rainforest, teeming with vibrant colors and enormous, beautiful flora. It was a significant contrast to the ominous dull white or futuristic chrome skyscrapers of the city. Their looming presence formed perfect rivals to the tall trees around them.

Boss Gareth watched one of the heirs to his throne from the balcony, commanding her squadron into drills. He withdrew from the terrace to find his other heir staring back at him.

He called himself Reynard. His skin was pale, his hair dark and streaked with red, and he wore a tactical vest that left a great deal of his fit chest bare. The sheathed hilt of an extendable whip remained coiled at his side.

"Boss," the man said. "You shouldn't spend long on the balcony. Dangerous days we live in. Always good to be careful." Reynard's voice now had a hint of mockery dabbed in it, but then again, it always seemed that way to Gareth.

"Spare me your false concern," Gareth said, removing his conical hat and admiring the shine of its edges. "As soon as I die, whether it be by your hand, my brother's, or someone or something else, I know you and Jade will kill each other for my spot."

173

He glanced outside again to find Jade, his other heir, training her troops. She had dark skin, dark-green hair, black garb, and wore a scarf that reminded Gareth of a soldier of the desert. A massive shield was in her arms, decorated with a green gem in its center, as well as two holstered sickles at both of her sides connected with a chain that wrapped around her, a kusarigama.

"Ah, but what of the Minotaur?" Reynard asked.

"He will not be going anywhere. He stays faithful as the right hand of the Syndicate's ruler, no matter who that is, as his many descendants have before my generation," said Boss Gareth. "What brings you here, Reynard?"

Before Reynard could open his mouth, gunfire erupted from outside, and the two rushed to the balcony to understand the commotion.

A blur of white sped past the street outside, and two members of Jade's squadron were cut down as it touched them. The others fired their weapons, but whatever had done its damage was gone in a flash. A moment of confusion followed amongst the troops until the white blur appeared again with a heavy, terrifying roar, unlike anything they'd heard before, cutting down another soldier.

Gareth leaped from the short balcony, landed with a steady roll, and approached Jade.

"What is this? What is going on?" he asked her in a fury.

It was not as if she knew what was happening, but she did not get to give an answer anyway. The

white blur appeared again, but this time it slowed down and stopped alongside the troops, revealing itself: it was but a lady completely clad in white, from her hair to her weapons to her clothing; even her vehicle followed the color scheme. Her sleeves looked like wings of pale, angelic and holy in appearance. She was mounted on a xenon motorcycle shining brightly, sleek and long in its design: two large, futuristic wheels connected by a thin frame.

Before the squadron could turn to her, she readied the longbow in her hands. As she pulled the string back, arrows of light manifested themselves in draw. She fired projectile after projectile with inhuman speed, white bolts dangerously soaring towards flesh. They flew over the heads of the troopers, and two landed precisely in Gareth's pauldrons. He clutched at the light arrows impaled in his shoulders, and they dissipated in his hands, leaving deep wounds behind. When he tried to retaliate, the woman in white was gone. The squadron had seen her, but she had disappeared from the messy scene so quickly, they had no time to react. A commotion burst out amongst everyone in the courtyard, as Boss Gareth, clutching the side of his neck where another arrow had narrowly skimmed, was escorted away on the shoulders of Jade and Reynard.

"What was that?" the Syndicate leader asked. "Who was that?!"

"I've heard of this before," Jade replied. "I've heard people call her 'Angel.' She's rarely seen, and her motives are a complete mystery."

"What else?" Gareth asked, clenching his teeth.

Jade shook her head as they approached the medical pavilion. "I don't know anything else about her."

. . .

The wheels of the White Heart jeep screeched in front of the facility's gate. The guards on the other side of Amber recognized her from before, and so they let her in, no questions asked.

She asked around for Xela, and her fellow Guardians' assistants led her to a laboratory room. Instead of her traditional black garments, Xela was wearing a simple lab coat, truly looking like a scientist now.

Xela was alone in the room, carefully investigating a red-orange vial of Reese's serum. She turned and stood at the sound of footsteps to find Amber looking back at her. The thanatologist's cheeks blushed as crimson as the liquid under her examination.

"Hi," she said, mentally kicking herself for almost stammering. "Look, I'm sorry about the other night."

She was shushed by Amber, who waved her finger at her. "Don't worry about it. We all make mistakes." Trying to change the subject, she asked Xela what she was working on.

"Reese gave me samples of his serum to experiment with. It has a healing component that I'm trying to find and isolate, as it might help in the revival process."

"Right. Science stuff." Xela laughed quietly. "I wanted to tell you that production on your thanatology center in White Heart begins tomorrow. They've found a lovely hospital long abandoned that might be in need of some refurbishing. Perhaps you'd like to stop and tell us how you want it to look."

Xela thought it over for a second. "Alright, I will come back tomorrow. Wait, why didn't you tell me this over your talker?"

Amber smiled and ignored her. "Good to know." Before she left, she quickly approached Xela, faster than the latter woman could react, and gave her a light kiss on her cheek. Had her heels not been on, she would have been forced to go on her toes to kiss the tall woman. "I mean, you didn't exactly give me any time to reject you, you know." With a sly wink, Amber then walked away, leaving a speechless Xela behind.

■ ■ ■

The prisoner's boisterous whistling was audible from across the hall, but his ears yet picked up the sound of footsteps in contrast to it. He sat up from his bed to find a group of guards approaching him.

"Stand, Weylin Graves," one of them said. "It's your lucky day."

He changed into some clothes the guards gave him, then found Amber by the gate as they released him, leaning on her trademark roofless jeep. She greeted him as he seated himself in the passenger seat, and before long, they were driving out on the streets of the sanctuary. It seemed like she had special privileges, as a general, to drive in the city.

He recognized a few parts of White Heart, as he had driven through it before. However, since he was no longer on the attack, he found himself strangely in admiration of the sanctuary. Any damage he or his comrades had caused seemed to have already been negated. The city's reconstruction efforts were impressive.

The general began to do a lot of talking, but Weylin didn't find himself listening much, his eyes overwhelming his other senses, the sights that the city-state had to offer captivating him. The architecture was astounding: everything was built in a similar fashion to White Heart's grand, legendary city walls, giving it the impression that it could outlast any attacker, and yet splendor saturated the style, as if everything created in the great sanctuary was built on pride.

Just before they reached their destination, they rounded a circle with a proud statue in its center. Weylin eyed it with heavy interest as Amber slowly drove the jeep past. It displayed the figure of an incredibly muscled woman standing with her arms akimbo. Her clothes were akin to that of the superheroes from stories Weylin remembered being fond of as a child, with the tight fabric all over her body hugging her muscles, a cape caught in the middle of its waving animation, a domino mask keeping secret the areas around her eyes, and, of course, her icon, the valiant anatomical heart etched on her raised chest. Just as it left Weylin's sights, he made out a name written on a plaque at her feet:

THE WHITEHEART

Finally, Amber rounded the jeep up into an alley, parking it there. She hopped out and led Weylin through the alleyway to what looked like a closed garage. When she opened it, however, there was much more than just a vehicle inside. It was the same armory Amber had shown Ezekiel and Reese some time prior; a plethora of weapons lined shelves and walls.

"Pick one. Take it as an olive branch. If anyone comes to White Heart with the intentions of destroying it, I want you to use it on them. And don't hesitate just because they may have used to be your friends."

Weylin wasted no time in selecting a submachine gun with a drum magazine from the corner of the room, equipping it and admiring it in his hands. Once he left the armory, Amber closed it behind him.

"Understand this, however," Amber said, turning to him. "If that weapon is ever used against this city or anyone who stands to protect it, I will destroy you."

Weylin nodded, his understanding accompanied by a significant amount of visible fear of the general.

As they exited the alley, they were privy to Eva and Reese walking by. The two noticed Amber immediately and greeted her, but once they realized the identity of the man next to her, they changed their

attitudes.

"Amber," Reese said. "What's *he* doing here?"

"*Weylin,*" she said, "is now working with us."

"You seriously trust that ex-Syndicate?" Eva asked.

"Reese is an ex-Syndicate."

"That's different," said Reese, his vexation growing. "I didn't try to terrorize the city you swore to protect." Hex cawed at Weylin with hate in his throat.

"I'm giving him a second and final chance."

"The story that you're weaving seems to repeat the word 'traitor' quite often. You sure you really want to use it again?" Reese asked the soldier beside Amber.

"Those are awfully fancy words for a brute like you," retorted Weylin.

Reese spit at Weylin's feet. "That'll be your last go at me," he said before he charged himself at him, and Weylin and Reese tumbled to the ground together.

"Stop! Stop it!" Amber yelled. She pulled Weylin away as Eva tried to pull Reese. Like a mad dog, Reese shook her off and ran back to attack Weylin. Before he could, Amber halted in front of him and whipped him with her pistol, leaving a small bruise on his forehead. "Behave yourselves!"

Reese rubbed his head and gave Weylin a final nasty look before scoffing and wordlessly turning to leave, steaming like a kettle.

CHAPTER 12:

They were quite short, and their red skin was not of a color the people of White Heart were accustomed to. They had mentioned to the guard at the gate the invitation they had received and had promptly been let in. The guard escorted them through the city, and though Reese and Eva had promised them that they were to be greeted with open arms, they could feel the heavy stares of the city-dwellers as they passed through.

They knew they had finally made it to wherever Reese and Eva had invited them when they saw the guard knocking on the door of a humble house. A short, hooded man answered, and the guard explained the invitation. Once he left, the short man removed his hood, seeing he was simply in the company of fellow Assossians. He signed the word *"Narha"* enthusiastically — the casual Assossian greeting.

I'm just like you, you see? Skullgem wished dearly he could have said the words, but a faint smile seemed to make them understand enough. He held up a finger at them, motioning them to wait, and looked around the house, finding Amber in the kitchen, stroking a halcyon Charlie.

Once she got to the door, she greeted Smoke, Blaze, and Burnellia. The trio was welcomed inside with a smile and a shake of hands.

"My name is Amber Leavett," she began, "General, Chief Executive Officer of White Heart's security, and the leader of the Guardians."

"My name is Blaze, and this is my brother, Smoke. We lead the Assossian resurgence." Blaze leaned in slightly towards Amber. "Those aren't our real names, though. They're just—"

"Codenames?" Amber interrupted. "I figured."

"What keeps giving it away?" the flame-haired Assossian murmured to himself.

"We wish to establish peace terms with your city," Smoke said, heeding his brother no mind.

"We don't ask for much," said Blaze. "Just your protection of our people."

Amber laughed. "You've come to the right place. White Heart is the best sanctuary Senia has to offer, you have our word! My only issue is that its other denizens may not accept you as well as we do. We have much work on making White Heart a socially equal home for all who call it such. I hope you understand, but also know that we, the Guardians, will treat you like family."

"We will take that risk," Blaze said, "as long as we're under your wings. We can no longer afford to be sitting ducks for the Syndicate. But you should know, there's more of us, many more."

"An army of Assossians will come to you seeking refuge," Smoke added.

"Bring all of them," Amber said sweetly. "Don't leave a single one behind. And if they can fight, all the better!"

They had not noticed Blaze's daughter slip out of the kitchen and into the living room, where she watched the red-haired girl from a window that showed the alley. Alyssa seemed focused on

184

something, as if she was meditating. She read silently from an ancient tome in her hands.

Burnellia made her way around the house and into the alley, watching the girl wordlessly for some time before chiming up: "Whatcha' doing?"

The red-haired girl opened her eyes and looked at the Assossian. "I'm concentrating."

"On what?"

Alyssa closed her eyes and raised her finger towards the cloudy sky, and a single flake of snow landed on it. Soon, more and more flakes fell, but they quickly melted before they could be properly admired.

Burnellia scoffed. "You're not going to tell me that you did that, are you?"

Alyssa scoffed back, gently placing her hand against a wall next to her. Ice crept alongside it, from her hand to the surface, frost trudging in a peculiar route. The cold sorceress closed her eyes, entrusting her emotions to paint a picture for her. Finally, a feeling inside told her that her work was finished, that her frost had fulfilled its purpose. She stepped back to find she had conjured a beautiful image of a massive snowflake of ice on the wall, towering above the two young women. "What about now?" she sassily retorted.

Unbeknownst to Burnellia, her jaw had dropped. After a moment of awe, however, she warned Alyssa to step away from her creation. Burnellia held out her palms, and a controlled fire spewed onto the frozen painting, melting it with no effort. The Assossian girl then closed her palms, and just like that, the snowflake was gone, replaced with blackened ash that slowly faded off the wall like dust in the wind.

Alyssa turned back to the other girl, and in a blissful glee, rolled up her own sleeves, revealing the blue hue of relic markings. She only now noticed the orange markings mirrored on the girl next to her, which camouflaged themselves neatly against her crimson skin.

"I never thought I'd meet someone else like me!" Alyssa exclaimed.

"I should introduce you to my father," Burnellia said.

They headed inside, eagerly chatting, but the snowflakes outside continued to fall, steadily, gracefully, as the ash drifted from the wall, peacefully, beautifully.

■ ■ ■

Smoke, Burnellia and Blaze were sent back to their forest base with a few White Heart security escorts to report to their troops on their successful new alliance.

Once Amber had seen them off, she returned to speak with the Guardians, gathering them together to speak with them as had become habit.

"Take note of what happened back there," she said, once they had all finally gathered around the kitchen table, referring to the peaceful exchange between the forces of White Heart and the Assossian resurgence. "I want you, just for now, not to be on the offense. Bring a message of peace and allegiance against the Syndicate to neighboring city-states and factions. We may be powerful on our own, but a threat big enough to put our existence in jeopardy is a threat that will be met with retaliation. First, however, we must be sure we have the power to bring such justice."

"Look," Reese butted in, practically cutting off Amber. "I get what you're trying to do here. But I'm afraid I can't help you earn the trust of these people. Not all of us are generals or public speakers or cult leaders."

"Watch it," warned Xela through gritted teeth.

"And I understand why you say that," Amber replied. "You think your particular skill set is only applicable to the field. But you helped earn the trust of the Assossians, didn't you?" Reese searched for a response, but quieted when he realized Amber was right. "That being said, I want all of you to help earn the trust of anyone you can. I didn't want to have to admit it, but..." She thought for a moment, forming a solid sentence in her mind before speaking it. "We are on the brink of total war against the Syndicate. With every coming day and each Syndicate attack, we grow closer towards it.

"I'm stalling time until we have gathered a sufficient amount of allies. If we jump into this war unprepared, it could very well mean the annihilation of White Heart, but our councilors grow more and more vexed by the Syndicate. So I ask of you to help me here."

"I could probably get Ezekiel and the rest of the ex-Syndicates to help us out," suggested Reese.

"It may not work," said Eva, "but I can ask for the help of Greenwood. I'd need White Heart's assistance, though; I'm kind of public enemy number one over there."

Amber smiled. "That can be arranged."

Skullgem tapped Brutus' shoulder to get his attention, then began signing. "I have many Assossian allies," Brutus translated. "I will convince them to come to aid."

Amber nodded with encouragement. "See? You're all capable of great things if you put your minds to them. Now go out there and make some friends. Show the world the power of the united."

■ ■ ■

The Chairman's office was unchanged since the last time Amber visited. It hadn't felt like long, but in truth, it had been a while since then.

As she entered, the Chairman looked up from a document. He motioned for her to have a seat opposite to him, and she slowly approached, nervous about something drifting on her mind.

"Hello, Amber," he said, as she returned the greeting mindlessly. "What are you calling to my attention today?"

"I wanted to request something of you."

"And what would that be?" He set his pen down and listened intently.

"I'm asking you to delay declaration of war against the Syndicate. Just until I can organize our army and make my alliances. Please."

"Amber," he started. "I understand you do this with the best intentions. But there are some things that are not in my control. I fear it may be too late to put war on hold."

Amber cursed under her breath. "There's something terribly wrong about this. I feel as if we're walking straight into a trap. I need you to trust me."

"And I do." His voice had grown more serious. "But you need to understand that there is nothing I can do in my power. Our council has made its decision."

"Chairman, please..."

"Will that be all, General Leavett?"

Amber sighed and slowly got up. "Yes, sir," she said. "That will be all."

■ ■ ■

"I have a bad feeling about this."

The hesitant voice sounded from Eva, now in the driver's seat of her van. Next to her sat Brutus, and behind her was Alyssa, all bearing anxious expressions as their mission loomed on the horizon.

Greenwood lay ahead in their sights, its glamorous, yet corrupted cityscape looming before them, the many mansions and sprawling, perfectly kept greenery visible. It was a partly cloudy day, the wind pleasant and cool, but the three Guardians were too focused to care.

"I'm sure we'll be fine," Alyssa assured.

"Easy for you to say, kid," Eva responded. "You don't have a track record."

"Well, I do. Just not here."

"Here's the plan," Brutus spoke, hastily clipping stun grenades to his belt. "I'm going to use these to incapacitate the guards."

"Once he does that, give 'em cold feet," added Eva.

"I'm sorry, I'm not quite sure I understand," the red-haired sorceress began.

"Do your freezy powers and stuff," quickly Eva said. "Just don't freeze their heads! I gotta be able to talk to them."

"Okay, okay, if you say so," Alyssa meekly spoke. With that, their mission was set to begin. Though they had clarified their objective, their dread and worry only worsened with every bump the van took on the path to the city-state. Despite this, they bravely drove on, headfirst into the den of sinners.

Their van was stopped at the main gate just before the looming city-state. Its walls were massive and sturdy, but nothing compared to those of their own proud sanctuary.

"Step out of the van, please," a voice demanded.

The trio looked up to find a rough-cut, intimidating guard staring back at them with a no-nonsense glare. They obeyed her promptly, stepping out and away with little hesitation. Other guards stepped up to check them individually, as Eva's van was brought under inspection.

"You've got some mighty fine weapons with you, sir," said the one inspecting Brutus. "May I ask just what is it you're doing with that much on you?"

He flashed the guard a smile, painfully disingenuous, but emotions were not his strongest suit. "You can never be too safe in a world like ours."

After removing his revolvers and machine pistol, the guard reached for his belt next. "What are these?" he asked, gripping the flashbangs in his hands.

"Stun grenades," Brutus clarified. "Here, let me show you how they work."

The guard did not expect the fist that shot towards his face, knocking him out cold. As he fell, Brutus reached with his other hand to snatch the flashbang, whose pin he promptly pulled and tossed towards the yet unsuspecting guards nearby. Alyssa and Eva, at the ready, averted themselves as a deafening blast accompanied a blinding glare. Brutus did so as well, as soon as he had taken back his weapons from the unconscious guard.

Alyssa took advantage of the guards' temporary blindness, and ice crept up from the ground, quickly encasing each guard up to the head in a frozen prison.

"Freeze!" The shout came from behind her.

"No, ma'am," Alyssa warned back, still not turned towards the guard with a gun in her steady grip. "That'd be your job!"

A shot rang out, a boisterous alarm to any ear in reach. As Alyssa wheeled around, frost trudged towards the guard that had been inspecting Eva's vehicle. A morphing, monstrous clump of ice engulfed the soaring bullet, storing it harmlessly in a frozen tomb. It continued on to swallow the Greenwood guard to the sound of her pleas for help, a wave of ice up to her neck, where it refused to climb.

Once Eva saw this done, she approached one of the struggling guards. He could only move his head, the rest of his body encased in frost. As she walked towards him, she removed her aviators from where they rested on the collar of her shirt and donned them on her face.

"Mind doing me a favor and delivering a message to whoever is in charge around here?" she asked the guard.

"Fuck you," was his response, which was followed by an attempt to spit at her. Eva quickly sidestepped it, and it foamed on the ground beside her.

"Well that was rude," she snapped back, and slapped him with the back of her hand. The gratifying sound echoed, leaving a red mark on his cheek as he screamed in pain. "Not so tough now, are we? Now, let's try this again."

■ ■ ■

The fog of the murky swamp surrounded the jeep as it lurched through the mud, passing massive, sprawling tree after massive, sprawling tree. Its headlights helped thin away the mist in front of it, paving a path of light that seemed to play with the vehicle, always running in front of it, just out of its reach. Far in the distance, the nostalgically cold, darkened sky brought a strangely comfortable shiver to her exposed skin.

With time to spare, Xela decided to head to her home in the middle of the mire to work on her research again, unlike the other Guardians, whom Amber had sent to help make alliances for White Heart.

As the fog parted, she noticed familiar lights ahead, feeling a sense of relief to have made it to her base despite the heavy brume playing with her vision. Only when she drew close enough to notice that there were no walls nearby did she realize that this was but a campsite. A busy campsite, at that; the commotion worked in her favor, silencing the sounds of the White Heart vehicle as Xela parked it behind a cluster of tents.

She sneaked out of her jeep and peeked out from behind the fabric of a tent. Though she could hear people nearby conversing, she saw no one. When she did, however, her heart seemed to stop; a soldier ran from one side of the campsite to another, and for the brief seconds Xela saw him, she recognized his dreadful black-and-white uniform, as well as the emblem of the two crossed swords emblazoned on it.

With utter silence and a skip of panic, Xela withdrew from the site, starting up her car and driving away, far away, stopping only when her instincts told her she was temporarily safe and her wits were slightly more composed. She reached for her talker, frantically rummaging through the seats, the compartments, the back, but to no avail. A deep sigh of disappointment escaped her lungs as she realized she had forgotten it in White Heart. Now, she was faced with a decision: was she to warn the fellow members of the Order, or alert Amber and the rest of White Heart of the serious threat this encampment would most certainly impose on them?

She decided it was best to prepare her group, as they were smaller and much easier prey for a large army encampment to capture. Xela did not like this in the slightest; the Syndicate drew closer and closer to them at a faster rate than before. It would only be a few days now.

A few more days, and Xela was sure they would spring their vile trap.

■ ■ ■

A black car with tinted windows sped through the streets of Greenwood, turning sharp corners at high speeds and darting past other cars with little care until it reached the city-state's gates, where it abruptly reached a halt.

A man in a suit stepped out, fixing his cuffs and approaching the odd group with a snarling expression equipped.

"You better have a damn good reason for wasting my time," he said.

"If it isn't the mayor himself," Eva said in an amused tone. He stopped a few feet from them, and from that respectable distance they conversed.

"That I am. You'd best get to your point, Evangeline Bates, before I wipe your sorry ass off the face of Senia."

"We want to establish peace."

The mayor raised his eyebrows. "Oh, really now? Are you sure you're not just worried we'll hunt you down for your crimes? You and your mentor have gotten on this city's bad side quite a few times."

"You misheard me. I said 'we.' As in, all of White Heart."

Greenwood's mayor gave an audible proclamation of disgust. "So now you're working for those stuck-up fuckers? Why would we ever make peace with them?"

"For protection."

The mayor laughed vociferously. "Protection, huh? From who? The wolves that roam outside the cities? Don't worry about us, we can handle them!"

"Ever hear of a wolf named *the Syndicate?*"

The mayor stopped laughing, his expression suddenly shifting to a damning glare, before he boisterously cleared his throat. His arm went towards his suit, and he reached for something inside it. "That won't be necessary."

"Oh no you don't," muttered Brutus under his breath.

It only took a second for the mayor to grab his pistol and aim it towards Eva. It took Brutus a fraction of that to place a hand on his revolver, draw it from its holster, tap the trigger back, and slam the hammer down with his other hand. For a brief moment, the mayor thought it was his gun that went off, but when the stinging pain of several fingers being blown off by a bullet from Brutus finally hit, he realized he couldn't have been further in the wrong.

In the moments that followed, a colossal wall of ice formed itself, separating the Guardians from the mayor and his henchmen. Alyssa's frozen shield was so thick that it stopped all the bullets from the volley they received.

"We need to get out of here!" Alyssa cried. "I can't hold this thing forever!"

"On it," Brutus casually said. He tossed a few grenades over the wall, both fragmentation and flash, leaving a window of opportunity. The trio hurried back to their van, jumping inside with haste.

"Don't even know why I fucking bother," Eva muttered, slamming her vehicle into reverse, then shifting it forwards and speeding away from the mishap in her home city. "He pulls a fucking gun on me the second I open my mouth! Can't believe I ever think people can change."

As Alyssa peeked out from the back window, she witnessed her giant ice wall collapse, and stole a final glance at the angered people of Greenwood, their weapons firing at the van to no avail.

■ ■ ■

The guards took up arms at the sight of the vehicle, but upon recognizing its driver, let her in without hesitation. Once safely inside, Xela motioned for them to close the gates with haste. They did so, but felt uneasy about it; something was clearly wrong.

"Is something the matter?" asked one of the guards.

Xela's black lips tightened. "The fog led me astray, and I stumbled onto a Syndicate camp."

The guard's eyes widened. "How far was it from here?"

Xela shook her head. "Not very. Prepare our defenses, I fear the worst. And get a messenger ready. We're going to need some help." He nodded and went on his way.

Half of the Order's headquarters consisted of a roofless base surrounded by sturdy walls. Residential houses were there, but most of the inhabitants of the facility lived underground, in a series of sprawling tunnels. The other half, which contained most of the research buildings, was covered by a gargantuan old tree. A hole in the tree had been carved out, hundreds of feet wide, as an entrance to the research district. All in all, the entire base was much like a small city.

Xela headed towards the back of the base, where the colossal tree stood proudly, as it had for centuries before her time. She made it under the cover the massive growth provided just as rain began to pour, then entered one of the buildings hugging the natural walls, finding herself in the room where most of the experiments took place. A few other scientists stood nearby, conversing amongst themselves. They greeted Xela, thrilled to see her.

"We need to pack up all this equipment as soon as possible," her serious voice spoke.

"Why?" asked one of the scientists.

They seemed glad to see her back home, but when Xela explained the situation and they realized she was the bearer of bad news, their expressions turned grim. "We need to move to the facility in White Heart," she said. She knew they would be reluctant to do so; some of them had lived here for years. It was the place they called home, and for many, it was the *only* place they could call home.

Their moment of thought was interrupted by an explosion that sounded from outside. Xela ran across the hall to the nearest window and peered out, her heart racing. The legion in the distance, emerging from the paludal smog, brought an immense pain to her chest. She cursed under her breath as her fellow workers followed her outside. White Heart had just been under attack; now it was their turn to survive the Syndicate's siege, and it had come much sooner than they had prepared for.

CHAPTER 13:

"How did the parley go?" Amber asked as Eva, Alyssa, and Brutus entered the house. Charlie picked himself up from the floor and happily trotted towards them, excited to reunite with his teammates. Alyssa knelt and set out a tired hand towards him, which the dog licked happily.

"Greenwood is not going to be our ally," said Eva.

Amber sighed. "They would have been useful. Are you sure you remembered to smile and shake the mayor's hand?"

Eva rolled her eyes as she set aside her rifle and backpack and collapsed onto the living room sofa. Amber disappeared into the kitchen and came back a few minutes later, a cup of coffee in hand. She placed it on the coffee table, next to Eva, who peeked up at it with exhausted eyes. The resting Guardian thanked her, her mouth muffled by the pillow she was stuffing herself under.

She didn't remember falling asleep, but when she awoke, Eva found the house dark. The lights had been left off, and the sky was in dusk, the red tint of Senia's sun painted across the heavens.

Eva hadn't touched her coffee; now it was cold and unpleasant. A note lay stuck to the side of it, which Eva peeled off. She turned on a light, and when her eyes adjusted to the sudden brightness, she read it to herself with a whisper:

*"Gone out to save Xela
and the Order. We'll be back
soon. Take care of Ire, and
take care of White Heart."*

-Amber

Eva couldn't believe her team had left to save lives while she slept lazily. She groaned audibly, upset she couldn't help. She felt selfish, but did her best to push those thoughts aside; she had no control over it. Still, the notion lingered in her head for a while. She decided that once she got back, she would let Amber know for future reference not to do the same thing in a similar situation. *If she gets back.* The thought made her heart ache. Perhaps checking on Ire would clear her mind.

She found him in Reese's room, his bedside lamp on, a thick book in his petite hands. He set it down as she slowly entered the room, a drowsy look yet about her.

"What are you reading?" she asked him, taking a seat on the bed.

"*Economic Patterns Throughout the Years: An Anthology,*" Ire answered, and continued to read.

Eva's eyes widened. "How old are you again?"

"Thirteen." His gaze didn't leave the book.

She figured she was way too tired to comprehend such a thing at the time. "You're very mature for your age."

"Thank you."

Eva looked around the room idly, her eyes catching the motions of a clock on the wall. "How late are you allowed to stay up?"

"Father lets me stay up as late as I wish."

She had expected such of Reese, so she rephrased her question: "How long does your mom let you stay up?"

After a short pause, Ire answered with: "I couldn't sleep."

Eva sighed, empathy in her heavy breath. "And what does your mom usually do when that happens?"

"She sings me a song. Sometimes she sleeps in my bed to make me feel better. Do you know any songs?" Ire had set aside his book now and lay on his side, watching Eva intently with his childish eyes.

There was one song from her childhood she had loved dearly, but that was so long ago. She took some time to recall the melody in her head and cleared her throat. She was no singer, so she decided to hum the melody. It was a beautiful song, a poem unbeknown to Ire about strangers, legends, and martyrs, about painters, pipers, and prisoners. The notes pouring out of Eva's mouth were waterfalls of beautiful sounds, smooth and legato, surprising even her. Her stare had moved from Ire to the clock during the song, and now when she looked back at the boy, she found his eyes closed.

Eva stopped singing, turned off the light shining beside Ire, and crawled into bed next to him, sighing as she closed her eyes and let sleep consume her again.

Xela's black combat boots splashed in a puddle of rainwater as she rushed to the gate. She motioned for the guards to close it, shouting commands left and right as she did. First, the steel barricades came down, followed by the two colossal walls, one interior and one exterior.

She witnessed a small object soar in the air and come down on the spiked walls of the base. "Grenade!" she shouted, a touch too late. A guard situated on the top of the walls who didn't hear her in time went flying and landed painfully on the inside of the facility. Xela and another guard ran over to help him, and the two carried the groaning, bloodied soldier to the medical pavilion.

Just as she set him down in the pavilion, a scrawny and short young man came up to her, stating he was ready to send off Xela's message. She commanded that he take a vehicle and leave through a lesser-known exit, make his way to White Heart, and alert a guard at the Eastern gate that the Order was in grave danger. She handed him her Guardian identification card, kissed him on his forehead, and wished him godspeed. The messenger nervously parted from her as he made his way to the back of the base, where the vehicles were kept.

The Syndicate had not yet made much progress on the destruction of their defenses, for which Xela was grateful. She headed up a raised ladder to the top of the wall, scythe in hand. A Syndicate soldier climbing a ladder leaning on the opposite side met her there. Xela removed a knife from her thigh-strap, took aim, and tossed it full force. It impaled her neck, a bloodcurdling shriek was heard, and she plummeted off the wall. Xela peeked her head out, glancing at the ground below, watching more Syndicate soldiers quickly take their fallen comrade's place.

"Amber, hear our cry," she whispered through her anxious breaths, as she ducked for cover.

■ ■ ■

Fortunately for Xela, Amber was listening.

A convoy of technical trucks and army vehicles made its way from White Heart into the thick marsh. In the front was Amber's jeep, Brutus and Charlie inside with her. Following behind were Skullgem, Alyssa, Reese, and Hex, as well as many guards and battle-ready soldiers.

Skullgem, in the back of an army truck surrounded by soldiers, unhappily held a heavy heart. He felt concern for his friend, as well as for the Order. Thoughts of arriving to little more than corpses flooded his worried mind. A particularly gruesome image of Xela's mangled body, lifeless and still, intruded his thoughts.

He shook his head, angry with himself. *No. Such thoughts would not defile my concentration now.*

He put his legs up on his seat, crisscross. His eyes shut, and he entered his brain to recollect himself.

After a successful meditation rid him of his stress, he watched behind him, where a few other vehicles took up the rear. He noticed a strange, black object following them; they were moving too fast, in too much darkness, for Skullgem to clearly make out what it was. At first, he considered it a will-o-wisp, nothing more than a trick of the light in a musty swamp. The idea didn't make much sense to him, however, as he knew for certain that they didn't move fast enough to follow a convoy. As he focused on it, it became unequivocal what it was: a figure was riding a strange, sleek vehicle, keeping pace behind the White Heart army.

With extreme speed, the wisp ditched the vehicle and hopped onto the caboose of the convoy, a technical with a turret in the back. Somehow, the figure's vehicle kept following a set path even after being abandoned. The figure then pulled away the soldier mounted on the turret, causing him to land on the path below. It was more obvious now, features clearing before his eyes as it drew closer: a dark-haired woman Skullgem had never seen before, a sword and bow stowed on her back, was engaging in battle with his allies. She was a threatening sight, and presented a danger Skullgem knew he had to deal with.

He vaulted from his truck and onto another vehicle, leaping down the convoy towards the woman now ready to fire the gunner's turret. Skullgem reached her just after she let out a few bursts of bullets at the other vehicles. The convoy seemed to take a halt as Skullgem threw a punch at her, knocking her off the truck.

As he approached her from above, she slashed at him with her sword. His armor saved him from a mortal wound, but it was not a painless blow she dealt him. As he clenched in agony, she swept his feet, knocking him down and the wind out of him.

While he remained incapacitated on the ground, a White Heart soldier grabbed the woman from behind and held her in a chokehold. She twisted his arm and hit his head with hers, and he let go and fell. She grabbed for her pitch sword and held it over her head, ready to cleave him in two, but Skullgem called himself to action.

The Assossian leaped in between the swing of the woman's longsword and the man on the ground. Dark clashed with metal and sparks flew. Skullgem's hammer took most of the hit, but he bled lightly from a few spots on his shoulder where some of the longsword had cleaved.

The encounter took enough time to enable more soldiers to come to their aid. Her vehicle, a strange, futuristic motorcycle seemingly with a mind of its own, drew towards her, not stopping even as she had boarded it at high speed. Gunfire chased her, but struggled to touch her. Like that, she disappeared into the fog as mysteriously as the character she was.

Skullgem had been caught up in the battle and did not notice that the shadow veil that masked his face had malfunctioned. He went to pick up the soldier lying on the ground, but the Guardian read surprise and awe on his face.

"You're Assossian," he whispered.

Skullgem, now realizing his hood was not working, simply nodded, pulling his hood further over his face to obscure himself.

"What happened? Who was that?" asked a familiar voice: Amber hurrying towards her fellow Guardian to understand the situation. Flummoxed by the woman in black, Skullgem struggled to give an answer.

■ ■ ■

The rain had stopped, and the red lights of dusk filled the sky, but the battle did not end.

Xela organized her guards into shifts in order to preserve energy. She tasked herself with bringing wounded soldiers into the facility's medical pavilion, but had previously served a long shift on the walls, the base's first line of defense.

She had already lost at least ten of her guards, but as grief-stricken as it made her, she did her best to postpone the mourning until later. Still, she kissed their dying bodies to show that she cared for them even in the very end. As she periodically ran from the wall to the medical pavilion, she warmed herself with thoughts that she would bring them back one day, if their research went according to plan.

Making her way back to the walls, she noticed from the view above a peculiar sight. For a moment, the siege stopped, as the Syndicate soldiers turned their attention elsewhere. A convoy, led by a vehicle familiar to Xela, was making its way towards them. She breathed a heavy sigh of relief, seeing that her saviors had arrived.

A deep bark pierced the sounds of scattered gunfire and steel clanging on steel; Charlie jumped from the front of the convoy and joined the battle. He pounced on Syndicate soldier after Syndicate soldier, as chaos erupted amongst the army.

Xela saw her chance. "Open the gates!" she yelled. "Prepare yourselves! Now we're on the attack!"

The guards of the Order did so accordingly, as the forces of White Heart distracted the Syndicate. Some guards saw it as an opportunity and quickly charged out with their weapons drawn.

Amongst the crowd, she saw familiar faces engaged in combat: Reese was firing his shotgun while his raven friend was next to him blocking bullets. Alyssa erected a column of ice and chipped off a large portion to use as an improvised spear. Even Weylin was firing away, a machine gun clenched tightly in his hands as shot after shot rang out.

Amber brought her vehicle to the gates, and Brutus stepped out. He grabbed for a machine pistol strapped to the side of his leg, a beautiful bringer of demise. It was sleek and black, save for the brown word scrawled upon its side: "UGLY." He fired it akimbo upon the disoriented army, bullets spraying like a deadly mist. As he covered her, Amber hastily parked the car inside the facility and rejoined them.

"I've never been happier to see you," said Xela to Amber.

Xela slowly backed up while Amber drew her pistol. "We're not out of the woods yet," the general said.

Brutus stood nearby, wasting bullets away, but he was stopped by a piercing pain in his left leg. When he grabbed his thigh, his hands touched a sickle embedded in his skin attached to a long chain that trailed into the thickness of the battle, past groups of soldiers fighting against each other relentlessly.

"Why is it always me?" he quietly growled, partially in anger and partially in pain, but certainly loud enough for Xela to hear.

He quickly reached to pull out the blade, but its owner began tugging, and with a mighty force at that. Brutus fell with a cacophonous "oomph" and began sliding across the ground, through clusters of soldiers of both factions fighting for their lives. When he finally reached the owner of the sickle, he found a green-haired, dark-skinned woman with a frown on her face staring back at him. She raised her heel and attempted to bring it down upon Brutus' chest. He caught it just before it made contact, and the two struggled for a bit before she leaped away and readied her shield in front of her. Brutus picked himself up and made haste to fire away, but her shield swallowed his bullets harmlessly.

The swing of Xela's scythe came just in time to help him, and the green-haired woman jumped back. She crouched and held her shield as if to fire a gun. Instead, a green beam of energy directed at Xela was fired through a cannon on the side of the shield. The Guardian was thrown back with tremendous force, hitting the walls of her facility and falling painfully as she clutched an arm to her stomach.

This gave Brutus time to attack once more, however, and he fired his revolver once again at her. She yelped in pain as a bullet grazed her sides, yet she was quick to pull up the shield again and retreat. She fled into the chaos of the battle, and Brutus retreated as well, making his way back towards the gate.

Amber rushed to help Xela, bringing her fellow Guardian to her feet and guiding her towards the inside of her facility. "I'll be fine," Xela said, lightly pushing away. "I'm not bleeding."

"That's good," Amber said.

"I'm just in tremendous pain."

"That's not good." As Amber spoke, a red-haired girl ran up to them frantically.

"Amber, I have another idea," Alyssa said, as Skullgem joined them with a keen eye watching for anyone ready to flank them. "I'm going to need you to trust me here."

"I trust you," Amber assured Alyssa, and the girl made haste to describe where they came into her plan and their job in it.

Skullgem, having overheard them, set to bringing it into motion. He ran to a cluster of White Heart soldiers and motioned for them to follow, bringing them inside the Order's facility, and they fired their weapons from there. Once they were safely inside, Skullgem went back to collect the remaining allied soldiers, who retreated to the gates at the sight of their comrades taking cover within.

As their allies flooded in, Syndicate soldiers closed in on the facility. The gates shut with a loud slam just as the last White Heart soldier made it in.

Once inside, Skullgem, Xela, and Amber pushed the guards and soldiers towards the back of the facility, where the great tree stood as cover. Alyssa remained by the gates, preparing to concentrate. A grenade flew over the wall, but Reese shot it down with his shotgun, and it exploded harmlessly in the air. As Alyssa built a wall of ice in front of her, she motioned for Reese to fall back and join the others. He grunted, desiring to protect her, but warily obliged.

Alyssa felt the stares of many behind her, but only a few knew what she was going to do. In preparation, she removed her sweater and laid it on the ground, then stood behind the wall and spread her arms. Her blue markings began to glow, and soon, her eyes did as well. Her hair and skirt started to flutter freely, the wind began to whistle, and light snowflakes quickly turned into a heavy blizzard until the White Heart soldiers, guards of Xela's Order, and Guardians watching intently from inside could not see her through the arctic blanket of dense snowfall.

They patiently waited for what could have been minutes, hours, days. Though they could not see Alyssa, they kept their worried eyes on the storm outside. Finally, the snow gradually slowed, the wind parting the white until the last flake fell.

The eager group flooded the uncovered part of the facility, slowing down when they noticed the hail that overwhelmed the ground. A dome of ice lay in the center of the facility, but Alyssa was not visible. Reese absconded from them and ran to the ice clump. He raised his shotgun over his head and hit the dome with its butt multiple times, until the ice finally shattered. He pushed the sharp shards away, and a few moments later, he emerged with a motionless Alyssa in his arms.

"She's alive," he assured the nervous faces. "But she's not conscious. It must have taken her a lot of energy."

They opened the gates to assess the damage and found the scene outside was just short of a massacre: bodies of Syndicate soldiers lay scattered on the ground, their heads bruised and bloody. Most seemed to have had escaped with their lives, but it was still quite incredible that such destruction had come from a petite, young girl.

A crew was sent to preserve the corpses of fallen soldiers and guards, both allied with White Heart and the Syndicate. Within a few hours, there was practically no indication that the base had hosted a battlefield, save for the red-stained, frozen clumps that had rained from the sky that yet remained.

■ ■ ■

As Alyssa rested in the infirmary, Amber and Charlie remained by her side. After waiting there for almost an hour, listening peacefully to the sounds of celebration outside, they were interrupted by Xela. She carried a curious red box in her hands.

"How is she?" she asked Amber, as Charlie, lying at her feet, got up and sniffed Xela. She responded by lightly petting him, and the dog waved his tail.

"Getting better," Amber answered. "Her body is relaxing, but she's still sleeping."

"Good to hear," said Xela, nodding her head. "Anyway, I wanted to thank White Heart on behalf of the Order."

"We serve to protect not only ourselves but those that fight by our side. It's just my duty, a present won't be necessary."

"Well, from one leader to another, I owe you one." Xela held out the box towards Amber, but the woman across from her shook her head.

"You don't owe me anything. I'm simply doing what I should be."

Xela's lips tightened. "If you don't take it, at least let me tell you what's inside."

Amber shook her head once more. "As I said, you don't owe me—"

"They're shoes."

In an instant, Amber snatched the box from her hands and practically tore it in half trying to open it. When she pulled out the sleek, black pumps, her eyes widened and her mouth opened. "What are these made of?" she asked, clearly in amazement. They were the same color as her usual heels, but something about how they felt and shone was much different.

"The same stuff in your dog's teeth," answered Xela, scratching Charlie behind his ears. "Try them on and click them together."

Amber did so zestfully. When she tapped the shoes together, two small blades protruded from their bottoms. She clicked once more, and they disappeared.

"You might also want to check this out." Xela took the titanium shoes from Amber and showed her their bottoms. A circular, metal disc had been placed under both of the heels.

"What do those do?"

"Reach your toes out a little bit more, but make sure you do it with both toes at the same time," Xela instructed.

Amber followed her instructions eagerly, and soon found herself slowly rising in the air. She reached out to balance herself, before realizing that the bottoms of the shoes were blasting small flares of energy, making her levitate. She moved her toes back and fell to the ground. Xela caught her arm and pulled her before she tumbled on her back.

"It might take some getting used to," she said. "But if you can master these, you'll be darting around faster than a bullet."

"Where did you find these?" Amber asked. "I don't even have a word for them!"

"Rocket heels?" she suggested, in a joking manner. "I had Reese's techno-whiz friend construct them just for you a few days ago."

Amber smiled and laughed. "Thank you." She hugged Xela and kissed her cheek with a slight giggle, her heart full of bliss.

Xela had never seen Amber so gleeful, but it was nice to remember that despite Amber's professional exterior, she could shed it easily when she was amongst friends and show her true colors. It made Xela laugh, as well.

■ ■ ■

Light came to the dark cave when the clandestine wall, posing as a dead end, revealed itself as an entrance for the woman in black, and she was met by the butler she knew too well. He looked a bit exhausted, but he put on the best smile he could manage when she rode into their secret home and greeted him.

"Hello, Janus," he said. As the woman in front of him disembarked her lightcycle, her wispy coverings went away, and her suit, weapons, and even hair swapped from black to grey.

"That's one of my names," she said sarcastically.

Thomas ignored her. "You're feeling useless because you couldn't have done anything to stop it, is that right?"

The base was a juxtaposition in and of itself: it was laden with stalagmites and dark corners, but also high-tech hallways and searing, white lights.

She shrugged and sighed, her eyes finding a sculpture of a pan balance seated on a grey pedestal. "Maybe."

He put a hand on her shoulder. "You have to remember, we are not here to turn the tides of battle. Once you prove to Èchelle that you are willing to obey as her prophet, then we will be allowed more influence."

"We're sitting ducks, Thomas. We had a chance right in front of us, and we let it slip."

215

He shook his head. "Patience, Janus. It is a virtue, after all."

"So?" she said disgruntledly. "I'm starting to question if our cause is even worth fighting for anymore."

"You know well enough why we do this." Thomas began to recite the oath that the two had taken long ago: "We are the watchmen of the passing of time. We are the past and the present, and we control the future. Balance will fail without us, and when balance fails..."

"Disorder takes over," Janus finished with a sigh. She stormed to her chambers without another word.

She sat at the mirror, admiring her grey clothes and grey hair. Angel, Wisp, Janus; she went by many names. Now she was adorning the look for when she was not fighting the Syndicate or White Heart; when her outfit leaned towards neither black nor white, but the grey in between. As she brushed her hair, she pondered whether peace on Senia would ever be possible.

CHAPTER 14:

Miles away, a feared leader sat on his throne, a group gathering in front of him. They were clothed in hoods and cloaks, their typical wardrobe, mercenaries whose own looks they cared little for. To them, their clothing was a reminder of who they were and where they came from. To Gareth, that did not matter, as it was a reminder that they were not truly from the Syndicate. He felt unsure about hiring people like them for such a critical mission, but he knew he had no other option.

"Aleegha?" called Boss Gareth in a booming voice.

A woman with white hair poked her head out from the crowd of thieves gathered in his throne room, seemingly having come from nowhere. She sported the thinnest body Gareth had ever seen, with her flat chest and slim arms, and the only weapons she carried were two krises. "You are the leader of this group?" The woman nodded and bowed, a stern look on her face. "You thoroughly understand exactly what your job is and how important it is?"

"With all due respect, sir, we are experienced thieves, but we are not rescuers," Aleegha said. "Are you certain you would like us for this job?"

"You are stealing my soldiers back from White Heart, are you not?"

Aleegha nodded once again. "Very well. You pay a fine fee, and our services are only the most professional you'll find in the business, I can assure you. For the price you offer, we can make a few...adjustments to our typical regiment."

"Excellent. You and your group are dismissed. I am counting on you to deliver as promised."

"And we will be counting on you to deliver as well," said Aleegha, grinning as she pulled her hood over her head before leading the rest of her group out of the throne room.

Before they departed, Reynard, standing next to Gareth with his arms crossed, decided to open his sly mouth.

"Sellswords?" he said, shaking his head. "My, we can surely trust them. I'm so glad that we're in such safe hands!"

"Enough," said Gareth, with a firm tone. "That is not how you speak to your superior."

Reynard rolled his eyes. "Perhaps I should at least get in her head, in case she gets any ideas."

"You're a fool," said Gareth, but Reynard had already left the room. He made his way to the front of the group, putting his arm around the shoulder of the hooded figure.

"You should know that if you fail," he began, leaning closer and closer to Aleegha's ear, "I will personally hunt down you and your group and make you all wish for death. Go ahead, test me. I've been looking for some new playthings to make mine."

He smiled, adding an ominously wicked giggle, and slapped the woman's rear, pushing her forward with a displeased grunt as he skipped away.

Gareth witnessed the whole scene, barely suppressing the cringe his body desperately desired to exert. If this was to be the future leader of the Syndicate, he feared for the day that might come.

■ ■ ■

Amber felt the heavy stares of the war council as she entered the room. She had just been given a seat on the council, and although she would not have much power, given that she already had enough authority with the Guardians, she was glad to at least have a say in the matters concerning White Heart.

She carried herself with important posture and sat with her back straight, legs together, hands folded in her lap, awaiting the discussion to resume.

"As we were saying, General Leavett," spoke one council member, "it is important that we take your team and put them on the front lines. It is time we bring ourselves to the attacking side."

"With all due respect sir," Amber responded, "I think that a counter-attack is just what the Syndicate wants. They're testing us, and we would be showing that we're not strong enough to hold our ground."

The council member that she contradicted shook his head. He looked ready to respond when a woman seated across from Amber took the words out of his mouth:

"They're testing us, and we must show that we're strong enough to fight back. Not only should we be on the offense, but your 'Guardians' should be the ones leading us into battle." She received a few nods of agreement around the table.

Amber was growing vexed, but tried her best to maintain a formal exterior. "They're called 'Guardians' for a reason. It is their job to defend, not attack."

"Sometimes the best defense is a good offense," said another member.

"Let's put it to a vote, shall we?" asked the blonde council member next to Amber. "If you wish to vote to send Amber and her Guardians to lead the frontlines of the offensive unit for our next assault on the Syndicate, speak 'aye' now."

"Aye."

"Aye."

"Aye!"

"Aye."

"It is settled then," a woman across from her decreed. The council members quickly shot up and packed their few belongings, to the shock and frustration of Amber. Some were out the door in seconds.

"Wait, wait!" the general shouted. "That's it? You've reached a decision already?"

A war council member turned to her. "That's it," he simply said, before turning again and fleeing the room with haste.

"Hold on a minute!" said Amber. "Where are we attacking? When?"

The man that sat next to her smirked. "Why, on Avalon, the Syndicate's home city, of course. And as soon as possible will do, General Leavett." He was the next to leave, and before Amber knew it, she was alone in the room, next to a massive table with no one to sit at but her.

She tried her best to repress her anger. She had felt in control when commanding the Guardians without interruption, but now that she had inevitably garnered so much attention, there were those that wanted to be above her. *These are the leaders of White Heart?*

She pushed the thought aside. Perhaps, when the war was over, she would clean up the city she so dearly loved. For now, she was still processing what the man had said to her: White Heart's war council clearly either wanted to see her dead, or had far too much faith in her.

■ ■ ■

"We're approaching," warned the helicopter pilot. "Now's the time."

Aleegha nodded to him, then glanced out the two windows on each side, finding the other helicopters trailing alongside their path, an airborne convoy. She closed her eyes, allowed her rear to fall unto the metal below her, her legs crisscross, and focused her mind. She couldn't see now, but she could feel the translucent markings on her arms pulsating, adopting a stronger beat than average as she strained herself to use her power.

"All choppers operating at maximum stealth," the pilot in front of her spoke into his headset. "We're good to go."

In the next moment, Aleegha's magical, transparent sheet blanketed over the choppers, as well as the soldiers and thieves inside them, as they approached the massive, sprawling city-state of White Heart. Her mind was meditated, her powers focused on keeping her allies unseen.

They could see the whole world around them as they traveled airborne at high speeds. She held her brave breath as she looked down, not finding her crossed legs or the floor of the helicopter, but rather the walls of White Heart as the convoy of thieves passed into the city-state silently. Eyeing ahead, at the far end of the city she found her objective: the large prison looming over the streets below, an ominous, raised cylinder that housed White Heart's most wanted.

Onwards above their enemies the flying machines soared, stopping once they were directly above the facility, and then descended. Aleegha exhaled as they quietly landed on the roof, ceasing the use of her abilities and making her people, as well as the helicopters they were using for the mission, visible again. Under the cover that the elevated roof brought them, the rest of the city could not see them.

Aleegha stepped out of the helicopter, taking in a breath of fresh air as the wind struck her. She crept to the edge of the roof and looked below, spying the courtyard of the prison crawling with armed guards.

"Ready?" she asked her team, as she slipped into transparency.

■ ■ ■

Alyssa threw a fist, but agile Burnellia sidestepped it. She grabbed Alyssa's arm and used it to pull the redhead closer to her, then swept her legs with a kick, dropping her to the ground.

"Alright, alright," huffed Alyssa, catching her breath. "You won that time."

Burnellia held out her hand, an offer to help the ice sorceress up. "Round two?" she asked, as she picked Alyssa up. She raised one of her muscled legs, almost like a crane might stand.

"You're that eager to lose?" Alyssa jokingly asked her.

A mocking snicker came from Burnellia. "In your dreams."

"Wait." Alyssa lowered her stance. "Before we start, can I ask you something?"

"Sure."

"Why do you use that pose?"

Burnellia's massive leg muscles eased as she lowered her weapon. "It's part of a fighting style I learned when I was young. Chororian, it was called, I believe. That was before I found out that the relic powers could be passed down genetically." She assumed the stance, this time with two columns of flame-wisps emerging from her palms. "It's a style that involves great agility and lots of kicking. Hence, the stance with one leg up."

"I'm sorry," Alyssa said, with disbelief pinging in her throat. "But what did you call it?"

"Chororian," her friend answered.

"As in, Choro?" interrogated Alyssa.

"Umm...yeah, sure. What's Choro?"

224

"Legend has it," began the ice-reliced teenager with wonder in her tone, "that long, long ago, there was a girl, who fought very similarly to the way you do now that I think about it, who was such a fantastic and beautiful dancer that she won over a powerful goddess' love from just the sight of her skills."

"A...goddess?"

"Ah, I didn't expect you to get it. Don't mind me, just being a nerd." Alyssa shook her head and smiled. "Alright, you ready?"

Rather than respond, Burnellia lowered her leg once more and pondered Alyssa's appearance: a blue tank top was in place of her sweater, and shorts were in place of her skirt, but she was still wearing her heeled boots. "Can I ask you something, too?"

"Sure, sure."

"Why are you wearing those boots? Specifically now, while we're training?"

Alyssa looked Burnellia up and down. "You're wearing boots, too." They were much thinner at the heels, but still boots.

"Balance," said Burnellia. "With the stance, and all that. What about you?"

Alyssa sighed. "These were the boots my father gave me the night of the last birthday he celebrated with me, the night he died." Burnellia's look turned grim. "I made a pledge to wear these boots, even in battle. It's stupid, I know, but it means a lot to me."

Burnellia shook her head. "I don't think it's stupid."

"Let's just continue," Alyssa said, not wanting the attention.

Following orders wordlessly, Burnellia picked up her stance, then leaped at her opponent, her legs a fury. Alyssa dodged her and managed an elbow to the other girl's gut. Burnellia doubled over before falling one her back.

"So that's how you want to play, huh?" Burnellia said. Without the use of her hands, she performed a kip up that immediately lead into a fast-moving roundhouse kick. Surprisingly, Alyssa malingered this move as well, managing to grab Burnellia's right leg. For a moment, their eyes met, silent, damning glares about them, and the next second Alyssa pushed the leg in her hand to the side. Burnellia hobbled away on her other leg, but before she could regain her balance, Alyssa gave a low kick that swept her to the ground.

"You win," Burnellia admitted with a struggling voice.

"Are you okay?" Alyssa said, concern in her words. She held out a hand to return the favor to her friend. "That one looked like it hurt."

Burnellia took Alyssa's hand and pushed herself up. "It did hurt. But, you know, we're at war. It's good to get used to the pain. I need to make myself stronger."

"Yeah, I get that," spoke Alyssa with a nod. "You want to do a tie-breaker?"

"Hold on, girls."

The familiar voice came from the back of the room. Burnellia and Alyssa turned to find Amber sitting by the exit, and they paused their training to greet her.

"How's it going, Ms. Leavett?" Burnellia asked.

"Good," she politely answered. Turning to the other girl, she said: "Alyssa, can you come with me please? I'd like to give a briefing to you and the rest of the Guardians."

Alyssa nodded and picked. "We're not done here," she said to Burnellia, walking away with a jestingly-serious stare.

"Uh huh," the Assossian responded, laughing lightly. Alyssa and Amber turned to leave, but before they could, Burnellia decided to speak up, not wanting to part from her friend: "Hey, Ms. Leavett, would it be okay if I sat in on this briefing? I'd be interested to see what goes on behind the scenes and all."

Amber shrugged. "I see no reason why not."

■ ■ ■

A light grunt escaped the thief as she crawled through the ventilation systems of the White Heart penitentiary, searching for the room she was to infiltrate. Finally, after trudging for some time, she came across a shaft that exposed the control room below her.

She eyed the poor warden below, who was surveying the inmates around her. The prison was built with a watchtower in the very center, a control room intended to provide ultimate view, as every cell was built around it.

Aleegha removed the shaft carefully, silently. She placed it aside and took up her krises: the wicked daggers, jagged and cruel, thirsting for spilled blood. The relic tribals on her arms once more brightened, preparing to be brought to use. First, her white hair, tied up messily, assumed invisibility, then her serious countenance, billowing cloak, loose tank top, dangerous weapons, baggy pants, all the way down to her boots; it all became completely unseen.

Now prepared to initiate, Aleegha's hand pointed toward the warden below her, her mind focusing. It did not take long for her to become as transparent as Aleegha was. She did not notice at first, intently studying the individual cells housing crooked prisoners, which gave the hired thief some time to approach. Aleegha silently leaped down into the watchtower, just as the warden exclaimed in horror at the sight of her own two hands not in front of her, though she could feel herself waving them around.

It was in this moment of panic that Aleegha was truly in charge, when she knew more of the battle than any and all pawns involved. The thief smiled as the warden shrieked, knowing that the mission was all in her hands from here. With deadly knowledge on just where to strike, she felt her krises plunge into the soft neck of her invisible opponent. There was no way the warden could have seen it coming.

Her screams quickly died down as clear blood poured from her ceaselessly, and she parted from their world. Wasting no time, Aleegha stripped the fresh corpse entirely, then exchanged her own clothes with the deceased warden's, assuring her powers would make it appear as if her disguise was not drenched in crimson. A keycard Aleegha pulled from the belt she had equipped, as she kicked the lifeless body under the control panel and abandoned the room.

■ ■ ■

"So you just let Charlie roam free?" asked Alyssa.

Alyssa, Amber, and Burnellia walked around the market district, which was apparently, according to Amber, his favorite place to visit. They couldn't blame him; the ambrosial aromas that flooded the area were quite tantalizing to their human noses. To a hound's, it must have been heaven.

"In a way," Amber said. "He may be a dog, but he deserves his free time as well. Besides, he knows this city by heart, and he has no reason to run away. He's still a Guardian, after all."

Burnellia suddenly stopped, catching something in front of her. "Amber," she started to ask, "exactly how much do you trust him?"

"Hmm?"

The Assossian pointed to an alley across from them. There, they found Charlie leaning over another hound that they had never seen before.

"Charlie!" Alyssa said, laughing. "You dog!"

The other hound, at the sound of shrill, mocking laughter, moved away from his grasp and ran from the scene, leaving Charlie standing in front of one angry woman and two girls chuckling amongst each other.

"Charlie!" yelled Amber, and the dog tucked his tail between his legs. "You can't just go around making love to every random dog you find off the

229

street!" She wished there was a better way she could have worded her outrage, but there truly was not.

"You make it sound like he's done this before," Burnellia said. "What a player."

"Yeah," said Alyssa, in between spurts of laughter. "At least take them out to dinner first!"

Amber glared at them. "You're not helping." Charlie whimpered and trotted next to them, and they abandoned the market. If hounds could blush, Charlie's face would have been crimson.

■ ■ ■

The banging of her fist against the wall next to the cell shook the inmates inside, all of them looking up to the white-haired warden with serene eyes of interest. A built one with hair in his eye donned a cool countenance, another was a bob-haired, pretty-faced boy sitting in the furthermost corner, and the ugly-faced heathen beside them looked as if he had never felt any emotion but anger.

"Jack Bahal! Brandon Derringer-Crimani! Mov Dormin!" she commanded. "Stand!"

They promptly obeyed her order, on their feet in seconds. Jack cracked his knuckles, a tiny, idle curtsy came from Brandon as he stood up, and Mov's scowl was as judgmental as ever, as the woman in warden disguise opened the cell door with the card she had stolen.

"Out," was her next command, followed by: "Come with me."

With silence, the three prisoners followed her around the noisy penitentiary. Many other guards they passed, and as they looked around, they found a frightful more posted on the other floors. A horrific stench followed them as well, somehow worse than the typical smell of the prison, but the three did their best to ignore it and march on.

She led them out of the main block, where most of the cells called home as they surrounded the watchtower, and away into a barren hallway.

"Where we goin', boss?" Jack asked her, as they walked with a sulk.

"Shut the fuck up." She responded. He promptly did as instructed.

To their curiosity, they were led even further down, until she stopped in front of a door marked *"INMATE POSSESSIONS."* With a swipe of her keycard, access was once more granted to her, and she hurried the Syndicate trio inside.

"The fuck is this?" Mov asked.

"Listen up," Aleegha commanded, as she stripped herself of her guard accessories. "I'm getting all of you out of here, and we're breaking out everyone else while we're at it. But you three have to listen now and listen well. Listen to whatever I tell you and do it without hesitation, and I promise to bring everyone here home. Fail to comply, and we all die. That clear?" They hastily nodded with nervous enthusiasm. "Good. Now find the shit they confiscated from you and let's get out of here."

They didn't need to be told twice, and all three changed with soldier-trained speed and no prevalent shame.

Jack dressed into his tank top, boxing shoes, and black shorts, then quickly wrapped his hands in his gloves. When he found his weapons, they were equipped likewise: brass knuckles clung to his beaten hands, on the left one inscribed "*GUTS*," and on the other "*GLORY,*" and a sawed-off shotgun clung to his waist.

Brandon's change in outfit was the most drastic: off came his prisoner attire, in place for a dancer's dress, crimson, short, and adorned with tassels, along with fancy heels, a beaded necklace, and a feather to top it all off. A double-shot muff pistol he held in one hand, and he idly and skillfully spun a fantastically crafted butterfly knife in the other.

235

Mov was buff and gruff in his vest and tie and dressed like a penguin, dandy and fancy, with a fedora to match. He grunted as he lifted up the belt-fed light machine gun in his hands, cocking it with a smirk to ready it for fire.

"You ready for some freaky shit to go down? I'm going to need you three to trust me on this one," warned Aleegha.

They weren't sure what to expect from the thief, but they quietly nodded after sharing a silent conversation of looks with one another. Aleegha nodded as well, seeing that the trio had mentally prepared themselves. With a wave of her hand, the thief drenched Jack, Brandon, and Mov in her relical magic, and their visages vanished away, though their bodies remained dormant.

"Where in the *fuck* did we go?" Though Aleegha could tell who had exclaimed the question, the other two had to guess who was speaking from his bitter tone.

"Quiet yourself. Nothing has changed, no one has moved, even your weapons are still in your arms, as you can feel," the thief briefed. "Mind yourselves, however, that you are simply invisible, not invincible. Follow my steps exactly, and as tempting as it may be, do not go anywhere else. Don't let anyone touch you, don't talk to anyone...pretend that you don't even exist, because as far as they know, you don't."

■ ■ ■

"Is this it?" asked Eva, as they entered the alley, referring to the door across from them.

Reese Black was called a foe by many, so naturally, he needed to find ways to protect himself. He kept many safehouses throughout Senia, including the one in White Heart that the three stood in front now.

"Yes ma'am," he confirmed.

A staircase led them downward after Reese unlocked the door, and they soon found themselves in a large, darkened room. He reached around the wall, flicked on a switch, and the room began to brighten. Slowly, the lights on the ceiling turned on, from one side of the room to the other, brightening with boisterous slams, until everything in the room was visible.

Despite a low roof, the room was very spacious, given how wide and long it was. Tables were lined up against the walls, and on them were weapons, many weapons; every kind Eva knew was visible. Rockets, guns, axes, saws, swords, spears, shields; the entire room seemed like Reese's dark fantasy of a candy shop, with him as the spoiled child. He smiled in a twisted manner, likely imagining himself using each and every one of them on his enemies, perhaps most of all on his only brother.

Eva could never understand him. She loved him dearly, but at times, as much as she didn't want to admit it, he terrified her. Still, she was very glad he was on her side.

"Alright," he said. He wasn't yelling, but he still startled Eva, who had lost herself in a train of thought. "Let's start packing these in your van."

"Right," said Eva, snapping back into reality.

．．．

They walked with both nervousness and excitement back to the watchtower, a disguised warden with a trailing trio following behind, the true guards unwitting of their intentions.

Her heart fluttered for a moment when she came back to the scene of two guards knocking on the door to the control room frantically.

"Should we go in?" she overheard one of them ask to the other.

"Hold on," his friend spoke. "Warden! You in there?"

"I told you," said the first guard, when no response they received. "She just went on break or somethin'. You worry too much."

"Nah man, I know her," he retorted. "Unlogged? On her shift? That's not the warden I know runs this place."

"What seems to be the problem?" the white-haired woman behind them asked.

They turned immediately. "We were just, uh..." one began, before his look turned to confusion. "Woah, what the fuck?"

"Shit!" exclaimed his comrade. "You're wearing her fucking—"

They were silenced with a draw of krises and a slash for their throats, making haste to choke on their blood and collapsing together as Aleegha assumed invisibility and entered the warden's watchtower.

"Wait here," her seemingly disembodied voice commanded the undetected Syndicate trio behind.

After some time, she appeared once more to them, clad in her own clothes, foreign clothes to them.

"You three!" Aleegha said quickly. "I need you to wait unseen, while I attract their attention. When you see your bodies and weapons returning to visibility, you fire like there's no tomorrow."

They posted up behind the walkway to the watchtower as Aleegha instructed, and she closed the door and locked it behind her. For further security, she blocked the entrance with a chair, into which she seated the warden's deadweight corpse. Now the fun could begin.

The stolen keycard fell into its slot in the control panel, and Aleegha smiled wickedly.

"CHECKING KEYCARD," announced a robotic voice to her. "ACCESS GRANTED. WELCOME BACK, WARDEN SANTIAGO."

"Warden Aleegha," she corrected, before quietly pondering out loud: "Huh, I kinda like the sound of that." Her eyes grew wide as she glared over the panel of buttons before her, a feeling of power washing over her. The force fields opened up before each and every inmate contained in the facility. Free from their cells, many were quick to take off with little hesitation.

Her pride was pushed away at the sound of banging on the door behind her, sudden pangs striking her ears. "Warden! What's going on?! Open up!" a muffled voice behind the door commanded.

"That's not the damn warden, I'm telling you!" came another, as the boisterous knocking only grew ruder. "We know you're in there! Open the fucking door right now!"

The sound of gunfire against the bulletproof door was barely audible, Aleegha's laughter drowning it away. More banging followed, relentless slamming now, and the thief could barely contain herself. The door's hinges began to bend, then drew close to snapping, before it completely tipped over like a domino.

A massive cluster of armed guards pointed their weapons towards Aleegha, who shot them a two-fingered salute. She swapped her visibility for the discreteness she had given the three Syndicate soldiers, disappearing from the views of her enemies in front of her.

Then, three emerged from behind the guards, one gripping a tiny pistol, another a heavy machine gun, and the last a booming shotgun. They morphed into a firing squad, wasting away bullet after bullet into a mass of flesh, ripping apart bodies, tearing away skin. Many had stood before them, but now there was nothing but a pile of bloody, mangled corpses littering the walkway, streaming their internal juices, dripping on cells below with little care, painting the prison red with their own sanguine fluids.

"Great job, guys!" shouted Aleegha as she came out from behind her cover. "I mean, you really showed them what for!"

"What now, boss?" asked Brandon meekly.

The thief smiled wickedly. "Go out there and wreak some havoc."

As Aleegha tended to her business, the three Syndicate inmates split up. Mov slowly walked to the stairs, peering around the cylindrical prison and firing at any guards his eye caught. Bullets descended from above, volleys firing from his heavy weapon as he rained death upon those threatening the escape of him and his fellow prisoners.

"If I could have your attention, please!" the thief's voice was heard. Aleegha had taken up the penitentiary's intercom system, and her booming announcement strayed into the ears of inmate and guard alike. "Today is your day, the day of your emancipation! Take up the fight against your shacklers and prove your worth, prove your freedom!"

Brandon vaulted from one floor to another, fearlessly jumping down railing after railing with impressive dexterity, his nimble, scrawny body darting across the makeshift battlefield with ease. After leaping onto one particular floor, he became witness to enemies locked in combat: a guard had taken up a nightstick, swinging it at two prisoners who slowly backed away, looking for a chance to strike. Toying his butterfly knife in his hands, Brandon took up a sprint to the guard, his pearls swinging and clutching his neck. From behind the guard he came, making no hesitation to plunge his weapon into flesh. The guard screamed in agony as again and again a blade sank and escaped, sank and escaped into and out of his exposed neck, blood shooting in every direction. As Brandon let the dying body fall, a rifle rang out, and he witnessed one of the inmates in front of him clutch herself as she took a bullet in the side. The soldier in a short dress took up his tiny pistol and shot his eyes to the platform across from him, finding a sniper running to cover. Brandon's outstretched arm followed his target's movement, his sights lining up, his aim adjusting to a shot. When he felt ready, he squeezed his trigger, watching as the guard across was stricken by a bullet in his arm. He pressed on yet, clutching his injury, trying to ignore the pain, trudging forward. With one bullet left in the chamber, the dancer-visaged Syndicate man tracked the sniper's movements, calculating once more, his aim a parallel. Another bullet screamed and away went the guard, falling onto the metal below as a projectile pierced the side of his head.

"For the prisoners that are allies of the Syndicate, you are especially in luck!" Aleegha continued. "I have come on behalf of the great Gareth Black, who anticipates your safe return home!" The thief's words were stopped as she turned to the sound of heavy footsteps behind her, her wary eyes finding a bulky guard wielding a sword taller than she. Her hand still gripped the microphone, her mouth yet prepared to spill more words, but she slowly took up a kris in one hand, readying herself for combat. "So take up the weapons before you, your own two hands, or any weapons you can scrap from the guards," she went on, "and fight!"

At this cue charged the swordsman, lifting his weapon to his side and attempting to strike hers. Their blades barely touched as she parried the hit, and again attempted the guard, again and again to no avail. Aleegha was relentless in her defense, successfully using a dagger no longer than a twig to prevent fatal blows from a terrifyingly large sword in flight. "Fight for your freedom, your liberty! Fight to save yourselves from these so-called 'sanctuary dwellers'!"

The swordsman bellowed a cry of fury as he raised his weapon over his head, preparing to strike with all of the force he had inside him. Before he could attack, however, two inmates appeared behind them, quick to come to aid. They grabbed the swordsman by his arms just as he was about to swing, prohibiting him from striking the thief down. They pulled him back as Aleegha watched, taking his struggling body out of the control room and onto the walkway. With a heave, he was tossed over the railing, weapon and all, his shouts of fear decreasing in volume before stopping altogether with a loud thud.

Meanwhile, on a catwalk below, Jack was engaged in combat as well. He had his fists up as a muscular guard across from him was likewise stanced. His opponent approached with a soaring punch that the quick-footed boxer sidestepped with ease, returning with a swift attack of his own. The guard stumbled back, as one of his comrades approached from the opposite side, behind Jack. This one seemed to pose a larger threat, as she was armed with a pistol in her anxious hands.

"Don't move!" she commanded with a shaking voice.

Jack slowly turned, raising his hands above his head, wondering how he was going to get out of this one. He stared into her eyes, desperate to read her movements, and almost sighed in relief when she lost her attention on him for a split second: up above them, Mov was laughing while he wrecked the prison with his machine gun, and the guard's aim quickly shifted to him.

However, with a ripe opportunity right in front of him, Jack was even quicker. He dashed forward, his fist flying out, striking the weapon directly out of his rival's hand. She stared at him in disbelief as the pistol fell off the railing and clattered harmlessly below, to which Jack frowned.

"Just not your day, is it?" he asked her with a shrug.

Her worried face gulped as the boxer reeled to punch. An impossibly fast combo hit her gut as Jack threw fist after fist in lightning succession. *"Onetwoonetwoonetwo,"* he gasped under his breath as he showed the guard what for. His flurry ended in an uppercut that did her done, causing her to go flying back and her consciousness to fade with a groan.

"Aghhhh!" shouted someone behind a panting Jack: his previous opponent letting loose his final war cry. The boxer, without turning to face the charging guard, drew his sawed-off shotgun and blasted him to bits before he nabbed the chance to draw close.

"Now, for those of you not with the Syndicate already, we present to you a choice," spoke Aleegha's serene, yet booming voice. "And I caution you take care in the decision you're about to make. You are free to go now, as you all know! However, I doubt any one of you will last long in the streets of White Heart, with

244

the whole city on a massive manhunt for your sorry asses. But if you wish for a home, then fight! The Syndicate will take you with open arms, so long as you are willing to take up arms for them!"

The thief slammed down on the control panel, and a large door on the bottom floor came down in the midst of battle, streaming the light of outside onto the faces of brawling prisoners. Quarrel ceased, as the few guards still standing were far too weakened to stop the stampede that followed. Aleegha, Mov, Jack, and Brandon rushed off, following behind the crowd of inmates that pushed and shoved their way out of what had been their containment.

Outside the prison, helicopters were parked, yet ready to take off, and Aleegha's band was in front of them, escorting the huddled, stomping masses to safety within the great flying fortresses.

"You three!" shouted Aleegha over the sounds of helicopter blades revving up. "Stay here! I need you to make sure everyone gets to safety! Take out anyone who poses even the slightest of threat!"

They nodded in unison, as obedient to their emancipator as ever, and took up their weapons with a tight grip. Aleegha ran to a smaller helicopter on the side that quickly took off, parting from the ground and the messy scene at the prison, and away they went.

While her fellow thieves pushed the sea of Syndicate to safety, the trio clenched their weapons, scanning their eyes for hostiles nearby. For some time, and oddly enough, none were willing to pose a threat to them, but just when they thought they were in the clear, they heard another droning alarm, singing along in harmony with the emergency sirens going off in the city.

A hog wheeled around, appearing out of nowhere, a blur to the Syndicate defenders, and stopped just to their side. Mov was quick to aim his machine gun, but Jack was quicker to halt him.

"Wait, wait!" the boxer called. "Look who it is! It's Weylin himself!"

"Oh, as if I'd fall for that! Why'd you think they took us away from him?" His focus never left his target. "He's one of 'em now, I know it."

"Put down your weapon," said Brandon to Mov calmly as he stepped in to side with Jack.

Just then, a barrier of guards armed to the teeth poured out from the exit the inmates had vacated, their heavy boots marching before kneeling shoulder to shoulder, a firing squad at the ready.

"I still want to call you three my friends, my comrades, my brothers. Please," pleaded Weylin, stepping off his motorcycle, the submachine gun gifted to him by Amber in his arms. "Don't make me do something I don't wanna do. Amber is forgiving, White Heart is forgiving. Lay down your weapons and come with me, please."

"Fuck you, prick!" was Mov's instantaneous response. "Boss Gareth's been nothin' but the best father we could ask for. Tenfold more caring than your awful general! This ain't gonna end well for you, old friend!"

"Funny you should say that, Dorm. I'm not the one who's outnumbered," Weylin spoke, pointing behind the Syndicate trio. "It seems your friends were quick to desert you."

"What in the fuck are you going on about?" Mov crudely demanded explanation with.

"Look!" exclaimed Brandon, pointing behind them. The helicopters were still there, and even the prisoners inside were visible through the windows on the closed door, but Aleegha's band had disappeared from sight.

"Alright, let's not make a mess of this," warned the ex-Syndicate. "Put your weapons down, and let's take you back in."

Jack frowned, partially in relief and partially in sympathy. "I'm sorry, Wey, but it's you that should surrender. Please."

"What are you talking about?"

"Behind you, buddy," said Brandon.

Weylin glanced around him, his confidence turning to anxiety. As he turned, his mind considered the worst possible outcome of what his ex-comrades were pointing to, and then imagination turned to reality, as he became witness to his firing squad at the slaughter of thieves regaining visibility. Aleegha's people sunk their many blades into Weylin's backup, and the guards crumbled with the groans of the dying. Before long, Weylin stood alone, surrounded by his enemies.

"You bastards!" gave Weylin with a feral scream.

"Go, go!" shouted Mov to Jack and Brandon. "I'll hold him off, you get out of here!" They wasted no time in heeding his command.

"No one is going anywhere!" came from Weylin, anger coursing in his throat. His focus shifted to the Syndicate trio, and before Mov could react, bullets soared from his rival's machine gun. In the few seconds Mov had given up his anger to assure his comrades made it out with their lives, he had been gunned down by the Syndicate traitor, holes bored all over his body. He crumbled to his knees, the machine gun falling out of his arms, light gasps escaping from his pouring lips stained red. His muscles eased, and he let himself fall to the ground and submerge in a pool of his blood.

Weylin reloaded his weapon with haste and turned to the corpses of prison guards littered behind him. Expecting to find Aleegha's band of thieves, his finger smashed the trigger with a shout, and a burst exploded forwards. His yelling ceased when he witnessed no bloodshed, and the sound of chopper blades whirring faster and faster forced him to turn. His head grew heavy as he saw the helicopters taking off, their hatches closing, and inside, inmates crammed and packed as tightly as could be, among them the faces of Aleegha's comrades, the grinning thieves. They drew further away, and Weylin armed himself to fire. Bullets bounced off the metal machines hastily, yet harmlessly, and away they escaped, off into the sky.

Weylin roared in anger, his lungs sore and aching, as he witnessed the dangerous prisoners and the cunning thieves abandon him, retreating to the man who had since become his greatest enemy.

■ ■ ■

The sirens began to shriek, their cries echoing through the streets of White Heart. "Again?" asked Eva. "What is it this time?"

Eva and Reese were loading the last of the weapons from the safehouse into the back of the van. When they finally completed the task, Reese, drenched in sweat, was quick to lock up the safehouse and hop inside. He turned on his talker and set it to the channel reserved for the Guardians. "What's going on, guys?"

Eva pulled the van out onto the street, focused on getting the weapons safely back to Amber's private armory, keeping a watchful eye on the road ahead.

Suddenly, seemingly out of nowhere, a hooded, robed figure materialized in the middle of the street, directly in front the van. Eva grunted loudly as she slammed the brakes. Reese paused his attempts to contact the other Guardians and angrily stepped out of Eva's van.

"Hey!" he yelled. "Who the fuck do you think you are?"

The figure did not answer, instead choosing to keep an eerie stance steady and make quiet breaths.

Eva could feel a terrible omen about. "Reese," she began. "I don't think you should…"

"You deaf?" he asked the figure, looking back at Eva in vexation, before confronting it with an angry pace.

"Reese!" Eva screamed suddenly as she witnessed the figure prepare to attack.

With extreme speed, the figure dashed towards Reese, cutting him off. Before he could react, it grabbed a few syringes from his belt. Reese swung with a heavy fist, but the figure ducked, then jumped on his back, injecting two syringes into his arms and pushing him into Eva's van with a crash as he yelled like a ravaged, savage beast.

He had only ever experienced the strength and anger that came from one vial of his personal drug, but never two shots at once. He could do little against the cluster of confusing emotions that barreled towards him now, save allow his body to rest before the rage would consume him.

Meanwhile, Eva snuck out of the van and made her way to the back, where she had left her rifle, cursing herself for not having it closer to her in case of emergency. When she finally had it in her hands, she noticed that the sounds of the sirens were now combining with the louder sounds of a fear-mongering vehicle above her. Eva looked up, watching as a helicopter soaring in the air somehow materialized right before her eyes. A ladder dangled from it, and it was drawing closer. Eva temporarily focused back on the figure, peeking out from the side of the van, and it was only then that she understood what was going on.

The now unhooded figure, with her white hair fluttering in the wind, took off with a handful of red syringes. She tangled herself in the dangling ladder, which raised into the helicopter, and with that, she was gone. As Eva aimed with her scope, she realized it was too late for tranquilizers, as she had nothing to fire at but the metal hull of an escaping copter. It was then that the rocket launcher glistened from the back of the van, ready to be used, seemingly winking at her with suggestiveness.

Reese was on the ground unconscious, but had he been able to, he would have already shot the flying machine out of the sky. In preparation, Eva grabbed for the weapon.

How many people were on board?

She took the launcher up in her arms.

She would bring them to utter destruction. Their bodies would never be found.

She prepared it for fire.

No one would even know how many lives were lost in the explosion.

Her lips tightened, and her palms began sweating profusely.

But did they deserve it?

Her nervous, shaking finger caressed a trigger.

Was it just to give them the permanence of death? And who was she to play the judge? Had she lived a moral enough life to have the right to take up the role of executioner?

"Damn it!" Eva shouted with a breaking voice, as she dropped the rocket launcher with a crash.

It was then that Reese began to pick himself up, panting heavily as he looked around for his target in confusion. Finally, he witnessed in the skies the helicopter soaring away, then disappearing before their eyes as quickly as it had appeared, vanishing into thin air.

He turned, spotting Eva with the idle rocket launcher next to her, a sorrowful look on her face. He gave her a heated, bitter gaze that shot genuine fear through her heart, fear of the man she loved; it was a fear of unpredictability, as one might fear a provoked wild animal.

"What is wrong with you?!" the angry man yelled, his muscles larger than ever, his veins visible through his tan skin, pulsing with a reddish glow. His voice was beast-like, brutish, raspy, and burning. "You had the shot, you should have taken it!"

Eva stammered, grabbing her rifle and backing herself up towards the driver's seat. As Reese yelled and cursed at her, she ducked into the van, frantically and furiously pushing her foot against the gas pedal. "Where do you think you're going?" she heard from behind her. "I'm talking to you!"

A sense of dread washed over her like a wave, her efforts to flee to no avail. Reese seemed to be holding onto the back of the van, and no matter how much Eva tried to move, he held a firm grip. Eventually, she could feel him lifting her van up and pushing his back against its bottom.

"Reese!" she cried, practically in tears of terror. "Please, stop this!" By now she was almost being lifted in the air.

Reese groaned as he managed to pick up the entire van over his head. He held it there for a moment, as the sounds of chaos played around him: Eva's pleading, blaring sirens, and a helicopter fleeing in the distance. Then, he threw the van with his fullest force, his loved one still inside.

Eva opened her door and leaped from the soaring vehicle. She turned around as she landed, witnessing the van she had practically lived in for most of her life, as well as Reese' highly explosive weapons, go up in a column of flames as the van was crushed against the side of a building.

Her hand moved to cover her mouth; this was not the Reese she knew and loved. Eva turned to run, the shouts of a man consumed by anger echoing behind her. She took out her rifle as she gave into a panicked sprint, firing it towards the man she never thought she would have to use it against. The tranquilizer darts did nothing to stop his ire.

Terror gripped her heart when she saw the raven following her as well. He closed in on her from above and dropped when he saw a moment present itself, slashing at her legs. She jumped for the balcony of a clustered house before Hex could cut her. She was vulnerable prey now; she needed to find help, and she needed to find it fast.

■ ■ ■

"What's going on?" a frantic Amber asked as she rushed downstairs. The sirens had been blaring for some time, but Amber had not yet received the distress call to notify her of the nature of White Heart's emergency.

Weylin stood at the door, panting. "General Leavett! A group of thieves just broke Jack, Brandon, Mov, and the rest of our Syndicate prisoners out of jail! They got out in helicopters!"

"All of them?" she asked.

"Yes," said Weylin with a nod. "A shootout erupted, and I killed Mov, but the rest escaped."

"You killed him? Wasn't he a friend of yours?"

"My ties with the Syndicate are long gone."

Amber nodded. "That's good to hear." She turned her focus towards the rest of the house, spotting Xela, Brutus, Charlie, Skullgem, and Alyssa awaiting her orders. "Has anyone seen Reese, Hex, or Eva?"

Just as she spoke her name, the brunette woman, seemingly coming from nowhere, pushed past Weylin and Amber, making her way up the stairs of the Guardians' home.

"Eva!" Xela yelled, but she paid her no attention.

"Eva, what's going on?" Amber asked, not receiving a response either.

A plan raced through Eva's head. The way Reese had reacted when he first met Ire...it was if he instantaneously forgot that he was the son he had not known about for more than a decade.

He was in his room, playing a game of solitaire on his bed. He looked up at Eva and gave her a small smile when she barged into his room.

"Hello, Evangeline," the boy said.

"Ire!" Eva yelled, her voice heavy. "I need you to come with me!"

"Why?"

She grabbed his hand and dragged him outside the house. Just in time, as Reese, with Hex perched on his shoulder, was barreling down the street.

"I need you to calm your father down, Ire. Do you think you can do that for me?" asked Eva, tucking hair behind her ear. Ire nodded, and Eva stepped back.

Amber walked up to her. "What's going on?"

"We got ambushed, and now Reese is going berserk," Eva explained. "We need something to tranquilize him. My gun won't do the trick."

"And you're sure bringing his son out will stop him?"

"Yes," replied Eva. "I'm almost positive. Ire is the only thing that can calm Reese down, save for a squad of Syndicates for him to brutally murder. I don't want us to be in the place of the latter."

Amber nodded. "I'm trusting you on this one."

Meanwhile, Reese was growing closer and closer. He barreled like a maniac, a loose cannon, an unstoppable train towards the lonesome boy in the middle of the street. Ire, however, remained eerily serene, his countenance perfectly neutral, almost disturbing the Guardians that watched on. A couple of feet away from his son, Reese raised his arm, and Eva could hear the fear-tinged gasps, as it truly seemed that he was going to swing his fist.

And he did, with all of his strength, but not a finger he laid on little Ire. His arm was outstretched just next to Ire's head, the punch carrying so much force that it briefly pushed Ire's hair like a carefree wind. Despite Reese's anger, he couldn't make himself hurt his son. His head fell downcast, as he didn't dare look his son in the eyes, his shame too great.

"Father," spoke Ire, in a soft voice. "Please stop this. You're scaring my friends. They're your friends too."

He put his hand over Reese's fist, pulling it downwards, and took his father in with an embrace. Reese hugged him back; the real Tyreesius, not the one consumed by drugged anger. It was the first time any of them had seen him cry.

CHAPTER 15:

The Syndicate leader removed his conical hat in the midst of the zephyr created by the wings of the helicopter. His black hair fluttered as the vehicle made a smooth landing on the helipad.

Out stepped Brandon, Jack, the rest of the Syndicate troops, and Aleegha's band of thieves, but not Mov or Weylin. As soon as Gareth shook hands with the Syndicate soldiers and thanked them for their service, he inquired about the missing soldiers.

"Boss," Jack answered. "Weylin betrayed our cause and joined White Heart. He murdered Mov."

Boss Gareth cursed and shook his head. "There is nothing more I hate than a traitor. He will burn, along with everybody else that fights on the side of that city. I am glad to see that at least we were able to save many others."

"Thank you, Gareth," Brandon said.

"Yes, thank you for not leaving us behind," Jack added.

"I will go to great lengths to ensure the safety of my people," Boss Gareth spoke. "I am sure it has been a long journey for everyone. Rest now, you have done a great service for your city. Just be ready to fight when duty calls you once again." The grateful soldiers parted with him then, leaving Gareth with the thieves.

"You have done well," Gareth said. "As such, you will be rewarded well. I have set aside as many credits as you could possibly ask for in return for your service."

"Thank you," said Aleegha.

"But I ask of you," added Gareth, "to consider joining the Syndicate. We are more than ready to take you under our shelter."

"I respect you very much," Aleegha said. "I see that you care for your troops and respect them, as I do with my people. I'll keep it in mind."

Boss Gareth nodded, beginning to walk away. "I hope to see you continue fighting against White Heart, Aleegha. You're quite the asset."

■ ■ ■

Eva wasn't surprised when Reese said he didn't want to sleep in the same bed as her that night and instead opted for the couch. Nor was she surprised when she woke up at noon and didn't find him there.

As she walked back to her room, she found Amber's door slightly ajar. The general's room was oddly neat and organized. Amber herself slumped over her desk, sighing as she idly arranged bullets in a row. Her hair normally ebbed down her back like a busy river of silk, but today it was quite unkempt. It was clear that the stress from yesterday had taken its toll on everybody.

When Amber saw Eva at the door, she did her best to smile, but it was very faint. "Good morning, Eva," she said quietly.

Eva returned the greeting, followed by silence as both Guardians thought of what to say next.

"Have you seen Reese?" Eva finally asked.

Amber nodded. "He took off a little earlier. Didn't say where. Probably went to a—"

"—bar," Eva interrupted solemnly. She thanked Amber and left to see the man she loved again.

■ ■ ■

It was said birds couldn't smile, but Hex often did when sitting at home on Reese's shoulder. Today, however, the raven seemed to be frowning. His friend was drowning himself in his misery, and there was nothing Hex could do to help.

A woman took the seat next to the massive Guardian. Though he was deep in his thoughts, he recognized her immediately.

"I'll have what he's having," said Eva, pointing to Reese.

After the bartender nodded and left, Reese spoke up: "I left most of my credits next to your bed. Should cover the costs of your van."

"I hadn't noticed," Eva said, "but I don't really care. I don't want you to pay me back."

"Please. Stop trying to be so modest. I absolutely destroyed something that meant the world to you. What's worse is that I did it in an attempt to kill you."

It was then that bartender brought her her drink, which she took a quick chug of and frowned at the taste. Eva sighed as she put it aside, and ran a hand through Reese's short hair. "Sweetie, you know that you mean the world to me much more than some stupid van ever could. Compared to you, it was nothing. And that wasn't you that attacked me, Reese."

"You know that's not true," he quietly spoke.

Suddenly, the sound of footsteps behind them almost made her jump, and the serious tone of a man speaking too close for comfort was not far from sending a shiver through her body.

"I'm not going to make a big deal out of this," a voice said from behind them. Eva looked at her two fellow Guardians to find a man leaning towards Reese's ear. "Step outside with us, please."

Part of her imagined Reese turning and brutally elbowing the man's face. As the man would crumble, clutching his bleeding nose, Reese would grab his shotgun and hit him with the butt. Then, he would turn to the man's henchmen, who were waiting outside, and rain bullets on them as Hex sat on his shoulder, protecting him from danger...

Reese stood without a word, but an exasperated sigh left his mouth as he stepped outside the tavern.

"Tyreesius Black," the man said with a stern voice, pulling out his badge, "you are under arrest on the grounds of disturbing the peace and attempted murder. You will be transferred to a maximum-security penitentiary effective immediately. Your raven and your son will be brought into protective custody..."

It was then that Eva stopped listening. She couldn't halt her mind from tuning everything out, her emotions reading nothing but disbelief and worry. The world as she knew it was crumbling around her, and all of it was unfolding within a matter of hours.

■ ■ ■

Steam arose from the shaking cup in Xela's hands as she brought it to the leader of the Guardians. It was Amber's job to take care of them, but sometimes, she was the one who needed care the most.

"I made you some tea." Xela handed the mug to Amber.

"Thank you," Amber said quietly.

"So, what's troubling you?" She put her hands gently on Amber's shoulders in a caring gesture.

Amber reached out to take Xela's hand, her actions mindless, her worries the only thing she could think about. "I just don't get it."

"Don't get what?"

Amber sighed. "I don't get the Syndicate. I don't get Gareth."

"What about them?"

Amber looked up at her. "I always thought they were the bad guys. That this was all just some battle between good and evil. Black and white. But I never considered things to be so...grey."

Xela shook her head. "I-I'm not following."

"The Syndicate authorized a top-secret infiltrate-and-rescue operation to break into our city, just to save their own. I haven't even heard of any of them before, save for the three we locked up, and our reports on them are almost empty. Just regular soldiers, the most of them."

"They did manage to turn Reese into a monster for a long enough time to wreak some havoc," Xela added. "And our prison is a mess right now. Lots of lives lost. Good thing you've got us on clean-up duty."

"Yes, but..." Amber struggled to find the right words. "Something just feels off, Xela. It frightens me."

Xela had no time to answer, as Eva fittingly ran up the stairs to the room just then.

"Amber!" she shouted. "Come quick! They just arrested Reese!"

■ ■ ■

"Under whose authority was this made?" Amber asked angrily, slamming her fist on the desk of the Chairman. Xela, Charlie, and Eva stood by her as she protested.

"Ease yourself, General," said the Chairman in a surprisingly calm tone. "And understand that there are some things not within my power."

"Since when was this not in your power?" Amber asked.

"As the war against the Syndicate continues on, the war council gains strength."

Amber shook her head. "That's unacceptable. At this rate, we'll turn into a dictatorship."

The Chairman nodded. "I understand your frustration, but I'm not going to speak out against my superiors. I funded the creation of your group, but I can't do any more for you."

Amber grumbled. "You can't? I think you mean you don't want to."

The Chairman sighed. "Perhaps you're right, General. Perhaps our war council is unfit for such power. However, if you're wrong about this war, you will suffer consequences. I will do nothing to stop you, but knowing these risks, I will not aid you either. Is that all? Are we clear?"

They had never seen Amber so angry and passionate before, her face red with ire and her fists clenched tightly. Xela took Amber's hand and led her out of the Chairman's room to avoid further arguments. As they left, she turned to her.

"We're willing to do whatever it takes to grant you whatever power you need," Xela said.

Eva nodded in agreement, seeing that Amber was now calming down, her breath steadying. "We trust you, and we know you'll do the right thing."

Amber smiled and thanked them. "The question is, how do we get that power?" Charlie gave a light whine, and Amber bent over to pet him thoughtlessly, her mind in a flurry. "I'll need time to make a plan."

■ ■ ■

The cheering and jeering of the enthusiastic crowd in the arena as Jack Bahal was pushed into the corner by his opponent only served to intoxicate his battle-fury even further.

He did his best to block the hits he took, allowing the other boxer to make her rounds as she wished. Tough as she was, Jack suffered through, and just when she took a pause, he slipped away. She attempted to strike once more, but her opponent was gone, behind her now.

She wheeled around just as Jack swung, his glove striking her face so hard he could feel one of her teeth coming loose. Her body collapsed to the mat just after the bell rang.

Jack shook his head. "C'mon ref, she can't even get up!"

"Ahhh, quit your bitchin'," came the struggling voice attached to the beaten body below him. His opponent picked herself up, and the referee shook his head back at Jack.

The Syndicate boxer gulped, swallowing his urge to argue, and got his mind back in the fight. His feet led him back to his corner, where he waited to hear the fateful words:

"Round 4!" someone shouted in sync with a bell going off. Jack was quick to walk into battle, faster than his opponent, eager to get the fight over with.

She attempted to take advantage of his speedy, willing approach and swung forwards once, twice, three times, Jack sidestepping all of them. He lunged forwards with a punch to her gut, and she stumbled back. When Jack approached again, she was ready, however, throwing a blow that he didn't expect.

He almost tripped backward in his failure to anticipate the strike, but was quick to steady himself with his agile feet. He broke from her then, taking a step back to mentally ready himself.

He was prepared when she began to follow. She struck Jack once more with a jab, just soft enough for his surprisingly rough body to ignore, and he allowed himself to adopt a monitored berserk. He threw fist after fist in machine gun fire, but not without steady rhythm to them. Finally, he finished the combo with a punch that left her staggering backward.

She was still then, her eyes shooting in every direction, as she fought to stay balanced. He could almost see inside her, her wit playing tug-of-war with her physical strength.

"Let me help you with that," Jack muttered under his breath. He took a few steps back, sighed, then leaped forward. His arm came all the way around, and from the moment of impact his hook struck his opponent, she was out cold.

A panting boxer drenched in sweat regained himself, then looked about the ring. Around him, he witnessed the crowd going crazy, and he heard the chant when his hearing came back:

"Jack! Jack! Jack!" he could hear them say. "Jack! Jack! Jack!"

He smiled there, in the locker room, just as he smiled when he prevailed and gloated in his victory.

"Great fight out there," said a stranger athlete passing by, snapping his attention back into the real world. He thanked her as she walked away, then took a swig of the water bottle next to him, before stuffing his face into his towel and wiping away the remnants of sweat, blood, and drool he had left on himself.

"I saw the whole thing," came another voice, startling him once more.

Jack turned to find himself face to face with none other than Brandon, dressed in his typical dancer fashion. "You were electric out there."

"Uh, tha—"

"Stunning, dazzling."

"Umm..."

"On fire, I might even say." Each time Brandon spoke, a pinch of extra wonder entered his voice.

"Thanks. It's good to see you, B."

"You too, sweetheart," the boxer's dancer friend spoke. "Mighty interesting of you to pick up another fight so soon. We just got back, you know?"

"Gotta make my money somehow." Jack's cool, casual voice was directly contradictory to Brandon's magical tone.

"You never rest, do you?" the dancer asked.

"You know what they say," the boxer responded with a shrug. "Ain't none for the wicked."

"Well, tell ya what. Any time you're feeling overworked..."

"I never feel overworked," interrupted Jack.

"Come see me perform," continued Brandon, ignoring his comment. "Most nights you can find me at the swing club on 46. I practically live there by now."

"I'll keep it in mind," said Jack with a nod, as he packed his things in his locker.

"Good to hear! I hope to see you soon," spoke Brandon with a smile, a singsongy voice, and a blow of a kiss. His stiletto heels clacked themselves into Jack's head as the dancer trotted away.

■ ■ ■

"Do you know the Syndicate's way of choosing a ruler?" Alyssa asked, hoping to get some words out of Amber, who stood next to her.

"I don't," said Eva, encouraging her.

266

"'Anyone who can best its current leader in a mock battle becomes a possible heir to the throne,'" Alyssa continued, reading from a book on the topic of their sworn enemies. "'If they lose, they are shown no mercy. If they win, once that current leader dies, the remaining possible heirs fight to the death, and the winner becomes the next ruler of the Syndicate.'"

"That's actually quite interesting," said Eva. She reached for a glass, catching Amber's blank stare. "Look, Amber, you need to relax. We've never seen you like this."

As if she snapped out of a trance, Amber sighed and rubbed her eyes. A little later, she said, "You're right, Eva. I'm really sorry. Maybe I need a break." She got up and gathered a few of her things, then parted from the teenager engrossed in her book and the headbanded woman with a frown upon her face.

"Where are you going?" Eva inquired quizzically, as Amber stomped away.

"To Xela. I'm going to let off some steam."

■ ■ ■

"Careful, careful," Xela warned, as she and her fellow workers removed the last portion of the brain from the lifeless body. Then, with the help of a man who fetched the preservation tube, they placed it inside for later experimentation.

She sighed, thanking her workers for their help, then began to pull off her goggles and gloves, only to find Amber waiting patiently outside the room. As Xela went to clean her hands at a nearby sink, the general followed.

"What are you doing here?" Xela asked with a smile.

"I came to spend some time with you," Amber stated. "Even if you're busy, maybe to just watch. I'm a bit scarred now, though, after witnessing that."

"What, me removing the brain from a corpse long devoid of life? What particular part of that is scarring?"

Amber gave a quiet and short laugh. "Why are you doing that anyway?"

"Oh, just changing some things up," Xela explained. "The brain is the most important organ when it comes to our research. I'm going to take it apart and learn about every little part that makes it tick. By next year, I hope to have brought at least one person back. Permanently. Or, at least, until they expire of old age!"

"That's interesting." She enjoyed it when Xela ranted on about her work, as Amber loved seeing the passion in her eyes. "When do you think you'll be done today?"

"I could just finish now," she said. "I may be the director of the Order, but I don't need to be here all the time. The people here are just as knowledgeable and trustworthy as I."

"In that case, I was wondering if you wanted to spend some time together, maybe get something to eat."

Xela nodded. "That sounds good."

"No, I *was* wondering. After witnessing that, I kinda lost my appetite," jested Amber.

The two laughed and smiled together. Xela removed her lab coat and took Amber's hand, and they left as one.

■ ■ ■

"He's sadistic and cruel. He clearly doesn't have a care in the world for anyone but himself. He only wants my throne for power."

"Then why don't you just get rid of him?" asked a sluggish Jade.

Gareth had paid a visit to her bedchambers, wishing to have a word with her. She sat in her bed, only half-awake, dressed in a nightgown and covered by wool sheets. Her prominent muscles were never usually so revealed, and her fit stomach could be seen through her thin sleepwear. Outside of her bedroom tower, a downpour beat down on the dimly lit Avalon streets.

"That would mean I would need to fight him, and I've lost to him before," spoke Gareth, removing his fabled conical hat and revealing the jet black hair underneath. "If he bests me, you and I, along with the entire Syndicate, including its civilians, will be at his mercy. And as I said, he has none."

Jade rubbed her green eyes. "Then what are you asking of me?"

"Our views may not mirror each other exactly," Boss Gareth continued, "but I would much prefer yours over the tortured views of Reynard Crudelis."

"Are you sure about this?" spoke a tired Jade.

"I've seen what he does on the field. He toys with his victims, the most twisted game of cat and mouse I have ever witnessed." Gareth caught Jade's eyes widening, seemingly in horror and amazement, as he spoke. "He lives only to humiliate others. He is a fox made human, cunning and manipulative. Jade, I want you to keep an eye on him, at the least. We cannot risk fighting him now."

Jade nodded. "I'll do my best, Boss. With all due respect, may I go back to bed now?"

"Be at ready, in case he challenges you to fight him," Gareth added.

Another nod from Jade. With that, Gareth bid her a good night and left the room.

Alone in her bed, she found herself quite uneasy. Jade thought much about Reynard, and whether she wanted to admit it or not, fear was the word that kept echoing in her mind. They were at war; the last thing she had expected to hear from Gareth was concern about a problem stemming from people who were supposed to be their allies.

■ ■ ■

"Perchance he for whom this bell tolls may be so ill, as that he knows not it tolls for him..."

Xela stopped reading the brown book, flipped through pages edged in a color that might have once glimmered in her eyes, and closed it to get a better look at the cover. The words had long been faded. "This looks ancient. Where did you find it?"

Alyssa smiled. "A bookstore. Just any old bookstore. It's amazing the treasures you can find in one. Anyway, I wanted to gift this one to you."

"Really?" asked Xela.

270

Alyssa nodded. "It's about philosophy and death and other boring and/or creepy stuff that I'm sure you'll be interested in."

Xela clenched her lips. "I'm going to let that one slide," she said with a light smile. "I promise to take good care of it."

Just then, Amber burst into the kitchen. Xela and Alyssa were surprised to see Ezekiel with her.

"Zeke thinks he has a way to get Reese back, everyone!" she announced to the house.

Xela turned to Alyssa, and Alyssa turned to Xela. "Let's hear it," they said in unison.

The Guardians seated themselves around a table, listening to the technologist explain his plan. "I've been working on this prototype for some time now," continued Ezekiel. "It's essentially a bomb, but instead of an explosion, it disables all electronics within an area."

"And then what?" Xela inquired.

"A loss of electronics would hopefully come as a good sign for the other inmates to start a little prison riot. Just to buy us some time. But we all know Reese can handle himself. He'll be fine."

"So we get Reese back into our safety," Xela said. "What happens after? He's going to need his weapons and his gadgets. He's surely going to need Hex and Ire."

"We'll make sure he knows where to find his weapons," responded Amber. "As for Hex and Ire, we'll take them in and rendezvous with Reese shortly after."

"This sounds incredibly complicated," commented Alyssa.

Xela agreed. "She has a point, Amber. What do we do then, once we have all three of them in our safety?"

"If we set this plan into motion a week or two from now, we'll have time beforehand to gather any troops we can," Amber said. "With these soldiers, we will make a large camp between White Heart and Avalon and unleash an attack on the latter from there. We're doing exactly what the war council wants us to do, anyway.

"We will stay in this camp depending on how well these attacks go for us. If we barely make a dent in their defenses, we retreat back to White Heart. Best case scenario, we constantly attack while waiting for more reinforcements. Once they get there, we launch a full-scale invasion of the Syndicate's home turf. We will stop this war before it escalates too high."

Xela shook her head. "No, no. I think it's just too complex. Too risky."

Amber put a hand on Xela's shoulder. "When have things not been too risky?"

CHAPTER 16:

"My name is Brutus McCallister." The words left his mouth in front of a crowd of soldiers at arms, looking anxious but ready to listen. The men and women in front of him knew they might die within the next few months, and they understood that this was to be one of White Heart's most dangerous missions to date.

Brutus continued on, reminding himself of that: "The man beside me is known as Skullgem, the Lionhearted. We are two of the Guardians, a specialist group led by General Amber Leavett. The following is a speech prepared by Skullgem, but dictated to me, as he is unable to present it in words. Today," Brutus paused to receive more signs from Skullgem, "he opens himself up to you."

Skullgem nodded, a small signal that Brutus was doing a good job so far, but stopped signing. He turned to the readied soldiers and pushed the small button on the side of his hood, near his neck. His hands reached towards his face, and he pulled his hood off. He had expected gasps or shouts, maybe even booing or clapping. All he received as a reaction from the crowd was...nothing. A silence that somehow made him feel worse than any other reaction would have. Perhaps it was because he was unsure of how they truly felt about his revelation. Still, Skullgem continued.

"My name is Geronimo Ao-Shi. Many years ago," translated Brutus, "I lived in a place where there

273

were few of my kind. Though some of my neighbors were accepting of me, others were not. They plotted to kill my parents. I was to die too, but they showed the slightest mercy and tortured me instead. That is why I cannot speak; they had my tongue ripped out. Before, I was good at convincing others that our people were not the enemy. My speech was my gift. Even after I lost it, I cared not to hate all humans for the actions of some, as they had done to me. I am not sure whether you consider me a friend or foe because of my race, but I hope we can get past something so trivial and focus on the true enemy, out there, attempting to destroy our city."

He saw the nods in the crowd; he was reaching them, as he had hoped.

Geronimo took Brutus' hand and raised it alongside his. "Skullgem and I are willing to fight by your sides against the Syndicate," continued the tactician with pride, speaking his own words. "But we need you to trust in us. We leave tomorrow. Ready yourselves; now we will bring the fight to them."

■ ■ ■

The boxer stared ahead at the club across the street, sighing as he threw his hands in his coat pockets. The drizzle of warm rain was pleasant, along with the darkness of the rainforest city-state, the moons above casting their lunar light on his cheeks, and especially the sounds surrounding him: cars driving home after a long night, their wheels pushing away the rainwater around them, and the songs, shouts, and singing arising everywhere around, sounding from clubs, homes, and the streets alike; how Jack loved the Avalon night-life.

He approached then, finding himself inside the club, and the jazzy melody entranced him further. A server took his coat, then led him to the small ballroom. He could hear the instrumental quiet just a tad, as they let the singer shine. A voice Jack barely recognized mused, soft words caressing his ears with a delicate touch:

"March winds and April showers, make way for sweet May flowers, and then comes June, of a moon and you..."

He could feel his heart flutter when he saw him on the tiny stage, illuminated by cool blue lights, in contrast to the warm red lightly covering his petite body: Brandon dressed in a crimson dress, loose and playful, short and showy, and yet all the while, he burned with passionate fire.

"March winds and April showers, make way for happy hours, and in the May time, June time, love time with you..."

He hopped off the stage, bobbed hair bobbing, allowing the violins, bass, clarinet, piano, and drums to take over the beautiful song. With a smile, Brandon approached Jack, his heels almost moving in tempo, his body swaying so much the boxer found it hard to keep track, and all the while, he was mesmerized. The ring was his arena, but here, where the music took over and the dance of battle exchanged for the dance of love, belonged solely to the man in front of him.

"Come dance with me," commanded Brandon with a bow, and yet the way his words came out was an art in and of itself.

Brandon rose towards his partner and turned elegantly to draw closer, finishing just in front of Jack with a gentle curtsy. He kept his arms open after his swift turn as he stood up straight, stiff, but inviting and almost enticing. His open hands motioned for Jack to come forward and mimic the position. Jack followed, hesitantly stretching out his arms and trying to mirror Brandon. The dancer beamed and playfully yanked him forward, placing his partner's right hand on his upper back, and firmly grasping his left, hoisting it into the air. Jack forced himself to keep his shoulders up and match Brandon's perfect posture. With a soft pace, Brandon began his own version of a foxtrot.

He stepped forward, his leadership on the dance floor evident, and lightly nudged Jack's right leg with his own, showing him that he was to do the opposite and step back first. Jack complied, but constantly looked down to make sure he was following the right steps. He repeated what he saw as they went in circles, *step, step, and together, step, step, and together*. Shakily, he got himself together, not without a giggle from Brandon, but a rather odd grin also stayed upon his face. Every time Jack found himself tripping, his dance master would only smile and bring the boxer back in line.

Brandon sped up their dance a tad as he could see his partner adjusting, encouraging Jack to go at it instead of overthinking. They continued with ease and traveled across the dance floor with elegance and pure fun. The foxtrot was a conquered beast until the two came to the middle, where Brandon winked, stopped, and turned out his leg almost completely to the side: an impressive feat reached only by the most esteemed of dancers. Brandon released his partner, then relaxed his body, letting his hips sway broadly, and the rest of his torso subtly followed. He didn't need to turn around to know that wanting eyes were staring. The dancer extended his right leg and put it down, then rolled his body. He executed an elegant ball chain as if it were nothing at all and fully swerved over, preparing for the walk back. He proudly poised himself and repeated the promenade back to his partner, showing pride in a closed smile. Brandon brought Jack into position, and as the song came to a pause, the boxer boldly dipped the dancer.

"Boxer boy's got some moves, hasn't he?" Brandon asked his partner.

Jack laughed and pulled his partner's tiny body up then, a moment in which they were face to face, admiring one another's beauty. "Absolutely nothing compared to what you can do."

Brandon couldn't help but be fascinated with the boxer, interest abounded in his hair, as he found it the centerpiece of the adorable visage he wore. Yet his muscles were quite the sight as well, and he refused to withdraw his small hands from them.

Jack knew his eyes couldn't stray from the dancer, he need not try. The boy in his arms perfectly captured the essence of feminine grace. His makeup was done with artisan skill, his wardrobe picked accordingly to bring out his beauty. Jack realized for the first time that it was truly an art form, how the dancer painted himself like he was his own canvas.

They could have stared at one another in admiration for hours, but an attraction pulled them closer, an urge to merge themselves and be together. Their lips caressed before they knew it, passionately touching, bridging their love for one another. When they parted after some time, they looked on each other with blushes and smiles. Then Brandon withdrew for a moment, walking slowly back with his eyes on Jack, and returned to the stage, gripping the microphone once more.

"March winds and April showers, make way for sweet May flowers, and then comes June, of a moon and you..."

Jack was seated at a table nearby and brought a meal, but forgot his hunger in his glee. His eyes couldn't flee from the man on the stage, and he felt nothing but his own heart beating as he looked on in admiration.

Time was forgotten, and as Brandon and the band behind him played song after song, the night grew old. Sometimes he danced, sometimes he sang, but no matter what he did, Jack found it lovely. The club slowly abandoned, save for the boxer, who had his attention glued. He was truly in bliss.

After playing their last song, a slow ballad of love that drew the party to a close, Brandon hopped off the stage and approached the boxer.

"Well, you certainly liked that, didn't you?" he said in his sweet tone.

"I don't think I've ever seen anything more beautiful," responded Jack.

Brandon smiled and laughed. "Thank you, sweetheart. I'm honored."

Jack smiled back at him. "Where are you off to now?"

"Home, I'm thinking. I've got a long day tomorrow."

"May I take you?" asked Jack as he shot up.

The boy in the red dress chuckled. "I don't think it'd be fair to say no."

Their coats were fetched, a cab called, and before long, the two were at the steps leading to the door to Brandon's home.

"I had an amazing night," said Jack.

Brandon stared at him, admiring his wonder, his splendor, then found himself embracing the boxer. Jack grunted out of surprise, then closed his eyes and hugged back. Their parting was slow, neither wishing to detach from the other.

When they were finally apart, Brandon sighed. "I guess this is goodbye."

Jack frowned at the words, as something felt off, almost melancholy, but nodded back in understanding. "Goodnight, Brandon."

The boxer turned, but nay did the dancer, who stared at the man walking away with grief. A pang of guilt struck him, and he swallowed a heavy gulp.

"Wait."

Jack stopped in his tracks, just before his feet touched the sidewalk. It was some time before he turned. Brandon approached then, his heart thumping, yearning to be with him. "I don't want you to go."

"But you have a long day tomorrow," Jack said. "Remember?"

"I don't care about tomorrow." There were tears in Brandon's eyes. "I care about being with you today."

"But—"

"I don't want to hear it." Brandon took Jack's hand with a firm grip, surprising even the muscular boxer with his strength.

"Where are we going?"

Brandon turned to face him, taking the boxer's hands in his. "Just one night. Spend one night with me, please."

Jack stuttered for a brief moment, then brought his nervous head to nod. "Okay, okay."

"It's been so long, darling," the dancer said, as he let him inside. "So long since I've felt that feeling of love. It's always been lust. I need something, someone to convince me that's not all I can feel, before it's too late, and just, the way you treated me..."

To Jack, Brandon was speaking fast, too fast to understand, his words cryptic. Jack shut himself up and allowed the dancer to do with him whatever his intentions were. No complaints came from him when Brandon led him to the bedroom, threw him on his bed, and leaped on top of him. His red lips cuddled everywhere on the boxer's fit body, often finding themselves coming back to his lips, his cheeks, his neck, his chest. All the while, he talked and talked:

"I missed this feeling. Not the feeling of pleasure, but the feeling of care. The feeling of being adored, and adoring in return."

Before long, Brandon moved his kissing lower some, stripping his partner as he moved. At this feeling of pleasure, Jack could barely hold in tiny gasps, save for the occasional few times the beautiful dancer would free his mouth to speak more:

"The line between lust and love is beginning to grow hazy. Odd, how others don't see it. I'm a whore to them, for searching for that understanding. But not to you, right? Isn't it love you feel, even while I do this for you?"

"I-I..." the boxer stammered, his mind barely able to think in his submissiveness. "I think I love you."

Brandon's laugh was both teasing and loving, somehow. "You're so cute," he said, as he placed himself on top. His positioning was careful, and when he felt the touch inside him, he let his body do its own moving. They breathed together, moaned together, as up and down the beautiful boy went. Jack had never known this before, to be with someone so knowledgeable in such a craft. Despite his efforts, he did not have it in him to save himself for much longer, and finally cried out when he was finished.

Brandon removed himself then, kissing Jack a few more times with all the love he could muster. He reached for his nightstand, finding the pack of cigarettes and lighter to which he always retreated nightly, and one found itself in his mouth before long. When he turned back around, he found Jack curled up, facing away, and smiled at the light snoring he heard coming from him. As he blew away smoke, he admired the boxer, his eyes glued to him. The shadows of the slitted windows presented the shining moonlight on his muscles, accompanied by the silence of the night.

The dancer found himself softly singing, his mind stuck in a loop from earlier tonight: *"March winds and April showers, romance will soon be ours, an outdoor paradise for two."*

Then, ready for sleep, Brandon doused the butt in its tray.

"Goodnight, Jack," he said quietly, as he embraced the boxer from behind and closed his eyes.

■ ■ ■

A green-haired woman carrying a large shield on her back walked up to the Syndicate leader, who was monitoring the scientists in front of them as they analyzed the samples of Reese's drugs brought by Aleegha.

"What's going on?" Jade asked Gareth.

"I need to find a way to negate the effects of Reese's serum to prevent my brother from posing such a large threat to us."

"Why not just replicate the serum so we can use it for ourselves?"

Gareth shook his head. "I refuse to put my soldiers through so much stress."

"You really do care about your troops, don't you?"

Gareth nodded. "Another reason why I don't want Reynard in my position."

"What was that?"

They simultaneously turned, surprised to find Reynard himself standing behind them. He took a noisy bite into a crunchy apple in his hands, chewing obnoxiously with his mouth open.

"What do you want?" Gareth asked, his tone harsh.

"I want you to watch your tongue," Reynard retorted, in his typical, flirtatious timbre. "I am not your enemy, Gar-Bear."

"I will leave that for me to decide," replied Gareth.

"Of course it's for you to decide. You're the leader of the Syndicate. Isn't everything for you to decide?"

Jade stepped in, deciding she had heard enough. "You assure Gareth you are not his enemy, and yet you mock him? You are a pitiful, dark man."

Reynard laughed in a manner akin to an unstable hyena. "Gareth, please curb your green whore. Ooh, I bet she'd look good in a leash and a muzzle."

"Enough!" yelled Gareth. He drew his longsword faster than Jade could stop him and swung the weapon over his head.

Steel clashed with steel, and yet Reynard wielded no weapon. Gareth's sword had stopped somewhere just in front of the cunning fox; it was if Gareth was striking an invisible foe.

Two krises materialized into vision before them, crossed in the pattern of an X; the only things standing between Gareth's sword and Reynard's body. Soon afterward, a hooded woman appeared, wielding the weapons.

Reynard took another bite of his apple and waved a finger. "You're a bit too slow there, Boss."

"Aleegha," said Gareth. "Have you no honor?" He pulled his blade away and stepped back towards Jade.

"Money is much more valuable than honor," she said sternly. "I'm sorry, Gareth. It's just business."

"I was willing to take you under my wing," Gareth replied. "But it seems you have taught me not to have the patience for sellswords."

"Maybe you don't," said Reynard, "but I do. Aleegha now serves to protect me, and only me."

Gareth shook his head. "I'm counting the days until I can cut you into two." He sheathed his sword angrily.

"Like I said, Gareth, watch your tongue," replied Reynard. "I'll let this slide, but you might want to be more careful next time."

Gareth looked ready to spit at him, but Jade pulled him away. He was at war with not just White Heart, but his allies as well.

■ ■ ■

"What's the status on the rest of the troops?" Amber asked Brutus as he walked into their house, along with Skullgem.

"We've got most of them ready to deploy. They're waiting in a large camp right outside the White Heart walls."

Amber nodded before heading upstairs. She found Eva in her room and motioned her over to the garage at the side of the house. "What are you showing me?" Eva asked.

"You'll see," said Amber, building suspense. She led Eva through an alley with a large, metal garage door at the end. "Are you ready?"

Eva shrugged. "I guess."

Amber smiled, grabbing a small remote control from her breast pocket. She pressed a small button, and the metal door slowly uncovered the surprise hiding behind it. Eva initially gasped, then laughed and smiled, clearly in awe of what stood before her.

Inside was a van, painted completely in white, the model identical to the one Reese had destroyed in his rage, save for different plating. A pink arch was covered over the top of the front windshield, mirroring Eva's pink headband.

"I call it 'Evan,'" Amber said. "It's spelled like 'Evan,' as in the name, but pronounced 'Eee-van.' See, it's a play on your name, Eva, and the word van..."

"Yes, Amber," replied Eva, chuckling loudly as she rolled her eyes. "I get it."

Amber laughed with her. "It's the same model as your old one, but it's covered in a special plating, like a tank, almost. Hopefully, it can stop an angry Reese Black, but we probably shouldn't test that out. It's even made to look like you!"

"I...I'm speechless." Eva turned to wrap her arms around the taller woman in a thankful hug. "How could I ever repay you for this?"

"Oh, please. Forget about repaying me. It's a thank you for your service towards this city. Besides, I'm not going to have you go to war unprepared. So I actually invented the first army van," jested Amber. "Why don't you see what it's like inside?"

Eva smiled, already climbing into the front seat. She put her feet up on the dashboard and rested her head in her arms as Amber left her to bask in her joy.

Inside the house, Alyssa and Burnellia sat together idly on the couch, having placed their arms adjacent to each other, comparing their relic markings. Besides the obvious color differences, they seemed to be identical. When Amber rushed into the room, they knew they had to temporarily part.

"I have to regroup with the rest of the army," Burnellia said to Alyssa. They hugged for a moment, and she wished Alyssa luck in freeing Reese.

"Thanks, friend," Alyssa responded, as she turned to follow the general. "I'm hoping we get to see each other soon."

Amber searched the house, finding Ezekiel in a room on the second floor that had been provided to him to use as a makeshift workshop.

"How goes it?" she asked him. He was tinkering with the device.

Zeke sighed. "It's as done as it can get for now, but it's not as permanent as I'd hoped it would be. It'll only work until they find a solution."

286

"Let's just hope whoever is in charge of technology and electronics over there isn't nearly as good as you are."

"Then I'm ready," Ezekiel said, nodding. "What about everyone else?"

"It looks like it," said Amber, a smirk on her face and a tone beaming with alacrity. "Let's start the show."

■ ■ ■

"It ain't sanitary to smoke in here," said Tyreesius Black, leaning on the wall by his bed cell.

The guard in front of the force field door that served as the only way in and out of Reese's cell put down his cigar and stared with disbelief at the hulk of a man.

"Fuck off," were the only words he gave him.

Reese chuckled. "That's no way to speak to your captive."

The man pulled a nightstick from his belt and tapped on the bars of the cell. "You got a mighty big mouth, big man. You asking for a beating?"

Suddenly, the sound of power dying down screamed at them. Lights flickered on and off, and soon, the entire building went dark, illuminated only by the lights of the windows spread throughout the penitentiary. Finally, the electrical doors to every cell in the prison turned off. There was a moment of uneasiness as the few prisoners crawled out of their cells, unsure of what was going on. They did not question it for long; many saw their chance to slip out.

The guard by Reese's cell saw it as his duty to watch the most dangerous prisoner there. However, the nightstick in his hands trembled as the man in front of him stepped out of his cell. The guard had not actually seen him in battle, but he had heard the stories.

As he stood towering in front of the guard, Reese uttered the words: "You still up for that beating?"

The guard stepped back. As the prison emptied out, he found himself alone, save for the hulking Guardian next to him. "You're not leaving," said the guard. Though he tried not to show it, he was deathly afraid, which Reese could tell from how the man's voice quivered with terror.

"Come on, bud. Let's not do it this way," said Reese. He made a *tsk* noise with his lips and closed his eyes, which the guard saw as his chance to strike, hitting Reese with his nightstick. A slap rang out as Reese's cheek reddened, but he did not flinch. When the guard attempted to strike again, Reese opened his eyes and yanked the nightstick away from him mid-swing. He raised it over his knee and broke it into two pieces, throwing the remains to the floor. When the guard raised his fists and didn't seem to want to surrender, Reese slowly approached him, taking whatever punch the guard threw at him without care. Once he was close enough, Reese ran behind the man and grabbed him, hoisting him several feet into the air. He gave him a crushing bear hug, the crunching of the man's ribs echoing through the prison. He screamed in pain, but Reese didn't seem to be done. "Up you go!" he said.

"No, no, no!" yelled the guard.

Reese did not listen, as he pulled the man over his head and leaned back, slamming him down into the floor. The suplex move left the guard groaning and moaning on the ground.

Reese made his way to where they kept the prisoners' equipment. He did not meet much opposition on the way there, as most of the other prisoners had darted straight to the exit, attracting the attention there. He found himself in a fairly large storage room, but thanks to a sheet left unattended on a wall nearby, was able to locate the bin that carried his things with ease. He smiled when he saw the shotgun, axe, and belt with the small teleportation device and his vials of rage serum, as well his clothing: the jeans, sneakers, shirt, and even the brown loincloth he wore over his pants. It had all been left untouched.

He found Eva in her new van just outside the prison gates. The guards by the gates all lay motionless on the ground, one or two darts in their necks. Her feet rested on the dashboard, and when she saw him, she raised her glasses above her eyes. As chaos erupted around them, Reese patiently walked towards Eva.

"Woah," he said when he was close enough for her to hear him. "What is this?"

Eva got out of the van and rubbed the shining white hood. "Amber had it made for me."

Reese laughed. "I love it."

Eva smiled and wrapped her arms around his neck. They shared a brief kiss, then decided they could not stay any longer, and departed with haste.

"I missed you, baby," Eva lovingly said.

"I missed you too." He sighed. "I'm sorry for what I did to you. I hope you can forgive me."

"Shhh." She quickly stopped Reese before he could continue further. "You don't need my forgiveness because that wasn't you that attacked me. It's the Syndicate that owes me an apology."

"You're sure it's them?"

Eva nodded. "Yeah, they hired someone to do the dirty work for them."

A hearty laugh from Reese. "Classic Gareth, always the pussy." After a long silence, he inquired about his son and his raven.

"Hex they put in a shelter," she stated. "Amber went to get him, while Ire they put in protective custody."

"Whose custody?" Reese asked.

Eva raised an eyebrow. "Take a wild guess."

■ ■ ■

"You want me to willingly hand over my child to you 'Guardians' while you go out to war?" Mary asked. She was clad in her lab coat, glasses, and damning stare, per usual. The three of them were in Mary's new home in White Heart, a generous donation from Amber herself.

"Essentially, yes," said Brutus, in a manner suggesting he was without social tact.

Xela shook her head. "He doesn't mean that Mrs. Black," she said.

"Don't you ever call me Mrs. Black again," Mary sternly said. "I am never to be associated with such a man. That's Dr. Mary to you."

"That man is the most dangerous and powerful weapon we have," Xela argued. "He could bring ruin to our enemies, but he could also bring ruin to us if we're not careful. Ire knows how to calm him down better than anyone else does."

"I couldn't care less your petty war. My son is more important to me." Dr. Mary scoffed and showed them her back. "Out of the question."

Xela made a noise that sounded closest to a growl. "If we lose this war, our city will be gone, and you will have no one to protect you."

"I could always bring Ire back to his true home, far from here."

Xela was beginning to grow vexed. "Like it or not, Doc, this is not a war you can avoid. If White Heart falls, the world loses its greatest sanctuary. No one will truly be safe, no matter what you wish to believe."

Mary took a moment to ponder this, then turned around, willing to negotiate a compromise. "Perhaps I will let him go, but on one condition: I go as well."

Brutus looked at Xela, and she stared back at him. "This will be very dangerous," he began. "We won't stop you from going, and we won't force Ire to come either, of course, but we'll do what it takes to get your permission."

"I used to work as a medic on the field. I had to be ready to respond at a moment's notice, and if I was a second late, which of course I never was, someone might have died because I didn't reach them in time," Mary said. "It's what I was trained to do. Now, it's been a long time since I've done that, but maybe it's time I find a job again."

She went off into another room and came back with her strange arm gadgets. They wrapped themselves around her wrists, and she cocked them in preparation.

Brutus nodded. "Thank you. We would be glad to receive your help."

"Where is Ire?" Xela inquired her.

"He's in his room," his mother responded, pointing to a door nearby.

There Xela found him, staring out his window with a smile.

"Hello, Ms. Zamora," he said, without looking up from the window. "What brings you here today?"

Xela approached him, placing a delicate hand on his back. "How would you like to see your father again?"

Ire turned to her with a bright smile, a childlike look of innocence. "I would like that very much."

CHAPTER 17:

"We are here," Brutus clarified. He pointed to an area on the holographic map in the middle of a forest with no particular landmarks to distinguish it. "White Heart is here, and Xela's Order is here." He pointed to two more points, both somewhat close to the first. "The Order is closer. They're willing to join us, of course, but getting them all here would be tricky. If they stay where they are and help us from there, the war council would have them arrested in an instant. For all we know, the council might already have its hands on them." He tightened his lips, considering their options.

"So we're planning a rescue mission?" asked the lieutenant. The notion had certainly crossed Brutus' mind, but he didn't want to say it aloud.

He sighed. "I wish we didn't have to use the word 'rescue.' This is still White Heart we're talking about. We may be in conflict, but they're far from our real enemies."

Upon the sight of a hound entering their tent, Brutus' eyes lingered away from the map, and he crouched on one knee as Charlie approached him. The hound wagged his tail in a gay and playful manner and frolicked towards him. Brutus stroked the dog's fur, and momentarily forgot the stress of his job. After a moment, Amber entered the tent as well.

"What's the story?" he asked her, picking himself up.

"Reese and Eva should be here within the hour. We're going to need Xela's Order here by tomorrow," Amber explained.

Brutus gave a hearty sigh, glancing over at his lieutenant. "We'll do our best to make it happen."

Amber nodded, patting Brutus' shoulder. "Good. I've got a lot of trust riding on you, love." With that, she left them to their work, and Charlie followed close behind.

"Now, where were we?" Brutus said, turning back to the map.

. . .

"Halt!" one of the guards on duty yelled. He and his comrade next to him crossed their spears, blocking their way.

"Oh come on," Eva grumbled. "You know exactly who we are. Do I have to bring Amber?"

Both guards frowned, but reluctantly let them through. The van passed them and slowly entered the newly formed camp. All the while, the guards seemed to be giving Reese the evil eye.

"I should expect them to hate me," he said. "I must look like a walking nightmare to them. For the first time in my life, I'm hating the attention I'm getting."

Eva shook her head, scoffing. "Don't put yourself down. The Syndicate is at fault for this. You know that more than anyone."

Reese didn't seem to agree. "It's my fault. My addiction brought this."

As the van drove slowly through the camp, he received more stares from passersby who recognized him. Now he noticed that they were not the same stares as those the bartender had given him the day he met Amber Leavett; it was not fear they felt, but anger.

"Please don't let this put you down," Eva said, frowning at the sight of a saddened, slumped Reese next to her. "You'll have plenty of chances to prove yourself." The man she loved said nothing, only sighed loudly.

Familiar faces finally found themselves in front of the van: Charlie, Xela, and Amber, with a large tent looming behind them.

"Great to see you all," Reese said, leaving the van, but the words left his mouth as he uneasily looked around, glancing at the civilians and soldiers and giving a pessimistic guess as to what they thought of him.

"We're very happy to have you back." Amber's smile, upon seeing his worry, soon left her. "Is there something troubling you?"

"Amber, I'm glad you've freed me, but I feel like a stranger here."

"What do you mean?" asked Xela.

"Maybe it's for the best if I don't fight with you guys. I'm a Guardian, and as a Guardian, it's my duty to be on the front lines; I get it. But would our people really want to fight with someone who just went apeshit on his own city?"

Amber put a hand on his shoulder, and she put back on a reassuring smile. "I'm sure you had the time while you were locked up to teach yourself to control your anger to some extent. If you think you can't handle it, then sit back and watch us fight from the sidelines. But if you think you can handle yourself, prove to these people that you're not a monster. Make a change." As she withdrew her hand, she retreated into the tent behind her. "Stay here for one moment."

When she came back, she was sporting a hefty glove with a familiar black bird perched on it. When the raven saw Reese, he darted onto his shoulder. In an oddly loving manner, Hex closed his eyes and softly rubbed his metal beak against Reese's neck. Reese smiled, stroking Hex's sleek feathers. It was a touching moment for the other Guardians to see the two partners reunited, and it made the rest of them smile as well.

Amber led Reese to his tent, where Ire lay napping on a sofa. Reese took a moment to stare at his resting son with loving eyes, then fetched a blanket and carefully covered the boy with it.

Amber let them be, allowing them privacy, and Reese and Eva found the bedroom they decided they would share. She set her backpack on the ground and placed her aviators on the bedside stand. Reese led Hex to the door, and the large bird promptly flew away, perhaps to scavenge the rest of the camp.

"I've been meaning to ask you something," she said.

Reese turned to face her. "Ask away."

She sighed, taking time to decide how she wanted to pop the question. "Are you sure you want to do this?"

"What are you talking about?" he said.

"We're getting ourselves caught up in the middle of a war. When I decided to become a Guardian, this wasn't exactly what I had in mind. I mean, war is nothing I was ever prepared for."

Reese seated himself next to her. "Then what did you have in mind?"

Eva shrugged. "I'm not entirely sure."

"Well, you said it yourself: we're here for each other now, and we've gotta help each other no matter what," assured Reese. "Through thick and thin." He reached a hand out to her cheek to lightly caress her, and she responded by taking it in her own hand. "How many reasons would you need to fight with the Guardians? We've done a lot for each other, after all."

"I guess you're right," she admitted.

"Of course I am, I'm always right," he joked, and after a laugh or two received a roll of Eva's eyes.

When a silence clouded the room, he leaned in slowly to kiss her, his hand still on her red cheeks. They closed their eyes and let their soft lips meet. He moved closer to her, she reached for him, and they fell down upon the bed together. A slight moan involuntarily escaped Eva as Reese's mouth moved lower down her body. She was quivering as she waited for him to make a move, but instead, Reese took a pause.

"Hold on," he said.

"What is it?"

Reese shook his head. "This isn't going to be like the relationships you've had before, right?"

"You mean back when I was a prostitute?" she asked, suppressing a snicker.

"I mean, I didn't want to say it myself, but..."

Eva laughed mockingly. "You're really stupid sometimes, you know that?" She straightened herself up, then hugged his chest tightly. "Look, Reese. I love you. I mean it. I love you with all of my heart."

Reese was stunned at first, nothing able to escape his mouth, but after a moment of collecting his thoughts, he embraced her and replied with the words: "I love you, too."

She grinned sweetly. "With all of your heart?"

"With all of my heart," Reese responded, grinning back.

When he sat up, she mounted herself on top of him, removing her off-the-shoulder shirt. Her movements were slow, but meaningful.

Wishing to contribute, he pulled her head towards his. He nibbled cautiously on her lips, and after he deemed that he had done that long enough, took off his shirt, tossing it carelessly to the other side of the bed.

"Hey," began Reese, "I love you."

Eva smiled and laughed cheerfully. "You already said that, dummy."

"I'm used to saying 'I hate you,'" he explained. "But 'I love you' also has a nice ring to it. I should use it more often."

She was now grinning so hard her cheeks hurt. "I'm honored to be one of the few to see the adorable side of Reese Black."

"Mum's the word," jested Reese, before their lips reunited once more.

■ ■ ■

The mature war council member coughed as he prepared his argument. Soon, the spotlight would be on him, and when it was, he needed to make sure he had their undivided attention. He fixed his already combed hair, black streaked with red, adjusted his glasses, and opened his mouth to begin.

"Ladies and gentlemen of the council, my comrades, my name is Marcus Crudelis. To summarize what has happened in the past few days, Tyreesius Black, the Guardian and convicted criminal has escaped from prison. Search crews have been sent out to find him within the city walls, but if he has already escaped White Heart, we certainly have an issue on our hands.

"I stand here to propose we expand our search. Our radio systems are offline at the moment due to some...technical difficulties, so we have no access to General Leavett and her army, which currently marches to siege on the Syndicate. An odd, convenient coincidence that Reese escapes just a few days before Amber leaves White Heart. An odd coincidence, indeed, and therefore I say we put our efforts together to find Amber's army. They can't have gotten far yet. It is more than likely that they helped Reese get to them, and even worse, helped him escape. It is clear that Amber cannot fight without this unhinged loose cannon, and yet she leads our front lines. Is it safe to say that Amber Leavett, the face of our soldiers, is a questionable role model? Perhaps it is time we find a new face."

With this, he left his case open to discussion within the council. The views of the party seemed to be mixed; some agreed wholeheartedly with Marcus, while others argued that Amber was still fit to command the army and that halting their approach on the Syndicate held too much risk. A vote was held, as matters have always been decided. Marcus gave an evil eye and a grimace to those who voted to leave Amber's army alone, but in the end, Marcus' argument prevailed. He now knew how capable he was of consuming the minds of others, but the sight of those that had escaped his influence angered him.

■ ■ ■

"The courageous people who have offered to take on this responsibility have made a decision that should be met with the utmost respect," Boss Gareth began. "They have decided to do what few in this world are able to do: to die with true pride. A White Heart army marches as we speak, intending to exterminate the people of this great city. I do not wish for a war to last years, decades, or possibly even centuries with no certain outcome. The time to end this is now. Therefore, I have made the decision to abandon our city as a trade for the survival of our people."

He looked up, finding his subordinates still heeding attention. "All of the citizens will leave the city, save the hundred who have volunteered to stay. Please understand that I do this with the best intentions. It is a very difficult decision even for me, but it is with a heavy heart that I say that it is what must be done. It's a tactic White Heart could never possibly expect. The volunteers who stay shall be known as The Hundred Lambs, from now on and here forth."

"Very well," one of the men amongst the group he was speaking to commented. "Where will we go once we take our leave? Would we ever come back here?"

"It is all planned out," Gareth assured. "We have already set up an encampment much closer to White Heart. Once their army leaves, we will launch a full-scale attack on their sanctuary. While there may be only some of their army to keep us at bay in our home city, we will be taking near our entire army. With this, White Heart will fall without effort, and even if our city falls, the forces there will not have the resources to keep control. Therefore, they will be faced with the option of staying there and being open to attack from us, or coming back to retake their city, which will be quite the arduous process for them, as you can imagine. At this point, we will crush the Guardians."

Gareth walked to a window and peered out of it, spying the colossal display hanging from a towering skyscraper outside. A faint, proud smile found him when he read the words on it: "The Hundred Lambs," followed by the many names of brave martyrs. "Yes, this victory is most certainly ours," he added quietly.

Still, he couldn't shake the queerest feeling of dread about him.

...

Flap, flap, flap.

The butterfly's wings were as red as her hair. It disappeared from view when it passed over Alyssa, but she soon felt it perch on her head. She didn't dare move, sitting frozen for quite some time. When it seemed to her as if the beautiful creature had made a nest in her hair, she slowly reached for the book on the porch chair adjacent to her.

"Hey, Alyssa!" a deep voice called.

When Alyssa turned, she knocked over the book and cringed at the ruckus it made. She sighed sadly as she watched the wondrous crimson creature flee from her, and her eyes didn't shift until the butterfly disappeared from her sight.

"What is it?" she asked in a dull voice, her eyes finding Reese and Hex before the porch.

"Have you seen Eva and Ire around?"

Alyssa shook her head. "I thought they were with you."

"When I woke up this morning, they weren't in my tent," Reese said.

"Sorry, I don't know where they could be," she responded with a shrug. "Maybe she took Ire out somewhere."

"Thanks anyways." With that, the man and raven left, leaving Alyssa alone to tend to her book.

She had been reading for quite some time, having found herself enthralled by the various other relics apparently scattered throughout Senia. She certainly did not notice Amber emerging from her tent, but when approached by her, Alyssa set her book down.

"Good morning," she greeted.

Amber rubbed her eyes, yawned, and glanced at her watch. "Looks like I slept in a little late."

"Mhmm," responded Alyssa, hugging her book. She followed Amber on a brief stroll to the main tent, where they found Brutus once again doing his job as a tactician. Amber slowly walked her way towards him and stood behind him and the holographic map he sulked over, putting a hand on his shoulder.

"Please don't tell me you've been up all night staring at this," she said.

"So what if I have?" was the defensive response she received. "I have a duty to do. You know that better than anyone else; you're the one that gave it to me."

Amber sighed. "You know the well-being of my people concerns me most. Relax, Brutus. Please."

The tactician considered it for a moment. He took one final glance at the holographic map before he turned it off, the blue hue of the projection dimming before disappearing completely. Brutus trudged away and plopped onto the bed in the next room.

Alyssa chuckled at the sight, but Amber, turning to the girl, didn't seem amused. "He's working hard, I'm glad for that."

"Maybe a bit too hard," remarked Alyssa.

"C'mon," said Amber, in an attempt to get them out of there. "Let's go find the others."

■ ■ ■

"I so wish this place had a bar," commented Reese. He passed a frozen bottle of beer to Eva, who promptly refused it. He was responsible enough not to offer a bottle to Ire, but did permit a sip or two from his own.

"We wanted to go on a little hike around the forests in the area," Eva explained. "I didn't want to wake you up, so I didn't suggest it."

"All good." He set down his beer and clapped his hands together. "Where are we going today?"

"I'm not sure," Eva said. "This is a really beautiful area. So scenic."

Ire sighed. "A shame war renders us blind to such splendors."

They left the van on a short cliffside overlooking the encampment and made their way into the forest. They didn't get far when they reached an incredibly large clearing about a mile wide, completely surrounded by barren, looming trees.

A bad omen struck Eva then, out of the black, and her heart grew heavy. She set her backpack aside to handle her rifle in her arms. Crouching low, she focused her aim on the other side of the clearing. Even with a scope, it wasn't clear to her exactly what she was seeing.

"What is it?" Reese asked.

"Shit..." she muttered, once the large, black objects came into view. Humanoid figures followed closely behind.

"What is it?" asked Reese, repeating his son's words.

"We need to go warn Amber now."

They didn't have to ask again; the tanks, trucks, and soldiers became visible as they marched into the clearing. They numbered in the hundreds at least, a stampede in the distance wearing painfully familiar outfits, and even the vehicles were branded with the telltale mark of crossed swords. It was instantly clear how big of a threat the approaching Syndicate army posed.

CHAPTER 18:

"How much time do you estimate we have?" Amber asked, cogitating her options. Her tone may have seemed calm to the allies around her, but she was doing her best not to panic inside.

"If we're lucky, a little more than fifteen minutes," replied Eva.

"Set up a few mortars and turrets by the border of the camp, across from where the tanks approach," commanded Amber. Brutus nodded and set to the task, leaving the tent and parting from the other Guardians. "How many tanks did you say there were?"

"I noticed about five," said Eva.

"Very well," Amber said. She turned to the rest of the Guardians. "I have an idea, but it'll involve us splitting up. I'll need to go with Charlie." They all nodded. "The rest of you must stay here and defend our encampment in the worst-case scenario that the first line of defense fails." She clapped her hands together loudly. "Let's get down to business."

The other Guardians drew their weapons and hurried away from the tent the fray, but Amber and Charlie split from them as intended. She searched for the ammo supply tent, and the hound followed close behind. Once she entered it, she pried open a special case, grinning at the stockpile of explosives she found inside.

Turning to Charlie, she told him: "It's your time to shine." He grinned back with a toothy pant.

■ ■ ■

"Fire!"

From the blaring command, mortars in a neat row sounded off one by one. Explosive shells soared into the air, only to fall back down on the clearing before them, but in retaliation, some of the tanks fired back. Most of the rounds soared between the thin trees, but an explosion rocked a larger tree at its base, toppling it over. Shrieks and screams were audible as the tree began to fall upon the squads of soldiers manning the mortars, yet it never touched them.

His veins were bulging and red, and the serum flowing through them was quite noticeable. Hex had gripped in his talons a White Heart soldier by her shirt and pulled her out of the way of harm, and the giant fallen tree was now on Tyreesius' shoulders. His body ached with tremendous stress, but with his incredible endurance, the Guardian found the strength to push back. His knees buckled as he ran forward, picking up speed while aiming for his target. Finally, he tossed the tree back at them, and it soared through the air, a terrifying sight to the Syndicate soldiers on the ground below, before landing on a tank, squashing it into an unrecognizable wreck.

Meanwhile, a familiar vehicle burst into the clearing. One tank diverted its attention, picking Eva's van as its new target, and its gun fired, an explosion rocking the van.

And yet, when the smoke dissipated, they were still alive, and the van was in still in one piece. Eva silently thanked Amber, realizing that the armor was as durable as the general promised it was.

She pressed on, plowing through the crowd of Syndicate soldiers. Eva didn't wish to say it aloud, but she was grateful that the soldiers leaped from her path; she wasn't ready to soil her hands just yet.

As she pulled behind a tank not focusing its attention on them, Brutus opened the back of the van and crawled onto the top of the vehicle. With a running start, the tactician leaped onto the massive tank as Eva drove by it. He opened the entrance hatch and tossed a fragmentation grenade to the soldiers manning the tank, then, making haste, leaped back to the van, which was speeding just ahead now. Bullets hit his shoulders and arms, however, and he clenched mid-jump, losing his balance and footing. He landed painfully in the back of the open van and slowly began slipping away.

Just as his boot touched the moving ground below him, he felt a force push against him. He turned to find Charlie nudging the back of his thighs with his head, doing his best to keep Brutus from falling out the back of Eva's van. His canine body seemed to be growing tired from the pushing and running, but he persisted until Brutus was finally able to pull himself to safety and close the back doors. The tactician was ready to collapse, but did his best to steady himself; the battle had only just begun.

Once he had seen that Brutus had safely made it back into the van and Eva was steering away from the fight, Charlie focused his attention on Amber. His sheer speed made him quite the difficult target for the approaching Syndicate soldiers, and he was able to locate Amber waiting behind the cover of a treeline for him. The hound darted ahead, pressing on, as Amber ran parallel to him at the border of the clearing and the dark forest.

When the hound ran close enough, Amber pulled an explosive mine, prepping it before throwing. She hurled it as an athlete might toss a discus, and Charlie leaped forwards and caught the device in his sharp teeth. He immediately set out for the nearest tank, and despite the enemy soldiers in every direction around him, Charlie pressed on. When he found one of the massive machines, he took a daring leap and slid under it. Charlie released the now saliva-covered explosive, and when he emerged from under the enormous vehicle, hurried away and let loose a massive bark.

Two Syndicate soldiers followed Amber into the deep woods after she had thrown the explosive to the hound. An intense chase ensued, the soldiers running after the White Heart general with their weapons out. Somehow, they lost her, and their pace began to slow when they realized they could not see the Guardian any longer. An eerie silence befell the two as their eyes scanned the trees packed around them. When finding the woman in blue came to no avail, they grew more frantic.

Meanwhile, an Amber hiding behind a thick tree clicked her shoes together, counting down quietly as she readied herself to strike. When she was ready, she leaped high into the air with the assistance of the rockets on her shoes and came back down upon the duo, the blades on her heels slicing through one soldier and the force of the impact causing the other to stumble backward. The remaining soldier grabbed for a gun, but Amber approached him with a spinning kick that knocked the weapon from his hands. He hastily picked himself up and ran off further into the misty woods. Amber watched him flee and pitied him, deciding not to give chase.

It was then that Charlie's fearsome bark pierced the sounds of gunfire and rumbling vehicles: Amber's signal. She took out her holo-tablet, finding a few buttons on a screen in front of her, and by pressing one, as if on cue, a great explosion detonated behind her. A tank in the clearing became a wreckage in flames.

"Another one bites the dust," she muttered under her breath.

■ ■ ■

The field medic let her boots carry her through combat, dodging bullets with the most impossible luck.

She witnessed a squadron of White Heart soldiers under fire ahead and ran to them with all her might. She slid on the dirt to reach them, readying a capsule in her pocket before tossing it skywards. It buzzed and droned, then stopped itself, airborne yet, opening itself up. A ray of green light dawned on the soldiers, with Dr. Mary watching as her contraption healed and eased their wounds. One soldier to the right took a beam strike to her shoulder, and she would have been crippled, but the doctor's healing brought her aid in her time of need, and she was utilizing her arm again in no time.

Moving on to others that needed assistance, Mary withdrew from the front lines and provided support from cover. Any moment she witnessed an ally take bullet or blade, she aimed the blaster hugging her wrist and fired a dart towards them, and it was as if they had never been stricken in the first place.

As she moved forwards with the White Heart army, joining the wave pushing away the Syndicate troops, she came across a White Heart soldier sprawled onto the ground, hacking blood and moaning in agony. "H-help me," she struggled to say, her voice quaking in pain.

The doctor threw another healing contraption into the air, providing herself cover and keeping the soldier alive.

"I'm going to die here, aren't I?" she asked the medic tending to her.

"Quit being such a baby," groaned Dr. Mary.

"W-what?"

"Are you a hero?" she asked her patient, as she prepped a ridiculously large syringe that would have been right at home in a cartoon depiction of booster shots.

"That's an awfully big needle, ma'am," the soldier commented with a gulp.

"Are you a hero?" Dr. Mary repeated, slower this time, with more emphasis.

"Y-yes," she reluctantly responded, a tad confused. "I'm a hero."

"Good," said Dr. Mary. "Because you know what they say…" Seeing that the soldier's wounds were treated to, she stood above her patient and aimed her syringe directly above her. "…heroes never die."

As the colossal syringe impaled itself in the soldier's arm, she screamed bloody murder, never before feeling pain like this. Mary watched as her serum flowed out of the needle and into the woman below her. Her pleas soon faded, and before long, she was simply panting. She picked herself up, took up her rifle, and like a woman born again, or perhaps risen from the dead, she charged back into battle with a voracious cry. The doctor watched on with pride as her patient broke through her allies' lines and took down Syndicate soldier after Syndicate soldier with impossible accuracy, terrifying speed, and utter fury in her veins.

■ ■ ■

"Charge!"

It wasn't clear who had said it, or whether he or she fought alongside the Syndicate or White Heart. It didn't matter much, as both sides obeyed the call.

Miniscule capsules littered the ground, and smoke hissed and puffed out from them. In a matter of seconds, a thick fog covered the field. Smoke reloaded shells into his launcher, preparing his weapon again, and the two sides clashed in front of him.

A bullet of fire flew through the air, parting the smoke around it. Its targets found themselves engulfed in flames, frantically screaming and running in a panicked manner, no particular direction in mind. More and more orbs of flame soared, as Burnellia and her father appeared from somewhere within the fog.

She ran to a fighting soldier, her leg flying at him like a blade, and he struggled to keep from falling as he stumbled backward. Her father witnessed a woman with a sword then appear behind Burnellia, shoving the smoke away as she shambled toward her target. Blaze flew at the Syndicate woman, the weight of his firm shoulder slamming her away. Flames licked at her, but she ran off before being engulfed in them.

Nearby, a tight group of three Guardians, comprised of a short, mysterious man with a hammer of justice in hand, a young redhead tightly gripping a frozen spear, and a tall woman holding a bloodied scythe, stood with their backs to each other, the three of them in the thick of the battle together, before splitting off to deal with their own threats.

Skullgem's nimble body allowed him to quickly dash from soldier to soldier, striking his opponents with mighty force. Alyssa was right behind him, using shields of ice to block the bullets and blades that dared to strike him. Xela was there too, and with every slash and stab she landed, a shower of blood followed.

Shouts and screams filled the air as women and men took up arms to either protect a military encampment or destroy it. Tents burned down, and the battlefield quickly became a graveyard for tanks. A sense of chaos had been instilled in all of them, and for the longest time, it wasn't clear to any of them who was winning. Both sides seemed to be stuck in a bloody stalemate.

Finally, a wave of helicopters approached the clearing from the direction the Syndicate troops had come. In fear, the White Heart soldiers withdrew, only to find none of the airborne death machines raining lead on them. Their missiles were poised and their guns ready, but none seemed to open fire. They hovered patiently as the remaining Syndicate forces fled. Once they made it back without much opposition, the helicopters turned and flew toward the horizon.

They left an encampment in flames. Although silence blanketed the army, no one needed to point out that it could have been much worse.

"What happened?" asked a confused Alyssa, making her way toward Xela.

"I think they've retreated," Xela responded. "And I think we've won."

■ ■ ■

"It was almost as if they thought we weren't worth the trouble," Reese Black said.

Amber had gathered all the Guardians together to speak with them personally in her own tent. They had all been thrown into confusion about what had happened, and considering how much they treated each other like family, she figured they would be able to make better sense of the situation if they discussed it amongst each other.

Brutus said, "They withdrew very quickly, but I'm not entirely sure why." He was lying on a bed, everything from his left shoulder to the fingers on his left hand covered in bandages. The bullets were ridden from his body quickly due to the help of Mary and Xela, but he would not be able to taste combat again until he had fully recovered and healed.

"It's not like they didn't stand a chance," Alyssa commented.

A silence then loomed over them; though they lost some of their army, they were certainly glad they had not lost more.

"How did they even know that our camp was here?" Xela asked.

"I mean, what if we have a traitor?" questioned Eva.

"Relax," spoke Amber. "Let's not worry about that now. Our troops are still recovering; let's not spark some paranoia. Here, I have something that may get our minds off of it."

She disappeared into another room and reemerged with a heavy blue cooler in her hands. Reese darted to help her when he saw her slightly struggle to carry it. She opened it, and the Guardians crowded around to see what was inside. There were a few bottles of beer, as well as soft beverages, lying in the ice.

"Nice," Eva spoke.

"Help yourselves," said Amber with a grin. "But do not tell anyone else about this. Our only cellar was destroyed during the battle. Consider it a special treat, courtesy of yours truly."

Help themselves they did. Reese eagerly grabbed two bottles of beer, while Alyssa and Ire were the only few to take sodas.

Xela drank a portion of her bottle and left the rest on a coffee table. She left them for a moment, finding a bench outside, in need of a moment to recollect her more personal thoughts, now that they weren't in grave danger.

"Something troubling you?"

She turned to face the voice, surprised to find Brutus. Though he was a Guardian just as Xela was, something about him made him feel more distant than the rest. Plus...

"You should be resting," she told him.

He ignored her. "What's the problem?"

"It's not important." His curiosity and stubbornness seemed to go hand in hand, she realized.

"Is it about Amber?" Brutus asked, joining her on the bench. He had a bit of trouble sitting, careful not to put pressure on his left arm.

Xela turned to him. "How did you know?"

Brutus shrugged. "Lucky guess. Is it that she's pushing you away?"

"That's two in a row," commented Xela. "Seriously, how are you that good?"

Brutus sighed. "It's because I've been in your shoes."

"What?"

"You heard me. I've been in the exact spot you're in. And that look in your eyes, when you gaze at Amber? I see myself in it."

A blushing Xela was a bit stunned to hear this. "How so?"

Brutus leaned back. "Has Amber ever told you that you weren't the first group of Guardians serving White Heart? Granted, you were the most successful so far, but you aren't the original."

"How many have there been before us?" she asked.

"Just one. Amber, Charlie and I are the only remaining survivors."

"I'm...I'm sorry to hear that," she said, offering words of consolation.

"A long time ago," he continued, his usual serious voice about him, "Amber loved a man. A friend of ours. And..."

"He broke her heart?"

"He broke *her*," he corrected. "He broke us apart, too."

The Guardian beside him moved a hand to her own cheek, ever so slowly. "What do you mean?"

"You weren't the first group to come along. Nah, there were the Guardians before you. We were smaller, just Amber, Charlie and I, along with a few others. One of us," a sigh from Brutus, "he took advantage of all our trust, yes, but more Amber's trust. And when the time came, we were betrayed in the worst way possible."

Xela was quiet for some time as she took in his words with a solemn stare. "Fuck," she finally muttered under her breath, in amazement at the tortured pasts her friends had lived. "I'm sorry, I just...didn't know."

"No, it's okay. Listen, I trust you, Xela. But please be careful with Amber. She's... a special case."

Xela nodded. "I'll be careful."

"No no no." He shook his head. "She really is special."

Xela thought for a moment before she inquired. "What are you talking about?"

"Amber isn't like you and me. She doesn't understand some things like we do, but she understands other things we don't. Sometimes she lives on a whole different plane from us."

"I'm not sure I follow..."

Brutus shook his head. "I really shouldn't have told you this. But I think it's important you hear it. The point is that Amber is fragile sometimes, and I just don't want you to be treading on thin ice."

Xela stared him down. "Do you want me to back off?"

"No, you should just be careful," Brutus stated. "In fact, I think she may have taken a bit of a liking to you."

"Really?" she asked, although in truth, she wasn't surprised to hear it. She took this in quietly, swearing she could see out of the corner of her eye a sliver of a smile coming from Brutus. A fraction of intimidation prohibited her from looking at him again, and so she mulled over her thoughts with his looming protectiveness for the general in mind. "I'll be as careful as I possibly can be, Brutus. Thank you." She did not glance at him as she turned and welcomed the lights of the bustling tent again.

"Don't mention it," he said nonchalantly. "Seriously, you'd do good not telling people about this conversation. I've got a reputation to maintain."

Xela was already gone, however.

■ ■ ■

She found her sitting on a chair, watching the conversing Guardians in front of her. "Amber!"

A smile from the general. "Yes, Xela?"

"May I have a word with you?"

Disappeared the smile. "Of course. I hope it's nothing too serious."

When Amber remained sitting, not taking the cue, Xela added, "In private, please."

"Oh," escaped Amber. "What's wrong with out here?" Her eyes glanced at the rest of the Guardians.

A beseeching frown followed. "Please?"

Amber sighed the quietest of sighs as she rose and allowed Xela to lead her into her own bedroom. When they entered, Xela paced as she gathered her thoughts.

"Xela, I'm not so sure we should..."

"Wait," she interrupted. "Please, I just want to say one thing." She turned, approached the general, and stared into her eyes, losing herself in their beautiful hazel hue.

"Just one thing?"

"Nothing more, I promise."

"Well?" Amber swallowed a deep breath. "What is it?"

"Now I know you've been hurt before," started Xela. "Now I know you've trusted people in the past

319

and they've let you down, I just didn't know that before."

"Xela..."

"I would have never pushed as hard as I did if I knew about what happened to you, and..."

"Xela, please." Amber's voice was growing guilt-ridden.

"And anyway, we're in the middle of a war. I should have known better than to let feelings get in the way."

As soon as she stopped talking, Amber dashed towards her, grabbing her hands and pulling her close in a sudden movement. Xela's petite, pretty mouth sat slightly ajar, and Amber couldn't get her stare off of it.

"I want to feel again," Amber began, still retaining her closeness to Xela's body. "No, I need to feel again. I'm sorry, Xela. I know I've been sending confusing signals, I know, but..." Her gaze shifted towards her anxious, tapping heels. "It's hard for me. I don't know what I want sometimes, and that frustrates me."

"Then maybe it's for the best that I give you some space," said Xela, moving away ever so slightly.

"No." Amber pulled her back. She abandoned holding Xela's hands in place for hugging her thin body. "Show me what I want."

"Show...you?"

Energetic nodding from Amber. "Show me," she repeated, shifting her gaze into Xela's eyes.

Xela slowly moved her arms, wrapping them around Amber's neck. The two Guardians were frozen for the longest moment, watching each other, studying the face of the other. Finally, Xela inched her head ever closer. Amber closed her eyes as the other woman approached. She ran her nails down Amber's body, slowly, carefully, shyly, but with only pure emotion. When their heads were nearly touching, she followed Amber and shut her eyes, too.

Xela neared Amber's lips, but there was no kiss. She hovered there, unwavering, not in tease but in hesitation. Her mind was astorm as she decided her next move, but Amber's sudden movement made that decision for her: the general pushed forward, and black met pale as their lips pressed together.

Then they moved in symmetry, a ritual of dance, and their hands soon joined along. Xela first, then Amber, using her body to understand her partner's.

Xela was thin, she realized, she felt even thinner than she looked. Amber held onto her arms, pale in complexion and scrawny enough to wrap her whole hand around, save for at her able biceps. Yet she was fascinated with her so, and her love grew stronger as she realized she was touching the prettiest person she had ever met.

Amber was shorter than she was, even in her tall heels, and Xela tried not to smile and blush at how hard her partner was trying to reach her. She knew she was a fit lady, but now that she was feeling her body, she realized Amber was more muscular than she imagined. Xela's hands went all the way down the other Guardian's sides, and stopped at her strong hips, settling on them as a resting place.

Then they parted for a brief moment, to be able to look again at each other. Both wore stupefied but desirous expressions, both stunned at the beauty of one another.

"Are you...comfortable?" asked Xela, quiet and shaky. It was the most nervous Amber had ever heard her.

She returned with the sweetest smile on Senia, and an awkward, love-filled nod. "I couldn't be happier."

"Do you want to continue, then?"

Another nod, this one even more energetic. "Yes, please."

A sense of glee found Amber, an unfamiliar glee of love. Her mind should have been in a flurry, her thoughts thrown about in disorder, but she stayed strangely calm. The only thoughts she focused on were the ones revolving around Xela: how she was just now noticing how beautifully her hair shimmered, how the touch of her cold hand and her soft movements aroused her, what her next move was going to be.

Amber carefully set the taller woman down upon the bed. Her knee slowly slid between her thighs, and it was Xela's turn to give a moan, but their lips never parted for long, as if they both feared what would happen if they did. Xela curled her leg upwards, and nails decorated in black dug lightly into the other woman's back.

"Hey, Amber!" a deep voice called. Reese walked into the room, his eyes tilted downwards. "You sure you ain't got any more beer? I'm *so* close to getting this really nice buzz." When he looked up, he found the sight of the two women in bed, Amber on top of Xela. Reese's blushing, aghast countenance read only shock. He turned silently, tossing one of his discs behind him. In a flash, he teleported back into the living room.

"Oh my," Amber said, her face red as well. "Tha-that's embarrassing."

"Should we go stop him?" Xela suggested, starting to get off of the bed. "I mean, the man's drunk, who knows what he'll say?"

"No no!" Amber said, a little louder than she expected. She shoved Xela back down onto the bed in a playful manner and gave her a sweet smile. "I'm pretty sure we just shocked him sober, anyway."

Xela giggled lovingly, and they continued.

It could have been a second, a minute or an hour later, but eventually, they relaxed and ducked under the covers of the blankets. Amber was curled up at Xela's breast, hugging her flat chest. When Xela peeked at her, Amber's eyes seemed to have already closed.

Xela found herself grinning, unsure as to why. It must have been the light breaths that Amber blew upon her as she brought herself to rest, or perhaps it was the way Amber seemed to smile in her sleep. Whatever the case, Xela was quite blissful at the moment, and she knew from then on that it was a memory she would treasure forever.

CHAPTER 19:

"These so-called 'Guardians' are a pox!" The slam of Marcus' fist against the table was an earthquake to the coffee mug of the man next to him. "They leave us in shambles by breaking free the most dangerous man on Senia, and yet you still protect him?"

The bald, older man raced to save his coffee from a hazardous spill. "With all due respect, sir, I only said that if they were to return from their current journey successfully, we shouldn't condemn them. Getting rid of the Syndicate is an exceptionally arduous and heroic task. Say they complete this, I think we should get past that they freed Reese Black. It's a chance for him and his comrades to prove themselves."

Marcus scoffed. "Are you hearing yourself? Forgiving our enemies? Forgiving traitors to this glorious city?"

The other man was beginning to grow nervous. "Since when were the Guardians our enemy? They still have the best intentions for White Heart. It was us that sent them out, no?"

Marcus shook his head. "I didn't want it to come to this, Mr. Brooks...that is your name, yes?"

"If I remember correctly, we are allowed full anonymity in the war council, and I was availing myself of this right."

"Alright, Mr. Brooks," Marcus continued. "You are weighing down this important meeting...nay, you are weighing down this entire council, dare I say all of White Heart itself. I say we take it to a vote. All in favor of exiling Mr. Brooks from White Heart's war council, please raise your hand." He raised his own. A flash of purple in his eyes, from behind his bulky glasses, so brief that it could have been missed in a blink. The bald man next to him felt confusion turn to fear as he questioned whether he saw the flash at all. He snapped out of his thoughts when he noticed the room was filled with raised hands. "Then it is settled!" exclaimed Marcus.

The man scoffed. "You must be joking. This isn't some childish treehouse club you're talking about here. You're taking advantage of every conflict this city will have. You can't just—"

He was interrupted when two guards seized him by his arms. Now angered, the balding man thrashed violently, his foot kicking the table. His mug tipped and fell with a crash, spilling its contents on the table. A puddle of coffee crept to the nearest edge, a waterfall soon to rain upon the protesting man's now vacant chair.

"You can't do this! You can't do this! You can't do this!" It was unclear if his words were actually being repeated or if it was just a persistent echo. Either way, Marcus was glad to see him gone. It only made his job easier.

"That's more like it," he said to himself contently. "Now, where were we?"

■ ■ ■

She awoke still in ecstasy from the previous night, a grin stretched on her face. As she sat up, she noticed Amber leaning on a chair, staring blankly. She seemed stressed, so Xela rose and lovingly embraced her from behind.

"Is there something wrong?" she asked her.

Amber wheeled around. "I'm sorry, I don't mean to bring this onto you. It's just..."

Xela waited for her to continue, but Amber lost herself in her own thoughts again. "It's just what?"

"Xela, Eva was right. There's spies in our very encampment," she began. "I can't believe I haven't seen it sooner."

Xela sat down at the bedside. "It's inevitable," she assured. "We have spies in the Syndicate, too. Such is war."

"How long has this been going on?" asked Amber. "I mean, I've been thinking about it; why would the Syndicate attack a purification plant? Surely there are other ways you can declare war...no, Gareth wanted to see the newly formed Guardians for himself...but how could he have known?"

Xela stood up slowly, placing a gentle hand on Amber's shoulder. "C'mon, Amber. You know this is just you letting it get to your head."

"I just want to be able to trust my own troops. Is that too much to ask for?"

Xela lightly laughed. "I admire you dearly. You're very gentle and very kind-hearted...but like I said, this is war. You can't trust everyone, even within your own ranks. Look, we just woke up. Last night was fun, right?"

The other woman sighed. "Of course."

Xela ran a finger through Amber's dark hair. "Yesterday was a stressful day. Let's just take some time to relax. It's healthy."

Amber gave her a light, understanding nod. She bit her lip. "I suppose you're right."

Xela began to dress herself. "C'mon, let's go find something to eat," sweetly she said.

■ ■ ■

Knock, knock, knock.

The heavy slams of a clumsy fist against deep wood rang out through the house. No response.

Knock, knock, knock. The boxer waited patiently, yet paced a bit back and forth out of anxiousness, his body idly repeating simplified versions of the movements he recalled from the ring. Now a frown was upon him, however, as he was yet to see the face of the one he loved once more.

Knock, knock— "What is it?" asked a moody Brandon as the door abruptly swung open.

"I, uh..." stammered Jack. He blushed, smiled, and stuck his hand out, presenting to the dancer a present. "I brought you flowers."

"Thanks," Brandon said, as he snatched the bouquet away with an agape mouth. "Listen, you should probably go." He could not stand to look in Jack's direction as he said it.

"W-what?"

"You shouldn't be here." The dancer's voice was hoarse, full of grief. It was nothing like how Jack had always heard it before, always bursting at the seams with energy.

The boxer shook his head quickly, nervously. "I don't understand...was I wrong to believe there was something between us?"

Brandon pushed himself to look, look into Jack's sullen eyes, and truly think about what he was looking into. "It's not...it's just..."

He could practically feel the waterworks boiling inside, ready to spill, as here he was, presented with his mistake. "What is it?" asked Jack, when he received no response.

"Please," pleaded Brandon. "I can't do this. Please go, Jack."

The boxer sighed, gulped silently, nodded his head with acceptance. "Okay," he said, turning away from Brandon, parting with slow, somber footsteps, not even his body willing to accept such misfortune.

"It's my fault," Brandon spoke loudly, stopping him in his tracks. "It's all my fault."

Jack slowly turned back around to face him, a sliver of hope now inside him. "What is?"

He exhaled, motioning Jack to draw closer, and the boxer obeyed. "The Hundred Lambs. Ring any bells?"

"Yes, of course," said Jack. "Boss Gareth himself came to me and asked if I wished to join the troops. I told him I'm not ready to die, not ready to give up everything. I thought I was when we went to White Heart, but...it scared me straight, made me realize that my life was still young."

"Who do you think he came to next, when you said no?"

A look of confusion found itself on the boxer, and then aghast disbelief. "You mean to say...? No..."

An unfortunate nod from Brandon. "You may not be able to see it from the facade I put on when I go on the stage, but I don't live the best life. I've felt alone, for most of it, and let me tell you, living a lonely life is not living at all. I jumped at the opportunity to serve my people because the only moments I don't feel alone are the moments I feel a part of something bigger than myself. But then I thought about you, Jack, and the night you gave me...I had never felt so alive, being with you. I wanted to experience life with you, but it was far too late then."

The tears had begun to stream when he started his confession, and now they were showering down uncontrollably. As he sobbed, Jack approached, wishing desperately to comfort him. "Brandon..." he began, his hand reaching for his lover's soft face, pretty and sweet, even when red with sadness. He flinched when Brandon retracted, moving away from him.

"This is all my fault," Brandon repeated, choking on his tears. "Please, please forget about me. Please pretend like we didn't have that night. Please, Jack, for your sake."

The boxer couldn't even react before the door slammed in his face. His heart grew heavy as he heard the dreadful sound of locking, Brandon securing himself to keep Jack away from him, for the boxer's own sake.

"I can't," he faintly whispered, but the dancer was gone.

. . .

Amber and Xela decided to have their breakfast at a spacious tent that had been erected to serve as a dining place and a bar somewhere near the center of the large encampment. Unsurprisingly, they found Reese at the bar, Hex on his shoulder as always, but the other Guardians were elsewhere. They greeted him and sat adjacent.

Many of Xela's Order were there; the extraction went simply and smoothly, all of them brought there in the morning with the technology they needed in the span of a few hours. Xela looked around the room, glad to see so many faces she recognized.

They were almost finished with their meals when a scuffle caught their attention. The conflict seemed to have been growing during the prior few minutes, beginning when a human hurled insults at an Assossian. It looked as if it was going to escalate into a brawl, with the Assossian readying a fist. Before he could throw it, someone else stopped his hand.

Reese had been quick to intervene, sidestepping in front of the man to take the brunt of the hit. He seemed to feel no pain from it, and thusly expressed no anger. Amber and Xela rushed to them to intervene as well.

"What's the problem?" Amber asked, hoping to get an answer from either side.

"The problem is him," the human said. "Him and his filthy brethren. Do you know what the Assossians have done to us?"

Amber nodded. "But this man is not guilty of any of it."

The angered human spit at the Assossian's feet. "He's just like the rest of them! They're all the same!" He was pulled away from the scene by Reese, who picked him up with little effort and brought him outside the tent.

Amber turned to the Assossian man. "What did you do to him?" It was only then that she recognized the grey hair and stern face.

"I have done nothing to him," replied Smoke. "He is simply a hateful man. *Galvoe*. Perhaps I have overestimated your soldiers, General. You claim to fight with good intentions, and yet you let people like him represent your front lines?"

She was a bit shocked at his response, taking it as a grave insult. "We, the Guardians, are the very representation of our army. We are the front lines. People like him are...nothing more than unfortunate inevitabilities."

The Assossian didn't want to hear it, instead opting to continue finding a way to blame her. "I believe keeping your troops in check is part of your job, General Leavett. It would certainly be inappropriate for the leader of our army to be slacking off, would it not?"

Xela noticed the anger in Amber's eyes, and she pulled her back slowly. Amber looked up at her to find Xela shaking her head slowly. *He's not worth it,* Xela attempted to convey. Smoke scoffed and left the tent in a hurry, failing so much as to glance at the crowd staring at him.

■ ■ ■

"Whatcha' doing?"

Skullgem almost dropped the paintbrush from his small hands. As he pulled it away from the wooden sign he had recently erected, the white paint dripped carelessly on the grass and dirt below. Burnellia stood in front of him, leaning with her arms behind her back. He looked around for the small clipboard that he had been recently carrying around with him; Brutus, due to his recent injuries, was not as mobile, and unable to perform as a translator. Skullgem didn't find it on the small boulder next to him where he remembered placing it.

"Looking for something?" Burnellia asked, revealing her hands.

Skullgem was relieved but slightly bothered to find the clipboard hiding behind her back. She handed it to him, and he began writing with a pen:

"Don't scare me like that."

She grinned and laughed. "Alright, alright. I'm just having a little bit of fun with you." Skullgem continued:

"I'm putting up some motivational signs."

Burnellia nodded. Skullgem kneeled back down, the paintbrush back in his hands. She watched closely and intently as he continued writing. After

332

many delicate strokes flew across the sign, he stepped back, admiring the words:

"We have won every battle presented to us. We have triumphed over every obstacle. The time to end this war is now."

"Such a way with words," commented Burnellia. "Well, it was nice talking with you. I'll see you around!"

What a strange girl... Skullgem thought as she skipped off, his mind lost in intrigue.

■ ■ ■

"Report!" commanded Boss Gareth from his seat on the steel throne in the massive encampment. To his right was the Minotaur, who had adorned his bronze armor. His fearsome, massive axe sat idle in his hands. He made no motions, save for a few deep breaths, and stared ahead at nothing, his eyes blank. Approaching Gareth was his right hand, Jade. She made her way in front of the throne to present what she had just learned of the battle.

"Many of our troops have made it back, Boss, but we lost most of our tanks," she reported.

"Probably wouldn't have happened if you hadn't resisted wiping them out."

Reynard emerged from somewhere behind a large pillar, and as his sight was presented before Gareth's eyes, the Minotaur let out a low growl.

"Excuse me?" Gareth said.

"You heard me," Reynard said. "You were so concerned about saving your precious troops that you never stopped to realize that sacrifices must be made."

"Need I remind you of the objective?"

Reynard scoffed. "No, you 'needn't' remind me—"

Gareth interrupted him. "The objective was to give them a victory. We want them to believe that they can win this war. It was *not* to destroy their entire encampment. We aren't capable of taking on a whole army now. Too much is at stake for such a risky attack."

"You had the chance, you imbecile, and you didn't take it," said Reynard. "Who cares what the objective was? You could have destroyed them, but you hesitated. What a leader you are. Boss Gareth, truly as unmatched and powerful as they say!"

Jade drew her weapon, aiming it at Reynard. The concentrated pulse of energy fired with great strength from the cannon on her shield. Reynard easily dodged it, and it made a dent in the column behind him.

"Jade!" Gareth cried.

She didn't hear him. She aimed again, but Reynard drew his electrified whip, and before she could fire, the tip of it smacked against her cheek. Jade cried out in pain, a red mark forming on her face.

"Jade! Enough!"

She reluctantly put her shield away. With that, Reynard pulled the whip back, and it constricted inside its handle.

"Tsk, tsk, tsk," Reynard said, wagging his finger. "Are you that feisty in bed? Perhaps Gareth might be able to answer me that."

Never before had Jade felt anger like she felt now. Gareth, however, put aside the insult and continued on:

"You know nothing of commanding an army, Reynard. I have made sacrifices, or have you forgotten? They await their deaths now in their own city, and they will bravely fight to the bitter end. That is the difference between you and me, Reynard. It pained me to see them this way, but I had the utmost pride in seeing them ready to take on the responsibility. Had you been in my position, you would not have cared, but you would not know what it would be like to be in my position, would you? You have no idea what it means to lead, as you see no difference between a leader and a dictator. Isn't that right, Reynard?"

He leaned forward in his throne, and his fist banged its side, all in one sudden, dramatic movement. Reynard smirked all through the long pause, and eventually, Gareth leaned back into the throne, uttering only: "I thought so."

■ ■ ■

The knocks upon the sturdy wooden door were ominous sounds to the man.

His head jolted up from his work. He looked around, the room dimly lit. It was now dark out, to his surprise.

He got up from his desk and trudged over to his apartment door, his eyes weary. His hand reached for the metal doorknob and gave a twist and a pull. Much to his surprise, he found none other than Marcus Crudelis standing before him.

"Mr. Brooks," he said, a false smile upon him.

"What are you doing here at this hour? How did you find out where I live?" the tired man asked, peeking down the apartment hall. "And that's not my name."

"My mistake," he said, "I was never good with names." The man opening the door waited as a brief silence found them. It was interrupted by Marcus, who took a step forward.

"I didn't say you could come in," said the other man, to which Marcus responded with by quickly shoving him to the floor. The tired man got the wind knocked out of him, and as he desperately tried to get up, Marcus put a dominating foot on his chest. The man struggled to get Marcus off of him, to no avail. After some time, Marcus raised an outstretched hand towards him, his eyes shining a strange shade of purple. "What are you doing?!" exclaimed the man on the ground.

"Stop struggling," Marcus commanded, his eyes twitching, his face beginning to sweat. If anything, it made the man struggle more. Eventually, Marcus sighed and stopped, his eyes returning to normal and his gaze slowly shifting idly to the wall, a gesture of disappointment.

"Please, stop!" A panicked shout arose from below him.

"What is it, Mr. Brooks? How can you resist it?" His foot slowly pushed downwards, squeezing the air out of the poor man. "What makes you so fucking special? Is it perhaps that you have a sense of righteousness instilled in you? A shame, on your part. Had I had more time, I would have kept you as my guinea pig. Unfortunately, time is not on my side."

He reached for something tucked near the back of his pants, slowly pulling out a pistol with a silencer attached to it. "Time may not be on my side, but righteousness is not on yours. This city is not as moral as they say it is, Mr. Brooks. You find yourself standing alone, to your dismay. A dramatic tragedy. 'Tis a shame no one will write about it; I will make sure of it myself that this is where your story ends." Marcus gave a long, ominous sigh.

"Please..." the downed man cried.

"It would have made a nice read," Marcus said, aiming his pistol downward. "Oh well. Goodbye, Mr. Brooks."

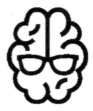

After the ring of the shot had broken the silence, Marcus noticed an unlucky witness stumbling backward behind him, perhaps a next door neighbor choosing to take a jog at the wrong time.

Their gaze met for a split second. The witness ran to his own door, desperately rushing to get it open. Marcus extended an arm, his eyes shining once more. The other man stopped panicking, stopped shaking the doorknob. He slowly moved his head toward Marcus, revealing eyes that glimmered in a dark purple. The kneeling Marcus motioned over to the fresh corpse, blood gurgling like a geyser from a hole in his head.

"Clean this up," he commanded.

The witness shuffled mindlessly to the dead man as Marcus got up and abandoned the scene.

CHAPTER 20:

It was unanimously decided that now was the time to move the encampment another step closer to Avalon, and within a few hours since the decision was made, the incredibly large convoy was almost ready to go. A few tasks were yet to be completed, so the Guardians and their close allies stayed behind to ready any final preparations.

"Here, let me help you with that," Blaze suggested, finding a man struggling with an elephantine box clearly too burdensome for him.

Panting heavily, he set it on the ground. After a few seconds of regaining his strength and leaning on the box for support, he finally responded: "I don't need any help." He picked up the box again, squinting and clenching his teeth. "Especially not from you."

"What was that?" Blaze asked.

Though the man was struggling with the box and spoke quietly, he was almost sure he had heard him correctly; he was simply in shock that such rude words had poured from his mouth.

Now a crowd was beginning to stare. People momentarily set their work aside to watch the arising conflict. The man once again set his box down. "C'mon man, take a hint," he said. "Just fuck off already."

"Do you have a problem with me?" Blaze asked angrily.

The man looked around the people gathering, amazed that Blaze was still speaking with him. "You daft or somethin'? Yeah, I got a problem with you. Maybe if I said it slower, it would go through your thick head. Do I need to do that for you, dumbass?"

"Hey, hey, hey!" The general, who had overheard the argument from nearby, decided it was time to step in. "What's the problem here?"

"The problem is that some people don't know when enough is enough!" the angered human said. "We don't need these red-skinned fuckers, and we never will!"

Amber then recognized him as the man who had scuffled with Smoke the other morning. "What's your name?"

The angry man looked her up and down. "What?"

"You heard me. What is your name?" she repeated, this time in a sterner voice.

"Nah." He shook his head and clenched his lips. "I'm not telling you anything."

"Disobeying a direct order? Harassing your fellow comrades for their differences?" She pointed to the dark woods behind them, on the outskirts of the camp. "Get out of here. Get away from my people. Get out of my army. You are no longer part of it, and you will never be part of it again. You embody every ideal we strive to fight against, and unless you admit your mistakes right here, right now, in front of me, and show me that you truly regret them, then you can find a place for your bigoted views elsewhere, in the lawless Borderlands, where they belong." Some of the rest of the Guardians began to gather behind her, including Charlie, who let out a menacing, low growl.

The man scoffed a few times, speechless, taken aback. He turned once again to the crowd around him, finding some eyes filled with pity, but most others with the prideful cheerfulness one feels when justice is righteously served. Then he fled, disappearing somewhere amidst the remaining tents. A few soldiers followed suspiciously behind him.

"We don't need people like them with us," Amber said out loud. "Alright everyone, back to work."

The crowd did just that, but the thought of what had just occurred floated in their heads. Amber left then, likely to continue overseeing preparations, and the topic of the exiled man eventually dissipated.

Burnellia approached Blaze quizzically just after the conflict. "Father, what was that about?" she asked.

"Nothing, sweetheart," he responded tenderly. "It's just that not everyone is as nice as our friends."

■ ■ ■

The convoy made steady progress as it stormed towards the Syndicate's capital. Sometime after noon of the third day, they took their first break. An overcast sky had plagued them for quite some time, but the first droplets of rain licked at their faces just as they stumbled upon an abandoned fortress. It wasn't very large, unable to supply shelter for their entire army, but it sufficed as a temporary base.

For years and years, it likely had gone without the touch of a human. Some vultures perched themselves atop the weathered stone walls, and

Charlie and Hex found great pleasure in chasing them away together.

Before they knew it, the drizzle had transformed into a moderate storm. They set up their tents quickly, hoping to find shelter before the rain worsened.

Skullgem and Burnellia found themselves darting into a nearby stone tower just outside the fortress' gates. Together, they walked up a spiral staircase and situated themselves on the second floor. Utterly drenched, they had to huddle together on one side, as a flimsy plank had resulted in part of the tower's roof collapsing long ago.

Burnellia peered out the window, her legs tucked behind her arms. Skullgem looked through the small satchel that carried most of his belongings, making a huff stuffed with disappointment when he found his notepad soaking wet.

Burnellia turned at this, immediately understanding his pain. "It's okay," she said with a reassuring smile. "You know, you're much easier to understand than you think you are."

He removed his hood and smiled back, then turned to watch the storm outside. Silence wedged its way between them again, and all they could hear was the *pitter patter* of raindrops and the occasional crack of thunder.

Finally, the young girl broke the quiet: "Do you think all that stuff he said was true? That mean man, I mean. The one that got into the fights with my father and my uncle."

Of course it's not true, Geronimo wished he could say. A simple shake of his head was the best he could give her. It would have to suffice.

"It's just..." she began, but regretted starting the sentence. "Nothing. It's nothing. I'm just letting it get to my head." She scooted closer to Skullgem, retaining her curled-up position.

Sometime later, the rhythmic falling of water upon their world meshed into a sleepy buzz, and Burnellia could not help but take to rest, leaning on the other young Assossian. Skullgem himself was falling asleep as well, but the sound of arguments stirring outside over the droning sound of rain shook him back awake.

Though the weather had not changed, it was slightly darker out, which he noticed when he peered out of the window. Something inside attempted to assure him that it was but a dream playing before his eyes, yet it certainly felt very real.

Keeping his breath still, making as little noise as usual, he witnessed the blood pouring from a guard's neck like a fountain. He gave a long gulp as he saw even more corpses strewn behind the first, soldiers killed not long before the guard.

The knife dripped a crimson trail as its holder made his way to the main gate, his large gang shuffling behind him. The hate strewn on their bloodied, tired faces made them look an army of revenants seeking vengeance. The soldiers posted at the massive wooden gate frantically closed it shut just before they could enter. The hateful gang took cover quickly, as a few soldiers on the gate's wall opened fire with rifles.

One man, hiding behind a bloodied tent, looked up at the tower. For a split second, his stare locked with Skullgem's, and the Assossian ducked as fast as he could.

Unfortunately, it was not fast enough.

Geronimo raced downstairs to bar the door, praying that the old wood would hold. He made his way back upstairs and shook the curled Assossian frantically. It took a moment, but she finally opened her eyes, slightly agitated from her sudden awakening. How she had slept through the expulsion of bullets, he had not a clue.

When Skullgem pointed to the window, Burnellia frantically looked out, fearing what her eyes would show her. A mob gathered in front of them, grim expressions strewn about many faces. At the front of the group was none other than the man who had conflicted with Smoke, repeatedly smashing his side against the tower's only door. Burnellia panicked and jumped away from the window, shuddering in fear for their lives.

"What do we do?" she asked.

Skullgem frantically looked around the tower for another exit, but found none, save for the thin window and the collapsed roof.

He pointed to the roof. It would be dangerous, but it seemed their best option. The other would be to stay and fight the horde, completely outnumbered.

She nodded and gave a long gulp. Skullgem found his way onto the awkward planks creating a makeshift ramp to the top of the tower.

The rainwater didn't help their cause, threatening the two as they climbed up that they might slip and fall down the stairwell below them. Steadily and slowly, Skullgem made it to the top first. He immediately turned to help balance the planks for Burnellia. Now the banging on the door stopped, replaced by the terrifying hacking of wood. It was not long before the hateful leader would burst through the door, his mob silently following behind. A shaking Burnellia was still only halfway up.

With paranoia coursing in her blood, she began climbing faster. Skullgem's hand reached her, but not before the angered humans below them now inside the tower noticed. A man raised a pistol, firing at the fleeing Assossians. Skullgem pulled Burnellia with all his might, but not before a bullet grazed her calves, ripping a small piece of her leggings away and tearing at her skin.

She screamed as she fell into Skullgem's arms, partly because of the pain and partly because they had lost their balance. Skullgem tipped over the railing of the roof, and as Burnellia raced to grab him, she found herself slipping and falling with him.

The tower was not very tall, but the fall, as well as the girl landing on him, knocked the wind out of Skullgem. They could see the soldiers ahead, opening the main gates of the fortress.

With Burnellia's bleeding leg and Skullgem's aching back, the gate to safety felt miles away. Some

346

of the posted guards ran to them and either helped them up or attacked the hateful mob pursuing them.

One of the guards attempting to buy them time succumbed to the charging crowd. He crumbled after being struck by a bullet in the chest, crying out in pain. His screaming, however loud, was still inaudible over the unforgivingly hard rain and thunder, as well as the gunfire from both sides. More guards were on their way, but the Assossians crawling to safety were still vulnerable.

Their hateful leader, charging from the front, saw his chance, just as Burnellia tripped over a rock on the ground. Her cheek grew even redder as it fell onto a wet boulder. A guard tried to help her up, but took a knife to the neck from the leader and tumbled backward. As Burnellia struggled, he pulled at her neck, launching her up. She now stood with a beast holding a bloodied knife to her throat.

Skullgem turned towards the gruesome sight. With a heartrending gulp, he swallowed the water pouring onto his lips. It could have been rain, tears, sweat, or perhaps even likelier, a salty and bitter combination of all three. He felt his hands clap together, almost in prayer, and he wanted desperately to beg for mercy, for an end to the violence. Unable to speak the words in his mind, he instead cried out loudly. A guard continued to drag him away, and he was unable to walk for himself or struggle against the help to save the Assossian girl, but the farther Skullgem got from Burnellia, the louder he wailed.

The girl's face read a fear she had never felt before. She gulped, the lump in her throat caressing the steel of the blade at her neck on the way down. She could feel the man breathing heavily behind her, as an angry bull might. All around her, the other hateful mob members gathered, jeering and shouting until they were but a droning noise of anger.

The White Heart guards behind them had weapons raised, but they refused to fire, afraid they might hit the struggling woman; they were at a draw. What sort of toxic chaos would unfold next was up to the man gripping the terrified Assossian.

And pick his poison he did.

After a swift motion in which the knife's steel was but a blur, a scarlet geyser exploded from Burnellia's neck in a sanguine display. Grief took hold of Skullgem's heart in a sudden painful pierce, and he shouted, screamed with all of the energy in his petite lungs. His aching cries of agony did not go unheard. Though he thought it was all over, it certainly, most certainly, was not.

Burnellia's eyes moved almost all the way to the back of her head. Blood bubbling in her mouth, she let loose the most bloodcurdling scream any of them had ever heard. As her heartbeats slowed their tempo, her orange relic markings did just the opposite, pulsing faster and growing brighter, to the point that they burned Skullgem's eyes, but nothing could bring him to look away.

Somehow still standing on her shaking legs, Burnellia convulsed violently, her body quickly growing hotter until a heat wave slapped the gang members behind her. Suddenly, she stopped, her arms now outstretched.

Then, without warning, she exploded.

It was a horrendous explosion: a hellish inferno that consumed her and the gang behind her. Those who did not get vaporized instantaneously quickly caught aflame.

With a speedy reaction, Skullgem escaped the guard holding him back, taking advantage of him being distracted by the Assossian's execution, and leaped for the two dead guards, dragging their corpses to the gate with every bit of strength left in his small body. He stole a glance behind him, finding none of the mob members remaining. Most were reduced to piles of ash, and the luckiest corpses were contorted beyond recognition in the great mess that had been made of them. An epic fire still burned, the heat of it slapping Skullgem's eyes, forcing him to look away.

The rest of the Guardians, along with Smoke and Blaze, gathered at the gate. Xela was quick to take the body away, pulling the lifeless man to the large preservation chamber somewhere within the camp. The others were quick to find their way around the fire and help bring into the ruins the guards at the front of the encampment that the mob had slain. No bodies of the mob members were to be found, save for a few blackened, charred remains of limbs scattered here and there.

When Blaze found them, Skullgem hastily signed a few words for him. Brutus jumped to translate, and as he did, he could feel Blaze's sadness radiating. The man who had just lost his child slowly parted from the others and walked towards all that remained of Burnellia. Immune to the flames due to his relic abilities, he trudged right into the ember, reaching the epicenter where his daughter's final moments had occurred and collapsing to his knees. He tried his best to cry, but the fire around him evaporated his tears before they could caress his cheeks.

With no body to recover, even Xela was powerless to help. Burnellia was gone, and nothing short of a miracle could bring her back to them.

CHAPTER 21:

She was somehow back in White Heart, on the street where she had first met Brutus and Charlie. This time, however, the street was completely empty, in contrast to its usual hustle and busyness. A dark and haunting sky added to the desolate feeling. It seemed like the entire city, in fact, was empty, perhaps even the entire world. She heard no sounds around her, near or far, save for the lonely, chilling wind humming down the street. And then a realization hit her:

She was cold.

The feeling was unfamiliar. Goosebumps, shivers, clicking teeth, frozen breath; they were all strangers to Alyssa, and now they gripped her menacingly.

The library lay in front of her, and she wanted desperately to go in. Though it wouldn't matter now, she felt more relaxed by the feeling of books around her. Books were knowledge; knowledge comforted her, and now was as good a time as any to seek comfort.

However, when she attempted to step onto the grand steps leading to the library, she found her feet literally frozen; she had not noticed it at first because her boots were the color of thick ice, but now her legs failed her, and a tinge of fear slapped her. Frost was apace creeping from the ground up. Her boots were high, but they did not go on forever; eventually, she felt the stinging, unkind pain of ice on bare skin. She did her best not to scream; for some reason, she did not want to disrupt the calm silence. The pain grew as it found its way up her skirt, then beyond, not stopping or slowing until only her face was uncovered. The sadistic frost then spread past her chin, past her lips, and into her mouth. It was only then that she felt the urge to scream, but when she realized it was too late, she wanted to scream even more.

There was stillness. Perhaps, under different circumstances, she would have enjoyed such a tranquil portrait, but she was alive now, frozen, unable to do anything but think, think and fear.

Then, without warning, she exploded.

Somehow, her mind was still there, but her body was not. She saw a familiar landscape, but just as the frost had slowly taken her body, it was slowly taking the world around her as well. First, it was her beloved library, pages of history books, forever gone to humanity, frozen in time. Then, it was the rest of the city: houses, vehicles, stores, streets, all engulfed in ice. Finally, Alyssa became witness to a world covered over by a layer of winter white, still and unmoving, cold and harsh, unforgivingly desolate and lonely...

She awoke with a heavy gasp, squirming, testing her ability to move again. Her body was fine, but her traumatized mind was not.

Had she been normal, unaffected by the relic taking over her body, she wouldn't have remembered the dream as well. It would have been forgotten sometime later that day, perhaps during breakfast, perhaps in the afternoon.

But Alyssa wasn't normal, and she knew it. Relic users faced much more vivid dreams than those without such abilities, a drawback she couldn't help but resent.

This dream would haunt her for a long time. She had experienced what Burnellia succumbed to: a body gone forever, destruction brought to everyone around her, a gruesome death unfit for her.

Would Alyssa suffer the same fate?

■ ■ ■

The framed picture shook in his nervous, red hands. There she was: his niece, in the body that he would never see again. Her human friends stood around her, smiles on all of their faces. The redhead was slightly taller than the Assossian girl. The young, pale boy was shorter, but not by much. While the two girls both donned toothy grins, he adopted a simple smile.

Smoke was ready to break into tears. As anger tugged on his hand, he broke the frame, small shards of glass sprinkling on his knees. He removed the picture with haste and proceeded to rip away the two humans. There she was, as Smoke preferred her to be, not surrounded by such hideous creatures.

"What do you think you're doing?"

The grey man turned, finding his brother standing over him. He reached and fumbled for what was left of the beautiful frame and picture, but Smoke refused to give Blaze the picture of Burnellia, holding it away like a stubborn child.

"Listen to me!" Smoke said, pushing him away. Blaze was giving him the evil eye, but was still heeding him. "You can't trust humans. You know we can't. Your daughter trusted humans, and look where it got her!"

"You must be kidding," his sibling replied. "That's what this is about? This is pathetic, Smoke. You're better than this."

"I am done with Smoke. Smoke was a chance I gave the humans to show me that they truly want us to live in harmony together. One chance, and it is gone now."

"They gave us shelter, care, protection...the people that killed her are not the people that we are under the wings of. Those people are dead, killed by my daughter herself in her final spark."

"If they were truly protecting us, we would not have been in this predicament," the grey man retorted.

"There are some things not even in their power, brother."

"Guardians, they called themselves. Some guardians they were."

"Listen to me!" harshly demanded Blaze. "They're not at fault for this! They didn't want this to happen!"

"And yet they certainly let it happen, did they not?"

Blaze's expression changed from frustration to concern. "Brother, please..."

"Did they not?" he asked again.

"Brother, you can't blame them for this!" A frustrated sigh. "They're not at fault! There will always be those amongst our ranks that we view as despicable. It is inevitable. But they're gone now, and we have much more important things to worry about. Burnellia is gone, yes, but to seek redemption for her death is foolish, and it will get us nowhere."

"Everything is their fault, don't you see?" The grey man said with clenched fists. "We cannot live in harmony if they are prevalent in our lives!"

"*We?*" Blaze said. "If we want to be as one, we cannot separate ourselves from the humans."

Smoke paced around the room, scoffing and sighing here and there. "No, no, you misunderstand. We are not like them. We will never be like them. The day I am one with them will never come, do you understand?"

Blaze groaned in outrage. "It is almost as if you don't want us to be equal to them."

"We are not equal. We have become the prey, and humans the predators." A long silence filled the room. Two brothers with conflicting views stared at each other, before the one clad in grey spoke again. "I am gathering the Assossians. Surely they know that the humans are not to be trusted."

Blaze's countenance reverted to anger. "*Exqo' enso eff!* You will stand alone!" he furiously snapped, as his brother walked away. "You will find no one, and you will die without anyone to understand your bigoted ways!"

But Smoke was long gone.

The troubled boss of the Syndicate stared back at the reflection glaring at him with crooked, black eyebrows in the shine of the polished Caliburn.

"Something wrong?" someone in front of him asked.

Gareth was used to the voice being proud and regal, but here it sounded touched with personal concern. He was a bit startled, having thought he was alone in the enormous throne hall, save for the Minotaur, who was so quiet that Gareth might as well have been alone anyway.

Gareth sighed. "War."

"Hmm?"

"War," repeated Gareth. "That's what's wrong. War is disgusting."

From in front of him, Jade took a deep breath. "And where, exactly, is this coming from?"

Gareth's eyebrows perked. "I wish I knew. Perhaps a sudden enlightenment. I am tired, Jade. Tired of hating White Heart. Tired of hating the general. Damn it, I'm even tired of hating my brother. I've hated Tyreesius for as long as I can remember." He left his throne and walked up to the green-haired woman, leaving his sword behind, and set his hands on her shoulders. "I am tired of hating."

Jade was unsure how to react, never having seen the leader to whom she devoted her life acting like this. When she stared at him with blank eyes and a gaping expression, he knew she couldn't understand. No one could understand him now, but perhaps if she took his place, she would. It was never that easy, unfortunately.

"Gareth, please," she said. "We're so close to the finish line. So close to victory."

"And what will happen when we cross that line?" he asked her. "Nothing changes. We could just as easily form a peace treaty with White Heart. I hear General Leavett is a forgiving person. I'm sure we can negotiate some terms..." His mind was in a frenzy, hopping from thought to thought. "But we will be no closer to getting rid of Reynard. He is the true enemy. People like him, who think that to rule over people you are to do it with an iron fist. People are complex. They need to be ruled over, but by someone who understands them. Not by someone like him, someone attempting to establish a suicidal hive mind. Slaves, he wants. And I've lost the fight, Jade. He's made a slave out of me."

Somewhere within the colossal throne room, a woman in a cloak, cleverly hidden as if she were invisible, heard the words. Aleegha was sure they would spark Reynard's interest.

■ ■ ■

A single encased ember burned over her tombstone. The flame had been kindled by Blaze's relic abilities, a small donation he had provided to commemorate his daughter. Amber promised a proper memorial in White Heart when their conflict had seen an end.

Most of them were unsure of how to feel. A memorial or a funeral was now alien to them after growing attached to Xela's sweet promises of science. Death was not a stranger, but it rarely presented itself without a body until now.

Nor was the young Assossian's death a glorious one, like a demise in the heat of an epic battle. She was slaughtered by merciless traitors, killed by the ones that should have been her allies.

Amber watched the fire intently from her window for some time, allowing herself to be engulfed in sorrow. Finally, she gave a deep sigh and turned to pack her belongings.

"Hello? Hello?"

She heard the sound, a quiet buzz foreign to her ears at first, then realized someone was speaking through the talker she had left on her bed. She scrambled to pick it up, responding to a frustrated Weylin back in White Heart. "Weylin? Is that you?"

"Yes, yes. Ezekiel stopped by and let me borrow his talker."

"What's wrong? You sound a bit panicked."

Weylin drew a breath. "I really gotta make this quick. White Heart's in trouble, Amber."

A frown found Amber's face. "What?"

"The war council has taken control over White Heart, and the crazy shit is that most people are just letting it happen. Seriously, Amber, I wish you were here to see this."

Her frown distorted her face now. "What are you talking about? How is this possible?"

"Look, I really wish I could give you an explanation here. The council's been getting greedy, ever since they let this shady guy in."

"Who?"

"Guy goes by the name of Marcus, that's all I know."

Amber's hand went to her mouth. She was stunned and silenced at the sound of the dreadful name, and forgot she was talking to someone for a moment. "Hello?" Weylin asked her. "Hello? What's wrong, General?"

"Sorry," apologized Amber. "It's nothing." Another silence found them, Amber losing herself in her thoughts again. "I think I have to go."

"What's going on? How close are you to the Syndicate?" he asked, attempting to change gears.

"Close," she hurried. "We've survived an ambush. Lost a lot of people. Some we've lost forever. But we're close. It won't be all in vain."

"You're doing good out there Amber, you remember that," responded Weylin. "Listen, I won't keep you waiting. You're busy, you've got an empire to take down." A tired sigh. "Good luck out there."

The sound of disconnection. She removed the talker and reached for the beret on her bedstand. She fluffed it neat and tidy, then donned it on her pitch-haired head. She then reached for her gun from next to where her hat had been, and a bullet-brimming clip. She clicked the small pistol's chamber back and loaded a magazine. With an effortless push, it clicked back in.

"Let's end this," Amber said to herself.

■ ■ ■

"Mercy," he spat, pacing back and forth. "We have sacrificed so much to get here, to be so close to destroying our enemies and putting an end to this war, and now he decides to show mercy? The man that is supposed to be *our* great leader?"

Gareth watched Reynard silently from the window above, the latter man speaking to the mob on a raised pedestal. Gareth cared less and less for Reynard as the days passed. The Syndicate may have already nearly won the war against White Heart, but Gareth had lost control of the Syndicate itself. He was sure Reynard would be the most horrid of leaders, but there was not much he could do about it. His people were slipping through his fingers like grains of sand.

"Don't mind him," a voice called from behind Gareth. He did not need to turn to recognize his personal advisor. Her bulky shoes thumped on the floor as she walked towards him.

"I no longer care what he says," Gareth responded. "Make him Boss of the Syndicate. Make him king of the world. He can do whatever he desires to with this shithole."

With that, Gareth turned to leave, off to an unknown destination. He thrust his sword into the ground and began to depart.

"You may not care," Jade said, stopping him. "But I still do. I care about this place. I can take care of you and your people. Let me fill in your shoes."

"I wish it was that simple," he said as he stopped, his words lavish in abdication. "It is not, however. You would need to kill Reynard first."

Jade clenched her teeth. "Then I will. If you can't get a grip on yourself, then I'll be the one to take the initiative."

Gareth wheeled around and gave her a surprised stare. "W-what, like now?"

She didn't answer with words, but her walking out of the throne room with a dramatic departure was answer enough.

After a short moment, he took his weapon back up again and chased after her, worry flooding his mind. The Minotaur followed suit, with the duty of protecting Gareth.

"Hey!" he heard the loud voice call from ahead. "If you're done spewing shit from your mouth, we have something that needs to be settled!"

Gareth found her outside, sharing the raised platform with the pale man.

"Is it a fight you desire, Jade?" Reynard asked, eager, practically begging for a resounding "yes." If there was any anxiousness in him, his voice did not betray it.

"It's about time I got rid of a parasite like you," Jade responded, unsheathing her sickles and spinning them around her. "I know how much you like attention, Reynard. Maybe your little crowd here would enjoy seeing you die."

He drew his whip, hitting a button on its holster, and electricity flew out from it in every direction. "You certainly know how to spark my interest," he said, lashing out at Jade. She ducked and dodged, and he missed.

When she saw a chance present itself her, she swung her kusarigama, her bladed, green chains, around her. The first swing cleaved his vest, the second barely grazed his exposed chest. He scuttled backward, and as she stopped swinging, he entangled her arm in his whip, dragging her toward him as sparks slapped at her violently. He grabbed at Jade's neck as she flew at him. As she squirmed, his grip only grew tighter.

Something sped towards him with violent velocity. Reynard had to jump back and release Jade so not to lose his arm, but his skin was still skimmed. Gareth's hat, with its sharp, moving blades, flew back after slashing at Reynard like a boomerang with a wide curve, denting itself in the planks next to the Syndicate leader's feet.

"What's he doing here?" complained Reynard.

Gareth walked onto the platform and helped Jade to her feet, the Minotaur trailing behind them. "I don't care about honor. I don't care about tradition. Whether or not I lose the respect of my people is beyond me anymore. All I want is to see you fall, and I'm going to make sure you fall hard." He picked up his bloodied hat and placed it on his head, running the edges of the blades along his finger.

"Three against one?" Reynard asked, shaking his head with a smirk. "Now that's hardly a fair fight!" His ensuing whistle pierced their ears, and as if on command, Aleegha materialized from invisibility behind Gareth, Jade, and the Minotaur.

Gareth drew Caliburn, Jade her green shield, and the Minotaur his bronze axe. The three had their backs to each other, surrounded on one side by the thief gripping her krises and by a cunning fox equipped with an evil smile and a whip on the other.

"You think we'll get out of this one?" Gareth asked Jade.

"We can hope," she responded in a quiet voice.

"Unlikely," commented Aleegha.

The Minotaur grunted.

"Shut up," said Jade, harshly. "You're still outnumbered."

"Not outgunned, though," said Reynard, his eyes darting from side to side.

Another grunt from the man in bronze.

"We going to sit and chat all day?" Jade shouted. "You like to keep things interesting, Reynard, don't you? Then let's make it interesting."

The Minotaur yelled ferociously, choosing his target and swinging his axe over his head with tremendous force. Aleegha flew back to avoid the attack. As soon as he recovered from the swing, the Minotaur spun the massive weapon around him. Aleegha held her daggers in front of her, parrying as she slowly walked backward. When she saw the chance, she disappeared from his view.

He grunted again, hoarser and angrier this time, as he felt the blades striking his armor, though he could not see them. After resisting strike after strike, the Minotaur, with a surprising reaction, threw his hand out, catching the invisible woman by her thin waist just as she was to attack again. Though he still could not see her, he could feel her fear radiating as he held her with a firm grip. He threw her at a nearby wall with fullest force, and Aleegha screamed as she clutched her side. With not enough strength to keep up her invisible state, she reappeared: first her krises, then her clothes, and finally her body. She saw the man in bronze charging at her headfirst with his horned helmet, and her instincts found her just before he rammed into her. She leaped, jumping off the wall and landing behind the Minotaur after using him as a footstool. She triggered more ire from within him when he had to pull his horns out from the wall that had been behind her with some struggle, letting loose a deep, enraged growl.

Meanwhile, Reynard faced both Jade and Boss Gareth. He found himself between the charging man with a claymore in hand and the green-haired woman running towards him with a shield. He dove away, searching for cover, putting some space between himself and the other two.

Until now, he had kept the large weapon he had stowed on his back a secret, an unfinished prototype. It begged to be used now, and the temptation was too much not to. Reynard drew the weapon, placing it upon his shoulder as one might hold a launcher. As Gareth and Jade stood in fearful confusion, Reynard propped up his weapon, a deep beeping threatening his targets.

"That can't be good," Jade said.

As if on cue, a rocket flew towards them with a screech, and they ducked for cover. The projectile missed, but looped back around to face them, and this time they were thrown off guard. It struck the ground before them, sparks of electricity flying chaotically and unpredictably.

Their bodies violently thrashed and flailed as electric currents surged through them. Gareth picked himself up first, standing in front of Jade to protect her as she collected herself as well.

Gareth removed his hat and threw it at Reynard once more, missing as the fox ducked. Reynard retaliated by unsheathing his own melee weapon, the surging whip. Gareth drew his longsword, and the two stared each other down, wolves ready to engage in combat for superiority.

Gareth charged, swinging his weapon in every direction with skill and fury, and even Reynard found it hard to keep up with his rival's attacks. He tried to sidestep most of them, but found himself receiving many cuts across his arms as he barely dodged potentially fatal blows. He patiently tried to read Gareth, deciding what pattern he was following. Indeed, he was able to predict Gareth flawlessly, so when his opponent struck a heavy blow with his sword and missed, Reynard was ready. His whip coiled around Gareth's neck like a snake around its prey. Gareth shouted, electricity coursing through every vein in his body, and Reynard sadistically laughed. Then, Gareth felt a short moment of ease as the whip loosened, no longer strangling him, and the electric current paused. His relief ceased when he felt Reynard yank him forward. The fox leaned in far enough until their lips touched, Gareth squirming uncomfortably. The crowd that watched from below laughed as he was mocked by a shameless Reynard.

Finally, Reynard pulled away, only to lift his own leg up, his knee violently hitting Gareth's groin.

"That's far enough!" Jade yelled. A beam of energy flashed from her shield, shoving Reynard against the wall. He and Gareth struggled to pick themselves up, with Reynard getting up first. He saw Aleegha push the Minotaur away, their eyes met for a second, and they nodded in syncopation.

Aleegha disappeared from sight, and Reynard lashed his whip at Jade, hoping to push her away. Gareth, meanwhile, struggled for his hat, the wind completely knocked out of him. The Syndicate leader reached it just as Reynard pulled up, locking his arms so he could not escape. Gareth's eyes met Jade's for a second, and she realized she could not help him anymore.

His head lurched upwards, and blood trickled and sputtered from his mouth. A hole in his chest presented itself, crimson liquid drops covering a knife-like shape. It was then that Aleegha reappeared into view, her krises stained with blood, already half deep within Gareth's stomach. Reynard then let him loose, and Aleegha withdrew her blades, only to brutally stab Gareth a few more times, perhaps for good measure.

As Gareth crumbled, he fixed his eyes on his true heir, the one to whom he had entrusted his life with. Out uttered his final words with a shaking breath towards Jade: "Only the sky and green grass goes on forever..."

A pause. A brief pause in which, to the green woman, it felt as if time had stopped, the world had slowed down.

"Gareth..." she muttered under her breath. Though a tough exterior was akin her, she could feel the salty, grief-brimmed tears swelling in her green eyes now.

"...and today...is a good day to die."

Reynard let his arms loosen, but he held a grip on the dying boss' head. The cunning fox let out a cackle as he tightened his hold, until finally, in one sudden motion, he snapped Boss Gareth's neck with a crack so loud all of Senia could hear it. The legendary claymore Caliburn dropped from his eased hands, and the fabled, bladed conical hat fell from his grip and rolled away.

Jade slowly stepped away from the sanguine scene, shameful tears forming on her face. Her sharp gasps were almost inaudible over the cheering of the sadistic crowd. She turned to the Minotaur, her last ally, to find him setting down his axe. With the assistance of his mercenary thief, Reynard had slain Gareth, and as such, the Minotaur had a new leader to serve. As Aleegha and Reynard gloated in Gareth's last moments, Jade fled. She ran through the crowd, arms grabbing for her everywhere. One found her neck, another punched her gut. She took out her chained blades, slashing at no one in particular. Blood showered in every direction around her, the blood of the raging mob around Jade. Her body burned as she sprinted with everything left in her legs, the shouting behind her feeling as if it would never disappear, the laughing mocking her ceaselessly.

It was a few hours before she stopped running, and she found herself alone, somewhere deep within the forest. The maroon hue that painted the sky, signaling dusk, told her to pause. She found herself crouching next to a large tree, panting heavily. Her expression was blank, her face stained with blood and tears.

Jade was more alone than she ever had been. It was her least favorite emotion, and here she was now, feeling nothing else.

CHAPTER 22:

As their journey continued, the landscape slowly changed from neat rows of dark cedars to a chaotic mess of beautiful flora. Days passed until they could see the massive skyscrapers in the distance near the ever-reaching colorful trees, signaling the large city-state that was their destination: Avalon, the home of their greatest rivals. Silence had followed them from the fort where Burnellia had been killed. Many wanted to get the arduous mission over with.

Amber leaned on a small rock with her leg, an army behind her. She surveyed the land between her and the city, a thick patch of dense forest, but nothing they were unused to trekking on. She stood at the head of a cliff, a beautiful waterfall roaring nearby. The Guardians approached her, standing by her side.

"We're close," Amber said softly. "So close." The others stood by as the sunlight flooded the grim expressions on their faces. In an attempt to lighten the mood, she decided to show them a trick of hers: "Hey, watch this. I've been practicing."

Amber walked to the foot of the tall cliff. She turned to face them, finding a few worried looks, but she herself kept nothing short of a comforting smile strewn on her face. She leaned back, arms outstretched, and let herself fall. Just before she did, she witnessed the rest of the Guardians scramble to the side of the cliff to get a good view.

She let herself plummet for a moment, enjoying the feeling of the wind around her. When the time came, she flipped once to fall feet first, reaching inward with her toes. Just before she hit the ground, her shoes pushed her slightly upwards with force, slowing her fall. When she was about a foot off of the ground, she stopped the flow of propulsion from her heels, landing elegantly. She looked up at her friends, giving a few bows. Even from here, she could make out their faint smiles.

It's a start, she told herself.

. . .

"Wake up!" Janus was in a deep sleep on her bed. "Wake up!" He repeated it a few times and had to shake her before he finally had her attention.

"What, what?" she answered, irritated.

"We need to act quickly," Thomas said. "Come." He led the sleep-deprived Janus downstairs with a tug.

"What's going on?" she asked as they walked.

"This will be an important decision, Janus Symmetra, so please listen. Gareth, the Syndicate boss, has been usurped. He was killed by one of his two heirs, the other disappearing into hiding. Reynard is his name, and he marches to White Heart as we speak. White Heart's army, having been split into two, stands no chance divided," he said, briefing her quickly. "On the other hand, Amber is on her way to the Syndicate's city, with her Guardians. She'll find few guarding it and an easy battle. Even if you intervene there, she will likely succeed."

"Very well, Thomas. Thank you for this," Janus responded, doing her best to realize the direness of

370

the situation and shake herself literally and metaphorically awake.

She walked away with a heavy gait, pulling herself to a special room and shutting the door behind her. It was a visually dull room, with the ceiling, floor, and walls painted in a neutral grey. However, no other room in the world was more important to her.

The only object in it, aside from a grey bowl filled with water in the center, was a grey knife, beautifully crafted and perfectly symmetrical. She found the dagger in her grip soon enough, as her shaking hands hovered over the bowl. Without hesitation, and with the most robotic countenance stuck on her, Janus slit her palms with the blade, not so much as blinking, let alone flinching, when the dark liquid trickled into the bowl. Clear water turned red as it mixed with the woman's blood. Janus closed her eyes and waited patiently, silently praying for another sign. When she opened her eyes again, the liquid in the bowl was pure white, the color of an angel's wings. Janus promptly leaned down, letting her hair slowly submerge in the bowl.

When her hair had dried, she walked back to her room. Her reflection in the mirror spoke kind words of her white, angelic hair, shimmering with beauty. From her closet, she picked out the outfit in white: a pale catsuit with angelic, wing-like sleeves, and white boots.

In a few minutes, she found herself in the garage, mounting the white lightcycle, a white longsword and a white longbow slung on her back.

She waved to Thomas as she left, with a sanctuary in her thoughts that she swore to protect.

■ ■ ■

Turrets and cameras focused on the mysterious, white vehicle, as its pilot took off her helmet, shaking down her pale hair.

"Who are you?" demanded one of the many guards at the gate.

Before she could answer, a man in an elegant coat and a cap stepped up to the front gate. He signaled to another man in a small post nearby, who promptly pulled a lever. The steel gates had been replaced by one of Ezekiel's prototypes: a transparent wall, a force field very similar to those utilized in White Heart's prison, simply repurposed to a larger scale. He motioned once again, this time for the guard to pull the lever once more when he had walked past the city walls. The guard reluctantly obeyed, a nervous stare about him.

"Ho, traveler!" the capped man said, though he knew she was no ordinary wanderer.

"Who are you?" the strange woman asked him.

The man in the white fedora made a *tsk* sound with his tongue. "I believe the question had been asked to you first. Give me an answer now, and I will give you one as well."

She nodded her head. "Angel."

"What was that?"

"Angel." A little louder this time. "My name is Angel."

"Weylin, White Heart commander," the man said, extending a hand, which Angel reluctantly shook. "Now that I know your name, why are you here?" He drew his weapon sternly, not ready to fire, but willing to make a statement.

"I don't have much time to explain myself, so I will need your trust here. The Syndicate's army marches here as we speak. Not just a small portion of it, either: they're going to hit you with everything they've got."

"What?" a disbelieving Weylin asked.

"The Syndicate has split. Boss Gareth is dead, and Reynard has taken the reins. The few still loyal to Gareth are protecting their city, unaware of his death."

Weylin scoffed, though he was quite frightened at the possibility that Angel was telling the truth. "And why should we trust your word?"

"I hear trust is an important value in White Heart, especially with people under General Leavett's command. I can't offer you much, however. It's your choice here: take me or leave me. You're going to be in a desperate situation soon, however, and I can tell you right now, you will need all the help you can get."

After she finished, there was a long pause, in which Weylin processed what she told him. Finally, he motioned behind him, and the gates opened once more.

Before he let her in, he pulled her close and whispered into her ear: "You step out of line, you get a bullet in your head. I can't make it any simpler than that. I really want to trust you, Angel. Don't give me a reason not to. As for now..." Weylin patted her on the back, glaring at her with a strange smile, "...welcome to White Heart."

■ ■ ■

"This is it," Brandon whispered to himself.

Just ninety-nine others were in his city now, a hundred proud Syndicate soldiers in total, either incredibly loyal or long prepared to meet their ends without hesitation, but most the former, and some a bit of both.

Most of them had gathered around the main plaza at the entrance to Avalon. One was at the front, the others facing him, their commander. Their boss had given them the choice of wearing either their personal outfit or the Syndicate's own. The commander was decked out in the latter, elegant black and white attire, with his striped fedora and his coattail suit blending in a roguish, rough way with the many scars across his body.

Brandon wore his favorite dress, the shimmering red one he had seduced the boxer in, and proudly sported a Syndicate fedora of his own, embroidered with the emblem of the crossed swords.

"The moment of reckoning is upon us!" screamed their commander, snapping the dancer-turned-soldier back into focus. "Our enemies come with the intentions of taking our great city, so let's give them a fight they'll never forget!"

A great eruption of applause exploded from anxious, excited soldiers eager to live their last moments serving their great empire. Brandon pushed himself to cheer with them, but something felt amiss. These people were his sisters and brothers, so why did he feel so distant from them, so different?

It was then that one of the sentries posted watch on Avalon's defenses shouted with all his might. "Commander!" echoed the yelp, growing more distinct as the applause from the soldiers below died down. "Commander, commander!" His chubby body ran down the wall's staircase and vaulted when he was a few feet from the ground.

"What is it, comrade?" his leader asked.

The sentry approached, his breath heavy. After a moment of recollection, he picked his head up and faced his superior.

"The Guardians, they're here!"

A wide grin slowly grew on the commander's rugged face as he smiled ahead, into the distance, past the sprawl of greenery surrounding them, from where their enemies approached.

"Stations, everyone!" the commander shouted at the top of his lungs. "Everyone to their places!"

The cluster of soldiers scattered like mice to their predetermined positions, frantic and hurried. The dancer quickly found himself waiting in an alleyway nearby, the soldiers in the street ahead serving as the front line, he to play the role of the ambushing assassin.

As he checked his weapons, he could feel his ear twitch, something odd coming to him in sound then. It seemed like a whisper behind him, but then it grew in volume, ever so slightly, until finally, he could hear:

"Brandon."

The boy in a dress turned to the darkened alley, watching a silhouette approach from the shadows, too far to be recognized. "Who's there?" he asked out loud.

As the daylight drifted onto the figure, Brandon began to feel a sense of disbelief. As he questioned if he was truly seeing who he thought he was seeing, the man opposite to him crept closer, his familiar face becoming more apparent.

"Brandon," the boxer repeated.

"Jack..." came the dancer. "Jack!"

He bolted forwards to embrace Jack, allowing the tears to flow without care. He was partly angry with Jack for joining him, but now that the two were together, Brandon realized how much he had missed him.

Jack returned the hug, and next the crying, lighter than the dancer's sobbing, but with every ounce of emotion.

"W-why did you stay?" asked the shorter man in heels, as they parted ever so.

"You found a purpose in me, and now I feel like I've taken it away from you." The boxer could barely look into his partner's eyes as he spoke. "Well, I found a purpose in you, and it was like nothing I've felt before. I'd give up anything just to experience it once more, absolutely anything."

"But Jack," cried Brandon. "You'll die here. You could have moved on, lived a happier life without me."

The boxer shook his head, then finally allowed his stare to meet Brandon's. He couldn't suppress the smile that formed on his bruised, yet generous face, the sweetest smile the dancer had ever seen. "I died the moment I heard you tell me of the sacrifice you were prepared to make. But then, I found hope again. If I could be with you for your final moments, and make them my final moments too...well, I'll be living more than I've ever lived, just then and there."

Brandon couldn't help but smile back, the makeup he had adorned already ruined from his tears. "I love you, Jack." The boxer tenderly embraced him once more then. "I love you."

Silence found them for some time, before Jack closed his eyes and spoke: "I love you, Brandon."

Their parting was slow, full of amour and emotion, but a sudden thought forged itself in the dancer's mind, one he could not help but speak aloud: "But...the Hundred Lambs...you'll be forgotten to history, Jack Bahal. Are you sure you want this?"

"Sweetheart," he softly said, nothing but love in his tone, "I want to be with you, I need to be with you, and nothing can change that. Perhaps if I'm lucky, then one day future historians will debate the myths of the hundred-and-first Lamb's existence."

Brandon laughed, wiping away the water on his reddened face. "Maybe."

The boxer lovingly felt the dancer's beautiful cheeks with his rough hands. "For now, I don't care if history forgets me. All I care is that you remember me, now and for the rest of your life."

■ ■ ■

"This is it!" Amber called to her army.

Avalon lay in front of them now, few trees blocking their view. It seemed as if the luscious rainforest had parted to grant them a path to the city, and now nothing stood in their way.

Reese unhooked a canteen from his belt, popping open its cap and chugging its content. When he finished, he let out a boisterous burp.

"Reese, are you drinking?" Eva asked in a shrill tone.

He glanced at her. "Yep."

"Just before we fight one of the most important battles of our lives?"

This time he sighed. "Yep." Eva glared at him with a painfully disappointed stare. "Oh, don't look at me like that. I do this all the time."

"You what?" Eva exclaimed, her voice getting higher as she grew angrier with him. As they argued, Charlie whimpered, and Hex cawed.

"I don't mean to interrupt your adorable couple fight," Xela said, "but we have a city to capture, remember?"

"We all recall the plan, yes?" asked Brutus aloud, as Skullgem, next to him, tightened his grip on his hammer.

"Right," said Alyssa, looking at Amber for confirmation.

"Alright," Amber said, nodding quickly. "Let's do this."

Alyssa aimed a ray of frost at the ground, and her allies watch her turn a tiny snowball into a clump of ice as tall as her before their eyes. Her work kept growing from there, until it was a massive frozen wall, nearly a hundred feet high. Her eyes shone a brilliant blue as she constructed their shield.

When she was finished, she turned to Reese, who had just finished injecting a syringe into his arm. After a pause in which his body found its strength, he pulled himself together. "Hit it, big man," Alyssa told him.

Reese cackled and cracked his knuckles before putting his palms on the wall. Despite the cold touch of ice against his hands, he felt no pain. He pushed the thick shield with all his might, and it slowly trudged forwards, with the army following close behind, covered by the giant wall of ice. When they were close enough, Eva readied herself, nodding at Amber. Amber nodded back, and Eva spread out her arms. She felt Amber's arms wrap around her chest, and soon after, they took to the skies. Using the propulsion from her heels, Amber carried Eva to the top of the wall, then set her down gently upon the ice. She flashed a brief salute to Eva, who returned the favor, before dropping back down and leaving the sniper to herself atop the gigantic sculpture of ice.

It was a staggering, jaw-dropping view. She was level with the tallest trees in the forest, and almost tempted to leap onto a nearby branch and explore the lavish scenery laid out before her, had they not been commencing with a very important battle at the moment. Senia's sky was stolen from a beautiful painting, shades of purple, red, orange, and yellow blending together perfectly. The army below and behind her was huge, the city in front of her vast. It was serene and quiet from up here, save for the occasional crack of a gun going off, in an attempt to break the ice.

Remembering her mission, she turned to the city with her rifle in hand, her sharp eyes instantly finding the posted sentries. In the blink of an eye, her mind had already calculated the shot.

She pulled the trigger, watching the first sniper on the wall of Avalon slowly fall, a dart in his shoulder. More and more soon followed, until no one dared hinder their progress except the ready soldiers at the gates of the city.

They pushed valiantly until they were at the main gates, truly massive walls, yet no more than half as tall as Alyssa's wall of ice. From below, Reese screamed and yelled like a wild animal as he exerted his massive strength into a final heave. He began to tip Alyssa's sculpture of ice over, Eva losing her balance above. She rode the wall down until the angle of its fall became too much for her, then leaped, flipping and somersaulting with her incredible agility to a sentry tower where one of the guards lay sleeping.

The wall fell, and the Syndicate guards ran for cover, hoping not to be crushed under the massive block. Ice shattered over the front of the Syndicate city, destroying the main gate, and the battle commenced.

Eva provided cover from above, occasionally leaping across the tops of buildings to change her position, firing into the fray, tranquilizing foes below her.

A Syndicate soldier, a bow in hand, shared a rooftop with her. She noticed him, but he was oblivious to her. She took up her rifle, ready to fire a dart into him, but he noticed her at the last moment. Before she could pull the trigger, he turned, bow drawn, and fired at her, surprising even her with his reaction. An arrow skimmed her thigh, and though a stinging agony struck her, she fought through the pain. Before he could load another arrow, Eva ran at him, delivering a powerful roundhouse kick. He stumbled back, then swung at her with his bow, missing sorely. Eva, with frighteningly quick action, struck her foe with her fists, forced him to clutch his stomach after sending a front kick his way, and finally sent him flying as she destroyed his chin with her a swing of her rifle. He was left on the rooftop, too weak to continue.

Far below Eva, Alyssa stood frozen, her eyes overcome by blue. Her red hair flew as a cold wind was called against the city. Blaze was beside her, his black hair fluttering carelessly, a blank expression on his face, with eyes glowing a red-orange, as a heat wave began to pick up. One half of the city shivered in the throes of a furious blizzard, while the other half burned and succumbed to a searing firestorm.

Steel clashed with steel, bullets against shields, axes against swords, scythes against spears. The Guardians were somewhere mixed into the fray, along with White Heart's foot soldiers, Blaze's Assossian troops, and the trained guards of Xela's Order.

In a nearby alley, two soldiers plotted their ambush. As Blaze and Alyssa slowly brought up the backline, approaching steadily as they brought chaos to Avalon, one of the two hidden in the alleyway lined up his sights with his small pistol.

With a split second reaction, Alyssa caught the ambushers out of the corner of her eye. She shouted Blaze's name to catch his attention, then erected a column of ice just large enough to block the bullet directed at the Assossian.

When Alyssa permitted her frozen construct to crumble, out came the two attackers, weapons in hand. One charged for Blaze on swift feet, his head ducking in his arms as he ran. The other, an elfin figure in a dress, picked Alyssa as his target, advancing with his gun in one hand and a small blade in the other.

The man with a boxer's stance was more skilled with his fists than Blaze, lunging at him and throwing blow after blow. The Assossian was able to dodge most of them, but every time he tried to strike, his opponent punished him with a staggering punch. After this kept up, Blaze realized that being on offense would not work, so instead focused on watching the boxer, noting his patterns, surveying for the perfect opportunity. Finally, after attempting to land a flurry of jabs, the boxer reeled in for a powerful hook.

Blaze was ready, however. His fist shot out to block his opponent's, grabbing the boxer's fist and holding him in place. Their gazes met, fire in Blaze's eyes, fury in the boxer's, before the latter screamed in pain, as his hand was catching aflame.

Next to them, Alyssa battled with the slender figure, who waltzed through his attacks with the movements of a prestige dancer. Swing after swing frisked towards the ice sorceress, her opponent's movements a blur, his butterfly knife spinning and soaring with precision, his feet kicking in rhythm. Alyssa did not fail to keep up, meeting every slash with one of her own, with the battle experience to match. With every parry, with every attack, her makeshift dagger of ice fractured, forcing her to construct a new one again and again.

After testing her out for some time, the dancer felt brave enough to pressure her further. His legs still moved in his particular tempo; he could not help but incorporate performance into combat, as if it were instinct. He almost threw Alyssa off guard when he drastically picked up his speed, even succeeding in drawing blood.

It was his dire mistake to take this as an opportunity to harass her further. Channeling her anger after failing to dodge one too many strikes, the Guardian yelled out loud, unwilling to lose her fight here. Her arms pushed forwards, and a blast of icy gust followed, pushing him back, away from her. He shivered as the frost crept up his dress, but did his best to shrug the cold off. Now at range from his opponent, he reached for the pistol strapped to his thigh. When he drew it, however, his face read disbelief; as he had parted his focus from Alyssa, the crimson-haired girl had constructed a frozen spear in her hand and had it poised, prepared to release it forwards. The dancer rushed to aim his sights, but it was too late, and in the next second, a stick of ice was impaled through his chest.

Blaze's opponent froze in shock just as it happened, even though his sights were not on the dancer. He broke from the fire-powered Assossian to understand the sudden pang in his heart, his heart shriveling when he became witness to a portrait of his partner in his final moments. The dancer fell to his shaking knees, his last breaths combining with his bubbling blood as they abandoned his lungs.

"Brandon!" shouted the boxer, a fury like no other resounding in his feral voice. "You...monster!" He slammed his knuckles together and turned to Alyssa, just as the frost in her hand dissipated.

A brutish beast of rage charged the scarlet-haired girl, who was too taken aback by his savageness to retaliate. He ran at her with a heavy hook, then punched again and again and again. As Alyssa doubled over from a blow to her stomach, the boxer prepared a stunning lunge, screaming at the top of his lungs as he readied a fist behind him.

The Assossian, however, was prepared to protect his Guardian ally, and when the burning orb formed in his hand, he tossed the fireball with all his might.

The boxer's fire was doused in a split second: just before his powerful punch struck Alyssa, a searing pain pierced his gut, though he was silent as he realized his circumstance. He looked down at his chest to find it open and gaping, light from the other side of his body visibly pouring through the burning hole inside him. Blaze emerged not far behind, his hand engulfed in fire.

The boxer could feel his consciousness beginning to fade, life beginning to desert him. The battlefield became a blur, and silence crept in, eerie but peaceful, but he had not quite made his peace yet.

Frantically, his eyes scanned around, and he knew he had found the man he was looking for when what fragments were left of his heart grew heavy. The boxer stumbled forward, trudging on with the last bit of strength left in him, then collapsed next to the boy in the red dress.

■ ■ ■

The blood from his gored chest slowly burst through where the hole had burned and the circulation had briefly stopped, and Jack, lying on the ground, felt the crimson liquid creep along his prostrate body.

He could sense himself slipping away, and made haste to focus his attention on his parted lover adjacent to him. His rough hands touched Brandon's sweet cheek, and Jack could do little more than admire his beauty, which he even in death retained.

The sight of the dancer, and the realization that this would be the final sight he witnessed on Senia, brought Jack the closure he so desperately desired. His life with Brandon was short-lived in the physical sense, but the moment Jack's life truly began, he knew, was when he first walked into his lover's club.

And here he was now, not long after. He was content with it all, content with his final moments, as to him, they were lived to the fullest.

"I...I love you," he whispered under a quivering, weak breath as he looked upon Brandon's empty stare, and then Jack's expression grew just as empty.

■■■

The fighting pressed on, however, far from finished.

A Syndicate soldier charged Amber, sword in hand. He narrowly missed her as she side-stepped away, and he charged again, but this time she used her heels to avoid him. The rockets on her shoes pushed her into the air, and she landed behind him, giving her just enough time to strike an elbow to his nape. Another soldier then took his place, running at her as well.

His swing was parried by someone who placed themselves between him and Amber: Skullgem, a hammer in his grip, retaliated with a blow hard enough to knock the weapon out of the other man's hand. He spun and swung with quick hits, bringing his opponent to the ground and knocking him unconscious.

Reese stood nearby unarmed, but with fists out and ready. Two soldiers jumped him then, trying their best to stay on him as if participating in a rodeo. He wrangled them loose, and two more took their place, but Reese grabbed them by their necks, pushing and punching others away. Anyone that attempted a shot at the massive Guardian was prohibited from doing so by Hex.

Another soldier jumped him, grasping the angered behemoth by his massive shoulders. The soldier tried to pull out a knife, but Hex turned to him with cruel eyes and pecked at the man with his metal beak, piercing into his skin like a drill. Once he felt the blood trickle from his head, the soldier screamed in agony and let go.

Xela soon found Reese, using her massive scythe to cut down a few Syndicate soldiers attempting to overwhelm him. One disembarked from Reese's shoulders, putting a rifle in her hands while stepping away from the action, turning to Xela and readying her aim at her.

The Guardian was ready before she was, however, putting aside her scythe and quickly reaching for her throwing daggers. She tossed one into the Syndicate woman's shoulder, throwing her aim off, and another into her arm, forcing her to drop her gun.

She frantically reached down to pick it up, but Xela was quickly upon her. The Guardian became a blur of blades as she spun and swung, her knives slashing and hacking with incredible speed. Finally, after being thoroughly drenched in her opponent's blood, she withdrew a step back and tossed a dagger into the Syndicate soldier's neck. Her rival fell slowly as Xela flipped her knives with style, tucked them back into her garters, and blew the hair away from her face. The Guardian then pulled her scythe again, charging off valiantly to fight another soldier.

A bark was audible over the heated firefight: the sound of a hound filled with a lust for bloodshed.

In the midst of battle, Charlie turned into a war machine on four legs, running with canine swagger and satisfying his ravenous hunger with every fang he sank. He spied a scene in the corner of his eye, and in the next second, he was leaping at a Syndicate soldier attempting to plunge a blade into a White Heart soldier on the ground. She let go of her weapon as Charlie bit deeply into her arm, the telltale red liquid pumping out of her. Then the hound moved on to another victim, leaving the screaming and bleeding Syndicate woman behind.

Elsewhere, Amber ran to Brutus, who was occasionally ducking from behind cover to fire his weapons. "How does it look?" he asked.

"In our favor," she responded.

As they hid from a wave of bullets, Amber noticed the big display on a few of the city's skyscrapers. Her curiosity got the best of her, and she peeked slightly to check what had caught her interest.

There were names, about a hundred in total, some crossed out with a big, bold "X." She watched as Reese, from nearby, grabbed a Syndicate soldier by her neck and tossed her effortlessly into a wall. She bounced off the steel surface and fell to the ground painfully, and when she failed to pick herself up, Amber noticed a name cross itself out on the huge board. A sudden feeling of unattractive remorse found her, sinking her heart and heavying her head with sudden realization. How many of those names were crossed out because of her?

■ ■ ■

"What?" Marcus asked, though he had clearly heard the words correctly.

"The Syndicate, under the new orders of Reynard, who has usurped Gareth, march here now," Angel repeated.

"No, no, no. That can't be true. How do we know we can trust you, anyway?" he asked warily.

The room was dark, and the war council members stood all around her, with Marcus at the front. He wore a damning look, complemented by his black and red hair and statesman's glasses.

Ezekiel and Weylin, who Amber trusted most in her home city, accompanied Angel on her visit to the council's chambers. They slowly drew their weapons, catching a few war council members slipping pistols and knives under the table.

"Mr. Graves, we don't tolerate people who march into our city and tell us lies. Why don't you do us a favor and get rid of her?" asked Marcus.

The bluntness and morbidness of the request hit him like a truck, as did how no one in the room questioned the command save for Ezekiel and Angel, For some reason, however, he was still compelled to raise his gun against her. Before Weylin knew it, his sight was precisely lined up with her fearful eye, and he was but a flick of his finger away from putting a bullet in her head. His hands shook, and he could feel worry radiating from her like a heat wave.

But suddenly, he dropped his gun, unwilling to give into the temptation.

"Ah, you're too weak," Marcus said, as he began to leave the room through a back door. "Very well. The

389

war council will dispose of her themselves, and perhaps you as well. Farewell, scum."

Angel, Weylin, and Ezekiel wasted no time in rushing out of the door behind them, gunfire sounding from behind them. They made a break down the hallway, but were stopped by a woman in work clothes chasing after them, knife in hand. She charged at Angel, the latter woman easily dodging the clumsy attacks. She sensed an unpleasant gaze from the other woman's wary and crazed eyes, close to a dark shade of purple. She wrenched the knife away from the insane woman, tossed it aside, and gave her a blow to her head that was sure to keep her temporarily incapacitated.

The trio fled the building through the main exit and was immediately greeted with the view of a sanctuary on fire. Corrupted guards drew closer to surround them, but the two archers readied their bows just as enemies closed in on them from both sides.

"On your right!" called Angel.

"On your left!" called Ezekiel.

They turned and crouched simultaneously, bows drawn and backs to each other. The two fired arrows in sync, hitting their unfortunate targets with skilled, practiced precision. Then they took after Weylin, who was already hightailing to the Guardian's home.

Along the way, they encountered few to stand in their path, promptly dealing with those who did. When they finally came to their destination, Weylin made a sharp turn into an alley, Ezekiel and Angel following close behind. They occasionally slipped unrestful glances behind them, assuring themselves that they weren't being followed.

Weylin did as Amber had done when he had watched her open the garage doors for the first time. The other two waited, an uneasy gloominess lingering over them like dark clouds. Eventually, a sentry running past the alley saw them out of the corner of his purple eye and turned to them with a rifle in hand. He was just ready to unload a full clip onto them when they ducked into the garage, the slow door eventually opening just enough for them to slip through.

The unlucky sentry was mowed down by their speeding jeep just moments later. Weylin, Ezekiel, and Angel pressed on as they sped through the crumbling city, eventually making it to the eastern gate.

"What the fuck just happened?" a frantic Weylin asked. Sorrowful sighs were the only responses he received.

The guards did not seem to be under the betraying influence, fortunately. After being filled in on the situation, they eagerly shut off the gate for the trio, and then, seeing no better option, stole a few vehicles from the main garage nearby and followed behind.

Angel permitted them to leave her behind as she searched the garage for her lightcycle. A smile found her when she encountered its friendly face, but then the sound of approaching vehicles made her heart heavy. She turned to find two motorcyclists barreling towards her, far down the garage, drawing pistols and firing relentlessly. Angel made haste to mount her own vehicle, but the two attackers were now in her way. She drove towards them, hoping a stray bullet didn't find her head.

When the gunfire stopped, her steadily approaching enemies unsheathed their swords, and Angel drew her own weapon, accepting the challenge. As if about to joust, Angel calculated a strike with her weapon posed. When they were close enough to her, she hastily pushed a button on her sword. The blade launched forward with frightening speed, an unwinding, durable rope of light attaching it to the hilt. The biker it was about to hit swerved to avoid the attack. At her cue, Angel quickly retracted the blade back to its hilt. When the biker changed his lane, it left the two of them on the same side; perfect targets for Angel. The swing of her sword was true, and both of her opponents fell in a curtain of blood, their bikes skidding far from them.

Angel scoffed, making haste to depart before anyone else challenged her. She left the garage behind, finding her way out of the burning sanctuary that was White Heart.

Meanwhile, the doomed city was on the horizon behind Weylin and Ezekiel. They wished to help, but knew they would certainly meet their demise if they stayed. They also wished to live another day, and unanimously agreed to regroup with Amber's army.

Weylin, sitting in the back, turned to the glorious city, now in chaos and flames. The great walls were once inspirational images to him, but now they seemed desperate and foolish; beautiful as they were, they were fruitless defenses against the enemies already inside his city. He pulled off his white-and-black hat and placed it on his heart. He was bleeding white on the inside.

■ ■ ■

The familiar skyscrapers of Avalon, once beautiful in their proud standing, finally presented themselves on the horizon through the thick rainforest trees, but she only felt anxiousness and fear. The sounds of warfare had haunted her ears for quite some time.

Jade mustered the last of her already exhausted endurance onto the final stretch. She had an aimless encounter to prevent, sacrifices with no meaning, the pointless battle that, to her dismay, had already begun.

■ ■ ■

Brutus fired a round of bullets from his machine pistol before he heard the clicking of an empty magazine. The soldiers that had been behind cover saw their chance and rushed out to charge the Guardian as he frantically reloaded his revolvers. Outnumbered, Brutus was easily knocked onto his back. A man in front of him raised a lance over his head, preparing to execute. A beam of green flashed from nowhere, however, pushing the soldier away.

Nearby, a Syndicate woman kicked at the hound, launching him backward. Charlie mustered his strength and pulled himself up, but the soldier lunged at him with a small axe. As she swung, Charlie bared his fangs, and his metal teeth parried with her weapon, sparks flying in every direction. The Syndicate soldier did not expect his block and stumbled back from the backlash of her swing. The dog saw his opportunity and pounced on her, his drooling, open mouth just above her, ready to rip her throat out. A green light illuminated him, however, and the next second he was flung backward, denting the wall when he collided with it.

"Stop!" a voice shouted. "Stop! Stop! Stop!"

It repeated seemingly without end, radiating desperation. More and more combatants drew their attention away from the battle, and more flashes of green knocked anyone willing to keep fighting away from their opponents. Eventually, the two sides paused altogether.

The green-haired woman struggled to present herself as she walked out from behind the remains of the gate, a massive shield in her arms. "Please, stop fighting! Gareth is dead!"

CHAPTER 23:

"You're telling me Gareth went through a complete change of heart just before he died?" a reluctant Reese interrogated.

"Yes."

"We're talking about the same Gareth, yes?" he asked in mocking disbelief. "Gareth Black? 'Boss' Gareth?"

"I know how farfetched it seems," Jade said. "I know how much you disliked your brother."

Reese burst out into laughter. "Disliked? What do you take me for? No, no no, please. There's no one in this terrible fucking world I hated more than Gareth Black, and I'm a pretty hateful guy. In fact, I bet you could trace all of my hate in some way back to him. I wish there was a stronger word I could use, but even then, it probably wouldn't be enough to describe what I thought of him. Dislike, however? Most certainly not enough, no ma'am."

"Look, there's always someone worse out there, and I'm telling you, Reynard is that man," Jade continued. "Whatever grudge you had against Gareth, I ask of whatever sense of good you have in you to get past it. Our original plan with him was to attack an unprotected White Heart, and hesitation could have possibly saved your city. There may be time still."

"What a fucking coward," commented Reese.

"Reese, that's enough," butt in Brutus, before turning to Jade. "What are you talking about?"

"There are only two ways I can earn your trust, one of which I have already done," she explained. "Our agreement was to pause the violence. Now Amber waits with the Hundred Lambs, all that remains of Gareth's army need I remind you, while I am here with you. The soldiers could instantly put a bullet in her head. It would be simple. It would cause so much confusion in your own army that it would be hopeless. Why haven't I ordered them to do this yet? It certainly isn't because I'm cooped up in here; I willingly made this trade. Reynard now controls the Syndicate, if we can even call it that anymore. He marches to White Heart at this moment, him and all of his forces. He has usurped Gareth, and once he destroys White Heart, nothing in the world could stop him from achieving ultimate chaos. Neither of us want that."

"So you're suggesting a temporary alliance?" asked Eva.

"Exactly. Once this is all over, I swear to you, we will leave you alone," Jade firmly promised. "The Syndicate will never again wage war against White Heart. We'll go our separate ways once the total destruction of Senia is avoided."

"I trust her," spoke up Xela. "I understand if you don't believe me when I say this, but I am working on technology that will allow me to bring back those that have fallen in battle. So long as you preserve the bodies of those slain today, I can promise you they'll come back to you, one day."

Jade looked to the other Guardians for confirmation. "Is she serious?"

"Believe it or not," said Brutus with a shrug. "What a world we live in."

"And you're suggesting to use this on our people? Well, it is certainly not an honorable death to die at the hands of your soon-to-be allies. This is extraordinarily kind of you, Xela, and I gladly accept."

A handshake ensued, and Jade and Amber's places were switched, Jade explaining the agreement to her soldiers and the Guardians to Amber.

"So that's what the big screen of names was about," said Amber after everything they had just discussed was retold to her. "A tactic by Gareth to make us feel like his soldiers were people, too. His final tactic."

Reese grimaced. "I certainly didn't feel any guilt." A caw emerged from his steady bird.

"Of course you didn't," Eva murmured.

"So what now?" asked Alyssa, who sat on a couch in the corner with Ire, her legs crossed. Charlie looked up at Amber as if he awaited an answer as well.

Amber glanced around the room, finding many familiar faces staring back at her. She closed her eyes and took a deep breath, then spoke when she opened them once more: "It's time we return home."

■ ■ ■

Marcus stood leaning upon the massive open gate. His arms were covered with permanent, purple runic tattoos, visible from far away.

The two brothers shared similarities; though Reynard did not have any runic powers, they both sported similarly structured faces and the same hair with the same red streak in it. The sight of them together, with their similar looks and their brotherly love, was an awkward sight to all but the two of them.

Reynard swirled and skipped like a playful child toward the reliced man, towards the entrance to the great city now under the control of his greatest ally, his cruel mind in twisted bliss. "Oh brother!" he exclaimed. "This is the greatest gift ever bestowed upon me!" He gave his sibling a strangely loving hug that surprised even Marcus himself.

Marcus laughed lightly and fixed his glasses. "Yes, well, anything for my baby brother."

Reynard may or may not have heard him, his attention focused in wonder on the city in flames around him. "Beautiful," he whispered with a hushed tone. "Absolutely beautiful."

"Listen Reynard," Marcus said, putting a hand on his brother's shoulder. "The Guardians are very powerful people, people I will not have any control over. You need to be prepared for if they come back to White Heart."

"Don't you worry, sweet brother," Reynard said in a remarkably cheerful voice, throwing in a wink for good measure. "I shall not let anyone take this away from me."

"It's strange," said Marcus. "I'm not able to control everyone. Some people are stronger than others, more able to resist it. As I had said, I would assume the Guardians to be strong enough. I fear my power is fading. Be careful, Reynard."

His brother nodded, taking note of his concern. "Everyone has a breaking point," Reynard added.

■ ■ ■

The smoky remains of what was once a city-state stretched for miles. Streets, houses, buildings; it was all now nothing more than charred outlines and broken memories. The walls were nowhere to be found, as if they had vanished into thin air. No inhabitants of the destroyed city were visible anywhere.

"What is this?" Amber asked. "And where is Greenwood?"

"This is exactly where it was," Eva said, a loud sigh overcoming her. "I guess this is all that remains of it." She knew will it had been filled to the brim with the corrupt and wicked, but it was still a place she had called home at some point in her life.

"Total war." It was Brutus who said it. "So it comes to this? They truly want chaos."

"Imagine what they could do to White Heart," said Xela. The morbid thought lingered in the air like a toxic cloud.

"Amber," Eva began. "If it's alright with you, I think I need a moment." The general allowed her to run off into the ruins of the city, with Reese and Hex following behind.

"Wait up!" Reese shouted after Eva. She was ahead, far ahead, her sneakers sprinting on the ashen, stone road, black as death. Nearly every building she passed was broken down, torn in two as if a giant had sliced through it.

Reese chased after her for some time, Hex flying alongside him, before he finally almost ran straight into an oddly static Eva. She stood directly in front of what seemed like a saloon, admiring the sign above it for some time before reading it aloud:

"The House of the Rising Sun," she spoke with a sigh. "It's been a while, old friend."

"You mean..." began Reese, staring in disbelief. "That's...the place?" Eva's only response was a silent nod as she approached her old brothel.

It was odd to see it deserted like this. The last time she had seen the small building, it bustled with festivity, full of love and lust played out in every room. Now, it was silent, dead silent, entirely empty, and carried the brooding atmosphere of a funeral home.

She walked around slowly, inspecting every nook and cranny to make herself recall what it had looked like before, before she left, before her enemies came.

After some time, she decided it finally fit to head up the great stairs to the bedrooms. She remembered how the madam always made them take their customers into their own rooms, as perhaps an attempt to establish just a touch more personal connection, save for those wealthy-pocketed souls that paid enough to spend a night with more than one of them.

She could barely glance in her own room. Though each was nearly identical, something odd protruded from hers, a strange feeling, and sure if it made her blissful or upset. Perhaps it was a queer mix of both. Her nostalgic high was broken by the sound of creaking behind her.

"Not. Another. Step," came a voice that she barely recognized.

Eva's breath froze. "Iggy?" she called out, before she turned around to face her old madam.

In front of them stood a boy lowering his bow, easing his stance. His weapon was a glimmering white...no, it was certainly made of marble, Reese deduced as he studied him. It had been decorated with various wooden engravings, the most prominent a large emblem on the center of his bow, in the shape of a heart surrounding a tree. Four fruits hung on the tree's branches, while one seemed to be falling off of it.

"Eva?" he asked, as he put his weapon aside. They stared each other down for a moment, then ran to each other, caught in a reuniting embrace.

"I can't believe it's you!" she exclaimed with a smile. "You look like you haven't aged a day!"

His blush was visible even through his makeup. "And I see you've still retained your beauty," he spoke in a raspy, legato voice.

"Ignatius, this is Reese," Eva said, turning to her fellow Guardian. The raven on his shoulder cawed loudly, as if he were sarcastically coughing. "And that's Hex," she added with a roll of her eyes.

"Pleasure to meet you," Reese spoke in his gruff voice.

"Likewise," Ignatius responded, though his words seemed empty, as he said them while deep in thought, studying Reese up and down. "He's your boyfriend, right?"

Eva stammered for words. "Uh..."

401

It was then that Ignatius approached Reese, then daringly placed his hands on the hulking Guardian's chest.

Reese suddenly felt himself in an even more awkward situation than Eva. "What are you..."

"Well, darling, you've got yourself quite the catch!" the old madam said to her, his hands moving to Reese's massive muscles. Hex eyed him with wary.

"Thank...you..." she slowly responded.

"Are you done?" Reese muttered, a hint of vexation in his voice.

Ignatius, sensing hostility, retracted. "I certainly hope you've been using what I taught you on him, sweetheart."

Eva smiled once more and nudged her mentor playfully. "Don't mind him, Reese, he's not particularly good at recognizing boundaries."

"No, I think I'm quite good at that," Ignatius said with a chuckle. "It's respecting them that's the tricky part."

She laughed along with him then, and the two shared a rare, gleeful moment in a gloomy time, but they quickly remembered where they were when they looked around to find themselves in a broken, ruined brothel they both used to call home. They couldn't help but witness their laughter slowly die down as sadness crept in once more.

"How have you been all this time, protégé?" Ignatius asked after a period of silence. "I bet your life's changed a lot since that Hangman fella took you in, right?"

"I've come a long way," she responded with a nod. "I split from him a while ago and found a group to take me in, but we're more like a family now. The Guardians, we're called, and Reese and his raven are in it with me. As of right now, we're going after the people that destroyed Greenwood, to put them to justice."

"Good on you," the madam said affirmingly, before staring at the ground with a pondering look on his face. "Hmm..."

"What is it?"

"The Guardians...I swear I've heard that somewhere, but for the love of me, nothing is coming to mind."

"Well, I hear we're quite popular nowadays," joked Reese.

"What about you?" asked Eva. "What have you been up to?"

"I can say I officially owned this brothel until the day it burned down," said Ignatius. "But now I suppose I have to live a new life."

"And where are you off to?"

"You know," Ignatius began, "there was a girl, long ago. I accepted that she was gone when I became a madam, but perhaps, hope is still out there. I can't believe I'm saying this, but I'm a bit tired of lust. I want some love in my life again, for a change. I'd fight your war with you, but I believe life has other things planned for me. I'm not ready to put myself in that danger yet."

"I understand. Go out there and find her. She might have been waiting for you this whole time, you know.

"I certainly hope," he said. "Well, for now, I'd best be going. It's time I go out into the world again. I've got a long way to go, and the Borderlands get particularly dangerous at night. It was good to see you, Eva, and good to meet your friends."

"Good luck, Iggy," she said as she embraced him. "I hope we meet again someday."

"One day, old friend, I'm certain we will," he parted with.

■ ■ ■

As off went Reese, Hex, and Eva, Skullgem tapped Amber's back, pointing to a section of the ruins some distance away that looked as if it was hiding something within it. Soon enough, soldiers and guards alike emerged, waving to Amber's army. The Guardians felt a wave of relief wash over them as they recognized the troops that had revealed themselves.

Reuniting was a rare gleeful moment in the midst of a gloomy war. White Heart troops kept wary eyes over the Syndicate guards and soldiers, most especially Jade, their new leader. Yet, they all understood that desperate times called for desperate measures after the new treaty was explained to them.

They took an hour to settle down and another to set up a perimeter for the campsite near the ruins of Greenwood. Ezekiel found Amber and asked her to gather the Guardians. She did so promptly, just as Hex, Reese, and Eva returned. Before long, the nine legendary heroes presented themselves in front of him.

"I've had a lot of time on my hands," Zeke began to explain. "And with what I've made during that time, I believe we can take back White Heart, I firmly do. You are the Guardians, and we are a combination of mercenaries and soldiers tortured by the system, eagerly awaiting your call to arms. Your sense of leadership is why we keep fighting; you are the ones that give us a sense of purpose, a reason to never stop. The corrupt dictators that now make our city their unrightfully claimed home don't have that. But that won't mean taking White Heart back will be a simple task, so I have devised the technology to make it easier for you brave souls.

"For you, Geronimo," he continued, starting with the first person in line, "I am quite proud of this one." He handed the shorter man a metal suitcase.

Skullgem flashed a few signs to Brutus. "He asks what it is," Brutus translated.

"You won't need to worry about having him to speak for you," explained Ezekiel, opening the suitcase. A few rods and wires were neatly tied up inside. "With this, your thoughts are translated into words that are displayed with a hologram hanging over your head. It's quite simple once you get used to it, and it's easy to turn off and on and remove, if necessary. Give it a try!"

Ezekiel proceeded to show Skullgem how his new contraption worked, asking him to remove his hood momentarily. A few wires were stuck over his messy hair, and Ezekiel put a collar attached to the wires on the Assossian's neck. He then motioned for him to put his hood back on. Skullgem did so, and before long, two simple words found themselves above Geronimo's head like a cloud:

Vaz eff.

Sounds of wonder passed amongst them, but Ezekiel had only just begun.

"For you, Eva," he continued, turning to her and handing her a white pouch, "this is small, but I hope you can see it put to use. Watch."

He grabbed another pouch and flipped it over, permitting the contents to spill on his palms. A glittery, pink powder spilled slightly from the gaps between his fingers like waterfalls of sand. He turned to a guard nearby, who put on a confused look. After an audible huff of Ezekiel's lungs, the guard waved his arms around as a cloud of pink plagued him. Before long, he seemed to struggle to keep himself up, and eventually fell to the ground. "He'll be out for two hours," Ezekiel explained. "Sleep powder. Just give it a good gust, and it should put anyone into a temporary rest. It's made with the same ingredients as your tranquilizers. Pixie dust, I like to call it."

She smiled at him and fixed her pink headband. "Thank you, Zeke." He smiled back; a brief smile, as if he was unused to appreciation, but enjoyed it. She received a suitcase as well, full of pouches of powder, and Ezekiel promised he would have more for her soon.

To Charlie he turned to next, petting his warm head. The dog sat patiently and regally, save for his loud panting. Another large suitcase was brought over to the hound by a nearby guard, who had to carefully step over the sleeping one. Charlie watched him curiously as he removed what seemed to be a sort of exoskeleton. There was a small helmet with wires attached to it, similar to Skullgem's newest gadget. The wires sprawled down into two strange, chrome tubes.

"What is this?" Amber asked. A low whine from Charlie, as if he wanted to know as well.

"Firstly, this helmet is made from a particular magnesium alloy; toughest and lightest metal I could find. It should protect him well. "Second, there are wires attached to the helmet and...these." He lifted up the tubes with some effort. "These are similar to the technology used in Amber's shoes and Hex's wings. As you can guess, something along the lines of jet propulsion."

"Rocket dog," Reese said, in a low voice.

"Uh, yeah, sure, why not," Ezekiel agreed, putting the hound into his new battle outfit. "Something like that." He looked around and spotted some empty space in a nearby clearing, motioned to Amber towards it. "Can you tell him to run over there?"

A slight nod from the general, followed by a whistle and a point, and obedient Charlie immediately ran down the clearing. After a few seconds, his pace picked up drastically, and soon he was soaring at incredible speeds. He darted around the clearing, lapping it in circles multiple times in seconds before returning back them, coming to a screeching halt before Amber.

Amber laughed. "Like mother, like son." Her "son" sat before her now, a cheerful look on his face and an outstretched, wet tongue hanging out of his mouth.

"For you, Brutus, I have this." This package came with no suitcase; Ezekiel simply handed him a small, black disc. "This is a map. Because you are White Heart's most important tactician, however, it's not just any map." He pressed a button on a very small panel to the side of the disc, and immediately, a holographic display presented itself, a flat landscape remarkably resembling the ruins of Greenwood. "This isn't all, though."

His fingers went through the display, and as he spread them out, the map zoomed in. They noticed markings, labeled with names, in exact formation in correlation to where they stood. Smaller chevrons signified White Heart guards nearby, even moving as they moved. "How does it work? Well, lucky for me, we're in a sci-fi/*fantasy* story, so for the sake of the reader, I'm gonna go with magic," Ezekiel spoke as he handed the map to the tactician. "You'll get used to it fairly quickly, I'm certain.

"For you, Xela, I don't have any physical technology to give you. However, what I have to offer is me. I will donate my effort and knowledge of technology to the Order until it has achieved its ultimate goal."

"Thank you," Xela said, "but there's something that needs to be done to seal the deal. Go on without me." She promptly rushed back to camp to fetch something.

To the heeled woman in the blue suit he turned to next. She stood straight and formal as she awaited her turn. He opened the next suitcase, this one the biggest and heftiest, and an alien gadget almost the size of Amber presented itself in front of her.

"This is a form of exoskeleton suit, similar to what Charlie has, tailored to fit your figure. It should aerodynamically compliment your heels."

"Not fashionably compliment," she jested.

Ezekiel chuckled. "It comes with built-in steel knuckles, great for punching, as well as a protective outer shell. If you're the leader of all of our forces, you should be well-protected."

"Thank you," she said as he put down the final suitcase.

"What about me?" Reese asked. He was practically fidgeting to see what Ezekiel had in stock for him.

"I, uhh..." Ezekiel thought for a moment, then shook his head. "I don't really have anything for you."

A frown from Reese. "Nothing?"

"Nothing."

"You sure?" Reese asked again, clinging to hope. "Try thinking some more."

Ezekiel sighed. "Besides your cybernetic guardian angel, you have grenades that grant you the gift of teleportation, a shotgun, an axe that always finds its way back to you, and a drug that grants you near-invincibility. What more do you need?"

"Oh, I don't know," said Reese, who sighed and seem to genuinely ponder his friend's question. "...I mean, a giant laser cannon would be pretty cool, if you ask me."

Ezekiel shook his head, wiped his brow, and sighed loudly. He ignored his immature old friend and turned to the redhead.

"For you, Alyssa," he said, pulling a blank journal from his coat and handing it to her. "I have this. I know how much you love to read, so I'm hoping you would like to have a chance to write as well, which is what you can use this for. I want you to promise me to write about all of our adventures in protecting and serving. Write every detail and anything you find interesting. May our stories never be forgotten."

Alyssa smiled, charmed and captivated. "I promise," she said, taking the journal and holding it in her arms cheerfully.

Xela returned just then, a makeup kit in her hand. "Hold still," she commanded Ezekiel, applying a special pencil to his face. After a while, she drew away, letting the others see her work.

Around Ezekiel's eyes were black tears. They streamed down his cheeks, much as they did with Xela and the rest of the Order. "What did you do?" he asked her, failing to hold back a giggle and a smile.

Her dark lips smiled back. "I made you one of us."

■ ■ ■

Skullgem found Brutus in the tactician's tent, where he now spent most of his time he was not occupied with battle. Brutus' eyes shone a hue of blue, the reflection of the holographic display casting its light over him.

Geronimo approached slowly, and Brutus turned to face him, powering off Ezekiel's gift so that he could give his attention to the fellow Guardian before him. For a moment, no other lights were on, and they were surrounded by complete darkness. Brutus trudged for the nearest lamp, turning it on with a few loud clicks.

Skullgem had removed his hood now. He reached for the button on his collar, and without delay, the red display turned on above his head. As his mind was blank, it shone crimson, but scribed no words, until...

Vaz eff.

"What are you thanking me for?" Brutus asked as he leaned on a chair.

Thank you for being there to help others understand me.

He almost saw Brutus smile. "I'm just doing my job, really," responded the taller man, as Skullgem began trudging towards him. "What are you doing?" Brutus asked, slowly moving back.

Before he knew it, the Assossian took up a sprint, running at Brutus and catching him in an embracing hug. It was unexpected, as he had always looked at the short man as a humble and wise person, not one to be bothered by emotions such as loneliness, as was made clear to him here. Before long, Skullgem pulled away.

I'm sorry. It's just that a life in which it is hard for people to understand you is sometimes a lonely one.

Guilt, utter guilt. Was it visible in the reflections of himself he noticed in the drops of sweat on Geronimo's face? Was it even sweat? Were they tears?

Brutus gently wiped the Assossian's cheeks. "Look, I wouldn't go down the road you're going down. It's full of bumps and ridges, and it's not a fun place. You're going to regret it later, trust me."

A frown, and a turn of his face toward the ground. Somehow, the guilt was worse for Brutus now.

Skullgem looked like a boy. There was the irony; he was always the wise, scholarly type to Brutus, save for now. He looked like an innocent child, a child stricken with sudden gloom.

Guilt, guilt, guilt. Brutus felt terrible. How could Geronimo even understand?

"You know what?" Brutus said. "I'm sorry. I'm sorry. I'm sorry I said that. I...I didn't know where I was going with it."

He sighed a very long, exhausted sigh. Silence filled the room, broken every few moments by another apology from Brutus. Finally, Geronimo felt it best to leave, but before he did, he stood on his tiptoes to reach Brutus' face. A surprised Brutus had no words for the gentle kiss that briefly touched his reddened cheeks. Geronimo parted with a smile before concealing his face with his hood and once more returning to the darkness outside the tent.

■ ■ ■

Her legs were crossed, and the blue heels on her boots tapped the ground repeatedly.

"Why do you always wear those boots?" Ire asked her friend.

Alyssa smiled and looked up from her book. "My father always told me that anyone that can in run in heels is someone to be feared." She chuckled lightly and gently, a sweet, miniature laugh. Her gaze moved directly in front of her, and Ire's followed.

Amber ran past their view, her heels blurs of black; the timing couldn't have been more fitting. She ducked into the next tent, and then she was gone, busy preparing for the important soon to take place.

"You look up to her," Ire noticed.

Another smile, and her long, red hair swirled as she turned to him. "She's the mother I never had." Silence settled as the boy took this in. "Can I ask you something?" A nod from Ire. "How do you do it?"

"Do what?"

"You're just so calm. I mean, we live in war, your parents hate each other with a burning passion…"

"Sometimes, Alyssa," he started, "you just have to let it all go. My parents, I love them, I really do, but my father thinks he's the strongest man in the world and my mother thinks she's never known what it's like to be wrong. Unless I want to be just another cog in a

414

system, another link in the chain, I have to be calm. I have to relax." She nodded, understanding. "Please don't tell them I said that."

"I won't, I won't, don't worry," Alyssa assured. "You're so mature, Ire, that sometimes I forget how young you are. You honestly seem older than your parents sometimes."

He shrugged. "We're all children on the inside."

"Alyssa!"

The girl turned at the sound of her name, and her eyes caught Amber waving at her. "It looks like I have to go," she said to him, picking herself up off the ground.

"Best of luck," said Ire, a slight grin forming on his young face.

CHAPTER 24:

We are the Guardians.

It started off as a whisper that escaped Amber's mouth. Her knees were shaking, just as they had when she first suggested her proposal to the Chairman, nothing short of an eternity ago.

We are the Guardians.

She found herself repeating it. The thought of the phrase hadn't occurred to her as she spoke it, but now that she did, she liked how it sounded. It brought her comfort and reassured her that they would win their city back.

We are the Guardians.

She had not said it that time. The words came from Brutus, who sat in the seat next to her, waiting within the helicopter that would take them to the battle of their lives.

We are the Guardians.

Alyssa, Xela, Reese, and Eva joined in this time. They continued to repeat the phrase, a crescendo that grew louder and louder. Skullgem chimed in, displaying the words over his head in red, as well as Charlie, who howled and barked, and Hex, who cawed boisterously.

What had started as a whisper now grew into a loud chant, audible over the sounds of a flock of approaching helicopters.

We are the Guardians!

Even as the flying machines hovered above the warzone, rockets and explosions ever-present in the sky, their chant continued. Soon enough, other squadrons joined in. From a whisper to a chant, from a chant to a war cry.

We are the Guardians! We are the Guardians! We are the Guardians!

As soon as the helicopter landed, out came six humans, an Assossian, a hound, and a raven.

Almost immediately, they were surrounded by enemy soldiers. The Guardians stood with their backs to each other, a circle of trust, of close friends and lovers, all fighting to protect each other and their city.

Darts from a rifle pierced the chaos of battle: Eva picking out target after target. Her enemies fell quickly, succumbing to a deep sleep. Her sunglasses slowly slipped from her nose, but she was careful not to let them fall, as her eyes darted from soldier to soldier.

A moment ago, no one had been in the spot next to her, but a second later, a tower of a man appeared alongside the caw of the smaller atrocity on his shoulder: blasts of buckshot flew from Reese's shotgun and into the armed mercenaries and soldiers around him, and Hex watched carefully for bullets that traveled in his allies' path, destroying them before they could bring harm to his friends.

It was almost easy to miss the man standing beside Reese, as he was but a shadow amongst them: Skullgem was now unafraid to keep his hood down, fiercely proud of his crimson skin, shining with battle-fury. He slowly spun, preparing to swing his mighty hammer with all the force in his petite, but strong body. The holographic shine above his head proudly displayed the words:

FOR WHITE HEART

Elegant silk twirled, a fascinating black blossom, before a dark woman spinning two daggers revealed her face: Xela poised her knives, then threw them both into the fray, and two soldiers in front of her with blades in their chests fell. She then drew her massive scythe, the long blade shining beautifully, daring any to challenge her.

Beside her, a barrage of bullets whizzing through the air carelessly: Brutus grimaced, no remorse in his cold expression, as he fired revolvers into the fray. His enemies found themselves crumbling to the ground in quick succession, falling victim to his deadeye draw.

A bark and a growl sounded nearby: Charlie poised himself to strike, and before long, was flying at the first hostile he saw raise a weapon against them, then the second, then the third. His unmatched speed made him a blur on the battlefield, his fangs finding foes faster than bullets barraging out of barrels.

The *whoosh* of a harsh gale, and the frigid touch of a blizzard: snow quickly piled up, and before long, hail rained down mercilessly. Standing next to Charlie, Alyssa's eyes shone a tint of light blue, and her crimson hair and blue skirt and scarf fluttered carelessly in the wind.

Rocket fuel burned boisterously as a woman descended beside Alyssa: Amber drew a small pistol, and the crack of her gun chimed in on the fray. She was an icon of leadership, and her body radiated dignity as she fought alongside her eight most trusted allies.

They were the Guardians, a family at arms. A city imprinted its image in their heads, the city that had brought them together, and now the city that they were bound to guard from danger, as they were always destined to do.

■ ■ ■

A grunt escaped Jade's lips as she felt the strike of her opponent's sword. Sparks flew in every direction as the swordsman held his weapon to her shield. She shoved him back, and he stumbled. When he picked himself back up, Jade readied her shield once more. The man never struck it again, however, as he crumbled to the ground, an arrow lodged in his nape. Jade's gaze met Ezekiel's as he readied another arrow. She mouthed him a quick "thank you" before hurrying back into the fray.

Ezekiel scanned the streets, finding a cluster of Reynard's soldiers firing upon White Heart guards behind cover. He pressed a button on his bow, and a blinking red light presented itself on his readied arrow, coupled with steady ticks. He fired at Reynard's troops, landing an arrow somewhere in the middle of the group. With a press of a button on his bow, Zeke's arrow exploded like a bomb, sending soldiers flying in every direction. Even Ezekiel flinched at the size of the explosion, but he picked up his weapon again upon seeing swift movement on the rooftops above him. His bow lowered when he realized it was but Eva sprinting from roof to roof.

A sniper on the same roof lay in her sights. As she advanced upon him, he picked himself up from his crouching stance, retreating back while opening fire on her. He missed sorely, as Eva dove downwards and rolled, then threw a few kicks at him. As he stumbled backward, she reached inside the pouch clipped onto her shorts and grabbed a handful of pink powder. With a deep breath, the remnants scattered in front of her, and the man quickly stopped firing. He dropped instantly, and Eva chuckled when she heard him snoring on the ground through his mask.

Down below, a familiar figure emerged from a vehicle that dropped him into the fray. His bronze armor and golden nose ring shimmered, and he lugged a massive axe on his shoulders. The sound of air angrily escaping his nose could almost be heard amongst the chaos.

Another figure, much shorter, set out to deal with this man. His hammer struck from the shadows, hitting the Minotaur's colossal chest. Skullgem saw a slight flinch in the face hiding behind a hefty helmet and a hairy beard; so the beast was not invincible, it seemed. The man retaliated with slow, yet frighteningly powerful strikes from his axe. Skullgem was quick enough to dodge most of the attacks, but one unfortunately slipped past him, and he went flying back as the Minotaur's massive weapon struck his mail. The Guardian already felt severely weakened from just one blow, and he struggled to pick himself up, until a sharp prick touched his shoulder, then another his back, and one more his neck.

Skullgem reached to feel what had pricked him and found himself pulling out empty syringes. Just then, a sudden burst of invigorating energy pulsed from within him, and he felt even more prepared for battle than before. He looked behind him to find none other than Dr. Mary pointing at him, her wrist blaster raised. Her aim suddenly shifted, however, and she fiddled with her weapon before firing again. The projectile missed Skullgem this time, and as the Guardian turned once more, he found a charging Minotaur suddenly stop, a syringe in his thigh. It had the opposite effect on him, temporary paralyzing part of his body, stopping him in his tracks, and giving Skullgem an opportunity to retaliate.

He finally got a good hit at the bronze man's jaw, but it only seemed to feed his anger. The Minotaur spit at Geronimo, blood and saliva splattering on the disgusted Guardian's chainmail. Now the Minotaur swung with all his might, but his axe chipped itself into the pavement of the White Heart street as the man with the hammer dove away.

Skullgem saw another chance present itself and stepped on the man's axe. Before the Minotaur could pull it out, the Assossian leaped, delivering a kick to the man's face and flipping away. He pushed off the angry bronze man with all his might, and as the Minotaur struggled back, Skullgem swung once again, this time at his gut, then, this time past his opponent, to deliver a smash of his hammer towards the Minotaur's nape. He staggered forward now, and

Skullgem spun his hammer as he beckoned the beast to attack him again.

"I got this, Geronimo," Skullgem heard come a deep voice behind him before he could pursue his opponent further. Reese Black trudged past the Assossian and towards the Minotaur, arms bulging with bright red veins, a raven on his shoulder. He shot an aggressive hook at the bronze man, and the Minotaur's helmet received a visible dent. Reese then charged upon him, grabbing him by his legs and lifting him into the air before spinning him around with ease. He picked up speed, the Minotaur struggling frantically as he was slung over Reese's back. Reese then suddenly stopped himself with a leap into the air and slammed the bronze man with all his force into the ground.

As the Minotaur picked himself up, he coughed, the wind having been knocked out of him. He felt Reese's cold hands on the back of his neck, ready to hoist him up, and the will to fight back triggered itself from within. The Minotaur reached for his great axe and swung it with one hand. Though he didn't hit Reese, the sudden attack surprised him nonetheless, and the Guardian jumped backward, tripping onto the concrete below.

Now was his chance; the Minotaur gripped the axe tightly and held it above his head, then let it fall back down onto the tall man on the ground.

A laugh: an unhinged, deranged, psychopathic laugh that grew mockingly louder. Blood dripped onto Reese's torso, but no axe lay in it. His hands had taken the blow, as he had grabbed the great axe as it swung down on him. His palms bled waterfalls, but Reese looked as if he felt no pain. He paused his laughter to give a whistle, and Hex darted in front of the Minotaur's face. The massive, armored man let go of the axe and swatted at Hex to no avail. The raven had rooted his talons into the man's chin and flapped his wings frantically in an effort to block his view. Another whistle sounded, and Hex fled. There was a brief moment in which the Minotaur was glad to have the annoying raven gone, but then he saw his own shimmering axe in Reese's arms, and he knew it was over.

Reese swung with inhuman strength, and the axe wound up in its owner's body, stuck somewhere within his head, ripping through most of his throat and the top of his chest. The Minotaur fell backward, a giant among men now fallen. The cybernetic raven perched on Reese's shoulder mimicked his partner's crazed laughter with loud caws, as the duo basked in the glory of the kill.

■ ■ ■

On the other side of White Heart, another battle raged. A great scythe swung through White Heart's residential district, flashes of sharp steel in every direction.

A group of soldiers surrounded Xela. She sliced at them in a matter of seconds, not a single bullet or blade scraping her, and bodies fell swiftly, one after another.

Then she grunted, as she felt herself get shoved from her side by another force. Her shoulder broke her fall, and she lay prostrate for a moment before getting up in time to see Jade's raised shield absorb the strike of a knife. A man had leaped from rubble that had been behind Xela, and Jade had pushed her away to save her life. The knife stuck itself in the slits of her giant shield, and the attacker frantically pushed to let it loose.

Xela quickly got up, aiming the scythe to point at him. With the flick of a switch, a spear shot from her weapon, and the man clutched his side in pain. Xela yanked it back, and he fell to the ground, too weak to stand up again.

"Thank you," she said, catching her breath.

"Just doing my duty," Jade responded, fixing her shield.

They turned to the sounds of crackling flame to find a wall of fire on the other side of the street closing in on them. A line of soldiers, all gripping relentless flamethrowers, approached slowly, as if attempting to control wild beasts. The sanctuary street was quickly catching aflame.

A sound, soft at first, rained from the heavens. Xela turned quizzically to Jade, who turned quizzically to Xela. It was an odd sound, something like the shrill scream of an extremely fast moving object combined with someone yelling at the top of their lungs. It quickly ascended in volume, a siren to their ears. The two women looked at each other again, then back up to the sky.

To their shock, an object moved at a terrifying pace towards them, something falling from above like a meteor storm. They dove for cover before it shot past them like a bullet, darting near the line of flamethrowers. One soldier was yanked and dragged into the sky by the mysterious blur. It pulled him into the clouds, and he was gone within seconds.

Jade stammered for words. "Was that who I think it was?"

Xela stared at her with her mouth open. "I'll be damned."

■ ■ ■

Amber Leavett pulled a soldier screaming for his life into the realm of the clouds as the sun watched from a distance. She only stopped rising once she was satisfied with their altitude, all the while her arms wrapped tightly around his chest. His weapon and his gear had fallen long ago, and now he was completely at her mercy.

"Just you and me, huh?" Amber asked as she let herself and her captive hover in the air, just above a fluffy cloud. "What a view, what a view."

"Puh...please!" It was a miracle the soldier hadn't fainted yet. He hugged her extraordinarily tightly, to her amusement.

"Alright, alright, I've had my fun," she said, before she yanked him loose and let him drop, then chased the descending soldier and his falling cry. She spiraled towards him, gave him a good few punches to his stomach when she reached him, and grabbed him by his shoulders with her firm grip.

They were right above White Heart now, back under the clouds, and Amber surveyed the city from her position. She found a needle pointing from a particularly tall spire and flew herself and the dangling soldier towards it. Once she was directly above it, she hoisted the man over her shoulder. Amber positioned him so that the back of his shirt gripped the needle tightly, and he was almost in tears now. She gave him a good pat on the head before returning to the battle.

■ ■ ■

"Look!" Xela gasped, pointing to another similar object, this one grounded, darting towards the soldiers. It slowed in front of one armored flamethrower-wielder, tackling her to the ground. When it lost its speed, no longer a blur to them, it was clear that it was none other than their fellow Guardian canine. Charlie ripped into the soldier's neck with his teeth before darting away again, making it out of the scene before the other soldiers could process what was happening.

Xela and Jade saw their opening and cut down the line of soldiers, receiving aid from Charlie as he darted in and out of the enemy ranks repeatedly. Even their flames were no match, and soon enough the ground became littered with the fallen. Jade and Xela stood before each other, their weapons stained, panting heavily. Charlie joined them as well, and soon, another familiar face.

Amber looked like an angel descending from the heavens as she landed in front of them. She walked towards them with a smile and a confident swagger.

"Not bad, huh?"

■ ■ ■

The jagged edges of two krises clashed with a spear of thick ice. With every few swipes from Aleegha, Alyssa had to conjure up another weapon, as the others shattered like glass.

Aleegha spun, her crooked blades flailing around her. A thin wall of ice, just slightly taller than them, manifested itself in front of Alyssa to block her attacker, sprouting up from the ground almost immediately when the ice sorceress willed it to. One of Aleegha's daggers went too far to Alyssa's side, however, and a lock of red hair flew upwards.

Alyssa flashed an angry look, and Aleegha grinned slyly. They continued their dance of combat, blades and spears flashing alongside the constant sound of ice breaking. At one moment, hoping to catch the white-haired woman off guard, Alyssa knelt quickly, sweeping Aleegha off her feet with a low kick.

As soon as Aleegha fell, a loud wheeze escaping her lungs, Alyssa crawled on top of her, a small dagger of ice forming in her tightly clenched hands. She tried to plunge the knife downwards, but to no avail; Aleegha held Alyssa's hands with an iron grip. As the two struggled, Aleegha saw a chance present itself when she noticed her weapons within grabbing space, and succeeded in reaching one of her own knives, the kris hungering for spilled blood.

Before she could strike, her hand was crushed with a cringe-inducing snap, followed by a scream and a wail. Brutus had lowered his boot upon her palms, and the kris dropped from her hand. Aleegha then made haste to kick at Alyssa, who let her guard down when she saw Brutus, and the girl fell off the woman. Brutus' foot slipped, and Aleegha began to pick herself up, but the tactician swung for her with his fists. Her dexterity permitted her to dodge the strike with ease, and she took her opportunity as Brutus recovered from his punch.

She slipped behind him, but when he turned to face her, he found no one. His eyes shot around, darting and scanning, but Aleegha was gone. He fumingly exhaled and drew his revolvers, sending bullets soaring in every direction, none of which struck his invisible target.

"Not so fast!" a voice shouted. A small object rolled on the ground, and when Brutus recognized it, he ducked and covered his ears. An incapacitating blast rendered him dizzy for a moment, throwing his senses into turmoil before he picked himself up. It had struck Aleegha as well, forcing her out of her invisible state.

Weylin emerged in sprint from nearby, a belt of concussive grenades strapped to his chest, as he placed a submachine gun in his arms and aimed his sights on Aleegha. She recovered more quickly than he expected, however, and darted towards him with her weapons at the ready. She struck his gun with her dagger, throwing his aim off, and the two found themselves locked in a duel.

Brutus witnessed this, and promptly pulled his machine pistol from the strap on his thigh, waiting for Weylin to part with Aleegha so he could get a clear shot at her. Just when the Guardian thought he saw his chance, he felt a stinging pain on his wrist.

"Don't be so quick to shoot!" a voice taunted him.

Unable to get his finger on the trigger, Brutus had no way of helping Weylin. He frantically yanked at something constricted on his hand, something shooting searing electricity into his body. He yelled in agony as he finally got it off, only to have it smack his face painfully before retracting back to its owner. He turned to see who had attacked him and groaned in disgust at the sight of Reynard approaching with a sassy gait, one hand akimbo, his whip in the other. He was snickering with his mocking hyena laugh.

"Not this freak," Brutus said under his breath.

"Hey, darling," Reynard called. "What say you and me have some fun?" He shot his whip at Brutus, only to strike a pillar of ice. His grin quickly turned into a frown of disbelief.

"You need to chill out, lover boy," Alyssa said with a smirk, as she appeared from behind the pillar. She approached him, Brutus at her side, and Reynard clenched his teeth, preparing for battle.

Some feet away, Aleegha and Weylin were still in the middle of heated combat. Aleegha launched herself at Weylin, krises in hand, attempting to stab his chest. He sidestepped her and kicked her back as she soared past him. Weylin raised his machine gun, and a barrage of rushed bullets began to fly towards her. Aleegha, however, quickly launched a kick at Weylin's shin. He stumbled to the ground before any of his projectiles found their target. As Aleegha pushed off the ground, so did her rival, and Weylin approached with a fist at the ready. He got on top of her and struck her face, first her eye, which turned bruised, then her nose, which began to bleed profusely. She dodged another one of his hooks, then slashed at him with her own weapons. He received a painful cut to his upper chest, and as he pushed her away, she tossed a kris into his shoulder, then leaped back on top of him.

Not far away, Reynard fought against Alyssa and Brutus. Alyssa came at him first, a frozen spear in hand. The weapon of ice she gripped was but a blur as she repeatedly swung it with impressive speed. Nimble Reynard was quick to dodge most of her attacks, but still found himself bleeding in various places from cuts he received.

Brutus was waiting, however, watching for the second Reynard dropped his guard. As soon as he saw the chance, the tactician ran at his opponent, trading spots with Alyssa. He flipped his revolvers so that their butts were raised, then he struck Reynard with them. The cunning usurper stumbled back, clutching his bruised head. Brutus spun his revolvers again, so that they faced Reynard, and opened fire. A relentless siege of bullets followed, but Reynard was ready this time. He raised his other weapon, the bulky rocket launcher, covering his body like a shield. He managed to block himself from most of Brutus' fire and found the strength to ignore the few projectiles that did pierce his body. As soon as Reynard heard the clicking of Brutus' empty clip, he swung his rocket launcher

430

with all his force. The blunt object struck Brutus just under his chin, and he went flying.

Alyssa was upon Reynard now, but once again, he was ready. She conjured an orb of pressurized ice in her palms, letting out a cry as she shot it towards her opponent. At the same time, Reynard crouched as he aligned his sights towards his target, then fired his rocket launcher. Alyssa's ball of stinging frost clashed with Reynard's rocket, filled to the brim with unstable electricity. An explosion of vivid colors, deafening volume, and epic proportions pushed both of them back as their powerful projectiles collided with one another. A thick, cold fog settled in, separating the two Guardians from Reynard.

Aleegha, still clashing with Weylin, noticed the cloud of icy dust that had formed nearby. She pushed her opponent back just long enough to see what was going on.

Her leader eventually emerged through the smoke, shivering, yet burned in many places. He was soaked in his own blood; the battle had taken its toll on him.

"The party's dying out, Aleegha," he called to her. "Take me home, please."

She nodded, running to join him, but Weylin was determined to stop them. He readied another concussive grenade, but before he could toss it, Reynard's whip shot like a bullet. It coiled around Weylin's wrist, and as the electrifying pain burned him, he screamed in agony. Reynard held him until he finally dropped the grenade, which proceeded to explode at his feet, harmless to Reynard and Aleegha.

The commander was left staggering from the force of the point-blank concussive blast his head aching, troubled and uneasy. When the fog cleared, granting Brutus and Alyssa vision once more, and when Weylin regained his senses, Reynard and Aleegha were gone.

■ ■ ■

His panting was muffled by the sound of the passing monorail train above him. Blaze ascended to the top of the stairs and onto the station platform just as the last of the civilians made it inside.

"Anyone left behind you?" the conductor shouted to him.

Blaze shook his head. "You're good to go. Just remember: stop at the station at the east gate. That's where the civilian camp is located."

"Understood." A nod from the conductor, and the train departed. Blaze got in a final glance the nervous civilians packed like herded sheep inside and felt pity for them. He hoped that they would make it safely.

Once the train left, Blaze was able to get a view of the street below him, and lo and behold, a soldier he spotted, sporting a bulky rocket launcher in his arms. The Assossian's burning eyes watched the man's as they followed the train's movement.

"Not today," muttered Blaze under his breath. An ember manifested in his palms, and he quickly hurled it beneath him. The frantic screaming of a dying soldier followed for a few moments, and then silence took over.

Blaze made his way back down to street level and hurried towards the center of the city, hoping to return to the battle. In a flash, a figure emerged from a nearby alley, putting itself in Blaze's way. He fired a weapon akimbo, and Blaze felt a blunt force suddenly knock the wind out of him before he could understand the situation. A canister bounced off his chest and rolled onto the ground for a moment, before exploding and clouding his vision with smoke.

A shadow manifested in front of him, against a wall of fog. Blaze coughed, his mind a flurry of panicked thoughts. For a moment, the shadow seemed to form the shape of a bird with great wings, and then the haze before Blaze dissipated.

It took him quite some time to recognize his brother. His clothing seemed similar, and but now he wore a gas mask of a malicious appearance. Goggles cloaked his eyes, tinted an unnerving red. It seemed as if a long nose pointed out from him, almost a beak. His brother also wore gauntlets now, made of a metal alien to Blaze. Smoke opened his palms, and flames of strange grey shade emerged.

Blaze spit, doing his best to land the projectile at his brother's feet. "*Atsi* is *my* thing."

"Where there is fire, there is smoke," the grey man said.

"Don't kid yourself!" Blaze exclaimed, chuckling through his pain. "You're nothing but a pitiful man stuck in my shadow. I'm ashamed to call you family."

"Smoke was your family. Your family is dead now, all dead. What was your brother has been replaced by the phoenix, *ahm atsiaag*, reborn into what he should have always been! And your daughter...you brought this *exqo'* upon her! Your trust killed her!"

Anger erupted Blaze's face. "Are you insane? Have you truly gone mad?"

"I've had enough of your talking!" The flames on his gauntlets burned brightly, more passionately now, a darker grey.

"*Galvehi*. You did not forget fire cannot hurt me, did you?"

"You are immune to fire. The human's *atsi*," responded Smoke, before he lunged and grabbed his brother's arm. "You are not immune to what I have unearthed!" Blaze screamed as a sudden agony struck him, squirming to push his brother aside.

The Assossian in orange clenched his charred wounds once he had wrangled away. "What did you do to me?" he questioned with teeth clenching in pain. His blood sibling only laughed morbidly. "You're sick," Blaze said. "Deranged. The very sight of the one who I used to call my brother disgusts me."

Out of reckless anger, the other man struck at Blaze, leaping and throwing his weight into a punch against the other Assossian's face. As his brother staggered back, the grey man quickly turned and held his arm out, smacking Blaze's cheek with a closed fist.

Once Blaze picked himself up, he threw an ember at his brother, sorely missing. Smoke then approached, slowly at first. "Get back!" Blaze commanded. He threw a fist at Smoke's gut, missing once more. His brother had sidestepped, and now grabbed hold of Blaze's arm. He pulled him close enough to land a jab to his forehead. Blaze once again fell back, witnessing his efforts come to no avail, as the man in grey approached him with a slow strut. "Get back!" Blaze said again. "Get back!"

He focused his energy on causing the street below to burst into flames until a wall of fire separated the two siblings. Smoke didn't stop moving towards him, however; in fact, if anything, he was picking up the pace. He darted straight through the wall of flames, yet no fire dared to cling to him. He sprinted towards his brother, readying a fist, before finally delivering a painful blow to his brother's jaw, the other Assossian too weak to dodge the attack. Blaze fell, and his sibling pulled the grenade launcher from his back. His knee went to his brother's chest, and Blaze coughed up blood.

"Open wide," the grey man said, shoving the barrel of the launcher into Blaze's mouth. He did not give his brother a moment to retaliate, and immediately squeezed the trigger.

Blaze made a choking sound, the sound of his throat sizzling. Smoke pushed hard against Blaze's mouth with his left hand, letting a burst of the anti-flames loose. He was even yelling now, putting all of his efforts into brutally making sure his brother could not come back. A mixture of blood, gas, and powerful embers combined in Blaze's throat, and his body quickly began to rot and boil from the inside.

Flames surrounded the entire street, and as the triumphant Assossian got up walked away, he gave no final glance at his brother's twitching, decaying body.

Finally came the frantic explosion of fire behind him, but the *atsiaag* was already too far away to be hurt by his brother's final spark.

■ ■ ■

A swarm of frantic civilians pushed down the street, fleeing towards safety. Brutus and Weylin led them to the eastern gate, making sure they used up any available space. After a while, the flood of innocents was safely inside, and a truck rolled up to the duo. Amber and Xela were at the front, and Charlie stood panting in the back.

"No luck?" Weylin asked.

Amber shook her head sadly, one arm lying on the steering wheel. "Unfortunately, it seems most of the population is either under Marcus' influence or deep in hiding."

"What about Blaze?"

"No word on him either. We're out of time, unfortunately."

"We can only hope for the best," Xela said sternly. "Is Alyssa ready?" Brutus and Weylin nodded. The tactician left to fetch the timid girl, finding her helping guide the civilians to safety.

"Alyssa!" he shouted, catching her attention immediately. She scurried over to him, her mouth hidden in her scarf. "It's time."

She nodded, making her way to the center of the district, running through the chaos of panic around her. Once there, she closed her eyes, now so used to the feeling that it was practically instinctual.

The pleasant chill caressed her body once more, and she let herself feel bliss.

She needn't look to feel the great walls of ice forming around her. They would protect the east gate, the section of the city that now housed innocents attempting to avoid a war that had found itself taking place in their homes.

The process was completed sooner than Alyssa expected. She looked on with pride as the dome of ice hugged and protected the remnants of White Heart, all above and around her and her closest allies. Now she truly felt like a Guardian.

EPILOGUE:

The Guardians stood in a unified line by the inner edge of the frozen dome, all prepared to face the dangers lurking inside their own great city.

Tyreesius Black was a monster, a brute of a man, a fearsome giant. The wicked raven perched on his shoulder, the scar that drained the pigment from his eye, his towering height, his massive muscles, and his assortment of gadgets and weapons contributed to make him appear a beast forged from nightmares. He grinned from ear to ear, unable to contain his excitement for his next battle. The spiteful berserker was nothing short of a terrifying sight.

Hex was the color of night, from his beak to his talons. The pitch-black raven seemed to smile just as his tall friend did, the two an inseparable duo of fearsome creatures. Various parts of the bird had been augmented with metal, making his wings, beak, and talons razor-sharp. Steel also covered his eye, the eye that held steady a damning gaze, forming a hexagonal shape over it. The haunting raven was nothing short of a terrifying sight.

Evangeline Bates was a petite, pretty woman, dressed in the fashions of youthful spunk. Her brunette hair shimmered in the daylight, and a pink headband held it together. With her white blouse and white shoes, she looked angelic, and her charming face radiated with sweetness, completed well by her bright, hopeful smile. Yet the rifle clenched in her arms warned that she was a capable fighter, and her eyes were already scanning, watching for targets coming from every possible direction, every possible angle.

441

Geronimo Ao-Shi was a shadow, a young man able to fit into the crowd with ease. A glassy, yet peaceful stare was hidden in a darkness cast by the hood hiding his head. He had simple armor, mail beginning to collect rust, yet his cape and hammer were icons of justice and heroism. He was quite short; shorter, in fact, than all of his human comrades next to him, and yet his presence did not lack in demanding attention. His skin was not visible in any spot, his clothing not willing to betray his true colors.

Xela Zamora had the appearance of a reaper, yet death was her greatest rival. Her black lips, dark hair, and sensual clothing made her a beauty, but her tall shape, wicked scythe, and countless daggers menacingly dared one to touch her. Tears of black streamed down her face, a haunting visage. She was an eerie, curious sight, and yet all she felt inside herself was curiosity.

445

Alyssa Lincoln was a young witch in modest clothing. A dull sweater covered her chest, a simple skirt fluttered around her, and her blue boots shimmered brightly, as if they were made of glass. Her long red hair stretched to her shins, a beautiful mane, and her sleeves were rolled up, revealing permanent markings on her body that pulsed bright blue. Gripped in one hand was a grimoire, her book of frozen arts, and out of the palm of her other hand a snowflake had manifested.

Charlie was a great hound, a shepherd dog turned war machine. His mouth was ajar, revealing a row of teeth adorned in a mysteriously glistening metal. The helmet on his head and the protective coat that hugged him indicated his readiness for battle; it almost seemed he was covered in an armored shell, the various gadgets on his body serving to boost his ferocity, and there was no remorse to be found in his angry eyes.

449

Brutus McCallister was a military man, stern and firm, cynical and unforgiving. Various guns and gadgets were scattered across his body, preparing him for every occasion, and he had equipped a thick coat and cool urban look. Two revolvers he had drawn, one tinted in red and the other in green, and a bulky machine pistol clung to his thigh. As their tactician, he was lost in thought, already imagining every possible outcome of the important battle that sat before him.

Amber Leavett was their dark-haired leader, a strong warrior capped in a beret decorated with four stars, clad in the uniformed garb of her high rank. An exoskeleton suit surrounded her body, stretching from her neck to her shoes. Her black pumps were quite extraordinary, fit to more uses than simply their style. She looked almost willing to take to the skies with a small pistol gripped tightly in her hand, but in truth, she was nothing less than ready to lead her people into the fray of battle.

Behind them stood White Heart and Syndicate soldiers, side-by-side for the first time in history, fierce Assossian warriors seeking justice, guards of Xela's Order wielding weapons as terrifying as their ghostly visages, even White Heart civilians willing to take up arms to defend themselves.

"Are we ready?" asked Alyssa, prepared to melt the dome of ice before them. When it opened, it would begin their crusade to defeat the enemies within their homeland.

Amber took a deep breath, then spoke: "Let's go!" she said, in a loud enough voice for her entire army to hear. "We have a city to take back."

 ALEEGHA

 ALYSSA

 AMBER

 BLAZE

 BOSS GARETH

BRANDON

 BRUTUS

 BURNELLIA

 CALF

 CHARLIE

 DR. MARY

 EVA

EZEKIEL

 HEX

 **IGNATIUS**

 **IRE**

 JACK

 JADE

 **JANUS**

MARCUS

 THE MINOTAUR

458

NILS

REESE

REYNARD

SKULLGEM

SMOKE

WEYLIN

XELA

Illustrations –

- Amber/Xela/Eva – *Goobermation* (Tumblr)
- Reese and Hex – *scruffyturtles* (Tumblr)
- Alyssa – *highviscosity* (Tumblr)
- Charlie – *mt-wolfy* (Tumblr)
- Brutus – *artsyroboartsies* (Tumblr)
- Skullgem/Boss Gareth/Jade – *ironscrewy* (Tumblr) / *@kaibootsu* (Instagram)
- Reynard/Marcus – *Trollskine* (Tumblr)
- Aleegha – *zaideaben* (Tumblr) / *@zaideaben* (Instagram)
- The Minotaur – Nick Rojas / *halomaster0517* (Tumblr)
- Ezekiel – Jess.K / *youre-my-art-blog-boi* (Tumblr)
- Burnellia/Blaze/Smoke – Suzanne Fieldberry / *beehivesansthequeen* (Tumblr)
- Dr. Mary – *teauija* (Tumblr) / *@teauija* (Instagram)
- Ire – *bibiriswamp* (Tumblr)
- Weylin – Yuliya Ganzha / *bsdrosinate* (Tumblr)
- Jack – *razaria* (Tumblr)
- Brandon – Megan Reynolds / *whatup-its-mgeezy* (Tumblr)
- Janus – *skyheaven1231* (Tumblr) / *@skyheaven1231* (Instagram)
- Calf/Ignatius – Racheal Fischer / *@noitey* (Instagram)
- Nils – Madeline Chadwick / macsartcommissions@gmail.com / *@skatethestars* (Instagram)

ACKNOWLEDGEMENTS:

This book has consumed the past four years of my life. It's been a journey, and I'm extremely happy to have shared that journey with several people.

Thank you to every single one of my friends that has pestered me for the past few months, asking about when and where they can buy this book. That's a hype train I rode the hell out of.

Thank you to Mrs. Marvilli, whose language arts project was what created Reese and began this crazy adventure.

Thank you to the many people that have contributed their edits and comments to this book, but thank you most of all to Jed and Mr. Robert Yehling, who really whipped it into shape, and Ms. Desireé Duffy, who saw something special in my book and introduced me to a cast of experienced and talented authors.

Thank you to the many wonderful artists who contributed their amazing talents. I can't stress enough how you all have breathed life into the book and made me feel even more attached to these characters as I crafted their stories.

This book would be nowhere without Ophelia, who truly brought purpose into it. Not only have we built this universe together, but she has been the emotional support that I couldn't have written this book without, and I am forever grateful for her presence in my life.

This book would also be nowhere without my family, who have financially supported this project and offered help every step of the way. A very special thank you to my mother, however, who knew from the moment I confessed to her I was writing a book that this was what her next four years should be dedicated to.

Harley Zed Mona is a seventeen-year-old Bulgarian-American high school student residing in Annapolis, Maryland. He was raised in New York City, where he began writing his first book, *"Our Guardian Renegade,"* at the age of thirteen.

He is a frequent daydreamer who spends his time writing stories, playing bass guitar, rapping to himself about his problems, and playing video games. He works on many of his writings with his girlfriend and fellow author Ophelia Zed Mona.

Follow him on Instagram! *@harley_zed*
Follow him and Ophelia on Tumblr! *zedmona.tumblr.com*

CPSIA information can be obtained
at www.ICGtesting.com
Printed in the USA
BVOW07s0854091217

502388BV00009B/368/P